BIGFOOT HUNTERS

TALES OF THE CRYPTO-HUNTER - 1

R. GUALTIERI

DEDICATION & ACKNOWLEDGEMENTS

For J.G. and L.G. They helped make this book possible.

Special thanks to: Alissa, Melissa, Anne, Matt, and Varia for their awesome early feedback.

PROLOGUE

G il Mercer loved camping. He couldn't remember a time when the prospect of being outdoors didn't cause a tingle of excitement deep within him. Something about being away from the normal hustle and bustle of society really called to him. He couldn't imagine a better place to be; a man in his mid-thirties experiencing the joy of birds chirping and deer dashing through the underbrush. He took a deep breath. The air smelled clean. It smelled right.

Having spent his youth growing up in Detroit, one wouldn't have expected him to have such a love of the outdoors. Most of the year, Gil had been a typical city boy enjoying the occasional after-school game of b-ball with his friends, watching TV, and causing the usual mischief of a kid his age.

Gil's mother, however, had insisted on a different course of action during the summer. Every year, she would sign him up with the *Boy's Club of America* or

I

the *Fresh Air Fund* and make sure he spent a good chunk of the summer months where there were trees to climb, grass to run through, and campfires to tell ghost stories around. She had claimed it would broaden Gil's horizons, show him there was a world beyond the asphalt and scarred building facades of their neighborhood. Gil wasn't stupid, though; he knew it was mostly to make sure that he didn't fall in with a bad crowd.

While school was in, his studies had kept him fairly busy. His mother would accept no less. However, once school ended, idle hands could easily become the devil's playthings. Gil had seen his fair share of friends get themselves into increasingly more serious levels of trouble from year to year. He'd come back at the end of each summer to find that some of them were in trouble with the law, some had become addicts, and occasionally one would just be gone – never to be spoken of again.

Some of the other kids from the inner cities had been bitter about being sent to camp. They'd complain endlessly of being stuck out in the boonies and do their best to find a way to be kicked out of the program. Not Gil, though. From the moment he had stepped off a bus and gotten his first taste of nature, he had been hooked. No matter how great the preceding winter had been, come June, Gil would be itching again for the outdoors. It was a love that had never left him.

It didn't matter even when there weren't others to share his enthusiasm. By his junior year in college, he had saved enough to purchase some decent gear of his own. That way, whenever there was a long weekend that didn't require him to go back home, he was ready. He'd pack up his gear in the old clunker of a car he had bought from his uncle and pick a direction. Any would do so long as no skyscrapers marred the view ahead. The wilderness was like a sort of soulmate to him. Girlfriends had come and gone, friends had moved away, jobs had changed, but the outdoors were the one constant in Gil's life. It was, he thought, his *rock*, for lack of a better term.

That thought caused him to chuckle as he walked upstream toward his little camp. He had spent the morning fishing in a spot he'd found during some cursory exploring. He had bagged a few keepers, but in the end had set them all free. Gil wasn't much of a cook and his wife, Maria, would have sooner filleted *him* than gut a bunch of fish.

He frowned ever so slightly as his thoughts turned toward his family. He loved them with all his heart, make no mistake. His wife was a lawyer for a global energy syndicate. She was the smartest, prettiest, and funniest person he had ever met. Sure, that last one typically only appeared after a good number of cocktails, but it didn't matter. For Gil, it had been love at first sight. After three years of trying to win her over, it had finally been love at about the thousandth sight for her. Shortly thereafter, they were married in the suburbs of Chicago. Gil had argued in favor of a honeymoon at Yellowstone but had been overruled almost immediately. They instead had spent a week on a beach down in Barbados.

If Gil had any regrets about marrying Maria, it

was that she did not share his love of the outdoors. During the course of their nine years of wedded bliss, he had made absolutely no progress with regards to changing her mind. Her idea of roughing it was a weekend of being pampered at a spa. To her, the woods were an insufferable hell of biting bugs, poisonous snakes, and all sorts of things that wouldn't bat an eye at eating her alive.

So, too, had it been with Carl. The birth of their only child had been nearly mind-blowing for Gil. Not only was he now a father, but his child was a boy, a boy to carry on in his footsteps and share in his interests.

Sadly, it had not come to pass. Carl was a great kid in almost all aspects. He earned good grades, was popular, and was even polite – a rare thing in children these days. He was everything that any parent could hope for. Unfortunately, he also shared his mother's disdain toward Gil's passion. Sure, he could convince his son to come on the occasional weekend layover, but the boy usually grew bored within an hour of setting up their tent. To him, Mother Nature had nothing to offer that could compete against his PSP.

Thus, Gil was forced to compromise, usually in their favor. He'd get a weekend here or there, and he'd always reserve at least three days out of his yearly vacation for a getaway. However, these were typically lone outings. Family trips almost always went in Maria's favor, especially since she was usually smart enough to plan them close to either a theme park or fairground. In doing so, she knew Carl was always sure to side with her. Gil had to admit it was hard to plan a good camping trip within walking distance of a killer roller coaster. Plenty of those places had dedicated campgrounds. However, they were often so congested and filthy that he would have preferred a week sleeping in his mother-in-law's backyard.

This year was different, though. For the first time ever, Gil had won the argument over the family vacation. He had offered his wife a compromise of two days in San Francisco in return for driving east through the Rockies and taking a week-long camping trip deep in the backwoods of Colorado. Neither Maria nor Carl had been happy about it, but even they had to admit that fair was fair. Both had promised to keep an open mind and try to enjoy things; Gil, in return, had assured them that if the campout was a disaster, next year they could have their beaches and amusement parks with nary a peep from him.

Unfortunately, three days in, it was looking like Gil might be forced to live up to his word. No matter what sights he showed them, his family had been unceasingly miserable. Truth be told, he was glad they had slept in today. His little fishing excursion was the first real enjoyment he had gotten so far on this trip.

The loud snap of a stick he stepped on brought Gil out of his reverie. It was silly, but it seemed to have nearly the same report as a gun going off. *No wonder*, Gil realized a few moments later. All had become silent around him. The chirps and chatter of creatures scurrying through the underbrush had disappeared. He stopped walking and looked around, suddenly glad he hadn't kept any of the fish he had caught. Silence like this usually meant a predator was near.

Gil was no fool. Loving the woods had meant learning about them, too. He'd heard similar silences before. Still, he wasn't particularly worried. A black bear would typically give a wide berth. As long as cubs weren't involved, they were often happy to leave people alone. An angry cougar could be a potential problem, but they were ambush predators, and the stream upon which he walked had a nice, wide bank. He was probably too far away from the brush to make a good target.

He decided to give it a few minutes. If things didn't go back to normal by then, he'd begin hooting and hollering. Most animals would think twice before charging a full-grown man making a boatload of freaky noise. Worst case scenario, he had bear spray in his jacket pocket. An eyeful would send even the ballsiest bruin running for the hills.

A low grunt from across the stream bed caught his attention. Gil turned and began scanning the area for signs of movement. The noise hadn't been a familiar one, but he wasn't fool enough to think he had heard every sound in Mother Nature's arsenal.

The grunt came again, this time a few yards to the left of where it had originated. A wild boar perhaps? He didn't think they were indigenous to these woods, but that didn't necessarily rule it out. More likely a feral pig. Gil didn't relish the thought of having to climb a tree, all because he had stumbled across a nasty side of bacon with an attitude problem.

Whatever it was, it was moving. It was also apparently aware Gil had heard it because, a few seconds later, it ended all pretense of sneaking about quietly. Leaves crunched and something moved past branches, snapping them as it went. Considering the sounds, something large was out there – and it was no pig.

Gil bent down, taking care to keep his eyes on the area from where the noises came. He picked up two flat rocks from the stream. At once, he started banging them together. The loud noise reverberated off the trees. It would have been enough to rattle the resolve of most bears he had come across in his adventures.

He stopped what he was doing and listened. There was silence for about twenty seconds, and then a sound carried back to him. It was the same noise he had just made. Was it an echo?

A moment later, it happened again. *Impossible*, thought Gil. Bears didn't bang rocks together. It would have been quite the task given their lack of opposable thumbs.

Almost immediately, all the tension drained from him. "Carl! That better not be you!" he yelled toward the bushes.

If his son was playing tricks, that gave Gil some hope. It meant he had finally given up on grousing in front of his video games and had decided to live a little. He was within spitting distance of their camp, so the risks were low. He'd go easy on Carl so as to not spoil what little progress had been made.

"Last chance, Carl. Come on out."

Still no response. Either the boy was being obnoxious – not unheard of – or it wasn't him. They were pretty far out, but this was still a known camping area. It was very possible he had stumbled across another hiker having a little fun at his expense.

The normal sounds of the forest finally returned. Whoever had been lurking there, having what they no doubt thought was a good joke, had moved away from the area.

Gil sighed. Assholes. Even in the big woods, you couldn't always escape them. He wasn't too upset. He had played his fair share of pranks on fellow outdoorsmen in the not-so-distant past of his youth. *No harm done*, he thought as he continued on his way.

He rounded a bend and could see the site about fifty yards away. *Odd*, he thought. Where were the tents? He should've been able to see them, especially the gaudy orange one he shared with his wife. It stuck out like a sore thumb in all but the deepest of woods. It was practically a beacon in the clearing where they had made camp.

Oh shit! He was afraid this would happen. Bored and miserable, they had gone and packed everything up in the SUV. He wouldn't have put it past them. They were probably thinking that if they put up a united front he'd have to cave and drive them back to civilization. Well, they had another thing coming. As far as Gil Mercer was concerned, a deal was a deal. He had no tolerance for welchers, especially in his own family.

As he got closer, he noticed things weren't as he had first assumed. The site wasn't stripped clean after all. Maybe he had caught them in the act.

No, there wasn't any movement. If they had been scurrying like ants to pack things up, he'd have seen them by now.

It wasn't until Gil reached the edge of the camp that a sinking feeling began to enter his gut. The bright orange tent was still there, after all. But it had been pounded into the dirt – flattened, actually – and was plainly missing a few large chunks. There was still just enough color left for it to be unmistakable.

A moment passed while this sank in, and then Gil dropped his fishing gear and sprinted full speed into the campsite.

"MARIA! CARL!" he began shouting as he circled the center of the clearing. Here, it became evident exactly how bad things were. The tents were destroyed and the sleeping bags torn apart. Debris littered the entire area. It looked like a tornado had hit. Hell, it looked like someone had dropped a bomb on the place.

Gil had never seen anything like it. He'd seen hungry bears attack campsites before. They'd make a hell of a mess – but nothing like this.

The thought of bears brought another uncomfortable feeling to the pit of his stomach. He forced himself to look more closely at the surrounding area. It didn't take him long. Gil was no tracker, but even he could see the rust-colored stains on the grass. It told a grim story.

Even so, he refused to believe it. It had to be something else. *The SUV!* He was sure of it. He'd go there and find them waiting for him, then they'd all have a good laugh and drive off together. He held onto that thought like a drowning man. It was the only thing keeping him on his feet.

He continued shouting for his wife and son as he raced to where their vehicle had been parked, about fifty yards away.

Gil ran through a copse of trees and tripped over something hard sticking out of the dirt. He pulled himself to his knees and saw it was one of the doors of their Dodge Durango. He immediately felt like he had stepped out of reality and into one of the horror movies that he and Carl would occasionally stay up late to watch. In the eerie silence of the forest, it was almost unreal.

The silence! Gil hadn't noticed it while he'd been shouting Maria and Carl's names, but now he did. The sounds of the woods had once again retreated into nothingness. For a few seconds, all he could hear was the beating of his own heart. Then he heard another of those grunts from earlier.

Gil turned toward the sound. Less than twenty yards away, just outside of the tree line, stood a nightmare. It was nearly nine feet tall and at least twice as broad as him, all of it muscle – hairy muscle.

It stared at him with red-rimmed eyes that bespoke of intelligence tinged with madness. Brown fur covered the creature from head to toe, except around its mouth. There, the fur was stained the same rust color as the grass in the campsite. The creature opened its mouth wide and let loose a roar that sounded as if it had escaped from the gates of Hell itself.

Gil's bladder emptied as the beast charged him.

The next two minutes were both the longest and last of his life. Much of what came out of his throat – while he could still make noise – was little more than inarticulate screams.

However, one thing was certain. During those few minutes, Gil Mercer loved camping a whole lot less than he usually did.

PART I

PART 1

1

*S*ince man first walked the Earth, people have seen
the unexplainable:

Lights in the sky, ghosts from the past,
monsters in the mist.

Do they exist, or are they just our imagination?

Science has scoffed at these stories ... until now.

My name is Dr. Derek Jenner, and I dare to believe.

Together with my team, I will find what is out there.

The truth cannot hide from me.

I am ... the Crypto Hunter.

"Oh, for Christ's sake, turn off that crap,"
Harrison said. "You're supposed to be packing."

"I like this show," Rob, his roommate, protested.
"And we're not leaving until this afternoon anyway.
Besides, who cares if we're late? Last I checked, they
don't shut the forest down if you're not on time. So
stop being so freaking anal." He turned back toward
the TV.

"Fine, have it your way. If you forget anything,

you're not borrowing it from me," Harrison said, resuming his own packing. "I don't know why you watch that stupid show anyway. It's not like they ever find anything." Despite his argumentative tone, he didn't feel any real annoyance toward his friend and frat brother. It was just part of the normal bickering they did on a day-to-day basis.

Harrison Kent and Rob Alieri were both juniors at Alamosa University. Harrison was a business major. However, he spent the majority of his time with either the lacrosse team or the myriad clubs of which he was a member. That was in stark contrast to Rob, who studied biology and could usually be found either in front of the TV or online – when he wasn't immersed in his textbooks. Harrison often joked Rob seemed intent on rotting his brain during those few moments when he wasn't busy trying to build it up.

"Don't be a hater. They find some cool stuff sometimes," Rob replied, still facing the TV.

"Oh yeah, I forgot about all the blurry photographs and redneck witnesses. Yeah, real cool," Harrison sniffed as he started rolling his sleeping bag, feeling a bit of regret that he wouldn't be sharing it with anyone for the next week. Things had been rocky between him and his girlfriend, Amy, for a while. That she had flat out refused to even consider the camping trip told Harrison maybe the writing was on the wall for their relationship.

He had tried not to let it get him down. They'd only been dating for a few months. If they were done, so be it. It wasn't like there weren't at least a few other potential prospects in his crosshairs either. He had a naturally athletic build and an outgoing personality, both virtues that meant he'd spent few Friday nights of his college career alone.

"These things take time. Besides, all they need is *one* good piece of evidence, and then BAM – the scientific world would be on its ear. I mean, seriously, wouldn't it be great if even one of them wasn't total bs? What if they found an actual thunderbird? Or what if that dinosaur in Africa turned out to be real?"

"What if my aunt had a mustache? She'd be my uncle," Harrison countered.

"Knowing your family, she'd also be your mother and your cousin."

Harrison couldn't help but chuckle. Rob had his own running jokes at Harrison's expense, his family tree being one of them. He couldn't argue against it either. He had at least a few cousins back East that he wouldn't be too surprised to learn had married their sisters.

"Besides," Rob continued, "did you know they had an episode of *The Crypto Hunter* last year that wasn't too far from where we're going?"

"Really? Let me guess, we're all gonna be anally probed by aliens before the week is out."

"Nope, it was about bigfoot."

"Seriously?"

"Yep," replied Rob. "They found tracks and hair."

"Tracks and hair!?" cried Harrison with mock enthusiasm. "Oh, well, that settles it then. There couldn't be anything else out in the woods responsible for that."

"Dude, keep an open mind. Besides, it might make for some good campfire stories."

"Planning on scaring Paula's panties off her?" Harrison joked.

Rob turned and gave him the stink eye. Unlike Harrison, he didn't exactly have his share of coeds to choose from. He was average looking at best, skinny, and somewhat introverted. Whereas Rob was plain, his girlfriend, Paula, was quite cute, though. He knew damn well he was dating above his pay grade and thus was willing to endure a little sexual frustration.

"I'm pretty sure her panties are welded on," Rob replied, a touch of annoyance in his voice.

Paula came from a devout Catholic family and was firmly in the *saving herself for marriage* camp, something she had made clear to Rob almost immediately after they had met at one of Ki-Beta-Phi's many yearly mixers. With the ground rules of their relationship set, they had been a stable, if perhaps trifle dull, couple.

"Wrong attitude, man. We're gonna be in the woods for a whole week. You gotta work on your '*me Tarzan, you Jane*' attitude."

"Are you kidding? I'm still not even sure how you dragged *me* into it. I hate camping."

"It'll be fun."

"Until we get mauled by bears."

"I thought it was bigfoot," Harrison replied as Rob flipped him the bird. "Besides, don't be such a pussy. Think of it as a rite of passage, a chance to get away from it all for a while. No books, no studying, nothing but good times with good company."

"Didn't *Friday the 13th* start off with a speech like that?"

"Yes, and until they all got chopped up by Jason, it was one big sex party in the woods. I could live with that."

"I'm pretty sure you won't be in too much of a *sex party* mood with your sister around. Or is there something else about your family you haven't told me?"

Harrison laughed. Though he himself had spent most of his life in the Denver suburbs, his parents were originally from West Virginia where they still had family. His had always been a close-knit clan, so reunions were held regularly. Though he was fond of his eastern cousins, even he had to admit they had a Hatfield/McCoy vibe about them.

The funny thing was that his sister, Daniella, seemed to be taking after them. She was a freshman, attending school in South Dakota – studying to be a forest ranger, of all things. It was she who had originally suggested the trip.

Harrison was typically neutral on the concept of camping. He had done a stint in the Boy Scouts and had gone rock climbing on more than one occasion, but that was about it. Regardless, he and his little sister had always been close – albeit not in the way Rob liked to joke – thus he had agreed almost immediately to go along. That Harrison was also a little over-protective of Danni and didn't like the idea of leaving her alone out in the woods – especially those as dense as where they were going – was also a factor in his decision.

Ironically, of the two, Danni was probably far

better qualified for this outing. Hell, this was her thing after all. Not to mention, she wasn't going to be alone, regardless of whether he was there or not. She was driving in with some friends, at least one of whom sounded suspiciously like a boyfriend. Harrison didn't like the idea of her being out there by herself, but he also found he wasn't particularly keen on her being with a guy – especially one who might wish to *get back to nature* with her. Thus, it had been he who had suggested they make it a group outing.

As Harrison continued to pack, he couldn't help but overhear the idiocy in which his roommate was engrossed. This episode was apparently set somewhere in South Carolina where they were searching for lizard men. He rolled his eyes at the concept. *Christ, the shit that some people would watch.* As far as he was concerned, so-called reality TV was a vast wasteland. He could think of dozens of better ways to spend his time than watching a bunch of clowns shout "Monster!" every time they heard a twig snap.

A quick check of his watch confirmed there was still plenty of time before they needed to be ready, so he decided he could let Rob finish his silly show before pestering him again. He was still somewhat amazed his roommate had even agreed to go. The guy wasn't exactly a survivalist on his best days. Harrison suspected it all had to do with Paula. He had discussed the trip with them while sitting together in the campus dining hall, and she had been surprisingly enthusiastic about the idea. As such, Rob couldn't exactly say no without losing points with her. In the end, he had agreed to it – albeit not without a good deal of bitching, at least whenever Paula wasn't within earshot.

Unfortunately, with spring break looming, Harrison hadn't had much luck with regards to getting others to join in their little adventure. Most of his friends were either going skiing or heading toward warmer climates. His only other recruit had been another frat buddy, Greg, although Harrison suspected he was only coming to get stoned in a place far from the eyes of the cops that prowled most spring break hangouts.

On the upside, a small group might not be a bad thing. His sister had rented a car for the drive down, and Harrison had his old beat-up Wrangler. Fewer cars in their caravan meant a better chance of getting where they were going without someone getting stuck once they were off-road. All in all, it was probably for the best.

Now if he could only get Rob to shut off the goddamned TV and get packed.

2

Two and a half hours later, the foursome loaded their supplies, including a cooler full of *refreshments*, into the back of Harrison's Jeep when they looked up to see a blue Nissan Xterra pull into the campus lot. Harrison spotted his sister in the passenger seat thanks to her mop of unruly blonde hair. Even if he hadn't, the arm hanging out the window and waving in his direction was a give-away. Harrison was impressed. She was actually early. Assuming her group didn't require much more than a pit stop to use the facilities, they could all be on the road within the hour. That gave them an excellent chance at making it to their destination before dark.

The other vehicle had just barely stopped when the passenger door flew open and his sister came running in their direction. Harrison noted that college life had apparently been good to her. Rather than put on the dreaded freshman fifteen that seemed to plague new students, she appeared to be in as good of, if not better, shape than when he had last seen her some months earlier.

He had barely enough time to register these thoughts before she launched herself at him. Unsurprised, he caught her in a big bear hug. "Oof!" he mock protested. "Just a little glad to see me?"

She laughed. "Always happy to see my favorite brother."

"Your *only* brother."

"At least you don't have to worry about any competition," she replied as he put her down. "So, are you all set?"

"Almost done. Come and meet your fellow wilderness freaks," he said, turning toward his small party.

"Hey, Rob!" Danni said as she approached. They had met a few times over the years and were on good terms with each other in a casual, "friend of a friend" sort of way.

"Good to see you," he replied with a nod.

"Danni, this is Paula, Rob's girlfriend," Harrison said. Paula gave a small smile in return. She was curvy, with auburn hair done up in a tight ponytail and dressed in functional, if plain, hiking clothes. Both her outfit and quiet demeanor immediately set her apart from Danni, who stood there beaming with her wild blonde hair, running shoes, and almost too short cut-offs.

Harrison wondered whether there might be tension on the trip between the two. Danni was outgoing to the point of sometimes seeming overly flirty, whether or not she meant to be. She was just that type of person. Paula, on the other hand, was fairly conservative. Whereas Danni might just chat with Rob for the sake of talking, Paula might very well perceive her to be a threat.

He made a mental note to monitor that situation as the week progressed. Being stuck in the woods with two fighting wildcats did not seem like a particularly fun prospect to him.

Up next in the introductions was Greg, who stood there looking every bit the casual slacker he was. Harrison liked him because the guy was almost always mellow. Little bothered him. At the end of the day, he was the perfect person to go on vacation with because he just went with the flow.

Harrison didn't fail to notice the appraising eye that Greg gave to his sister, but that didn't worry him too much. Danni was a little bundle of energy. It was doubtful whether Greg would be able to keep up with her, even if he got the opportunity to try – which wasn't likely because Danni had brought company of her own.

"So, what about your friends?" Harrison asked, noticing that her companions had parked and were now approaching. There were two of them. The first was a pretty girl of Asian descent. She was a bit taller than Danni, with a similar athletic build. As she got closer, Harrison couldn't help but notice several appreciative glances she was giving the third member of their group. Harrison turned and found a similar look on his sister's face as they approached.

So this is the guy Danni mentioned. His first impression was of a man who had watched one too many Westerns as a child. He had deeply tanned skin, almost mocha in color, and wore faded jeans, moccasins, and a fringed deerskin jacket. He rounded out the look with long black hair tied in what looked to be ... yes, it was actually a *feather*. Harrison wasn't usually the judgmental type, but something about this guy's appearance seemed to scream that he was trying too hard. Although, he conceded internally, he might be slightly biased due to the longing gaze his sister wore plainly on her face.

"I want you to meet my friends," Danni said, peeling her eyes off the male half of her contingent long enough to make introductions. "This is Allison Chan."

"Hey, guys!" Allison replied with a big smile. She seemed friendly enough to Harrison. It didn't hurt that she was a looker, too. If not for the fact that she seemed to be enamored of the guy in their group, he might have considered the possibility of getting to know her a little better. Oh yeah, if those thoughts were flitting through his head, his time with Amy was definitely coming to a close.

"And this..." continued Danni, indicating her male companion, "is Wild Feather."

"*Wild Feather?*" Greg quipped with a slight chuckle.

A slow, even voice replied, "It is the name given to me by my people."

"Your people?" Harrison asked, a bit more skepticism in his tone than he had intended.

"Wild Feather is a Comanche," Danni said with just a touch of defensiveness. "He's Native American."

"I know who the Comanche are," sniffed Harrison, struggling to control the eye-roll he wanted to give her. He stepped forward and offered his outstretched hand. "Nice to meet you."

Wild Feather reached out and grabbed Harrison's forearm instead. "It is a pleasure to meet the brother of the fawn. I look forward to us communing with the Great Spirit during this journey."

Harrison couldn't believe it. This guy was piling on the bullshit in layers, and his sister – not to mention her friend – seemed to be swallowing it hook, line, and sinker. Even Paula seemed to be giving this guy a much friendlier smile than she had afforded Danni.

Harrison was thinking his earlier instincts about being over-protective were spot-on. If he left his sister alone with this guy, they'd be having an orgy under the moonlight by the end of the first day.

A nagging voice in his head reminded him that Danni was an adult and could therefore have as many orgies with as many people as she damn well pleased, but he ignored it. He decided to make it a point to keep an eye on Wild Feather. If he accidentally happened to do any cock-blocking along the way, well, that would just be a damn shame.

He momentarily considered unpacking the cooler from his car. The less *liquid courage* around for this guy, the better. On the other hand, ruining everyone's fun wasn't a particularly great way to start this trip. Besides, he had little doubt that Danni and her group had packed their own libations for the weekend. She was still underage, but Harrison wasn't an idiot. Such things hadn't stopped *him* from drinking when he had first started college. Danni was every bit his equal in terms of resourcefulness. The fact that she was an attractive female – something Harrison had a little trouble admitting, considering her relation to him – probably made it all the more easy for her.

Okay, that settled it. The cooler would stay. No way was he going to play the buzzkill for this getaway. He'd just have to keep his eyes open and make sure there were plenty of tents to go around. Besides, if she had really wanted a romantic weekend alone with Geronimo here, she wouldn't have invited her brother – not to mention her friend Allison – along. Unless, that is, his sister was now into some freaky stuff, a thought which Harrison really wished hadn't popped into his head.

Allison broke the potential awkwardness of the moment by asking, "You guys need a hand loading up?"

Cute *and* friendly. Yeah, he would definitely not mind getting to know her better. Still, best not to look a gift horse in the mouth.

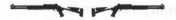

With the extra hands helping out, they were finished packing within fifteen minutes. A final check of their gear sent Rob running back for a few missed items. Harrison was tempted to give him an "I told you so!" for his troubles, but managed to refrain. It gave the rest of them a chance to hover over the hood of Danni's rental and go over the map. They'd be using

GPS for the majority of the trip, but considering their destination was a bit nebulous, they all agreed it was probably a good idea to have a non-technical backup. Besides, as good as a GPS was, Harrison had seen them fail on more than one occasion, usually just at the point where he had absolutely no idea where he was.

They'd take Route 160 the majority of the way. It would take them west into the Rio Grande Forest Reserve. From there, they'd turn north onto a narrow logging road for at least another hour. Their last taste of civilization for the week would be a remote little town called Bonanza Creek, assuming it was even still there. Harrison had never heard of it. Hell, the GPS wouldn't even acknowledge it as a destination. However, it was on the old Rand McNally map laid out before them, little more than a speck deep in the woods, but there nevertheless. It was probably not much more than a dirt road with a few buildings, but it would give them a chance to stretch their feet and maybe grab a bite to eat before four-wheeling it the rest of the way.

"Why this place, Dan?" Harrison had asked when she first mentioned it.

She had replied with barely contained enthusiasm, "A friend of mine went hiking around there for a few days last year. It's supposed to be beautiful. She said it's like stepping back in time to another era."

"And?"

"And what?"

"There's obviously more," he had pointed out. His

sister wasn't particularly good at hiding things when she was excited.

"Okay, fine. My friend said there's an abandoned ranger station out there. If we can find it, it'll be like exploring a haunted house. How awesome would that be?"

Harrison had to admit that it sounded potentially cool. Despite his active life at school, a little adventure seemed like a good thing. He could feel a glimmer of excitement at the possibility of doing some exploring in a place where they were highly unlikely to run into other people.

They agreed upon their route and then on the passenger split. Due to its roomier capacity, Greg would ride in the Xterra with Danni and her group. Considering the appreciative glances Greg had been making toward her, Harrison wasn't surprised when he didn't exactly balk at this proposition. Harrison's Wrangler, though old, was equipped with heavy duty tires and a tow-winch. He would take the lead once they got off-road. If there were any obstacles his vehicle couldn't make it past, then they wouldn't risk the other car in an attempt to do so.

By the time Rob made it back to the group, they were ready to climb in and start their engines. Adventure awaited.

3

T he ride out of Alamosa was fairly uneventful. Most of the departing spring-breakers were headed in other directions. Though camping and hiking were popular in the area, this time of year called the younger demographic toward where crowds of their peers would be gathering. Those who chose to stay local would most likely have their eyes set on the ski slopes. Others would be flying out toward points sunny and sandy. As such, the two car caravan had Route 160 more or less to themselves once they got past the town of Monte Vista.

After a few hours on their route, they began to leave civilization behind, the evergreens on either side of the road beginning to grow denser with each passing mile. Even so, it was a pleasant drive. Light traffic coupled with good company was enough to put all the travelers in a cheery mood. If asked, most of them would have probably agreed it was a particularly fine day to be young and on an adventure with friends, both new and old.

Eventually, Danni's Xterra slowed. Harrison knew they were searching for the turnoff that would signal their final wave goodbye to the modern world. Their GPS was no doubt telling them they were close, but you couldn't count on street signs or a nice, wide turnoff way out here. What they were looking for would amount to little more than a slightly wider than normal gap amongst the trees. Pick the wrong one and they'd end up backing out and trying again, assuming they didn't get stuck first.

They were in luck, though. As they came upon the dirt road, they saw fresh tire tracks leading the way into the wilderness. From the look of things, it wasn't as untraveled as they had assumed it would be. It was either local traffic going toward Bonanza Creek or, worst case scenario, they'd be sharing the woods with a few other campers. On the upside, at least there was no mistaking the road when they found it.

Danni's car pulled to the side to let Harrison go first as planned. It seemed to be an unnecessary precaution, though. The road was a little rough, but it was dry with firmly packed dirt. There was nothing even remotely challenging about it for either vehicle. Even as the miles wore on and the terrain became rougher, they were able to maintain a fair pace.

Harrison had to admit he was surprised at the time they were making. Normally, he'd have expected at least a few downed branches to force them to stop. It appeared, however, that whoever had recently traveled this road had already taken care of that job. He wasn't about to complain, though. He'd take a relatively smooth ride over grunt work any day of the week.

Nearing the halfway point, Harrison spotted flashing lights ahead. As they got closer, he could make out the red and blue lights of a police car. It was heading in his direction fast, a little too fast for the narrow road. He pulled the Wrangler off to the side as far as it would go without bumping the thick foliage that surrounded them. He checked the rearview and saw the Xterra doing the same. Last thing they wanted was a collision with a cop in a hurry.

The car, a Ford Taurus with a police bubble on top, slowed as it came upon them, but just enough to pass without scraping itself along the side of anything. It passed them, with only inches to spare, then accelerated again back toward the main road.

"He was in a hurry," Rob commented from the passenger seat.

"Yeah," replied Harrison. "This isn't exactly the Autobahn. Wonder what's going on."

"Maybe some campers got eaten by wolves," Paula joked from the backseat. She knew Rob wasn't particularly easy about this type of trip and was pushing his buttons.

"Not funny," he retorted, taking the bait.

"Aw come on," Harrison said. "Would the Crypto Hunter be afraid of a few scrawny canines? Hell no. He'd probably take an out-of-focus picture and declare them werewolves."

"Bite me."

"Relax," Harrison said with a sigh. "It was probably just an accident on the main road. Maybe someone hit a deer."

"What was he doing all the way back here?" Paula asked.

"Beats me."

"I think it makes sense," chimed in Rob. "The place we're heading toward is probably not much more than a ghost town. Might not even be big enough for their own police department. They probably check in every so often."

"Guess they don't have a good doughnut shop," Paula quipped, eliciting groans from her two traveling companions.

Bonanza Creek had been founded in the early twentieth century by a prospector looking to incite a new gold rush. Unlike other boom towns, though, it had never really taken off. No more than a handful of nuggets had ever been procured from the surrounding countryside. Even during the best of times, the town's population had never swelled past a few hundred. With no major source of precious minerals and little arable land for farming, the town had quickly settled into a tiny haven for lumberjacks, hunters, and families who appreciated the quiet.

Even though none of the travelers were aware of this history, the size and rustic conditions spoke volumes toward its story. Entering the town proper, little more than a good-sized clearing in the woods, it was evident this was a whole other world from the one they had left only a few short hours ago. To Danni, it vaguely resembled Walnut Grove from *Little House on the Prairie*, which she used to adore as a child.

Only the occasional satellite dish sticking from the rooftops broke the illusion of quaintness. Everything else seemed like a hole in time had just opened up and deposited the town there.

Almost everything, she thought as she spied a pair of sleek black SUVs parked in front of a bait shop. Each towed an empty trailer, and next to them was a large van similarly devoid of color. The three vehicles were neither old nor in disrepair. They weren't local, either. Gleaming "District of Columbia" license plates stared back at them from the bumpers.

Danni thought that a bit odd as they drove past. It would be one thing for locals to be there. Hell, she could even imagine hunters or hikers from neighboring states making their way to these parts. But to traverse almost two thousand miles just to come to this little backwater town? There were far more interesting places in Colorado to travel that distance for.

Oh well, their business is their own. She indicated what appeared to be a general store to Wild Feather. A few aged pumps sat outside of it. *That's convenient*, she noted. They could gas up, stretch their legs, and grab a few last-minute supplies before starting the final leg of the journey. From what her friend had told her, the logging road ran through the town and would get them a few more miles into the woods before they'd need to park and head off on foot. From there, they'd be on their own.

The prospect excited her. *Perhaps for more than one reason*, she mused as she glanced at Wild Feather from the corner of her eye.

Both cars pulled in and their occupants disembarked. A sign instructed them to pump their own gas, then pay inside. Greg volunteered for gas duty as the remainder of the group met up outside the doors to the store.

"So, should we see if Ma and Pa Olson are tending shop?" Danni asked in a playful manner. When she got nothing but confused stares back, she sighed. "Never mind," she said and walked inside, silently lamenting how culturally bereft her companions were.

The interior of the shop wasn't quite as quaint as the outside. Half of it resembled a modern day 7-Eleven, complete with a slushie maker. The other half appeared to be a mishmash of general goods. There were camping supplies, a rifle rack, gardening equipment, and even a small shelf full of video games. It was no Walmart, Danni considered, but for a town of this size, it would probably suffice.

Speaking of nicely sufficing, she noticed her brother immediately perk up as a shapely female stepped out from behind the counter. She was tall, at least five-eight, wearing close fitting jeans and a loose blouse. Her hair was a medium shade of brown and done up in a functional ponytail. She wore no makeup, but she didn't really need to. Judging by her appearance, Danni put her at late twenties, maybe early thirties. Not quite up in the cougar range, but judging by her brother's glances, Danni doubted

Harrison would have objected much if this woman decided to make him her plaything.

"Well, aren't we turning into the little tourist trap?" the woman mused, approaching them. Seeing the confused expression on their faces, her tone changed. "Sorry. It's just been busier here these past few days than it usually is. Welcome to Bonanza Creek!"

There were murmured thanks from the group as a whole, except for Wild Feather, who did some hand gesture and a nod of his head. To Harrison, it looked vaguely like something he had seen in a kung-fu movie. He mentally chided himself upon that thought. He really needed to get over it. If his sister was into this guy, then that was her business. They weren't in junior high anymore. He didn't need to watch out for her. Besides, at the moment he had more interesting things to watch.

He turned to their shapely host. "Thanks. We're just passing through. Some gas and maybe a few bags of chips, and we'll be on our way."

She shrugged. "Passing through? You're a bit far from the highway."

"We're going camping for the week," he continued, wondering why he felt the need to justify himself. What was it about a pretty face that made guys want to confess as if they had just committed a crime?

"I kind of figured," she replied with a grin. "I was

only teasing. Just make sure you're careful out there. We have enough shenanigans going on right now."

"What do you mean?" Danni asked.

"A couple of hikers got lost *again*. That's why it's been busier here than usual. The state troopers and some of the locals have been combing the woods looking for them. Been keeping everyone on their toes."

"Again?"

"Yeah, it usually happens at least once or twice a year. Some idiots head out with no map, compass, or common sense – probably thinking they'll somehow get cell service out there if they get lost. But this is the third time in two months. We seem to be attracting the stupid ones lately. Must be a leap year," she joked.

"Well, if we see anyone, we'll help if we can," Harrison replied.

"Just make sure you don't wind up with them. People are starting to get a little testy about it."

"Don't worry. We're all geared up," Danni said, pulling an old analog compass out of her pocket. "Besides," she added with another glance toward Wild Feather, "I think we have an ace in the hole with us."

Wild Feather again just nodded and replied in that same slow tone he kept using, "Yes. I have walked the path of my forefathers many times. The spirits have never failed me."

Danni and Allison practically swooned in their shoes as he spoke. Hell, even Paula seemed to be making doe eyes at him. In fact, the only female present whose facial expression wore the same dubious look as Harrison's was the shopkeeper. That cemented her coolness in his book.

"Yeah, okay..." she replied in a doubtful tone. "Well, spirits aside, I have just about everything you'd need to survive out there: sleeping bags, bear spray, trail rations, you name it. If I were you kids, I'd double check my gear before heading out. Pick up anything you think you might need. Trust me, it'll be cheaper than the bill the state will hit you up with if we need to come out and save your butts."

That last part was said with a smile, but Harrison had little doubt there was truth behind it. It was one thing for accidents to happen, but the authorities tended to take a dim view on people getting lost on account of their own stupidity. He'd heard of hikers being hit with heavy fines when such things had happened. Truth be told, he didn't really see an issue with it. Sometimes an idiot tax needed to be levied – he just preferred it not be on him.

"I think we're good," he replied, "although it probably wouldn't hurt to stick around for a little bit and do one last inventory. I don't suppose you'd like to help make some suggestions for anything we might have missed?" Even as he said that last part, he regretted it. It probably sounded like one of the lamest pickup lines ever. No doubt he'd be hearing about it later from Rob, and probably Danni, too.

The shopkeeper appeared to consider this for a moment. If she had a snide comment to make, she kept it to herself. Finally, she answered, "Okay. Just be warned, I might go a little nuts on my suggestions. I do have a business to run, after all."

Inwardly, Harrison breathed a sigh of relief. He was normally a pretty cool character with the ladies. It was unlike him to sputter like an idiot.

It was definitely time for him to move on. No point in delaying the inevitable. He'd break it off with Amy the second he got back to school. He had known couples to break up via text message or Facebook, but that struck him as excessively tacky. Even in this modern world, there were some things that needed to be done in person to maintain one's integrity.

But that was for later. For now, he got to spend some time with a helpful stranger who just so happened to be easy on the eyes. He decided he might as well enjoy it – although, perhaps he'd try to keep the lame come-ons in check while doing so. No point in embarrassing himself further. Otherwise, it could wind up being a long week for him.

4

One half hour, two full gas tanks, and maybe a hundred dollars' worth of extra supplies later, they were making final preparations to get back on the road. Kate, the shopkeeper, had been fairly impressed by their overall preparedness. She had told them that over the years she had seen far too many campers heading out with barely a sleeping bag to their names. Nevertheless, she had given them some decent suggestions to add to their already sufficient gear – and maybe a few nonessential ones, too; business tended to be slow in Bonanza Creek.

They had loaded up on extra rations, a second water purification kit, a hand axe, and a machete. Harrison wasn't quite convinced on that last one. After all, they weren't going on an expedition through the Amazon. However, in the end, it could prove useful ... maybe. Besides, Kate's smile was pretty intoxicating. If she had wanted to, she could have probably taken him to the cleaners as long as she kept batting her eyelashes.

"We about ready to go, or do you want to stare at the counter girl's ass some more?" Rob finally asked.

"Robert!" Paula exclaimed.

"What? Don't tell me you didn't notice. Jeez, I thought he was practically getting ready to propose to her."

"Asshole," Harrison huffed with a grin. He didn't think he would be getting out of this without at least one shot in his direction. He was just surprised his sister didn't get a dig in as well before climbing back into the Xterra with Allison, Greg, and Wild Feather. Actually, upon thinking about it, it made perfect sense. Considering the way her eyes were practically glued to him, Harrison could have taken a piss right in the middle of the store and Danni might not have noticed.

Speaking of the devil, Harrison could see Wild Feather sitting in the driver's seat of the Xterra. No doubt he was busy filling Danni's ears with some bullshit about how he wished it were a horse instead. Why was she unable to see through all of his crap? He was very obviously playing her.

Of course, on the flipside, why was he so busy harping on it? Harrison sighed and once again reminded himself that she was an adult.

"Are we going, or are we just gonna sit here all day, staring out the window?" Rob asked, breaking him out of his reverie.

He's right, Harrison mused. Plenty of time to mull

it over once they had set up camp. He was putting them at risk of not making it in before dark. If that happened, then he'd really have to hear about it.

He gave a wave toward the other vehicle and started his engine. He pulled out, and it quickly fell in line behind him. From there, it was only a few minutes to find the far end of the town and the beginning of the logging road as it led into the increasingly dense forest.

Once they started down it, Harrison actually felt a sense of relief. Concentrating on the trail ahead required more than enough effort so that he was able to put images of his sister and Wild Feather *communing* with nature out of his head.

Whereas the drive into Bonanza Creek had been relatively free of issues, the road – if it could even be called that – on the far side of the little town proved to be somewhat less friendly. They went no more than a mile before they came across their first obstacle, a downed branch. It wound up being small enough so that both vehicles could drive over it with no problem. Unfortunately, it was just a precursor for what awaited them as they journeyed further into the wilderness.

A short time later, they rounded a bend, and Harrison immediately hit the brakes.

"What the hell happened here?" Rob wondered out loud.

Harrison couldn't help but agree with the sentiment. For dozens of yards in front of them, large branches – and in some instances whole trees – lay strewn across the trail. It looked as if either a bomb or a small localized tornado had hit the place.

Harrison shut off the Wrangler and got out. He heard the Xterra stop behind them and its doors being opened, but he didn't pay it any mind.

He stepped over to where the first tree, not really much more than a sapling, lay and examined it. The tree appeared to have been bent down until it had broken. Looking further down the path of destruction, he could see similar markings on many of the other downed trees. That made no sense. The damage seemed to come from both sides of the road, and if it had been a tornado, it would have snapped them all in the opposite direction back toward the forest. This seemed more ... deliberate.

"The forest spirits here are restless," Wild Feather said behind him, offering what Harrison found to be an exceptionally non-helpful suggestion. Still...

"Something sure as hell is," Harrison commented.

"Yeah," responded Rob, also coming up behind him. "Looks like someone dropped a herd of elephants off in this place. You guys ever seen anything like this?"

Harrison shook his head. "Nope. What about you, Feather?"

"Once, on a vision quest, I..."

"Can we forget the spirit bullshit for now?" he snapped. "Have you seen anything like this, yes or no?"

Wild Feather seemed to be at a momentary loss

for words. "No." He quickly composed himself and added, "I will perform a blessing here. Perhaps that will ease the tension from this place." His normally easy tone was gone, however. To Harrison, it sounded like he was making it up on the spot.

"You do that," he said before turning back to Rob. "Come walk with me. I think we can make it over most of this, but I want to be sure."

As Wild Feather began chanting something unintelligible, just in time for the girls to join him, Harrison and his roommate began to step their way over the debris.

Most of the destruction looked the same to him, as if something had bent the trees to the point of breaking. He was beginning to suspect the possibility of a bunch of drunken yokels with ATVs and tow chains when Rob stopped and pointed out something.

"Are those scratch marks?" he asked, indicating one of the trees that still stood by the roadside.

Harrison stepped forward to look. It took him a moment to see them, and it wasn't surprising why. He had been looking from the ground level up to about his own height, but the gouges were higher, about seven feet up. There was also a chunk of bark missing from right in front of them, as if something had grasped the tree and simply ripped a piece out.

"There's more," Rob added, pointing out a few other trees at the far end of the debris field. "I think I read somewhere that bears do that."

"Would have to be a pretty large one," Harrison countered.

"A Grizzly?"

"Doubt it. I don't think they're native to this area. Black bears are, but it would have to be a big one."

"Pissed off, too," Rob added.

"Yeah, *really* pissed off. Either that, or he had buddies to help him with this. I don't know..." Harrison trailed off as he continued staring at the wreckage.

"What are you thinking?"

"Personally, I think someone's screwing with us."

"With us? Why?"

"Maybe not so much with *us*, as screwing with anyone trying to come this way. Look at this place. Do you really think one animal did all this? I'm thinking it's probably a couple of people trying to make it look that way."

"Why?"

"Who knows?" Harrison sighed. "Maybe they're growing pot in the woods and want to keep people out."

"Don't tell Greg that. You'd be giving him a new purpose in life."

They both chuckled, then began to make their way back to where the rest of the group was waiting. While it was definitely weird, Harrison was convinced it was the work of people. An animal doing all of this seemed doubtful to him. If there were freak weather conditions that could do such a thing, he had never heard of them. Either way, it wasn't an insurmountable obstacle course. He had no doubt his Wrangler could traverse it. Danni's rental would probably be okay, too, as long as they took it slowly. The biggest risk, as far as Harrison could see, was the possibility of a punctured tire.

However, he quickly realized perhaps there were other risks that he hadn't taken into account. Once they rejoined the group, Paula ran up to Rob with a slightly wild look in her eyes. "Maybe we should just go home," she said in a small voice.

"What are you talking about?"

"Wild Feather," she whispered. "He said this was the work of the wendigo. It's an evil forest spirit that..."

"I know what a wendigo is. You're kidding, right?"

She lowered her voice even further. "He's an Indian. They *know* these things."

Harrison had been close enough to hear her, and he shot his roommate an eye-roll. For the past few hours he had been thinking that, before the end of the week, he was most likely going to have a nice, long chat with this Wild Feather dude. Now, he wondered if he'd make it through the day before telling this guy to cut the shit.

For now, though, his main concern was to nip this in the bud. His sister had been looking forward to this trip, and as far as Harrison was concerned, unless she changed her mind, something stupid like a bunch of downed branches wasn't going to stop them. "Rob and I checked things out," he said in a voice loud enough to get everyone's attention. "It should be passable as long as we take it slow."

"That's good to hear," replied Danni, her tone

upbeat. "Just to be safe, though, I think we should do one car at a time." Smitten or not, he knew his sister was a smart, down-to-earth girl. He doubted she'd give much credence to any bullshit ghost story.

"What did this?" Allison asked. She was standing next to Wild Feather and, judging by the look on her face, she had been at least partially taken in by his "wendigo" crap. Harrison had no issues with using a good ghost story to get into a girl's pants, but this was different. Wild Feather appeared to be genuinely scaring some of the group.

He shot Rob a glance, hoping his roommate would take up on it. He needed a little backup. Otherwise, their imaginations could wind up running roughshod over each other. Finally, he said, "It looks man-made."

After a moment, Rob, having taken the cue, jumped in. "Yeah. I think I saw some tire tracks on the other side. Probably some assholes with a full bottle of Jack and too much time on their hands."

Allison and Paula both turned toward Wild Feather, as if expecting some brilliant rebuttal. Neither Harrison nor Rob knew Allison from a hole in the wall. However, both of them noticed Paula's reaction toward the newcomer. If he said the wrong thing now, things had the potential to turn ugly.

Fortunately, Wild Feather was either smarter than he looked – or just lucky – as he replied, "I feel a darkness about this place. But perhaps it is the taint of men and not spirits. I am still but a student of my people's ways."

That settled it right there. The tension drained from the group, or at least from the girls, and they set about righting their situation. It was decided that the majority would take their packs and walk to the far end of the downed trees. Harrison and Danni would pilot their respective vehicles, now with their reduced weight loads, across the obstacles.

Once the others had grabbed their stuff and made it across, Harrison started up his Wrangler and put it into low gear. It was slow going as he tried to make sure he didn't shred his tires on any sharp branches or protruding rocks, but fifteen minutes later his wheels touched down onto the dirt at the far side.

Then it was Danni's turn. The Xterra was almost as capable off-road as Harrison's vehicle, except it was outfitted with stock tires made more for the highway than for hard trails. She took it even more slowly than her brother. About three-quarters of the way through, one of her back tires got caught between two logs and lost traction. For a moment, it appeared the rest of the group would need to come back and give her a push, but then the other three wheels caught and she powered over the obstacle.

A few minutes later, they were all loading themselves back up into their respective rides. They were no worse for the wear, but Harrison noticed with some regret that they had eaten into their remaining daylight. Whatever cushion of time they had started off with was now greatly reduced. If they came across any further delays, they'd be hiking to their destination in the dark. He wasn't particularly frightened of that notion, and he knew Danni wouldn't be either. He wasn't sure about the others, though, especially if Wild Feather started in with his "spirit" crap again. If that happened, they might wind up camping out in the vehicles and starting again at daybreak.

5

R*age! He couldn't remember when he had felt anything other than a seething hatred for all things. Perhaps he had always felt this way. It seemed as if he might. Yes, it was likely so. Rage consumed his being now as it had always done. The only way to quench it was to unleash it upon anything he came across.*

He had torn apart countless of the four-legged things. They were timid and cautious, but they were stupid, too. They died bleating in fear as they were ripped to shreds. So, too, had some of the small chattering things in the trees been far too curious for their own good. They had come down to investigate, only to be torn in half and eaten even as they still twitched.

The meat didn't quell the rage, but he felt a need for it regardless. A small part of his fevered brain seemed to remember feasting upon roots and berries, but those memories must have been a lie. There had always been the rage, and it demanded that flesh and blood be his sole sustenance.

He walked through the woods aimlessly with no direction, no purpose. In that, too, there was only rage. He vaguely remembered a territory he had once kept with others of his kind, but that was no more. He had eventually savaged them with teeth and nails in response to their worried grunts. Now he was alone. His only companion was the anger that seethed within.

He slashed at a tree trunk as he lumbered past. He seemed to recall that this had once been a way to mark his passing. Not too long ago, he had done the same thing in a long, narrow clearing. Instinct had momentarily overcome the rage in his mind, and he had started marking trees to denote his domain. Then the rage had descended again, stronger than ever. The trees themselves seemed to mock him. He had killed a great many of them before the bloodlust abated. It had not been satisfying, though. Trees did not bleed. Trees did not scream.

A memory of the recent past reminded him that the two-legged things were a different story. Though they were small and weak, they were satisfying. They ran, they fought, they bled, and they screamed. Oh, did they scream. Their death wails were an agony of sound to his sensitive ears, but one that called to him nevertheless. Their flesh was fatty and foul-tasting, yet he craved its taste anyway. Yes, they were worthy prey.

Sadly, he didn't encounter them too often. Their territory did not usually overlap with his kind. However, sometimes they were stupid and wandered away from their clans. Such a thing had happened recently. More than once, in fact. He wished for it to happen again and *again. No amount of screaming could satisfy him for long.*

He considered journeying to one of their clans in the night. There, he could kill and feast as much as he desired. But even in his current state, he was still cunning. He knew the two-legged things could be dangerous. They sometimes carried objects that hurt. If he attacked a large group of them, they might be able to fight him off, might even be able to wound him. No, best to stay away for now until the rage demanded such action. Then, and only then, would he perhaps chance such a thing.

For now, though, an odd sound filled his head. It was a low, constant growl just at the edge of his perception. Perhaps another creature was challenging his domain.

No, two creatures. There were definitely two of them. Maybe they were battling each other for dominance. Yes, that could be it. It would all be for naught, though. Whichever was the victor would fall to his might, for there was nothing in the woods — no, nothing in the world — that could stand against him.

He stopped to listen again. The twin growling continued, but now it appeared to be moving off. One might have conquered the other and given chase. Perhaps, but there was still something strange about it. Then he realized what it was. The pitch of the two creatures never changed. Surely, had they been battling, there would have been a rise and fall to their vocalizations. No, this was a constant growl.

And then recognition came to his ravaged mind. He had heard this sound before. This wasn't the growl of two creatures battling. It was the sound of the beasts that the two-legged things sometimes moved about in. They were fast and had inedible armored shells, but they were stupid, no more than slaves to the two-legged things. But if so, then that meant more of the two-legged things had wandered into his domain.

His stomach growled as the need for their repugnant flesh once again filled his brain. He would feed, but first he would make them scream.

He would make them scream for a good, long time.

6

Luck had once again smiled upon the group. Following their earlier delay, the remainder of the trip down the secluded logging road was fairly uneventful. A few scattered branches were all they had come across, and those had been easily traversed.

At last, the road began to peter out. The path they followed became little more than a narrow trail through the woods. After another half-mile, the trail, or at least the drivable part, ended in a clearing.

Harrison exhaled a small sigh of relief once they parked and began unloading their gear. There was still enough daylight left to hike west for a few miles, then set up camp. As long as the tents were up and a fire was going, everything else could wait until morning.

The portable GPS was still getting a strong signal. That was promising, although the maps of the area were preloaded. Even if reception failed, they should be okay.

He shouldered his pack and grabbed one of the coolers. The load was heavy, but not oppressive. He was in good shape and doubted he would be doing much more than breathing hard by the time they made camp.

Once he and his friends were geared up, Harrison locked the Wrangler and pocketed the key, inwardly smirking at the thought of being carjacked way out here. He then checked on his sister's group. They were likewise finishing up with their packs and dividing their supplies amongst them. With a bit of smug satisfaction, Harrison noted that Wild Feather's gear was surprisingly modern-looking – despite his constant "spirit" mutterings.

"You guys all set?" Danni asked. She was fully loaded up and almost appeared comical, considering her size compared to the gear she carried. If she was feeling any discomfort, though, her face didn't show it.

There were nods all around. Everyone looked ready for the adventure ahead and, despite their earlier mishap, they seemed in high spirits.

"Okay. I'll take point with Wild Feather," she said, much to her brother's annoyance. "Harrison, can you take up the rear and help any stragglers?"

Harrison considered protesting. He knew his sister wasn't stupid. No doubt she had seen the tension he was directing at her wannabe boyfriend and was attempting to keep them apart for the time being. Still, she had a point. He knew what he was doing. If Rob or Paula started to lag behind, it would be a good idea to have someone there to make sure they didn't get lost.

"I've got your six," he finally said, suppressing the sigh he wanted to give. As long as they were moving, his sister was probably safe from whatever *vision quest* Wild Feather was planning for her. For now, making sure none of the group fell behind – or stopped for a toke break, in Greg's case – was his top priority. There would be plenty of time to play cock-blocker later on. Of that, he had no doubt.

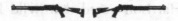

As the sun began to set, the temperature started to drop. The exertion of walking was keeping them all warm so far. Soon enough, though, it was going to start getting chilly. They were in no danger this time of year, but if they didn't get a fire started, it was going to be a long, uncomfortable night, even for those who had the benefit of a little body heat to be shared.

Harrison chuckled a bit at that thought. The first people who came to mind were Paula and Rob, being the only official couple on the trip. Unfortunately for his friend, Paula wasn't likely to be sharing any heat anytime soon, at least not until there was a ring on her finger. Harrison personally hoped Rob wasn't prepared to go down that route yet. There was nothing wrong with Paula, per se. He liked her well enough, their clashing beliefs aside. He just didn't particularly favor the concept of anyone tying them-selves down before they really had a chance to live.

This brought to mind his own soon-to-be-single status and he actually felt relieved at the concept. While Harrison had no qualms about settling down one day, he planned on giving himself a few good years of fun first.

The group stopped up ahead, pulling him from his thoughts. Catching up, he saw they had entered a small clearing. It wasn't much, maybe twenty feet by another forty, but it was definitely enough for all of their tents and a good fire.

"We here?" he asked to nobody in particular.

Danni answered, "I think so. Coordinates line up with what my friend gave me. Wild Feather likes it, too."

I bet he does.

As if in answer to Harrison's thoughts, Wild Feather replied, "The ground here is wholesome. There is harmony with the spirits in this place."

"Well, let's get with the harmony, then," Allison replied with a giggle. "I'm getting cold."

Amongst them, they had brought four tents. For the sake of speed, though, they decided to set up only three for the night. Danni and Allison would share one, Paula and Rob would take another, and the three remaining guys would share the largest. Considering Paula's stance on things, that more or less guaranteed that nobody needed to worry about any excess nocturnal activities over the course of that first night.

Danni, Harrison, and Greg set up the tents. Paula and Rob began to collect firewood from the edge of the clearing, an easy task as it had been a fairly dry week. Wild Feather and Allison worked on the rest of their supplies – hanging up the food just in case any bears happened to be in the area, then starting to cobble together dinner for the group.

Working diligently, within an hour they were more or less good to go. The tents were up with the sleeping bags inside, a fire was going, and a modest meal was heating up over the flames. As darkness descended, they lit a few Coleman lamps at the edges of the clearing to provide some extra light. That done, the campers began to gather around the fire both for warmth and a little relaxation. All in all, there was a content mood amongst them, their earlier trouble along the logging route completely forgotten.

"Well, we made it," Allison said, her pretty eyes twinkling in the firelight. "I don't know about the rest of you, but I think this calls for a toast."

"Just one?" Danni asked.

"Well, maybe two or three." She laughed and walked to the nearest cooler, pulling out two six packs. "Any takers?" she asked, receiving nods from all around the campsite.

As Danni took hers, Harrison said, "I'm afraid I'm going to need to see some I.D., miss."

She flipped him the finger and casually replied, "I.D. this, big brother," eliciting laughs from around the fire.

After the bottles had been cracked open and several long pulls taken, Wild Feather spoke up. "This reminds me of the old days. The braves of my tribe would sit around the fire as brothers."

"What would they do?" Allison asked, undressing him with her eyes.

"Many things. Most nights, they would tell tales of the spirits. Sometimes, they would make a war counsel. Other times, they would pass the peace pipe around the circle."

"I think I can help with that last one," Greg said. Unsurprisingly – at least to Harrison and Rob – he pulled two blunts from his jacket pocket and held them up to the group. "Who's for a little 'peace pipe' action?"

Under normal circumstances, Harrison might have joined in with the *peace offering*. He knew Rob probably would've done so, too, but tonight they both had personal demons to deal with. For Rob, it was obviously the presence of his girlfriend. While she wasn't a one-hundred percent stick in the mud, they had never known her to go for much more than a drink or two, much less any chemical enhancements.

Harrison, on the other hand, had a desire to remain mostly sober so as to keep an eye on Wild Feather. He just didn't trust that guy around Danni. He knew a player when he saw one, and he also knew a bullshit artist, too. He wasn't enamored of his sister becoming another notch on this guy's teepee.

In the end, only Allison and Wild Feather accepted Greg's offer. Harrison wasn't sure if Danni declined because she wasn't into it or because he was around. Either way, that was fine by him. If she kept a clear head, she'd be less likely to fall for any mystical bullshit tossed her way. Also, as one of the more experienced campers in the group, it was likewise probably a good idea to keep her wits about her until they became more comfortable with the area.

Thus, they sat around the campfire. They talked, they drank, and some of them smoked. The conversation was amiable enough and, Harrison's misgivings aside, even he found himself beginning to relax, although a part of him was pretty sure it was a mild contact high from the marijuana smoke wafting around the group.

After a while, Allison stood up. She grabbed a flashlight and announced, "Nature calls."

Paula replied, "I think I'll join you."

"Figures," Rob mused. "Even in the woods, chicks have to pee in a group."

Paula slapped him playfully on the shoulder, then the two girls walked toward the tree line.

"Don't go far!" Danni yelled after them.

"Do you think you should go with them?" Harrison asked.

"Not really," she replied. "Allison knows what she's doing. I'm not saying anything she doesn't already know."

"Yes," Wild Feather said, "she has told me of her many walks in the woods of Pennsylvania. She is as home in the forest as a doe."

"And what about you, Feather?" Harrison asked. "You seem to know a thing or two about being in the wilderness."

"It is a rite of passage amongst my people. When I came of age, I was sent out from my tribe with nothing but my wits. I was expected to survive for seven moons in this way."

"I thought it was the Spartans who did that shit," Greg replied in a lazy voice.

Wild Feather appeared momentarily taken aback by that. "All people of warrior mettle have similar customs," he quickly replied.

A little too quickly, perhaps, Harrison noted. Maybe it was the joint he had been smoking, but for a second there, Wild Feather's demeanor seemed to crack a little. Greg's seemingly innocuous comment had caught him by surprise. Harrison was tempted to ask whether he had stolen that idea from the movie *300*, when he was interrupted by the girls' abrupt return.

"I don't think we're alone out here, guys," Allison said, approaching the fire.

"Well, yeah. There are deer all around this area," Danni replied. "Not to mention..."

"I know *that*. I meant people. For a minute there, I saw lights off in the woods."

"Are you sure?" asked Harrison. "That shit Greg carries is pretty potent."

"I saw it, too," Paula said. "It was weird. There were these red lights shining around out there."

Allison nodded. "I pointed my flashlight in their direction, and then they just disappeared."

"It was probably some hikers," Harrison said. "Sometimes they'll use a red light because it doesn't screw with night vision."

"I think you mean hunters," Danni countered. "Most hikers out after dark are more interested in seeing what's in front of them."

"Why do you think they shut down when we saw them?" Paula asked, a little of that earlier nervousness starting to creep into her voice.

She's proving to be jumpy out here, Harrison noted. He gave what he thought was an easy shrug. "They're probably out here without a license. If they saw you, it's a good thing. They'll be heading away from us. It's not like we're exactly being subtle out here."

"It saddens me when people must resort to poaching," Wild Feather said. "I can only hope they put to good use whatever they take. My people have never been wasteful with the land."

Allison took that as cue to sit down next to him. "Don't let it get you down. Not everyone respects nature like we do." If she noticed the eye-rolls that both Harrison and Rob made, she didn't acknowledge them. "I know," she continued. "Since we're all gathered 'round the fire, why don't you tell us one of your tribe's stories?"

"Aren't we supposed to be telling ghost stories?" Rob asked.

"My people have many tales of the spirits," Wild Feather replied. "Some of them would qualify as your ghost stories."

"Tell us one," Danni said, moving to sit on his other side. Harrison felt a prickle of annoyance as she did so. He was not overly keen on his sister being the bread in a bullshit sandwich.

"I have an appropriate one. It is a tale of the wild man of the woods. What my people call sasquatch. Many moons ago..."

"Hold it!" Rob interrupted. "What *your people* call sasquatch? I heard that the word sasquatch was just a made-up bastardization by some guy in the seventies. No Native Americans ever called it that."

"Way to go, Rob," Harrison commented with perhaps a bit more glee in his voice than warranted. "Who'd have thought that stupid 'Crypto Hunter' show would pay off?"

"You watch that crap?" Allison asked.

"What? It's a good show."

"It's always the same," she complained. "They never find shit at the end of it."

"It doesn't matter. At least they keep an open mind. I think it's cool that someone is out there looking into this stuff," Rob replied a bit defensively. "Besides, how would you know they never find anything if you don't watch it?"

It was hard to tell in the firelight, but Allison's face appeared to flush a little. "Fine, you got me. The guy who hosts it is kind of cute." Danni raised an eyebrow in her friend's direction. "What? He is. Oh, who cares about that dumb show? Come on, Wild Feather, tell us the story."

He appeared to hesitate for a few seconds, or at least to Harrison it seemed that way. Perhaps he hadn't anticipated Rob's challenge. Finally, though, he said, "The truth is, my people have many names for the hairy men of the woods. Most are difficult to pronounce, but they all speak of the same thing: a forest spirit made flesh – a creature that protects the land and those who live in harmony with it. However, this spirit can be wrathful to those who would seek to defile the balance. My great grandfather used to tell of one such defiler as we sat around the fire, much like we all do today."

Harrison looked around at the collective faces. All

of the women, Paula included, were giving Wild Feather their rapt attention. Rob was listening, too, although probably for another chance to jump in and question his authority on this subject. As for Greg, judging by the glazed look in his eyes as he peered into the fire, he was in his happy place.

"What happened?" Paula asked as Wild Feather continued with his dramatic pause.

"Once, long ago, before the coming of the white man, when the buffalo were still plentiful on the plain," he began, "there was a man in the tribe. He was a powerful warrior, one of their fiercest braves, but he was also prideful. After many victories in battle and countless successful hunts, this man began to boast that he had no equal. He could defeat any man and take his wives and horses. He could kill any beast and claim its flesh and hide. He laughed that the spirits were but smoke to him, and he had made far too many fires to be fearful of smoke."

"I know what you mean, brother," Greg chuckled, taking another toke.

"The elders of the tribe chastised the warrior. They said his pride would be his downfall, that he should give offerings to the spirit world so they might forgive his arrogance. But the man just laughed at their entreaties. He told them that he had earned all of his possessions by the strength of his own arms, so why should he owe the spirits anything?"

"After the shaman's warning, his pride grew, and he decided that perhaps the spirits owed *him*. Thus, he set out to take what was theirs. He began to chop more wood than his fire needed. When he hunted, he would kill more than his family could eat, then leave the rest for the birds. In all things, he grew wasteful. The elders, seeing what he was becoming, began to pray for him behind his back. They knew that the spirits were getting angry at the man's umbrage."

Wild Feather paused again, making eye contact with all three girls, one after the other.

"Finally, the Great Spirit sent one of the hairy men down from the mountains. The beast was already fearsome, but the spirits imbued it further. They made it swift so that not even the deer could outrun it. They made it strong so that not even the bear could stand against it. They made it powerful so that no arrow could pierce its hide. Its cries could be heard in the village when it was still many moons away. The tribe grew fearful as the beast approached, its howls of vengeance growing louder with every passing day.

"Finally, the elders came to the prideful man and pointed at him. 'This is your fault,' they said. 'The spirits are punishing us all for your wickedness.' But the man laughed and told them, 'It is just another animal. I have slain the buffalo. I have slain the bear. I will take my bow and arrow and slay, too, this beast so that I might bring back its fur to warm me by the fire.' The next day, the prideful man packed up his weapons and set off into the woods to meet the creature face to face." At that, he stopped telling the story and just stared into the fire.

After a few moments of this, the girls chimed in with squeals of, "What happened next?"

Finally, after another pause – overly dramatic, in Harrison's opinion – he continued. "None know.

Some say the creature overtook him and carried him off to Hell, where the spirits continue to punish him for his arrogance. Others claim the man slew the beast, then set off to challenge the spirits themselves. They say that he still walks the woods to this very day, such is his wrath. It was never truly known. All anyone in the tribe knew was that the beast's screams ceased and the prideful man never returned."

"And then Jason and Michael Myers walked out and slaughtered the campers," Greg added, laughing at his own joke.

Paula, ignoring him, gave Wild Feather a wide-eyed look. "So, do you believe the story?"

Before answering, he fed another branch into the fire, causing embers to rise up in the air. "My people have a great many stories. Some are told to frighten children, but others serve as a warning to men. When I became a man, I went on a vision quest, as all of my ancestors did. In it, I saw many things. Things that give me reason to not doubt my elders."

"What kind of things?" Harrison asked.

"They are not meant to be spoken of. Each vision quest is for the brave who sees it, and him alone." He then turned back to Paula and spoke in a low voice. "But I have seen enough to believe. I think the hairy men are out there. I can sense them. They watch us. Perhaps they watch us even now."

Paula shivered. Rob put his arm around her, most likely as much a defensive gesture as to keep her warm. As he did so, Harrison could have sworn he saw her pull away from him ever so slightly. Rob seemed to notice it, too, no doubt beginning to question the wisdom of coming along on this trip.

Harrison decided that enough was enough for now. "Well then, let them watch us sleep. I'm tired, and we have a lot of walking to do tomorrow." He stood and stretched. "Unless anyone else has any tales they'd like to freak us out with, I'd suggest we all try getting some rest."

Danni stood up as well. "Harrison's right. Things will be easier with the camp set up, but we still have a lot of hiking ahead of us this week. We can save the hangovers for another day."

One by one, the group acknowledged their logic. They all cleaned up – even Greg, despite being a bit wobbly on his feet – then retired to their respective tents. Little did they know, Wild Feather was not too far off the mark.

They *were* being watched.

7

G reg was asleep almost instantly. He climbed into his sleeping bag, giggled for a few moments, then started snoring. Harrison smiled when he saw how quickly his friend had passed out. Greg liked his weed, but the dude had no tolerance whatsoever.

Harrison bedded down on one side of him while Wild Feather did the same on the opposite end. In the dark, Harrison couldn't help but smirk. Wild Feather's sleeping bag was definitely not what one would expect. It was brand new and heavily insulated. He might talk a good game, but he wasn't exactly roughing it out here.

Still, Harrison considered, he had done a lot of assuming in the past several hours about the guy. Now that they had a moment away from the girls, he figured he should at least try to talk to him. Who knows? Wild Feather might turn out to be less of an asshole than he seemed to be.

"You awake, Feather?"

"Wild Feather. And yes, I am still awake."

No shit. "So, how do you know Danni?"

"I met the fawn at the beginning of this semester in an ecology class."

"Yeah, about that. What's up with the whole 'fawn' thing?"

"Your sister has both the grace and purity of one," Wild Feather stated.

The purity thing is the part that bothers me. "So ... how long have you guys been dating?"

There was a pause before Wild Feather replied. "Danni, Allison, and I are just friends. We are kindred spirits."

Harrison couldn't help but notice that he dropped the little pet names this time. Wild Feather definitely wasn't stupid. He apparently realized that treading lightly was probably the smart thing to do around Harrison with regards to his sister.

"That's good to know. That's the way we should keep things out here ... nice and friendly." He hadn't meant it to come out as a threat, but he realized it probably sounded that way to Wild Feather. *Oh well,* he thought as he drifted to sleep, a smile slowly playing out across his face.

"You know, there's plenty of room in here for two," Rob said. He held open the flap of his sleeping bag and gave it a pat.

"We've already discussed this, Robert. You know

how I feel," Paula replied, climbing into her own bedroll and proceeding to zip it shut.

"Jeez. I just figured we could cuddle for a while."

"I'm not in the mood. I'm tired, and Harrison was right: it's going to be a long day tomorrow. We should get some sleep." She quickly turned over and began making exaggerated breathing noises.

Rob didn't buy it for a second, but he could tell she was in a mood. He just hoped it would pass. Although, considering the eyes she seemed to have for Danni's friend, he had a bad feeling about it all.

Sleep was a long time coming for them both. Thoughts of Wild Feather ran through their heads. For Rob, it was an amusing fantasy involving him being eaten by a bear. For Paula, it was thoughts of him running through the fields, tomahawk in hand. She pictured him wearing nothing but a loincloth which, in turn, caused a small shiver in her own loins.

"I don't think your brother likes Wild Feather much," Allison said, lying across the tent from Danni.

"Nah! He's just overprotective. Not that there's anything to be overprotective about."

"Of course not. We're all just friends."

Allison and Danni had been fast friends ever since they met. Even so, there had been some strain as of late. They both had their sights set on Wild Feather, and each was aware of the other's interest. They had discussed it and had outwardly taken a *"may the best girl win"* attitude with each other. Inwardly, though, they were both attempting to vie for an edge in his affections.

Wild Feather, for his part, had been maddeningly neutral. At times, Danni wondered if he might not be stringing them along, enjoying the attention. However, those were fleeting thoughts as she was genuinely convinced of his good intentions.

Still, she considered, it was never a bad idea to try and stack the deck. "Speaking of my brother, I caught him checking you out a couple of times."

"Oh? I hadn't noticed," Allison lied. The truth was, she thought Harrison might make a pretty good consolation prize if things came down to it. She had considered that it might be fun to have a tryst in the woods with a guy she didn't have to compete for. Still, she had her eyes set on Wild Feather, and until such time as he made his decision, she wasn't about to be distracted.

Well, all right, maybe an hour of distraction would be okay. After all, nobody had to know, and she was fairly sure Harrison wouldn't go bragging to his sister about a little dalliance in the woods. No, that would be weird. Best not to let Danni know any of that, though. "So, what did you think of Wild Feather's story?"

Danni couldn't have cared less about the story itself. She no more believed in bigfoot than she did trolls or fairies. It was the story teller who was important to her, as well as the way he told it. There was such passion and conviction in his voice that Danni couldn't help but get goose bumps during his telling of it. However, she answered with a casual, "It was okay."

"Yeah, I thought so, too," Allison said before turning over.

They both drifted off, thinking the other was a bad liar.

Several pairs of curious eyeballs viewed the campsite from just outside of the clearing. They continued to watch as the conversation in the tents died down and the fire outside slowly gave way to cooling embers.

8

"Slow down, Danni!" Rob yelled. Despite the coolness of the morning, he was already sweating hard. She hadn't been kidding last night. Even with most of their gear back at camp, the pace was quickly getting to the less athletically-inclined amongst them.

"Seconded!" cried Greg. He was in better shape than Rob, but was still suffering the after effects of his indulgence the night before. "This is supposed to be a vacation, you know. Not boot camp."

"Fine!" Danni called out from ten yards ahead. "Be a bunch of wusses." She, Harrison, and Allison stopped and waited for the rest to catch up. While they did, Danni uncorked her canteen and took a sip of water. Even she was a little winded, although she wasn't about to admit it.

She had woken early, light barely peeking over the horizon, and had roused the rest of the group. She couldn't help it. This was their first full day out in the woods, and she had no intention of wasting a second of it. To her surprise, Allison, normally an early riser, had been the first to grouse about it, complaining of sleeping like crap.

"I felt like we were being watched all night," she had said.

"Well, yeah. We do have four boys along with us," Danni had joked as she packed up her sleeping bag.

"It's not that. Things just didn't feel right. Who knows, maybe Wild Feather's story freaked me out more than I thought."

That's a bit odd, Danni had thought. Allison was no stranger to camping. Being creeped out wasn't her usual forte. Still, between her sighting of those poachers and the story, maybe she had been spooked. The generous tokes she'd taken the previous night had probably not helped in the paranoia department either.

Despite that, within the hour she had somehow gotten them all ready. They had a quick breakfast, secured some supplies, then marked the coordinates of their camp on both GPS and map. Following that, Danni had led them in the direction of the old ranger station she meant to explore.

Five miles later, they neared the coordinates her friend had given her. Unfortunately, some of them were starting to lag badly.

"Relax," Harrison said, bringing Danni out of her reverie. "If this place is still standing, I doubt it's gonna pick right now to crumble into dust. Besides, if I have to carry Rob back because you destroyed him on our first day out, I'm gonna be pissed."

"Yeah, yeah," she replied offhandedly as the others caught up and unshouldered their packs.

Paula sat down on hers and took a sip from a water bottle. After a few seconds, her breathing had slowed enough for her to say, "It's so peaceful out here."

"Yes," replied Wild Feather, leaning against a tree next to her. "In the silence, you can almost hear the forest spirits whispering to you."

Danni was about to chide Harrison for the look he gave Wild Feather when a thought struck her. It *was* quiet. In fact, other than their breathing, she couldn't hear another sound. That wasn't right.

Her eyes caught Allison's. They were showing the same questioning look.

"You're noticing it, too?" Allison asked.

"Noticing what?" Harrison replied.

"Listen."

"I don't hear anything," Greg wheezed.

"I think that's the point," said Harrison after a moment. "We should be. There's probably an army of squirrels alone right above our heads. There are lots of things that should be making noise right now, but they're not."

"Do you think it's us?" Allison asked, purposely looking toward Greg and Rob as she did so. "We haven't exactly been subtle."

"Maybe," Danni replied warily. "Let's keep still for a few and see. If so, things should start up again fairly quickly." She grabbed her pack and started rooting through it. "But just in case..." She pulled out a can of bear spray.

Both Paula's and Wild Feather's eyes went wide, and they immediately began rummaging through their own packs. While they did so, Harrison bent down and picked up a sturdy stick.

"What are you gonna do with that?" Rob asked.

"Scare it off." He raised the branch and smacked it on a nearby tree. It made a sharp report in the quiet forest.

"I can do better than that," Allison said. She pulled an air horn from her backpack just as there was a loud *CRACK* off to their left. The brush was too dense to see, but it sounded as if it were about a dozen yards off.

Harrison turned toward where the noise had come from. "Don't wait for my invitation."

"Hold your ears. This is gonna be loud." She raised it and pulled the trigger, causing an earsplitting bellow to blare out across the woods. As it subsided, she said, "There. That should scare off any..."

An ungodly roar, even louder than the horn, shattered the stillness around them.

It was followed by a splintering crash. It didn't take a genius to realize that a tree had just come down.

"What the fuck!?" Greg yelled as another crash came. The look in all of their eyes told the same story: there was something out there, and they had just pissed it off.

"Follow me, and stick together!" Danni ordered, quickly shouldering her pack. The rest of the group didn't need to be told twice. She checked her GPS and strode off into the woods, the others following closely behind.

"I don't think that was a bear," Allison gasped, following Danni's lead.

"No shit, Sherlock!" Wild Feather snapped, all traces of calm gone from his voice.

If he had ever known such rage before, it was lost to memory. He had approached the two-legged things silently, as he knew he could. They were stupid things with poor instincts and couldn't sense his movement.

He had planned to take one and scatter the rest. It did not matter. They could be hunted down easily enough. However, he had not expected to be challenged. As he neared them, a battle cry unlike any other rose up to meet him. The noise had stopped him in his tracks and shot waves of pain through his head. It was like another of his kind had bitten clean into his skull, so much was the agony. Regardless, the challenge could not go unanswered. To do so would be a show of weakness. Others might challenge his dominance, and that could not be allowed.

He had answered the challenge with a cry of his own, then the rage had taken over. So incensed was he that he unleashed his fury at everything around him. Branches snapped. Trees were felled. Dirt and rocks were thrown. It was minutes before he realized that he was once again alone. The two-legged things had moved off. Their challenge had been a bluff. They were weak after all. He had planned to savor the hunt, to enjoy their screams. Now he would make them all scream at once as he rent them limb from limb. But first he would salt their meat with fear.

He began to lumber in the direction of their scent, giving up all pretense of stealth.

Danni checked the GPS again. They were headed in the right direction. As they fled away from the source of the – whatever it had been – Harrison dropped back to make sure there were no stragglers. Danni wanted to protest, but her brother was more than capable. Thus, she was surprised when he caught up to her again.

"How are we doing?" he asked with obvious false calm.

"Maybe another quarter of a mile. Why?"

"You don't want to know," he answered in a low voice she could barely hear.

He was right. She really didn't want to know. Unfortunately, she was long past that state of blissful ignorance. Whatever they were running from was coming after them. "How bad?"

"It's making a lot of noise, but doesn't seem to be gaining on us ... yet."

As if in response to his statement, another roar split the air behind them. It sounded hundreds of yards away, but if it had snuck up on them once, it was probably capable of doing so again.

"Don't let anyone run off," she said.

He nodded and again fell back, but he needn't

have bothered. After that last cry, the rest of the group were crowded so close that Danni could have practically piggybacked them all, had she been strong enough.

Something was not right. He stopped and sniffed the air. For just a moment, the breeze had stilled and he thought he had smelled another scent from behind. Had one of the two-legged things broken off from its clan and tried to flee?

He sniffed again. The scent was gone. Whatever it had been had been faint, just barely there. Now that the breeze started up again, he could once again smell the two-legged things he was pursuing. He could smell their bodies, but best of all, he could smell their fear.

They knew he was coming. They knew that they were being hunted. If he could have understood the concept of a smile, he might have allowed himself one at that thought. As it was, he screamed again and once more began to stalk his prey.

"We are so screwed!"

"You got that right, brother," Greg replied to Wild Feather as they fled.

"Shouldn't we be trying to head out of the woods, not deeper into them?" Paula wheezed.

She sounded out of breath, but at least the effort was keeping her from settling into a full-blown panic attack, Danni noted. If they stopped, she was sure that would change.

"The cars are back in the direction of that thing," Danni replied. "And there's fifty miles of forest in every other direction. Trust me, this is our best bet." *I hope,* she thought.

She was trying to keep a positive attitude. Wild Feather had already lost it, and Allison was keeping unusually quiet. If either she or Harrison freaked out now, that would be it. The rest would scatter like doves. Fortunately, her big brother seemed to be doing his part. The least she could do was follow suit. "Just another hundred yards," she said before adding another silent *I hope*. She quickly checked her GPS again and trudged onward.

Near the back of their close-knit group, Harrison was making sure he didn't lose anyone. It was one hell of an effort on his part. Every instinct he had was telling him to cut loose and make a run for it. Inside of his head, the old hunting joke that ended with "*I don't need to run faster than the bear, I just need to run faster than you*" kept replaying itself. Suddenly, it didn't seem so funny. Still, he couldn't live with himself if something happened to one of his friends because of his selfishness. He had been raised better than that.

"How are you holding up?" he asked Rob, who had begun to fall back a bit.

"N-not good," his friend stammered. "You might have to drag me the rest of the way."

"Don't worry. I would," Harrison reassured him before looking back over his shoulder. He could still hear it coming. Whatever it was, it wasn't making any attempts at stealth anymore. It also didn't appear to be catching up to them yet.

It was the 'yet' part that worried him, though. Harrison wasn't a betting man, but if he had been he would have put money on it being able to overtake them anytime it damn well pleased.

"What the hell is it?" Paula asked, lagging but still doing better than Rob.

"Has to be a grizzly," answered Harrison.

Rob coughed. "I didn't think they were around these parts."

"Neither did I. But have you got a better answer?"

"I might," Rob said with a small tired grin.

"Don't start that shit," Harrison growled. "Everyone is freaked out enough as it is."

Rob, for his part, decided to follow that advice and concentrate on running instead of talking.

Danni wasn't a particularly religious girl. However, as they entered the clearing, she could have gladly dropped to her knees and thanked any of a dozen different deities. Her friend's coordinates had been faithful after all. At the far end of the clearing, partially overgrown but still standing, was the old ranger station she had been seeking. It was a small, one-story structure. Danni was once again reminded of Little House on the Prairie as she spied it, although the forest was about as far from a prairie as you could get. It appeared to be an old log cabin. It had seen better days, but still looked pretty damn solid to her eyes.

"There!" She pointed. The rest of the group followed her outstretched hand and saw it, too. A small chorus of cheers arose behind her. That was good. She was pretty sure at least a few members of the group were about done for. This would hopefully give them enough of a morale boost to get inside and bar the entrance with whatever the hell they could get their hands on.

Oh crap! What if the doors are locked?

Why would they be? she asked herself. This place hadn't been used in years, from the look of it. Why lock up an abandoned structure? It's not like anyone had to worry about looters out here.

"Are you just gonna stand there gawking?" Paula asked from behind her, startling Danni out of her thoughts. She had a point. Getting torn to pieces in sight of their potential salvation, all because she was busy worrying about whether or not the doors were locked, wouldn't be a particularly grand way to go.

She found the energy for a quick sprint. As she started running, she heard the others following her lead. Within the space of seconds, she made it to the dilapidated front porch and tried the door.

It didn't budge.

Oh God, it is locked a voice inside of her head screamed. For one small moment, Danni felt panic welling up. It threatened to bubble over until the rational part of her mind realized that the knob had turned when she tried it. Realization hit, and she put her shoulder into the door.

"Help me! It's stuck," she pleaded as her friends caught up to her.

Harrison dragged Greg up to the door with him and gently pushed his sister out of the way. A couple of good shoves by the muscular young men, and the swollen door began to groan open an inch at a time. Finally, after what seemed like an eternity, the opening was wide enough to allow access.

"Ladies first," Greg wheezed in a bad attempt at humor. He stepped aside and gestured toward the entrance.

The others had just started to move when another ungodly scream shattered the silence around them.

As one, the group turned back in the direction whence they had just come. They watched in stunned horror as the creature stepped from the tree line.

For a few seconds, silence once more descended. Then Rob asked Harrison, "So can I start that shit now?"

9

At the sight of the creature, Paula's nerve broke. All thoughts of the potential safety in front of her vanished from her mind, and she did the exact opposite of what she probably should have. She turned toward the other end of the clearing and began running. Most of the group was too frozen at the sight before them to notice. Even Rob was too busy muttering, "Sonofabitch, bigfoot is real," to himself to pay her much attention.

Fortunately, Danni still had her wits about her. "I'll get her," she barked before taking off after Paula.

That snapped Harrison out of it. He yelled, "Danni!" before noticing that the creature's eyes were tracking the two fleeing females. It bared its teeth, and long foamy ropes of drool began to spill over its lips.

Oh shit. It's gonna charge them!

Thinking fast, he cried out to his sister, "Don't stop! Keep going!" and started waving his arms at the beast. "Hey! Yeah you, you ugly fucker!" He bent and found a good-sized stone which he whipped in the monstrosity's direction. The projectile fell far short of its mark, but it had the desired effect. The creature once more turned its head toward them. For a moment, it seemed confused, then it tilted back its head and let loose with another scream.

Uh oh. I think I pissed it off.

The beast charged forward. He turned back to the remaining group and yelled, "In the cabin – NOW!"

He had been right. One of the two-legged things had issued a challenge for dominance earlier. He had been distracted by the sight of two of them fleeing before him. Females, from the smell of it, but then the alpha of their group had begun screaming and jumping. It even had the nerve to try to attack him. The females must have belonged to it.

The two-legged thing was stupid. He did not want its females for mating. He had no interest in that, not anymore since the rage had descended. Still, he would allow no quarter for such a small, weak thing to challenge his domain. He had planned to kill them all. This one, though, would die badly.

He returned the challenge with a cry of his own and sprang to meet the upstart.

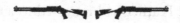

Most of the others didn't need to be told twice. They piled into the old ranger station as quickly as they could. The lone holdout was Rob, who was just now beginning to notice the rest of them. "Where's Pau..." he managed to get out before Harrison dragged him into the cabin.

"Grab whatever you can and barricade the entrance with it. That thing's coming," Harrison said, putting his shoulder against the door and pushing it shut. He had been hoping to find braces for barring the door. *Aren't log cabins supposed to have those things?* All he spied, though, was an old slide lock at the top. It would be better than nothing, but just barely.

He slid it home, then turned around. In the dim light of the cabin, he saw Greg and Allison pushing an old rotted desk across the floor. He quickly got out of their way so they could shove it against the door.

"Windows!" he shouted.

"On it," Whereas before, during the chase, Alison had seemed utterly stunned, Harrison was grateful to see her on the ball now. Whatever her shock had been, her survival instinct was apparently kicking in.

Greg, hungover or not, was in the game too, grabbing more dilapidated furniture to pile against the door. Unfortunately, the same couldn't be said of the rest. Rob just stood there, looking confused. Between his exhaustion, the creature outside, and his girlfriend running off, he had reached a point where he just couldn't process it all. He wasn't the worst off, though. Wild Feather had retreated to a corner of the dark room, where he huddled in the fetal position.

They were in luck in that there was only one small

window facing the front. Even better, it had an intact wooden shutter. Allison swung it closed, but not before muttering, "Oh shit."

"What?" Harrison asked.

"I'd get away from the door, if I were you."

In response, the entire cabin shuddered as the creature impacted with the heavy door. Their makeshift barricade held, if just barely. Unfortunately, a heavy splintering noise came from the door itself. Harrison put his back into the meager fortifications to give it a little more strength. Seeing his lead, Greg did the same.

Again, the beast hit the door. More wood splintered, and they felt the barricade start to move. It was like trying to hold back a Mack truck. Another second, and the two young men were going to be flung like rag dolls, but then it stopped.

A few moments went by, and then there was another roar – close, but not quite at the cabin's door. It was followed by several low thuds against the side of the structure.

"What the hell?" Greg gasped.

Allison chanced a peek through a gap in the shutters.

"What's going on out there?" Harrison asked.

"It's going nuts," she replied, a tone of disbelief in her voice. "It's pacing back and forth, beating its hands against the ground." She paused then added, "Now it's throwing mud at us ... oh wait. I don't think that's mud."

"Just keep an eye out and let me know if it's gonna try again," Harrison said as another roar split the air. "Greg, brace the door with anything you can find. Use the packs, too. They're not much, but they'll give it some weight. Rob..."

"Paula's out there," Rob replied in a dazed voice.

"I need you to concentrate," said Harrison, stepping up to him. "Danni's with her. They're probably a mile away by now. She's okay as long as that thing is here with us. For right now, we need to worry about ourselves. Now I need you to pay attention. You're the one who's into this shit. What do you know about this thing?"

The question brought Rob back to his senses. He thought for a second, then answered, "Not much. Nobody really knows anything about it. It's not supposed to even exist. Why don't we ask *him*?" He pointed toward Wild Feather, still huddled in the corner.

They walked over to where he crouched. "Hey, man, are you still with us?" Harrison asked. He received no answer to his question. After another moment, he sighed then added, "Sorry, but we don't have time for this crap." He reached down, grabbed Wild Feather by his jacket, and hauled him to his feet. That seemed to snap him back to reality a bit.

"Is it gone?" he asked in a shaky voice.

"No," replied Harrison. "I need to know what else your people know about this thing," he said while more thuds sounded from the front of the cabin. *The shit's really hitting the fan now.*

"What do you mean?" Wild Feather asked, his eyes darting between Harrison and the door.

"That story you told yesterday," Rob said. "What else do your people know about sasquatch?"

"*That!?* I made that shit up."

"What do you mean 'made it up?'"

"Exactly that!" Wild Feather mewled. "I don't know anything about that fucking monster."

"What was all that crap about spirits and hairy men of the forest?"

Wild Feather seemed on the verge of losing it again. He started sputtering, "H-how the hell am I supposed to know? I grew up in Chicago. My name is Phil. I just do this shit to get laid."

For a moment, there was silence in the cabin, save for what filtered in from outside.

"Well, that's just great, *Phil*," Harrison replied at last, releasing his grip and turning toward his roommate.

"I am *so* gonna kick your ass when this is over," Allison growled from the window.

"Save it for later," Harrison barked. "Rob, let's see if there's a back door to this place."

"Uh oh! I don't think there's time, guys. It's coming back," she said, catching their attention.

"Oh crap!" muttered Harrison. He quickly dragged Rob over to where Greg was trying to reinforce the miniscule barricade.

They braced for impact. None came. Instead, Allison jumped back from the window with a shout. Glass shattered, and the shutters blew off their hinges as a huge hairy arm came plowing through it. Allison fell to the floor as debris rained down. However, the grasping claws of the creature managed to miss snagging her.

A chorus of screams broke out from the group as the muscular arm began reaching around, searching as the creature snarled outside. Allison backed up to where Wild Feather once more cowered. He didn't even acknowledge her in his panicked state.

Amidst the chaos, an idea popped into Harrison's head. He pulled his backpack from the barricade and began rummaging through it.

He found what he was looking for just as Rob muttered, "Oh crap."

Harrison turned and saw that the creature had grabbed onto the window sill and ripped it, along with a chunk of wall, out. If it couldn't get in through the door, it was apparently going to try making its own.

Not on my watch, he thought, momentarily curious as to where this clearly insane bravery was coming from. He pushed those thoughts aside, though, as he pulled the machete from his pack. In an instant, he had stepped to the side of the window, still out of sight of the creature. The next time it started pulling at a piece of wall, he swung with everything he had.

He caught the creature flush on the wrist. The blow would have been enough to lop a man's hand clean off; however, Harrison watched in horror as the blade sank an inch at most into muscle and bone before stopping. There was a horrific scream of pain from right outside. In this close proximity, it was loud enough to leave a ringing in all of their ears. The arm pulled back, almost wrenching the weapon from Harrison's grasp, but he held true and yanked it free with a spray of blood.

There was another roar, then an oversized fist burst through the wood not a foot from Harrison's head. He had succeeded all right ... succeeded in pissing it off again, he grimly noted to himself. This wasn't good. If that thing could smash straight through the walls whenever it wanted to, then they didn't stand a chance. Their barricade at the door was little more than a joke.

"Allison!" he yelled, ducking out of reach of the grasping hand. "Find a back door, now!"

To her credit, she only hesitated for a moment before running toward the rear of the cabin. Harrison wished her luck. Unlike the monstrous ape at the front door, they had little chance of knocking down a wall. If it turned out there was no other exit from this building, it might very well become their tomb.

10

Taking Harrison's lead, Greg left his place and began searching through another of the backpacks. This left Rob as the sole person bracing the front door. *I might as well open up and let it in, for all the good I'm gonna do here,* he thought, watching Greg heft the axe they had purchased back in Bonanza Creek. *Great! That'll probably be just slightly more effective than thinking bad thoughts at it, but any port in a storm,* he mused as Greg took up a defensive post on the opposite side of the window as Harrison.

"There's no back door," Allison cried out to them.

"Of course not." Harrison muttered with a sigh as he waited to see what the creature would do next. "Greg, don't get too close to the window!"

Sadly, he was a second too slow in his warning. The beast's still bleeding arm shot through again. Greg managed to sink the axe into its massive bicep, but not before its grasping hand closed on his shoulder. Before he could do much more than open his mouth to scream, the arm pulled back. The window wasn't originally designed to be wide enough to accommodate a person of Greg's size. However, with the wood around it already heavily damaged, he was roughly pulled off his feet and through the portal, widening it even further.

Harrison made a mad scramble to grab for his friend, but the creature was both faster and stronger. He peered through the ruined window in time to see Greg thrown some fifteen feet out into the clearing. He landed in the high grass and flipped end over end before disappearing from view. The creature was at the edge of the porch, looking toward where it had flung him. It took one slow step in that direction.

"Oh shit."

Rob noticed, from his vantage point at the barrier, Harrison appeared to be tensing up his body. He realized his friend was actually considering what was sure to be a suicidal plan of action. Before he could make a move, though, Allison called out again.

"There's a cellar!"

"What?" Harrison asked.

"There's a trap door in the back room. Looks like it leads down to a root cellar," she replied, joining them in the front again. "Where's Gr..."

"Get everyone down there and lock yourself in as best you can."

"But..."

"Do it!"

They could all hear the tone of finality in his voice. Tears sprang to Allison's eyes, but she nodded anyway. She started toward Wild Feather, then stopped. Turning back to Harrison, she said, "Here, take this." She pulled a can of bear spray from her pocket and tossed it to him. "It's not much, but..."

"Thanks," he replied, then added with a smirk, "Heh, maybe I can use it on myself so I don't see it coming."

"Wait a second," Rob said, leaving his place at the barricade. "What the hell are you..."

But he didn't get a chance to finish. Harrison had already climbed out the window.

The creature was almost to where Harrison had seen his friend land. It appeared to be actually savoring the moment. This didn't seem the behavior of a dumb animal to him. In many ways, that made it even more frightening.

Stepping off the porch, he got his first good look at the beast. It was even larger than he'd thought. Covered in matted brown fur, it was nearly nine-feet tall. He couldn't begin to guess at its weight, but it had to be several hundred pounds, most of it dense muscle by the look of things.

Am I really gonna do this? he pondered right before springing into action. He had planned to run up behind it and swing the machete at its neck before it knew what was happening. As he got closer, though, he noticed that the creature didn't seem to have much of a neck to swing at. Its head appeared to sit almost directly upon its massive shoulders.

He was contemplating another target, maybe the back of its leg, when the creature turned to face him. The thing might've had the appearance of a large humanoid, but, as Harrison grimly noted, it definitely had the superior senses of a wild animal.

He stood there, not ten feet from the monster, feeling a little foolish as he brandished his meager weapons at it. The creature looked at him with red-rimmed, watery eyes. Harrison met its gaze. For a moment, it was a standoff between man and monster.

A memory from several years earlier flashed through his mind. It was of a trip to the zoo he had taken with his family. As they stood there watching the gorillas, his father had told him how, in the wild, staring down a silverback was the exact opposite thing to do if you wanted to keep living.

"Oh crap," he muttered before being drowned out by a roar of such primal fury that his knees began to buckle. He didn't think human emotions applied to this thing, but if they did, it sounded angry – *very* angry. It raised its club-like arms and charged.

Be safe, Danni, he thought as death rushed at him.

Just then, a sound like thunder resounded in the air around him. A moment later, a splash of something warm sprayed across his face. At first Harrison thought it must be his own blood as the creature tore him limb from limb. Then realization hit: he was still in one piece.

The creature had stopped less than two feet from him. Harrison immediately noticed two things: a bewildered look on its face, and a gaping wound in its right shoulder, about three inches in diameter.

Holy shit! I think someone just shot it. That thought was followed by a less hopeful realization. He was no hunter. Hell, he had never even fired a gun before. Nevertheless, he was certain that as ugly as the wound was, it wouldn't even come close to being fatal to the beast. Thus, before any thoughts as to the insanity of what he was about to do could slow him down, Harrison raised his left arm and unloaded the bear spray right into the creature's eyes.

The result was immediate. Whereas the surprise of being shot had momentarily stunned the creature, the spray caused it to go completely wild. It screamed again as it brought its hands up to its face. In that same instant, it took off running.

Unfortunately for Harrison, he was close enough to be shouldered aside as the monster ran blindly for the tree line. If he had ever wondered what it would be like to be the tackling dummy for the Denver Broncos' entire defensive line, he now knew. He flew back and landed on the ground, the wind completely knocked out of him. All he could see was the sky, but he could hear the screams of the monster as it crashed through the brush, soon drowned out by another loud gunshot.

Several seconds passed until he felt he could breathe again. He gingerly started to sit up, feeling as if every inch of him was bruised. He may have felt like a truck had run him over, but he was also aware that he was still alive.

Harrison had just gotten to a sitting position when he saw a hand in front of him. He took it and was pulled to his feet. He stood and found himself staring at a well-built man in his mid-thirties. There was something oddly familiar about his face. It took Harrison maybe a second to pull the memory up, and then he said, "Hey! You're that guy from TV."

"Yep, and you're that asshole who just ruined my shot."

11

"G reg," Harrison gasped, finally steadying himself on his feet.

"Relax. We're checking on your friend."

It was then that Harrison realized the newcomer wasn't alone. Three other men, each heavily armed and carrying a variety of gear, milled about. Two of them were crouched approximately where Greg had landed.

"I don't know whether you're brave, stupid, or both," said the man who had helped him up. "Spraying an angry squatch in the face, haven't seen that one before."

"Squatch?"

"Short for sasquatch." The man held out his hand. "Derek, Derek Jenner."

Harrison was still somewhat stunned, though whether from the hit he had taken or the sudden appearance of his apparent savior, he wasn't sure. He shook the man's hand before he even realized he was doing so.

It was only then that the fact he was still alive really started to sink in. He felt a coldness seep into him as he came to the realization of just how close to death he had been. He tried to shake it away. Going into shock wasn't going to help him or his friends. That thought pulled his mind back from the dark place it wanted to go. He disengaged hands with the stranger and walked over to where Greg lay.

"Is he..." he started to ask.

"Dead? No. Pretty banged up? Oh yeah," one of the men, thin and about middle-aged, said. "All things considered, though, he should probably play the lottery when he gets back home."

"How bad?" Harrison asked.

The thin man continued tending to Greg. "He has a fractured arm, a few cracked ribs, and maybe a concussion. One thing's for certain, once he comes to, he's *not* gonna be a happy camper." He unshouldered a pack and started pulling medical supplies from it. As he did, he spoke to the second man, a burly bearded fellow who resembled a stereotypical lumberjack. "Help me set the arm before he wakes up."

Seeing that his friend was being cared for, Harrison's thoughts returned to the others still in the cabin. They hadn't come out, which meant they had probably taken his advice about the root cellar. He started walking back in that direction.

"Where are you going?" Derek asked, catching up to him.

"I have some more friends inside." He moved to the window. "Door's barricaded."

"I would hope so," Derek responded, giving him a boost.

Harrison landed with a grunt, and the other man hopped in after him. "That's one way to renovate the place," Derek remarked, surveying the damaged wall.

Harrison walked toward the rear of the cabin. He scanned the room in the dim light, then spotted what he was looking for. In the middle of the floor was an outline in the wood, with a recessed handle in the center. He walked over, reached down, and gave it a pull. It didn't budge.

"Locked?"

"Seems that way," he replied.

"Smart."

Harrison knelt over the trapdoor. He banged on it a few times, then yelled, "Open up, guys! It's gone."

After a moment, there was a sliding sound, then the door began to inch up. "Don't! It could be a trick," Wild Feather said in a panicked voice from below.

"Yeah, Phil," he replied, "it's me, bigfoot, doing my best Harrison impersonation." That elicited a sharp retort of laughter from Derek.

The trapdoor swung open, and Allison's head appeared. Harrison helped her out, and she immediately threw her arms around him. The gesture caught him by surprise at first, but then he hugged her back, glad for her warmth.

"Get a room, you two," said Rob, next up the ladder. He had just made it out when he spotted the other man in the room. His jaw immediately dropped wide open. "Holy shit! You're Derek Jenner." He turned to Harrison. "Dude, it's the Crypto Hunter."

"Yeah, I kinda gathered that already."

"You're the Crypto Hunter!" he repeated.

"Yes, indeed. Dr. Derek Jenner, at your service."

Harrison ignored the exchange and yelled down into the darkness, "Coming, Phil?"

"Is it safe?"

"Just get up here. Unless you'd prefer we leave you behind."

Within moments, the faux Native American was scrambling up the ladder. Once he was out, Derek surveyed the group and asked, "Is that everyone?"

"Yes..." Rob started to say. "Err, no! My girlfriend is still out there."

Harrison could have smacked himself upside the head. In all the confusion, he had forgotten about Danni and Paula. "My sister, too. They ran when that thing came after us."

"We have to go after them," Rob said, starting toward the door.

Before he could get more than two steps, Derek caught him by the arm. "Not so fast," he said. "None of you are going anywhere at the moment. For the time being, consider yourselves detained under my authority."

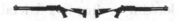

"Detained?" Harrison, Allison, and Rob asked as one.

"Yes, you heard me. Until we have a chance to

sort things out, you're all officially in my custody."

"No offense, dude," Harrison replied, "but last I checked, being on a low-budget cable show didn't come with that kind of power."

Derek smiled, showing off his straight white teeth. "Just for the record, that *low-budget show* has been the highest rated thing on the Adventure Channel for the past three seasons. But you're right. Even pay cable doesn't come with that many perks. On the other hand..." he said, fishing something out of his pocket, then showing it to the group. It was a badge. "The U.S. government is more than capable of delegating that kind of authority. Any questions?"

"No way! Let me see that," Rob said.

"As you wish, citizen," Derek replied, handing the I.D. over to the group for inspection. He was enjoying this part. He always did.

"U.S. Forest Service, Department of *Cryptid Containment*!?" Harrison read. "No offense, but there's no such thing."

"Yeah, I'm pretty sure it's a crime to impersonate a federal officer," Allison commented.

"Indeed it is," Derek said. "However, I think you'll find that if you call in my badge number there, it checks out just fine. Unfortunately, we're a bit out of cell range. Regardless, I can assure you," he continued, looking them all in the eye, a dead serious tone in his voice, "that if you do *anything* to step out of line, you'll be looking at time in a federal prison."

Harrison opened his mouth to protest, but Derek interrupted him. "Besides which, we have guns. Do you?"

There was stunned silence from the group, then he added, "That wasn't meant to be a threat, just a fact. Do any of you really want to go running around out there unarmed now that you know what's waiting?" Again, he was met with silence. "I didn't think so. Now, let's go gather ourselves together. You can tell me about your friends, and then we'll go take care of this business."

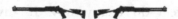

Derek helped them dismantle the barricade. The campers retrieved their packs and followed him out into the clearing. The two other men Harrison spoke with had managed to get Greg back to his feet. His arm was splinted, and his head was bandaged, but he was alive. The third man from the group was nowhere to be seen.

"How's the patient?" Derek asked the thin man as he walked over.

"He'll need a hospital eventually, but I think he'll be good to go for now. What about the rest? Anyone else need patching up?"

"The one in the deerskin jacket is going all basket case on us," he quietly said, motioning toward Phil, who stood silent and wide-eyed. "The rest seem to be handling things okay."

"Got it." He proceeded to pull a syringe from his well-organized pack. He walked over to Phil and put a hand on his shoulder, causing the younger man to flinch.

"It's okay," the thin man said. "This will help calm

you down."

"Very mild sedative," explained Derek to the group. "Will mellow him out, but not knock him out."

Harrison nodded, then said in as calm of a voice as he could, "That's all fine and good. Now about my sister..."

"We're taking care of it. One of my men is trying to pick up their trail. Once we have it, we'll go after them, but we'll do it my way. If any of you go running off blindly, there's probably gonna be a bunch of dead bodies in these woods by the end of the day. That thing isn't playing around. You understand?"

There were nods all around, except from Rob, who asked, "Is it Woodchuck?"

"Huh?" Harrison grunted.

Derek, on the other hand, smiled. "I see we have a fan." He turned to the others and explained. "Chuck *Woodchuck* Wayans is my tracker. Good man, formerly with the U.S. Army before signing on with us. Trust me, if it's out there, he can find it. Word of advice, though, don't call him Woodchuck to his face. Unless, that is, you like spitting out your own teeth."

Rob looked confused. "But I thought that was his nickname."

"No. He can't stand it. The network gave it to him. Said it made him more approachable. Trust me, it's only for the cameras." Derek then gestured toward the other two men from his group, but Rob was one step ahead of him.

"That's Mitchell, the team medic," he said excitedly, pointing toward the thin man, the perils of his friends momentarily forgotten. "And that big guy is Francis, their cameraman."

"Interesting camera," Allison commented, noting the large rifle he was holding.

"Yeah, about that," Harrison said, "I can't help but notice the lack of a show being filmed here. I don't suppose you're about to tell me I've been punked."

"We can discuss that later." Derek pointed toward the tree line. As he did, a short, powerfully built African American dressed in camouflage fatigues stepped out of the brush and walked toward them. As he came closer, the group wrinkled their noses at an odor that hung about him.

"Game scent," explained Derek, noticing their expressions. "Speaking of which, Mitch, once you get that kid fixed up, everyone needs to be scented."

The medic gave a thumbs-up, at which point Derek directed the campers in his direction. He then headed toward the man in fatigues, motioned him to follow, and kept walking. Once they were far enough away from the others, he asked in a low voice, "How's it look, Chuck?"

"It's weird, DJ," the other man replied. "The two runners took off in a straight line. Pure panic. A blind man could follow their trail."

"Is the squatch going after them?"

"That's the odd part. It's heading in their general direction, but it's acting erratically, making a hell of a mess along the way. It's like every ten yards or so it has to stop and punch out a tree."

"You know these rogue males can get a little squirrelly, Chuck. That one in the Cascades led us on a hell of a chase, remember?"

"It's not like that. Like I said, this one is erratic. It's barreling through there like a freight train. Hell, one of those kids could probably track it down. I'm not sure, man. There's something off about this one."

"Well, let's keep it to ourselves for now. The main thing is that we find it and take it out. That thing's killed at least four people so far. Much more, and the local government won't be able to keep a lid on it."

"I hear you, boss. Don't worry. It's not getting away."

"Good. Let's see if we can find those girls before it does. Take point. We'll move in five."

Derek Jenner addressed the group of shaken, but still very much alive, campers before him. "Okay, listen up. This is the way things are gonna work. That stuff you were sprayed with is squatch ... sasquatch musk. It stinks, but it'll keep that thing out there from immediately recognizing you as human. Since it seems to have a mad-on for people, I think we can all agree that's a good thing. But smell is only half the equation. I need you all to be quiet. You move when we move. You talk only when we say it's okay to talk. You follow those directions, and we'll all stay alive."

"What about..."

Derek cut Harrison off. "Your sister and friend are our number one priority right now. We have their trail. Running through the woods hollering our heads off isn't gonna help them. It's only going to bring eight-hundred pounds of angry ape down on our heads. We'll find them as quickly as we can. Okay?"

Harrison nodded, hoping it would be quickly enough. Rob seemed to still be enamored at meeting his TV hero, but it would be only a matter of time before panic for Paula bubbled back up to the surface.

"Good. Chuck and I will take point. You, Harrison, right? I want you behind me. Mitch will walk with the rest of you, and Frank will have our six. That's the way we go. For now, quiet conversation is fine. When I give the signal, though, that means zip it."

Derek spent a couple minutes going over some hand signs with the group. They seemed like fairly smart kids to him, especially the one that had gone toe-to-toe with the squatch. If he could do that armed with just a knife and some pepper spray, then he was probably reliable. It was the rest Derek was worried about, especially the kid dressed like Sitting Bull. Even with the sedative, he looked like he was ready to bolt for the hills. He mentally noted that Frank would probably need to pull double duty, guarding their rear and keeping an eye on that one.

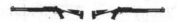

"Are we all set?" There was assent from all, save one.

"How about you, Tonto? Ready for a hike?" The purposely insulting question had the desired effect. Phil glared hard at Derek for a second, but then simply nodded. Harrison tried, albeit not too hard, to suppress a smirk.

Derek and his tracker set off. The rest of the group followed. As they started walking, Harrison turned to his friends to assess them. This Jenner guy had pretty thoroughly taken charge of the situation, and he was glad to let him keep it. However, this trip had been partially his idea and he felt responsibility for his friends.

"How're you guys holding up?" he asked them as a whole.

"I feel like hammered shit," Greg replied, his arm in a sling and the contents of his pack spread out amongst the others. "But I have to tell you, the doc here has some good shit in that bag of his." He hooked a thumb toward Mitchell. "We should definitely party with this guy sometime." Everyone chuckled, including the medic.

Harrison was glad to hear his friend was in good spirits, although he could tell by the look on his face it was an effort on his part.

"Physically, I think we're pretty good," chimed in Allison. "Mentally..."

"I know what you mean," replied Harrison grimly.

She walked up next to him and placed a hand on his shoulder. "Don't worry. We'll find them."

"I know," he responded before silently adding to himself, *I just hope we find them first.*

12

D anni finally caught up with Paula. Fright and adrenaline had given the scared girl a boost of energy, much like it would a gazelle fleeing a lion. At first, Danni had attempted to keep up with her as she fled through the woods, but Paula had refused to listen to or even acknowledge her. Eventually, she had let her own pace slacken to conserve energy. Danni wasn't exactly a tracker, but she had spent her fair share of time in the woods and knew what to look for.

Besides, Paula had been making absolutely no effort at anything other than running. She ran straight and true, so Danni had been able to follow her with little problem. Broken branches here, foot-prints there, a swatch of torn clothing every once in a while ... all of it finally led her to Paula. Her reserves spent, she had collapsed against a tree; where she remained, eyes closed and breathing heavily.

Danni approached quietly. She simultaneously

put one hand on Paula's shoulder and the other over her mouth. She didn't think the creature had followed them, but there was no point in taking the risk. As expected, Paula's eyes opened wide and she attempted to let out a shriek, muffled against Danni's palm.

"It's okay. It's just me," Danni said in a soothing voice. She herself was tired and scared, but since there was nobody else to fall back on, she would have to be the calm, collected one for now.

Eventually, Paula's eyes focused and she nodded. Danni removed her hand and sat down next to her. She pulled out her canteen and took a swallow of water, then offered it to the other girl who drank with no hesitation.

When she was done, the two sat together in silence for a few minutes until Paula whispered, "Is it gone?"

"I think so."

"Did the others follow?" Without warning, she broke out into sobs. "Oh God! Rob! I left Rob."

Danni put an arm around the other girl. Despite that, she wasn't particularly happy with how Paula had panicked, causing them to split up. Then again, a bigfoot attack hadn't exactly been on any of their agendas that day.

Thinking back on it, it almost seemed surreal now that they had put some distance between themselves and it – she hoped. She was still somewhat surprised that she hadn't completely flipped out as well. All things considered, she could probably forgive Paula for losing her cool. "I'm sure he's fine."

"But that thing..."

"Harrison is with him. He wouldn't leave Rob. I know my brother."

"Do you really think they stand a chance against that thing?"

Danni didn't want to say what she was really thinking. The thought was far too painful to even consider. So instead, she replied, "Trust me. It'll take a little more than an oversized gorilla to stop Harrison. Besides, Wild Feather is with them. I'm sure *he* has a couple of tricks up his sleeve."

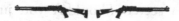

"Can we go home now?" Phil whimpered.

"Come on, that's not something the *prideful man* would do. Where's your bow and arrow?" mocked Allison.

Though inwardly Harrison was chuckling, now was probably not the time for any browbeating. "Enough of that," he chided. "We're all coping as best we can. We need to stay focused for now."

Fortunately, Rob was on hand to change the subject. Despite his endangered girlfriend, he was still all starry-eyed with regards to their current company. "So, when are you guys gonna start filming this?"

"We're not," Mitchell replied.

"*What?* You're kidding me, right? Forget the stupid Adventure Channel. If you get that thing on video, we're talking the cover of Time Magazine here."

"I know."

"Then why? I mean, you don't even seem all that excited to know that bigfoot is real."

"That's because we've known about them for years," Derek replied over his shoulder.

"Years? Then what the hell is the show for?"

"The show is our cover," Derek said cryptically.

"It's also a second paycheck. Don't forget that," Francis called from the rear, eliciting a chuckle from Mitchell.

"I don't get it," Harrison said. "If you know bigfoot is real and you know that they're killers, then why keep it a secret? Shouldn't you just warn the authorities and let them come in guns a-blazing?"

"They don't," replied Derek.

"Don't what?"

"They don't kill people, at least not normally."

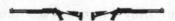

His arm was on fire, much like his mind. So much pain. So much rage. He would kill his attackers. Kill them and suck the marrow from their broken bones.

In his madness, though, he was careless. He moved to and fro through the trees, first one way and then another, nearly aimless. Every few steps, he would stop to vent his rage against whatever was nearby. For many minutes, the process repeated itself. His wounded arm blazed with pain, but was otherwise functional. Such was the resilience of his species.

Some small part of his brain contained the race memories of the past. Long ago, his ancestors had lost a great war against the two-legged things. They were smaller and weaker than his kind, but they were clever. They had learned to use the sticks and rocks of the forest as weapons against their larger, stronger adversaries. In time, his ancestors had also learned these skills, but by then it had been too late. They were too few by that point, and thus they had retreated deep into the forests, where the two-legged things did not go. They became scattered and reclusive, but their exile had also caused them to grow strong. As time passed, they became larger and more durable, better suited to their harsh conditions.

In contrast, the two-legged things, though still clever, became physically weaker over the eons. Ten of them could not stand against even one of his kind. Even a cub could easily subdue a two-legged thing if need be. Nevertheless, it rarely happened. They were strong, but they were also peaceful ... at least most of them were.

The rage returned. Within the space of seconds, his memories flickered out, and once more all he knew was anger. The cause wasn't important. He destroyed another nearby tree, but then stopped. He sniffed the air. The two-legged things that had harmed him were back the way he had come. Their scent was also somehow now in front.

Fewer of them ... the females he had smelled earlier. He would kill them first as a warning to the others. When they broke and ran in fear, he would pick them off one by one. Then the feasting would begin, but first the screaming.

"Oh really?" Harrison asked. "I don't think this one got the memo about not attacking people."

"You have to understand," Mitchell explained, "sasquatches are not all that different from humans. In fact, they're probably our closest relatives on the planet."

"Gigantopithecus," Rob stated proudly.

"Actually, that's wrong," Mitchell corrected. "Just sensationalist claptrap, really. Gigantos were big, but they were more like oversized gorillas. Oh, and they only lived in Asia. Based on what we know, I'd say squatches are more of an offshoot of a creature called Megathropus. They were large hominids, not too far off the genetic branch from Homo erectus. In short, they're big, hairy kissing-cousins of Homo sapiens..."

"They could be the Jolly Green Giant for all I care," Allison interrupted. "What's your point?"

"My point," he continued, "is that these creatures have a lot in common with us. They're smart. They live in families. And for the most part, they're pretty okay with the concept of leaving us alone if we do the same. Except..."

"Except?" asked Rob.

"Except that, like people, sometimes you get a bad egg in the bunch."

"That's where we come in," Derek said. "When a cryptid goes bad, it needs to be taken care of."

"I couldn't help but notice you said cryptid, not just bigfoot," Rob replied.

"Smart boy. Let's just say that there are more things in heaven and earth..."

"That still doesn't explain the cover-up," Harrison said.

"Slave labor," replied Francis.

"Huh?"

"Exactly that," he explained. "If the world as a whole learned that these things existed, before you knew it you'd find them working on construction crews or being forced to mine minerals."

Allison rolled her eyes. "Oh, you mean just like you see all the gorillas out there paving roads today ... oh wait, you don't."

Mitchell laughed at that. "She's got you there, Frank. I told you that slave labor argument was bullshit."

"So what, then?"

"They only tell us so much, kid," Derek stated flatly. "If you're a philanthropist, you might say that it's because these things are rare and the government figures the best way to protect them is to deny they exist."

"And if I'm not?"

"Then you might argue that it's in the best interest of some large corporations to keep things mum because otherwise we'd have large swaths of natural resources closed off as sanctuaries."

"At least that sounds more honest," Allison replied.

Before anyone could comment further, Chuck reappeared from the brush ahead. He came over and whispered to Derek. They conversed for a few seconds in muffled tones before splitting up. Derek turned back to the group, while the tracker ran off ahead of them again.

"Actually, what it sounds like," he said in a somber tone, "is that our squatch has found your friends."

13

Once upon a time, he cared for stealth. In what seemed to be a former life, he had been docile and curious, as the others of his kind were. He had been more than capable of sneaking right to the edge of a campsite unseen, observing the occupants for as long as he pleased, then stealing away into the woods without the two-legged things being any wiser.

Then the rage had come. For a time, he was able to push it aside in favor of caution. There had even been moments of clarity when he had once again merely been curious. That was all over now.

The last few scraps of sanity had fled his tortured mind when he had been shot. The pain of it, combined with the seemingly endless fire burning in his head, had made certain of that. All that remained was the rage, and the rage commanded that he abandon all caution. Only the killing was important now.

The faint whispers in the back of his head that had

been telling him to sneak up on his prey, take them quietly, then retreat to the mountains to lick his wounds, had gone silent. The fever had finally claimed that part of his brain.

Danni noticed that Paula had been dozing off – the poor girl had finally reached her limit – when an ungodly scream erupted from the forest. It was the creature, and it was close...*too close.*

The noise brought Paula back to full consciousness, and before Danni could clamp a hand over her mouth again, she screamed with everything she had.

"It's coming for us!" she yelled, that wild-eyed panic setting in again.

It is now, Danni thought ruefully as she pulled Paula to her feet. "Can you run?"

"I don't know."

"Well, I guess we're gonna find out." She was every bit as scared as Paula, but she knew deep down that if they both succumbed to panic, it was as good as over. She quickly unshouldered her backpack, taking just enough time to grab a bottle of water and a knife. *Fat lot of good it'll probably do me,* she thought before tossing the rest of it aside. She regretted leaving it behind. If they got lost with no supplies, they might be as good as dead.

Another bellowing roar sounded.

On the other hand, if they didn't move fast, they'd *definitely* be dead. She likewise pulled Paula's pack from her shoulders, then looked her in the eye.

"Do you want to live?" she asked the other girl.

Paula gave a small nod in return. She was a frightened rabbit, but she was still in there somewhere.

"Good. Then we move fast, but we do it my way. If you run off, I can't help you. Do you understand? If you don't do what I say, then that thing is going to catch you and kill you."

Paula whimpered pitifully, but then nodded again. Danni hated herself for saying it, but in Paula's current state of mind, the only way to reach her was to scare her even worse. She had little doubt the creature could find them wherever they fled, but she had no intention of making things easy for it.

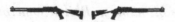

They were getting closer. Where the creature's path was still erratic, they had been following a straight line in the general direction it was headed, right toward the two girls. Another of the squatch's cries from somewhere ahead confirmed this.

Even though they were closing in, Derek still found himself a bit troubled. He and his team had hunted down rogue sasquatches before. Hell, during mating season the year before, they had been on the road nonstop for three whole months. But there was something weird about this one. Its behavior was just *wrong*. Even a rogue male gone full-on psycho would normally still be a little cautious. It might kill any human who entered its territory, but then it would fade away back into the woods. This one had thrown all caution to the wind. It was like a tornado on two legs.

A few days prior, he had seen the damage it had done along the trail leading away from Bonanza Creek. Such savagery was almost unheard of.

He had once come across two clans of squatches warring with one another over territory, and even then there hadn't been anything like this. There was definitely something wrong about this one, even more so than usual.

"You guys can kill it, can't you?" a scared voice asked.

"Huh? What?" Derek asked, coming out of his reverie.

"You can kill it, right?" It was the Indian-looking kid. *What was his name ... Phil or something?*

"Don't worry about it. We have it covered," he replied, turning back to the trail.

"He's right," Mitchell said. The kid was obviously scared out of his wits, so a little reassurance wouldn't hurt. "That's a Browning BAR safari rifle Derek's using. It's loaded with .338 magnum shells. You could take down an angry rhino with that thing if you needed to, and there's more where that came from." He patted the rifle hanging from his own shoulder. "Relax. We've done this before."

"So, if you've done this before," spoke Harrison, "what happens to us after you've killed that thing?"

"Isn't it obvious?" Derek asked, checking his rifle. "We interview you for the show."

Kate Barrows, the owner, manager, and only employee – outside of occasional counter-sitting by her father – of the Bonanza Creek General Mart, locked the door of her establishment and put the *Out to Lunch* sign in the window. The name of the store had been her little joke after renovating and reinventing the old feed and grain shop her father had signed over to her. It was a little too modern for your typical small town general store, yet it had just a bit too much hometown flavor to be considered a Quickchek or a 7-Eleven. It was also the largest store in Bonanza Creek, although that wasn't saying much.

Regardless, it was all hers, and she loved every second of it. Sure, she'd never retire rich from it, but she set her own hours and had a good relationship with almost everyone in town. Those were the things that counted, as far as she was concerned.

She was in a fine mood as she walked the quarter-mile toward her home. While she hated to profit off the misfortune of others, whenever hikers went missing her business went up. The local authorities would be in need of batteries to fuel their flashlights and coffee to fuel their bodies. In addition to that, not only had Old Man Gentry's Social Security check arrived for the month, allowing him to pay down his tab, but those college kids from yesterday had also resulted in a pretty healthy sale.

She remembered that one of them had been eyeing her up. He had been kind of cute, too. Kate allowed herself a momentary blush at the thought, but no more. He must have been ten years her junior. She was single and, truth be told, a little lonely. In Bonanza Creek, the pickings for eligible bachelors were meager, indeed, but, she wasn't quite ready to play the cougar card yet. Maybe if he had only been five years younger...

She pulled herself out of that little fantasy as she approached her house. It was a small, one-story ranch, but, like the store, it was hers. She had been raised there and had left only long enough to attend two years of community college. Her mother had passed away shortly afterwards, and she had returned to keep her aging father company. Whereas some might have resented doing so, she hadn't considered it an inconvenience. After a few years in Denver, she had grown to miss the quiet of her little hometown. She would have returned eventually. Her mother's passing had just hastened an inevitable decision.

A few years later, her father had decided to retire. Shortly thereafter, he signed over everything to his daughter, including the family home. As he had told her, part of it was trusting that his little girl would do right by him. The other part was a desire to screw the bastards in the state capital out of their slice of the pie when he passed from this mortal coil. Since then, he had seemed content to spend his days fishing or sitting out back, smoking his pipe. He often told her it was like being a kid again, but better. He had no responsibilities and also no parents to tell him when to go to bed.

As Kate neared her front porch, she realized something was wrong. She was almost always greeted by her Bluetick Coonhound, Gus. Whereas her father might be out casting flies at one of the many streams in the area, Gus was a homebody. He never strayed far. "That's because he knows where the food is kept," her father would always joke.

For now, though, the dog was nowhere to be seen, nor did she hear his distinctive baying off in the distance. *Oh well, maybe he's found a squirrel to chase.* She stepped onto the porch. It was only as she was pulling the keys from her pocket that she noticed the blood on the wood beneath her feet.

The two-legged things were close. He had made certain they knew he was coming for them. The stupid things might actually believe they stood a chance.

He could take them whenever he wished. He would tear them asunder. He would feast on their flesh and their fear. Perhaps he would even take his time, maybe cripple one and let it watch while he ripped the life from the other. The thought almost brought joy to his mind as he began to focus on the anticipated kill.

"Interview us?" Harrison asked incredulously. That was not quite the answer he had been expecting.

"Later," Derek turned and said. "We're getting close now. From here on in, I want silence until we bag this big boy." He heard a sharp intake of breath from the one they kept alternately calling "Phil" and

"Wild Feather." Derek made a mental note to ask what was up with that. For now, though, he couldn't have that kid messing things up by getting into a hissy fit. "Frank, come up here with me," he said, thinking it through. "Mitch, I want you to hang back about ten yards. Keep the peace."

Mitch nodded back knowingly. He knew exactly what Derek was talking about, although he didn't like it. The hunt was always so much easier when they didn't have to worry about making it a rescue mission, too. Armed or not, none of them liked the idea of going after this thing one man short. Physically, these creatures were the apex hominids of the world, possessing the strength of an adult gorilla combined with near human-like intelligence. That didn't even take into account the fact that this one was acting weird. However, Derek knew Mitchell wouldn't protest. These kids, especially the twitchy one, needed a set of eyeballs on them.

Francis came up from the rear and joined him. Together, the two of them doubled their pace and began to put some distance between themselves and the group Mitch was now tasked with babysitting. Within a few paces, they were lost from sight in the dense forest.

Derek pulled a Bluetooth earbud from his vest pocket and put it on. The others would be doing the same. Once he gave the signal, things would move quickly ... though whether for good or bad remained to be seen.

The two-legged things were stupid. Even had he not smelled them, they had been pathetically easy to spot. Though he had no names for color in his guttural tongue, he knew that the two-legged things were often adorned in patterns and shades that were alien to his home. These two were no different. His eyes, well attuned to picking out anything that didn't belong in his domain, spotted them as they attempted to cower in the brush.

The red haze of rage descended upon him. Any thoughts of savoring the kill emptied from his stricken mind. He mustered all of his considerable speed and leaped upon where they hid. Everything else ceased to be of importance as he began to tear them asunder. The fabric of their meager coverings tore with ease. He began to claw, to rip, to rend ... eager to hear their screams.

Kate's mind was in a panic. At first she thought that perhaps Gus had caught a possum, but there had been too much blood for that, and then there were the footprints. Barefoot tracks in the blood led off the porch where they appeared to head around back.

Kate followed them. Had her father injured himself somehow, then wandered off in a daze? That had to be the case. If so, she needed to find him quickly.

In her haste, she failed to realize that the prints were far too large to belong to her father.

Something was wrong. The two-legged things had not struggled. There had been no blood. Worst of all, there was no screaming. The rage subsided just enough for him to realize his error.

These were not the two-legged things. It was just the discarded coverings that some carried upon their backs. He had been tricked. He roared his frustration to the forest around him and once more began to sniff the air.

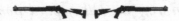

Paula and Danni both heard the beast's screams. It had worked. Just as they had been about to bolt, Danni had come to a realization. Their backpacks likely carried their scent. They could possibly be used as a decoy. She had hidden them in some bushes and instructed Paula to drop to the ground and roll in the dirt. She had done the same. It wouldn't be much, but it might obscure their scent just enough to draw it to the packs, allowing them to put some more distance between it.

She just hoped it would be enough.

He roared again in frustration and confusion. He had not realized how dull his senses were growing. He was having trouble picking up a scent. He exhaled, blowing a wad of thick mucus from his nostrils. He was only able to gain a few clear breaths before his sinuses again became

obscured by the viscous fluid; however, even muted, his senses were still keener than the two-legged things'.

He sniffed and listened. Finally, he caught something. It was small, no more than a branch breaking, but he heard it. Somehow, the stupid things had gotten behind him. They would pay for their trickery.

Those are a couple of smart girls, thought Chuck Wayans. He didn't have a clean shot, but he could see enough to know that the girls had left their backpacks behind for the squatch to find. Still, something about it bothered him. Squatches were smart, very smart. There's no way it should have fallen for the ruse. There was also no reason for it to waste time destroying the packs when the girls were obviously on the move. Chuck was beginning to question whether this particular squatch might be a tad retarded when he saw it turn in the direction where he was hiding.

Although he was sure the nine-foot creature hadn't seen him, he reflexively took a single step back. He heard the crackle beneath his foot even as he tried to stop himself. It wasn't much, no more than a twig. A man at that distance wouldn't have even heard it. But the thing that was out there was no man. The unearthly silence of the creature's presence was broken as it let out a bellow and charged.

"Sit down, and don't make any noise," Mitchell commanded the group. He had heard the creature screaming, then Derek's voice had blared in his earpiece, "It's going for Chuck!" It had seen them. It was an effort for Mitchell not to bolt in the direction of his team. He knew, though, he'd help them best by doing the job he'd been tasked with.

As for the others, Greg didn't need much convincing from Mitchell. He slumped against a tree, panting heavily and in obvious discomfort. Rob and the cute Asian girl likewise did as they were told.

Mitchell was pleasantly surprised to see the other hiker, Harrison, put a hand on Phil's shoulder and guide him down. That one was keeping his wits about him surprisingly well. Clever, too, he noted. In appearing to give comfort, he was also making sure the other kid wouldn't have a chance to run.

Mitchell knelt next to them for a moment and looked the pseudo-Indian in the face. "Whatever you do, don't make a sound. You don't want that thing to find us, do you?" It was reverse psychology at its finest. The kid was scared to death and probably ready to bolt at a moment's notice. So instead of trying to downplay that, which would have only resulted in a lot of running and screaming, Mitchell used the fear to push him past that and into a place where he'd hopefully want to do nothing more than curl up into a little ball ... a quiet one at that.

Harrison, seeing what the medic was doing, gave him a small smile of gratitude. Despite their status as *prisoners*, he began to feel hopeful. Now all they had to do was keep from getting killed.

He was just beginning to think that might actually be possible when the shooting started.

14

D erek and Francis heard the commotion ahead. It sounded like all hell had broken loose. First there was the bellowing of the creature, then the angry growl as it abruptly reversed direction. Derek had barely enough time to yell a warning into the radio before he heard the shot. It was Chuck's bolt action rifle. As the thunderous noise died down, he expected to hear quiet return to the forest. Instead, he heard screaming, human screaming.

Without hesitation, he and Francis brought their guns to bear and raced forward. The shot had only come from a few dozen yards ahead at most. Derek silently cursed himself as he ran. This situation was rapidly turning into a giant furry clusterfuck. The second that thing had started acting all squirrelly, he should have pulled back his team and done some more recon. Instead, they had charged blindly ahead, confident in their knowledge of a creature that nobody on Earth really had all that much knowledge about.

He had hoped to come out into a clearing and line up a clean shot at the squatch. It was wishful thinking, and he knew it. Instead, they both pushed their way past a thick bramble of bushes and ran almost straight into the arms of the enraged beast. Up this close, it was massive – a hairy locomotive on legs.

Both parties were surprised. Derek and Francis dove to the side, losing any possible shot they might have had. The creature, in turn, clumsily swung one of its massive arms at the two men, just barely missing them.

Derek managed to land in a dive-roll to put some distance between himself and the creature. Francis, however, was not so lucky. As he landed, his legs became tangled in the underbrush. He skidded to a halt, still within reach of the monster. Derek saw the creature in full as it turned toward his cameraman.

My God, what's wrong with it? he asked himself as it reached a bloody claw toward his friend. Derek hated to waste ammo, but he didn't have time both to save Francis and line up a clean kill. Still on the ground, he raised his rifle in the creature's direction and squeezed the trigger.

He got lucky. A spray of blood erupted from the beast's side. It grunted in pain and backed up a step. Derek had a moment to hope he had gotten a lung, but then he saw a flash of white from the bullet wound. *Dammit!* He had done little more than graze a rib. All he had done was tick it off.

"Frank, move it ... now!" he yelled, scrambling back to his feet.

His cameraman, not being stupid, rolled onto his back and brought his own gun to bear on the creature. In the close proximity, he didn't have time to raise the barrel. He pulled the trigger, and a chunk of the creature's right thigh exploded.

Gotcha, motherfucker! thought Derek as the massive beast lurched backwards. Unbelievably, though, it still refused to fall. He briefly wondered how in the hell it was still on its feet, though the question didn't matter. All he cared about was that it not *stay* on its feet.

He raised his gun and took aim as the creature roared its defiance at them.

Danni at first had led Paula in a direction perpendicular to the one they had originally come. From there, she had zigged and zagged, hoping to make their trail as difficult to follow as possible. She knew deep down it was a futile effort. No human could hope to evade an active predator for long in its own habitat. Regardless, she owed it to herself to at least try.

She was more or less dragging Paula. The girl somehow managed to stay on her feet. She was too tired to do much more than pant and let out the occasional whimper of fear, but Danni considered that a small blessing. Less noise was a good thing for them.

She had begun to think it might be working. The

creature's cries hadn't sounded any closer, and, if anything, seemed as if it might have turned in a different direction. Nevertheless, that seemed liked false hope to her. Their best bet was to keep running and hope for a break — maybe some rocks they could climb or a stream where they could further dilute their scent.

Danni was still weighing options in her mind when she heard the first shot. She stopped, and Paula nearly bowled her over.

"We have to keep..." she panted, near hysteria.

"Shh!" Danni commanded. "Quiet! Don't you hear that?" Earlier, while running, she thought she had heard gunfire, but she had convinced herself that it was just wishful thinking. Now, there it was again. She didn't dare to hope that maybe someone was shooting at that thing. Still, Allison thought she had seen poachers the night before. If there were people with guns out here, and they could find them, their chances might improve dramatically.

"I don't hear anything. Danni, we need to keep running before that..."

Another shot filled the air. No mistaking it. Someone was shooting at something. It was hard to tell with the way sound bounced around in the forest, but Danni would have bet it had come from the direction they had run from.

"That's gunfire," she said to Paula. It took a second for it to sink in, but then, for the first time since the creature had appeared, something other than panic shown on the frightened girl's face.

"Wild Feather and Harrison?" Paula asked

hopefully.

"Not unless they were secretly packing heat. No, there's someone else out here with us. Since they have bullets and we don't, maybe we should try to find them."

"No! It sounded like they were coming from where that monster is."

"I know. I don't like it either," Danni replied. "But if we keep running this way, we're going to lead it *away* from the hunters. I don't know about you, but I can't keep this pace up forever. If that thing is gonna catch us, I'd prefer it happen when we're surrounded by plenty of hot lead."

Paula seemed to weigh the options, although Danni knew what decision she would make. She had purposefully phrased her words that way. It was either facing a possible death in an attempt to save themselves or a definite death if they kept running. Finally, she nodded.

"Okay, good," Danni said. "Let's take this slow and careful, conserve our strength a bit. Eyes and ears open. If we run into that thing, we bolt like hell. If we find the hunters first ... well, let's try to not get shot."

Kate ran around the back of her house as quickly as she could. As she feared, though, her father was nowhere to be seen. She checked the back porch for more blood. Not seeing any, she let herself into the house.

"Dad!" she yelled. There was no response. A wave of panic began to spread inside of her as the silence stretched out.

Again she screamed for him, louder this time. She was considering where next to look when the door to his bedroom flew open and he stepped out.

"What the hell are you yelling about, Katey?" Richard Barrows asked in a grumpy voice.

Kate breathed a sigh of relief, then flung her arms around her father. "Dad! I was so worried. Why didn't you answer?"

"Can't a guy take a nap without everyone thinking he's gone and dropped dead?" he joked as he disengaged from her and rubbed his eyes. "What's the matter? It's not like you to go around hollering and screaming like that."

Kate forced herself to take a few deep breaths. Now that the excitement was over, she needed to think rationally again. "Sorry, Dad. There's blood all over the front porch. I saw some footprints. I thought maybe you had hurt yourself."

"Blood? That mutt of yours probably just caught himself a rabbit," he said, turning toward the front of the house.

She followed as he made his way through the living room. "That's the thing, Dad. I don't know where Gus is."

"I wouldn't worry. He'll be around soon as he gets hungry," he replied, opening the door to investigate. He stepped outside and took a look around as Kate joined him. "Holy Christ. Make that a lot of rabbits. Looks like a slaughterhouse out here, Katey."

"I know, Dad."

"You piss off anybody down at the store?"

"What!?"

"You deny credit to someone? Maybe one of those Bachowski boys? Those Polacks are all a little off in the head."

"That's not nice, Dad. And no, I haven't denied credit to anyone. It's been a good week."

"Not that good." He looked around, then spotted the bloody footprints. "Who the hell made these?"

"I don't know. I thought they were yours."

"What would I be doing walking around bare-foot, girl? Not to mention," he said, putting one of his booted feet down next to a print, "last I checked, I wasn't wearing size twenties."

Pain flared everywhere: in his brain, his shoulder, and now in his side. That was nothing, though, compared to the fury that erupted from his leg. Back before the fever had taken his mind, he had known about the fire sticks. He did not have a name for them, but his race was well aware of the dangerous tools the two-legged things often used. Two-legged things that carried these fire sticks were to be avoided at all costs. Whatever they were, they were capable of killing without touching. One of his own could easily snap the neck of any animal it caught, but the two-legged things didn't need to catch their prey. They could bring death from far away, even further than one of his kind could hurl a stone.

But that was before. The part of his mind that used

to remember those things had begun to liquefy. Now all he knew was that his leg was in agony and he could no longer put his full weight on it. The two-legged things had wounded him badly, crippled him even. How could this be? Did they not realize this was his forest, that here he was supreme? He might be laid low from his wounds, might even eventually die from them; however, he would tear the two-legged things apart before he let that happen.

There was a second shot, and then, a few moments after, a third followed by a tremendous bellowing scream. The group all looked at one another for a few moments. None of them needed to be psychic to know what the others were thinking. With the first few shots, they had all been hoping that it was over. Now, with the advent of the roaring, they were all wondering just how badly they were screwed.

Even Mitchell was feeling a bit worried. Three shots, and it *still* wasn't down? That was very unusual.

The battle was momentarily forgotten, though, as all of their attention was drawn to Phil. "Oh God! It killed them," he said, starting to rise. "We need to get out of here!"

"Jesus Christ, dude..." Rob started, but Harrison held up a hand to silence him.

He put his other on Phil's shoulder to try to calm him down again, but this time Phil swatted it off. He stood up and looked ready to bolt.

"Easy there, son," Mitchell said, stepping in.

"Screw that!" Phil barked, his voice rising in both volume and pitch. "I'm not sticking around and waiting for that fucking thing to kill us all."

"Listen, kid..." Mitchell replied, moving to block his potential escape.

Unfortunately, Phil had reached his breaking point and was beyond reason. He shoved Mitchell away. It wasn't particularly forceful, but it caught the medic by surprise. He stumbled and went down.

It apparently surprised Phil, too. He stared at the downed man for a second before turning to run. Before he could bring his foot down for the first step, though, he was tackled from behind. His hesitation proved to be his undoing.

Harrison was at least twenty pounds heavier, and thus the smaller boy hit the ground. Unfortunately, Phil was in the grip of panic and proved difficult to subdue. He squirmed against Harrison and, as he did so, he started screaming at the top of his lungs. It was a desperate, keening wail with no discernable words.

Mitchell got back to his feet. "Shut him up!" he hissed through clenched teeth, although nobody was able to hear him over the pitiful screeching.

Finally, Harrison had enough. He let his frustration boil over. All thoughts of Phil's deceit as Wild Feather and, even worse, his entreaties to get into Danni's pants were concentrated into one swift, savage action. He drove his fist into Phil's jaw with everything he had. The other boy's eyes rolled into the back of his head, and he at last fell silent.

"Effective," Mitchell noted with a tone of admiration in his voice. He started to thank Harrison before he was again drowned out – this time by something much louder than Phil.

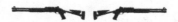

Derek took aim with his Browning rifle while Frank struggled to his feet. The creature had backed up into a tree and was using it for support. "Come on, let's make this count," he said.

He aimed for the creature's right eye, exhaled, and slowly pulled the trigger. Just as the necessary force to fire the gun was applied, a manic screeching filled the forest. Derek was an experienced outdoorsman, but he was still human. The sound, a high-pitched scream like a scared teenaged girl might make, caught his attention and threw his aim off just enough. The bullet grazed the creature's head and sent a shower of bark flying as it impacted with a tree behind it.

"Frank!" he yelled as the creature lurched in their direction, using the nearby foliage to keep itself from falling. *Damn, these things are smart ... too smart.* It began to close the gap between them.

He turned his head to find that his cameraman had regained his footing and was lining up a shot. Just as Frank pulled the trigger, the screaming abruptly ceased. Nothing but a dull click sounded in the renewed silence. The gun had jammed.

Oh yeah, that fucking figures.

There was no time left for a proper sighting. Derek brought up his rifle again and aimed as best he could at the creature's center mass. It was nearly upon them when he started to squeeze the trigger again.

15

Three shots rang out in quick succession. As their echoes faded, silence descended once more. Mitchell stood up from where he had been checking on Phil. The boy was still unconscious, but aside from a possible cracked jaw, he'd probably awake with little worse than a headache.

Harrison, still cradling his bruised fist, motioned for the rest to stay down as they waited to see what would happen next. Everyone did as told, except for Rob, who bounded over to Mitchell's side.

"Did they get it?" he asked the older man.

"I hope so," Mitchell replied. He then tapped his headset. "Derek, are you there? Come in."

No reply came, so he tried again. He was about to do so for a third time when Francis stepped from the bushes, a somber look on his face. "Derek can't answer you."

There was a moment of stunned silence until he

smiled. "Because he's too busy checking out the big bastard we just nailed."

Mitchell let out a sigh. "Asshole."

Rob thought it was hilarious and a grin spread wide on his face as well. "All right! The Crypto Hunter lives to hunt again."

"You had us worried there. We thought that thing killed you all," Harrison said.

The smile fell off Francis's face. "It almost did. That was one mean motherfucker, I tell you. Derek missed his shot ... oh, by the way, whichever one of you was screaming like a little girl, *thanks a lot for that* ... and then my damn gun jammed."

"So, what happened?" Allison asked, regaining her feet.

"Derek unloaded in its chest with his last two rounds. Blew holes in it big enough to put your fist through."

"We heard three shots," Mitchell said.

"Exactly," Francis continued. "The damn thing was just too stubborn to die. Was about to club us like baby seals when Chuck suddenly appeared out of nowhere and put a bullet into the side of its head. He's gonna need help, by the way, Mitch. That thing gouged a couple of good-sized chunks out of him."

"On my way," the medic replied, beginning to gather his supplies. "Can you stay with the kids?"

"No problem," Francis said. "I've had enough ugly for one day – although if any of them wanna tag along and check it out, now's the time to do so."

"Hell yeah!" Rob exclaimed. "You couldn't stop me if you tried."

"I'll go, too," Harrison said, stepping next to his friend. He wanted to see for himself that the thing was dead. If so, that meant his sister and Paula were out of immediate danger. They were still lost in the woods, but, oddly enough, that seemed like a minor inconvenience compared to what they had just experienced.

Unsurprisingly, Greg opted to stay put, the strain on his face still evident. Allison decided to join Harrison and Rob. Although she had no desire to see the creature that would surely haunt her nightmares for years to come, she had even less of a desire to be around Wild Feather ... *Phil*, she mentally corrected herself. No way was she falling for his crap again. She couldn't believe that she would have gladly slept with him up until only a short while ago. It disgusted her to no end that it was apparently part of his plan all along. *Guys can be such pricks,* she thought, following the other two.

As she walked, though, she found her eyes drifting down toward Harrison's ass. It wasn't all bad, she mused. Where Phil had turned out to be a major disappointment, Danni's brother had stepped up to the plate like a true hero. He was cute, too, which definitely didn't hurt. She had been so enamored of Phil's bullshit that she hadn't even given it much consideration. Now she began to entertain those thoughts, a smile crossing her face. *Maybe I should give him a hero's reward.*

The trio followed Mitchell through the forest. Within a few short steps, the party members they had left behind were out of sight. They only needed to walk a couple dozen yards, but in the dense woods, a hundred feet might as well be another planet.

A few minutes later, they stepped past some trees and caught sight of Derek. He waved them over. The scene looked like something out of a bizarre *CSI / Tales from the Crypt* crossover. Blood and viscera were everywhere. A massive body lay on the forest floor, gaping wounds covering its legs, torso, and head. A few feet away, Chuck sat propped against a tree. He was breathing heavily and holding a bloodied hand over his midsection.

Mitchell immediately unslung his bag and went to check on his companion. He bent down and slowly pried Chuck's hand away from the still dripping wound. He examined it briefly, then began cutting away the tattered material around it.

"How bad?" the wounded man asked.

"It's ugly, but I think you'll live. What happened?" Mitch asked.

"I got sloppy. Fucking monster heard me and charged," he gasped. "Missed my shot like a newb fresh out of basic training, and then Frankenstein over there caught me a good one in the gut."

"I'd say you got lucky," Mitchell replied as he began cleaning the wound. "I don't think you'll be impressing the ladies with your washboard abs anytime soon, but it doesn't look like he got anything major."

Derek pointed the three campers toward the body. "Look, but don't touch." He turned back to Mitchell. "How's Chuck?"

The medic glanced up from his work. "He'll need to be stitched up properly once we get back to town. I can field dress him for now, though. I guess we won't be able to get rid of him just yet."

Chuck laughed and then winced. "Screw you, man."

Derek chuckled, too, but then lowered his voice. "Mitch, when you're done, I need you to check out the squatch."

"Looks like he's dead to me," Mitchell responded in a glib tone.

"No shit. Seriously, though, there's something majorly wrong with it. Never seen one act the way it did."

"What do you mean?"

Derek hesitated. "If I didn't know better, I'd say the damn thing was insane."

"Insane?" Mitchell asked, keeping his tone low so the others wouldn't overhear. "Are we playing sasquatch psychoanalyst now?"

"Fine then, maybe it was sick or poisoned," Derek countered. "All I know is that something was definitely not right with it."

"Doubtful. We've never even seen one of these

things with so much as a case of the sniffles. Then there was that report in the archives. You remember that?"

"The one from that crazy defector?"

"Yeah, well, according to him, the Russians caught one of these things in Siberia about thirty years back. Supposedly, they tested the crap out of it: small pox, malaria, all sorts of nasty stuff. Found that it had an immune system like a battleship."

"Anecdotal evidence at best," Derek replied. "Besides, the rest of his account read like a cheap horror novel."

"They really should have double-checked that cage."

"Tell me about it," Derek said, then lightened his tone. "I don't know. Maybe I'm just getting paranoid in my old age."

"I'll check it out anyway, just to be sure. Get some blood samples and a brain biopsy ... assuming all of it isn't splattered against the trees," Mitchell replied, kneeling so as to continue tending to Chuck.

Derek turned back toward the three campers. No doubt they'd have lots of questions. He might as well field them now before he had to silence them all under a mountain of non-disclosures. They'd all know the truth, but wouldn't be able to do anything with it. Even if they decided to talk, it's not like they'd be believed. That was part of what the show was about.

"Ugly bastard, isn't it?" Derek asked, stepping up next to the body. Harrison and the girl, Allison, were staring at it in awe. The geeky kid, Rob, seemed like he practically wanted to jump onto the corpse and hug it. *Ah, our core demographic,* thought Derek.

"It's freaking amazing!" Rob exclaimed. "You hear stories about how big they are, but damn. This thing makes Andre the Giant look like a midget."

"I'm just glad it's dead," Allison said, a look of disgust on her face.

"Don't be," Derek replied. "I'm not entirely sure it was his fault."

"*His?*"

"Well, yeah." He gestured toward the creature's groin.

"Oh." A blush rose in her cheeks.

"What do you mean that it's not his fault?" Harrison asked.

Derek shrugged. "We're not sure yet. We need to run a few tests."

"Who cares what was wrong with it?" Allison commented. "Like I said, I'm just happy that it's dead and that there aren't any more of them around."

Derek raised an eyebrow in bemusement. "I agree that this one needed to be put down, but I wouldn't be too sure about that second part."

"What do you mean?" she asked, her eyes opening wide.

"It's nothing to worry about," he said. "These creatures are social animals, much like gorillas – or even humans."

Rob asked, "You think there's a pack of them out there?"

"Considering how close they are to us, we tend to think of them more as tribes or clans. But yeah, I don't doubt there's a small population in the area."

"Oh God!" Allison gasped.

"As I said, don't worry about it. These things are mostly peaceful. They want to avoid us as much as we want to avoid them."

"This one sure didn't."

"It was an aberration. Now that it's gone, the woods will quiet down again..."

The sound of movement off in the brush interrupted him. Branches broke and leaves crunched as something approached.

All of their heads snapped toward the direction of the disturbance. "You call that quieting down?" Allison asked, her eyes wide with fear.

"I hear voices!" Danni whispered as they made their way through the foliage. That cemented in her mind the outcome of the battle, for a battle it surely must have been.

After the first volley of gunfire, she had managed to convince Paula to follow her. It was a calculated risk, a very large one ... a potentially very large *hairy* one. Nonetheless, she felt their chances of survival were still better than continuing to lead the monster on a merry chase through the woods, a chase that they would eventually lose.

At first, she had been nearly as petrified as Paula. The thought of turning around and walking straight into that thing was utterly terrifying. Every fiber of her being screamed at her to keep running.

Then the shooting had begun in earnest, followed by the thing's enraged cries. That erased any doubt about it. The hunters had come across the monster. The only question was: *who would win*? She desperately prayed it was the guys with the guns. If not, she hoped that they were at least able to badly wound the beast before going down. If that didn't happen, she and Paula were toast.

It was only after the gunfire ceased and silence once more returned to the forest that she dared hope for the best. Although not entirely convinced herself, she had reassured Paula that the creature was either dead or driven off. It had made no attempts at stealth during its pursuit of them. The fact that she couldn't hear it raging through the forest now was a good sign ... or so she hoped.

As they continued onward, she thought she heard voices; however, she kept silent about it until she was certain. The woods could play tricks on one's ears. The chattering of squirrels could sound like a conversation as the sound bounced around. Now, though, she was certain as to what she was hearing. Those were definitely voices, and she could tell Paula had heard them, too.

She opened her mouth to let out a warning. The possibility of being shot was still a concern. However, before she could do so, the other girl bolted, the hope of being rescued far outweighing any caution. Danni muttered a curse and went after her, chasing Paula for several yards in an attempt to slow her down.

She had just managed to grab hold of her jacket when they burst through some bushes and found themselves staring down the barrel of a very large gun.

Derek silently cursed. He had been only a few ounces of pressure away from blowing the girl's head off. It was only his instincts that had saved her. A jumpier man would have perforated her – *them*, he saw now there were two – full of holes.

"Jesus Christ!" he spat. "You have no idea how close you just came to a face full of .44's."

The girls paid him no mind, though. Their eyes immediately went to the enormous corpse lying on the ground before them. Before they could do more, they were practically knocked over by Harrison, Rob, and Allison.

"Danni!" Harrison yelled, grabbing his sister and lifting her off her feet. Allison joined in, too, putting her arms around them both.

Rob's greeting for Paula was a bit more subdued. He gave her a quick hug before turning and dragging her over to the dead monster. "You gotta see this," he said excitedly. Paula, for her part, was too stunned to do much in the way of protest. The girl's mind had finally reached overload. The lights were on, but nobody was home.

Danni finally pulled away from the embrace. She

looked around, first at the body, then at the others. A look of horror crossed her face. "What about Wild Feather and Greg? Did this thing..."

"They're both fine," Harrison reassured her.

"Well, Greg is," Allison countered. "Phil's kind of a basket case."

"Phil?" Danni asked.

"I'll tell you about it later. Let's just say we've both been a little stupid lately."

Danni had no idea what she was talking about, but she didn't care right then. All she knew was that she, her brother, and their friends were all still alive. That was what mattered.

It was only then she realized exactly how weary she was. She leaned against a tree to try and catch her breath. Harrison stepped forward, a look of concern on his face, but she waved him away. "I'm fine. Check on Paula. I'm more worried about her."

He hesitated for a moment. Physically, she looked okay, but mentally ... well, it would be a long time before any of them were totally fine again. Now, though, was probably not the time for them to all start talking through their troubles.

Finally, he nodded and turned to find Rob – noticing him still talking to his nonresponsive girlfriend. Harrison sighed, noting his roommate was utterly clueless, then walked over to the couple. "Rob, why don't you let the doc check on her?" he said, motioning to Mitchell.

"Medic," Mitchell corrected, still tending to Chuck. "I'm a registered nurse. Never got around to that doctorate, unlike our esteemed host over there.

Anyway, I'm just about finished here. Bring her over."

Mitchell stood from where Chuck still rested. He had bandaged up the injured man as best as he could. The tracker didn't appear to be in immediate danger, so Harrison walked Paula away from her overly excited boyfriend and toward the medic.

Rob, for his part, didn't really notice. He was still studying the corpse. After a moment, his brow furrowed as a thought popped into his head. "Hey, I just realized we never smelled it coming." He took a deep breath through his nose. "This thing doesn't smell great, but it doesn't reek either. Aren't they supposed to stink?"

"That's the skunk apes down in Florida," Derek said conversationally, as if discussing the weather. "Same species, but their fur is usually matted down with stagnant swamp water. Makes them smell like month-old rotten eggs."

"But everyone says..."

"That's just media hype and hysteria, kid. People assume they're supposed to stink, so when they see one their mind fills in the gaps after the fact. Suddenly, they're sure they smelled it coming a mile away."

"Either that, or they're getting a whiff of the load they just dropped in their pants," Chuck replied from where he lay. He laughed at his own joke, then groaned in pain.

"That, too," Derek replied.

A few minutes later, Derek walked back over to his medic. "How's the girl, Mitch?"

Mitchell pulled something out of his pack. "She's in a bit of a fugue right now. Scared beyond the capacity for rational thought, would be my guess. Go figure." He turned his head and shouted, "Hey kid! You might wanna drag yourself away from the squatch and get your butt over here." Then to the rest, he announced, "Everybody, hold your ears ... this could get loud."

Rob walked over, a sheepish look on his face, and put an arm around Paula.

Mitchell cracked open the smelling salts and waved them under her nose. For a few seconds, there was no reaction, then her eyes began blinking rapidly. A moment later, a high-pitched scream of "OH GOD!" came bubbling out of her throat. Despite Rob's efforts to comfort her, several more shrieks escaped her lips before she finally broke down in pitiful sobbing.

Sound can carry far in the woods if it bounces just right, especially if things were as deathly quiet as they currently were. Paula's screams echoed through the forest for quite some distance.

Eventually, they reverberated through a small

hollow, within which was a crude bed of leaves and moss. Something stirred within as the sound hit its newly sensitive ears. The fever had gripped it only hours earlier. It had lain down to sleep, hoping the bad feeling would pass. It hadn't. It had instead worked its way further into the creature's brain, slowly eating away at its peaceful nature.

Its eyes opened. The noise was causing it pain. For some reason it couldn't understand, the only thing it wanted to do was find the source of the sound and kill it.

PART II

16

Derek instructed Chuck to take the kids to where they had left Francis and the others. He wanted them all back together – no stragglers this time.

Chuck, unsurprisingly, balked when Harrison tried to help him up for the journey. He still had an Army mentality and didn't like the thought of relying on civilians, despite being one ever since retiring from active duty. However, that mindset also meant that Derek, as his commanding officer, was easily able to overrule him.

Derek and Mitchell hung back, crouched over the corpse, examining it. It was the unglamorous part of the job, one that others were usually surprised to see him doing. Whenever Derek introduced himself in conjunction with the show, people usually assumed he had some bogus mail-order PhD in cryptozoology. The truth, though, was somewhat more mundane – if still a bit surprising to some.

Derek had a doctorate in zoology and had begun his career as a researcher, studying the habitat of endangered howler monkeys in the Amazon. His aspirations hadn't been any more grandiose than finding a way to save a harmless creature whose home was slowly being destroyed. Ironically, he was now tasked with killing other endangered, albeit far less harmless, species. *Funny what fate and a chance one-in-a-million meeting can do to a person's life*, he often thought.

Now was not the time for a stroll down memory lane, however. He shook his head and got back to the task at hand. "What do you think, Mitch?"

"The big fellow was definitely not feeling at the top of his game."

"That's probably a good thing."

"Not arguing."

"I'm telling you, though, it looked sick to me."

"I know that, Derek. We've already been over this."

"Great apes can get a lot of the same diseases that humans do, you know that."

"Yes, and if this thing were a gorilla, I'd be all over that theory. But it's not."

"I'm well aware. Trust me, I'd enjoy facing down a pissed off gorilla a lot more. But still, the question remains: what the hell was wrong with it?"

Mitchell stood up and stretched. He retrieved his pack and started pulling equipment from it. "Beats me. As I said before, maybe it ate something." Derek started to open his mouth, but Mitchell held up a hand. "But I'm going to find out for certain."

"How long do you think it'll take?"

"I can use the mobile lab in the van to run most of the tests."

Derek shot him a smirk at the mention of it. Mitchell had argued against the van when it was first offered to them some months back.

"And yes, you told me so. Don't rub it in. Anyway, the CDC has an office in Denver. I can link up with their computers and probably have some answers in three or four hours."

"It'll take us at least six just to get back to it. We left it in that town."

"Fine. Then we'll have answers in about *nine* hours. Now, do you want to waste more time arguing about it, or do you want to hand me my drill?"

They stepped from the bushes. For a moment, there was nothing but silence. Then the knowledge that their group was whole again, that they had all survived, began to sink in. Greetings, as well as cheers of triumph, rose up from the little clearing. The feeling was euphoric ... for most of them.

Harrison, Danni, and Allison went to check on Greg. Though obviously still in pain, his spirits were high now that he saw the others were all right. He even began to joke about how surviving a fight with bigfoot with nothing more to show than a busted arm was a new source of pride for him. They all laughed when Greg immediately started flirting again with Danni. She rolled her eyes but couldn't help smiling, too.

Rob, too, was ecstatic. With the danger over, he began pelting his captors with question after question regarding sasquatch and whatever other mythical monsters came to mind. He was firmly in the throes of what Harrison would have deemed a major nerdgasm. Fortunately, both Francis and Chuck were likewise in good moods and indulged Rob's eagerness ... for a few minutes, anyway.

Unfortunately, the good cheer was not universally shared.

"Get away from me."

"Listen, I'm sorry I hit you. I..."

"What part of *fuck off* did you not understand?" Phil asked, turning his back. After a few moments, Harrison took the hint and walked away.

Phil rubbed his aching jaw. Even so, the pain from the fist-sized bruise adorning his cheek paled in comparison to the damage he had suffered inside. He was ashamed of himself for how he had acted, but his feelings for the others had been forever darkened by the experience.

They had embarrassed and belittled him in his time of weakness. As far as he was concerned, his charade had been little more than harmless fun, yet they had treated him like a pariah. Now he remembered some real lessons he had learned growing up. On the streets of Chicago, disrespect could not go unanswered.

There would be no forgiveness.

Rob had been so enthralled that he failed to notice his girlfriend wasn't holding up very well at all. That Paula was bone-tired was the least of her issues. The encounter with the creature had shaken her to her very core. There was no room in her beliefs for such a thing to exist. It was an affront to her faith. Surely a just and loving God wouldn't allow such an abomination to walk this earth. Yet it had been real, and in the end it had been bullets, not prayer, which had defeated it. What that told her, she still wasn't sure.

Derek and Mitchell rejoined them a short while later. Soon the entire group, seven campers and their four escorts, were setting off on the long trek back to camp. Once the small talk finally petered out and everyone began to concentrate on the hike ahead, Harrison asked, "So what happens now?"

"We walk out of here and get our injured the medical attention they need," Derek replied, keeping pace with him.

"I kind of figured that. I mean, what happens to *us*? You did technically put us under arrest."

"You're not under arrest," Derek replied. "You're just in custody until we can get all the paperwork sorted out."

"'*Paperwork*'?" He lowered his voice so the others couldn't hear. "I really hope that's not some code word for shoot us all in the head and bury the bodies."

Derek snorted out laughter. "You watch too many movies, kid. If that were the case, we'd have just let that thing eat you for lunch, then mopped up later."

"Okay, I'll buy that."

"It's the truth. When I said paperwork, I meant it. We're talking signed affidavits swearing your silence on the matter ... under penalty of treason."

"Don't they usually execute people for treason?" Danni asked from behind, where she had been eavesdropping.

Derek turned his head toward her and smiled. "Not unless you were selling nuclear secrets to that squatch."

"So then, what if we refuse to sign?"

"This is the U.S. government we're talking about," Derek explained. "Believe me, they have a way of making your life miserable. You could find yourself on the no-fly list. Cops might suddenly show a lot more interest in you on the highway. I don't handle the details. I just know that the suits in D.C. have a way of getting what they want."

The siblings appeared to consider this. Finally, Harrison said, "So what was that earlier about interviewing us for the show?"

"Exactly that. You're all eyewitnesses. Outside of a few of the more sensitive details of what happened, it'll make for great TV. The Adventure Channel loves that sort of thing. Adds drama to the show."

"We'll wind up looking like crackpots, is more like it," Danni groused.

"There's that, too," Derek replied. "No offense, but it fits right in with the affidavits. Think about it. If you appear on a show like mine, ranting about bigfoot, who's gonna believe you – aside from the other crackpots?"

Harrison chuckled and Danni gave him an eyeful. "You think this is funny? Mom and Dad are gonna think we've been doing drugs out here."

"Well..." Harrison replied, thinking back to the previous night. "Anyway, that's not what I was laughing about. I was laughing because it's so damn perfect. It basically hides the truth in plain sight."

"Now you're getting it," Derek said with a tone of admiration. He was finding this Harrison character to be likeable. The kid was smart and kept his cool. If they ever needed an intern for the show, he'd have to give him some consideration.

Phil continued to sulk alone near the rear of the group. He kept back from the rest as far as their chaperones would allow. He had no desire to be amongst them anymore. He kept his eyes down and his mouth shut. His darkening thoughts were only interrupted by a female voice saying, "Hey."

He looked up to find that Paula had joined him. She had bags under her eyes, and her hair was unkempt. She looked as if she had just been chased by the devil, which wasn't too far from the truth, now that he thought of it.

"Hey," he answered back sullenly.

"Are you okay?" she asked in a listless voice.

"No."

"Neither am I."

"Why don't you ask your boyfriend for some comfort?"

She sniffed. "I'm finding myself not liking him too much right now. He just doesn't get it."

"Yeah. I'm pretty sure he'd have married that thing if given the opportunity."

To his surprise, she actually smiled. He managed a quick grin in return before he resumed trudging along.

After a few moments, Paula spoke again. "I don't believe them, you know."

"Believe what?"

"What they were saying about you."

"What's not to believe?" he said, then spat on the ground.

"Them," she said. "It doesn't take a genius to see they've been jealous of you since we met up yesterday, Wild Feather."

"I don't think they're jealous anymore."

"Sure they are. I bet they were just looking for an excuse to take you down a peg. And the fact that Harrison cheap-shotted you like he did was just an asshole thing to do," she said, raising a hand and putting it on Phil's bruised cheek.

He was momentarily taken aback by this, but then he smiled and replied, "Thanks."

"No problem. Hey, it's a long walk back. Do you have any more stories for me? I'm starting to like this Great Spirit of yours."

17

T he group split up after returning to the campsite. Derek and Francis needed to pack up their own base camp, which was, coincidently, only about a mile further north. Mitchell and Chuck stayed behind to help the rest get back to Bonanza Creek. This served the dual purpose of acting as escort while also ensuring the wounded were treated in a timely manner.

While they packed their gear, Harrison began to notice the oddness between Phil and Paula. The cold shoulder from the faux-Native American wasn't surprising. After all, Harrison wasn't too sure he'd be all that chummy either with someone who had slugged him. The rest of the group, though, hadn't been overly harsh to him during the walk back. Regardless, he had pointedly stayed away from almost all of them.

Paula's behavior, however, concerned him more. She seemed to be on better terms than ever with Phil.

Though they appeared to be casual, he could see the little looks and smiles they had been passing each other. Normally, he'd say it wasn't his place to interfere, but Rob was his friend. He was also acting hopelessly clueless about the whole thing. Not surprising, considering the circumstances, but not good either.

"How's it going?" Allison asked from behind him.

"Hmm?" Harrison muttered as the question began to register. "Oh, sorry. Caught me daydreaming."

"Anything good?"

"Nah, not really. Just thinking how much of a bust this trip has been. And now we have house arrest to look forward to. Not turning out to be quite the Spring Break I had imagined."

She smiled. "It hasn't been all bad."

Harrison raised a quizzical eyebrow.

"Okay, it's been *mostly* bad. But look on the bright side. Nobody got killed, we got to meet a minor celebrity, and we learned that bigfoot is real."

"A little too real," he said.

"True. And I also got to meet you."

"Oh yeah. Me, the guy who almost got us eaten by that thing."

"Don't sell yourself short. First of all, this wasn't entirely your idea. Danni picked the place ... and no, I'm not blaming her. But you should be proud. You kept it together. In fact, you're the only reason I didn't completely break down and cry myself out. What I'm trying to say is thank you. You were a real hero out there." She leaned over and planted a kiss on Harrison's cheek. Before he could respond, she gave him a wink then turned around to finish packing.

All thoughts of his roommate's wayward girlfriend evaporated from his mind as he watched her walk away. His eyes strayed a little further south than they should have as a smile found its way onto his lips. Perhaps the trip hadn't been such a bust after all.

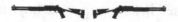

The exchange didn't go unnoticed. Phil quickly and chaotically stuffed his gear into his pack. He didn't care if it was neat or not by that point. Once finished, he had sat down against a tree and kept out of everyone's way. However, he wasn't blind. He saw how Allison spoke to Harrison and how the asshole had responded. *He probably planned this. Wanted what was mine and did whatever he could to embarrass me and take her away.*

Phil then glanced in Danni's direction. He regretted not bedding her when he had the chance. If he had acted, he could have had them both several times over by now. Instead, he had enjoyed playing them against each other, teasing things out until it became too much for either of them. Now it was over. He'd be lucky if either of them ever spoke to him again. *I don't care. Bunch of filthy twats. I wouldn't piss on them if they begged me.*

His thoughts turned to Paula. He had no real feelings for her. He wasn't sure he had feelings left for anyone at that point. He felt dried up inside, like a husk. It was like that creature had literally scared everything out of him.

It wasn't a bad thing, though. In its place was left a vacuum, and in that cold emptiness he felt like he was thinking clearly for the first time in a long while. He wouldn't waste time playing games with her. She seemed receptive to him, and he planned to make the most of that. Best yet, whatever he did with her would hurt her little twerp of a boyfriend. In turn, that would hurt Harrison.

Oh yeah. He could feel himself hardening at the thought of what he was going to do to Paula.

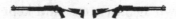

What Phil didn't realize was how little effort would be required. She, too, had packed her things quickly, if more neatly than he had. Since meeting him, she had been somewhat enamored of Wild Feather. For starters, he was exotic, which was exciting to her. She had grown up in a middle class Catholic family, the middle child of three. She had tried to be a good little girl and live up to her parents' stern teachings. That had meant going to church, remaining chaste in all things, and making sure, that when she started dating, she only brought home men who would meet her parents' expectations.

Still, that didn't mean she never fantasized. Often times at night, she would lie there thinking of the things that men, men her father would deem undesirable, might do to her. She imagined herself walking the streets of Queens, only to be dragged at knife-point into an alley and then violated by a Negro with a huge black penis. She envisioned going to a dance club and falling under the spell of a hot Latino who would later seduce her in some cheap motel room.

Now she found herself indulging in a new fantasy. She had never considered being taken by an Indian, but, ever since the walk back with Wild Feather, that's *exactly* what she had been thinking. She saw it clearly in her mind's eye: her, hiking alone in the woods, coming upon him in a clearing. He'd be wearing nothing more than a loincloth and war paint as he put a tomahawk to her throat and forced her to undress. Then he'd take her like the savage he was, her cries for help going unheard as they gradually became cries of ecstasy.

Now, for the first time, she found herself seriously considering one of her fantasies. She had held Rob in a mediocre light for some time now. He was smart and funny, but ultimately he bored her. Her parents adored him, though, and thus she had continued to date him, not to mention tolerate his pathetic attempts at pawing her. Hell, to make her parents happy, she would probably have eventually married him and then be forced to tolerate his pathetic attempts to fuck her.

But now that had changed. That horrible creature had been an offense to her and every belief she held dear. Rob should have been equally offended by its existence. Sure, he loved watching that stupid little show, but she always assumed he had about as much belief in those things as she did in the teen dramas she favored. Instead, he had been practically orgasmic regarding the creature. It was like a slap in the face. How dare he show more attention to *that thing* than to her?

She was still fuming about it when he came over to check on her.

"Almost finished?" he asked, shrugging on his pack.

"Oh. I think I'm quite finished," she replied emotionlessly before once more turning her thoughts toward Wild Feather and his loincloth.

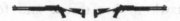

Once Danni had finished packing her equipment, she went over to check on the injured men. Greg and Chuck were sitting off together, both resting against the same tree. Her concern for them quickly dissipated, though, as she approached and caught the end of a dirty joke Chuck had been telling. The two guffawed at it but quickly stopped when they saw her approaching. *Two peas in a pod,* she thought, not unkindly. If they were well enough to laugh, that was a good sign.

This trip had been mostly her idea. Now that the excitement was settling down, she could feel a massive thunderstorm of guilt threatening to roll in. She knew it was silly. Everyone here was an adult. They'd all come of their own accord. Still, she couldn't help but think that people had gotten hurt because of her. Greg and this other man had been injured physically. She was also well aware there were probably deeper scars starting to form in a few of them, particularly Paula.

She tried to remind herself that it might all very well just be in her head. She and Allison had been on better terms in the past few hours than they had been in weeks, especially in light of how they had both been played by Phil. Then there was her big brother. If he had come down on her with a guilt trip, she didn't know what she would have done. Though she wouldn't admit it, even under torture, she had always idolized him. Fortunately, he hadn't thrown even a smidgeon of blame at her. If anything, he seemed to have come through this stronger than ever.

As for the rest, it was obvious that Rob was having the time of his life. Phil ... well, she wasn't sure what to think there. She was still sorting those feelings out. Regardless, she was pretty sure that whatever might have been there was gone now. She could handle him being scared. His deception, which Allison had brought her up to speed on, was a bit too much to handle, though. Still, there was plenty of time to sort that one out later. For now, there were more important matters to take stock of.

"Something funny?" she asked the two men.

"Nothing," Greg replied, leaning against the tree with his good arm. "The Chuckster here was just telling me a joke."

"Chuckster, eh?" the other man seemed to consider. "Okay, guess I can live with that. Better than that Woodchuck bullshit. God, I tell you, Derek has us do those stupid comic book conventions a few times a year. Says it's for the fans. Then I have to sit there all day listening to geeks ask me, '*Hey, Wood-chuck, can I get a picture?*' Fuck that."

For some reason, Greg found that uproariously funny. Danni wasn't sure why, then she took a breath through her nose, smelling a familiar herbal scent in the air.

"Greg!" she scolded.

"Don't be mad at him, little miss," Chuck said with a smile. "He was just sharing some happiness ... for medicinal purposes only, of course. Kill the pain a bit."

Greg looked up at her and tried to make puppy dog eyes, but he wasn't quite able to keep the grin off his face. Eventually, he dissolved into giggles.

Danni put her hands on her hips and tried to look disapproving. Deep down, though, she was relieved. If these two were over here sharing a joint while laughing at dick jokes, then perhaps that was a hopeful sign. Despite everything, she actually felt a smile forming on her lips.

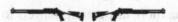

They were aware of the intruders in their territory. They were always aware when such things happened. In the past, they would go out of their way to avoid the two-legged things. Something in their memories told them it was a wise thing to do. Occasionally, they would be seen when their innate curiosity got the better of them. Even rarer, one of the young males might chase them out of their territory during rutting season. For the most part, though, their existence was one of

avoidance and stealth where the two-legged things were concerned.

Then the fever had come. At first, it had only affected the young male. Little by little, he had become erratic. Finally, he had begun to violently lash out at the others of the clan. They were mostly a tolerant species, and it wasn't until many of them bore wounds that the Alpha had acted and driven him away. By then, it was too late. Most of them had been infected, and as the violence inside of them began to awaken, the rest soon followed. The rage claimed the entire clan, the sole exception having been a cub savagely beaten to death by his mother after he nipped her too hard while nursing.

While most were not so far gone yet as the young male had been, a few had since wandered away in a daze. They had not been seen for at least a day. Those that remained, however, still understood order within the clan. They still followed the Alpha.

Thus, when the Alpha began to lead them toward the intruders, they did not disobey. They were still curious, but their curiosity was now tinged with madness. They would observe the two-legged things, but when they acted, it would not be to drive them away. The two-legged things would never be allowed to leave their territory.

"Are you sure it was a good idea to leave the body out there?" Francis asked, hoisting his camera.

They had returned to their own camp to pack up. Without Mitchell or Chuck, their load was heavier than usual. Fortunately, they didn't have far to go. It would slow them down a bit, but it wouldn't be oppressive.

Derek shrugged. "What else were we gonna do with it? I sure as hell wasn't going to carry it back to town, and we didn't have all day to bury it. Besides, within a few days nobody will ever know it was even there. Scavengers will take care of it."

"But I thought you said it was sick."

"*Might* be sick. Mitch disagrees. He thinks it could just be food poisoning."

Francis laughed. "Oh, please. I had some bad Chinese food last month. Gave me the Hershey squirts, but I didn't go around killing campers because of it."

"Yeah, but we still don't know too much about these things. A bad case of indigestion might put them in a much fouler mood than you or I," he replied unconvincingly. He was trying really hard to make himself believe in that theory, but it just didn't sit well. He had worked with animals for far too long. He was certain it had been sick, and Mitchell had humored him by taking the tissue samples. Derek just hoped he was wrong.

"So, what if it *was* sick?" Francis asked, echoing Derek's thoughts.

"Probably no matter," he answered distractedly. "The big predators won't touch a squatch, not even a dead one. Beetles and maggots will take care of most of it, and I'm not too worried about them."

"What if it wasn't the only one infected?"

There it was – a question that Derek had been

desperately trying not to think about. He didn't even want to consider it. They could handle a rogue squatch or two. But a whole clan of them? It was a bad thought. Even though he had seen creatures that few other men had, there were still some things that frightened him.

"I wouldn't worry," he finally replied to Francis, forcing a smile. "There's almost no chance of that happening. So, are you up for getting some filler footage as we bug out of here?"

"Always, chief." As the camera switched on, the lens panned across the canopy. "What about the trap cams?"

"Leave them for now. We can come back in a few days and grab them ... oh, and don't call me 'chief.'"

"Good point. I'll save it for that Indian wannabe we saved," Francis said with a chuckle before concentrating on his filming.

As they walked, Derek began reading some pre-written dialogue for the camera. It would need to be redubbed later during editing, but it kept his mind from wandering back toward questions he didn't want to think about.

18.

Kate Barrows was performing inventory in the back of her shop. It was mindless work, and for the most part unnecessary, considering her clientele was small enough that she was well aware of who bought what from her store. However, it kept her mind busy and away from thoughts of the blood on her front porch.

Her father had volunteered to mop it up. He didn't seem particularly perturbed by it, being of the mindset that the perpetrator was probably Joel Bean. Joel was a large man, a former lumberjack who had retired once he had lost a few too many fingers. Since then, he had a tendency to spend his days drunk and his nights passed out wherever he lay down. Her father figured he had probably cut his foot while drunkenly stumbling about and then somehow had made his way to their place.

"What if he's badly hurt?"

"I wouldn't worry," her father had said. "It'd take

a lot more than a bleeding foot to put that lummox down. There's so much whiskey in his blood that he probably doesn't need to worry about infection either."

Still, Kate was worried. Not so much for Joel, but her dog Gus was still missing. What if her father had been partially right? What if Joel had come over to her place in a drunken stupor and Gus had bitten him? He wasn't a vicious animal, but any dog could be a little protective of its territory. What if Joel had fought back and hurt Gus? She didn't think that scenario likely. He wasn't known for being violent, whether drunk or sober. But still, she hated not knowing. It was causing her mind to start making things up.

Fortunately, she wasn't given the opportunity for further wool gathering as, just then, she heard the front door open. She peeked out from the back and saw Grace Clemons walk into the shop. Grace and her husband, Byron, lived at the far end of town, although, considering the size of Bonanza Creek, that was still easily within walking distance of the store.

"Afternoon, Grace," said Kate as she walked out. She was on fairly good terms with the Clemons family. Grace and her husband mostly kept to themselves, but they were usually friendly enough, and they always paid up front. None of that mattered much to Kate at that moment, though. She would have probably welcomed a distraction by a mangy coyote walking into her store.

"Hi, Kate," Grace greeted her. "Sorry to bother you, but have you seen Mark?"

Kate knew she was talking about Mark Watson. In a small town like Bonanza Creek, it was easy to know such things. Mark ran a nature blog about the forests and natural resources of Colorado. It was popular with tourists and locals alike, allowing him to make a modest living off advertising revenue. However, that probably wasn't why Grace was looking for him. Mark Watson was also the closest thing to law enforcement Bonanza Creek had. He served as a part-time deputy. The town wasn't large enough to warrant a full-time police force, so, technically speaking, Mark reported to the sheriff's office down in Pagosa Springs.

"Last I heard, he was out again with that search party," she replied to the older woman.

"They're still looking for those fool hikers?"

"Yeah. It'll probably be at least another day or two, assuming they don't find them first."

"I swear," Grace said, "they should make people take a common sense test before they let them step one foot into the woods."

Kate chuckled. If anyone would know, it would be Grace. She and her husband were both avid sportsmen. They spent a good deal of their spare time out hunting elk. Over the years, Kate had heard other stories about the two. The rumor mill would occasionally flare up regarding other less savory activities about the couple. She'd never had any problems with them, though, and usually dismissed it as the gossip of small town folk with nothing better to do.

"What do you need him for, Grace?"

"Something killed my chickens," the woman said,

an edge of anger working into her voice. During the off season, Grace supplemented the lack of game meat by raising poultry at her place. She had no problems telling anyone who listened that she and her man were practically self-contained out in their forest-side home.

"A fox?"

"Not unless it was the biggest damn fox since the days of the dinosaurs. Whatever it was, it ripped into our coop like a runaway freight train. Tore the poor little things to shreds."

"Oh, maybe a bear then?"

"That's the damnedest thing, Kate. If it was a bear, we'd have known about it. Byron put up motion detectors last year to scare them off. Anything bigger than a squirrel comes into our yard, they get lights and an alarm."

"So, when it went off..."

"It didn't. That's why I'm here now instead of first thing this morning. The damn alarm never went off. At first I thought maybe a fuse had blown, but when I went to check, I found the entire thing was destroyed. Something tore the control box right off the back of our house. I don't know about you, but I've never seen a bear clever enough to do that."

"Neither have I," replied Kate as she found herself confronted with the second mystery of the day.

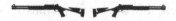

Joel Bean woke up in the woods. That in itself was not particularly surprising. It had happened many times before, especially when the weather was clear. On those days, he'd bundle himself up, nice and warm, and wander over to Ben Reeves' place, the Bonanza Creek Bar and Grill which served as both the local tavern and liquor store. Joel was a drunk, but he wasn't a fool. He knew the forest well from working in the lumber industry for years, before being forced to go on permanent disability, and had no intention of freezing his fool ass to death in it.

He'd started the night drinking at Ben's before getting nostalgic for the good old days, as he often did. At that point, he had paid Ben for a fifth of Old Granddad and had wandered off into the night to toast his former profession before eventually settling down against a tree for a snooze. Now, as he blearily looked up and noticed the position of the sun, he realized that perhaps *snooze* wasn't the correct term. From the look of things, he'd been out for a good twelve hours, not that it mattered. It wasn't like he had anywhere to be.

He pulled himself to his feet, picking up the nearly empty bottle beside him. "Waste not, want not," he said to himself. He drank off the last few swallows of whiskey before stuffing the empty bottle into his coat pocket. He was a drunk, but he wasn't a goddamned litterbug. He then unzipped his fly and proceeded to take a nice, long piss.

Joel hummed some Lynyrd Skynyrd while he relieved himself. He was still urinating when he realized that the humming was all there was. There were no other sounds around him. In fact, in the silence, he sounded comically loud.

Just my luck, a goddamned bear, he thought irritably as he zipped up. *Better scare it off.* Joel had come across numerous bruins during his years as a woodsman. The blackies didn't frighten him in the least. They were usually just as happy to avoid a scuffle and go on about their business.

"YAW!" he yelled at the top of his lungs, waving his meaty arms above his head as he did so. Joel was a big man, almost six-and-a-half feet tall and well north of two-hundred and fifty pounds. By waving and hollering, he knew he made himself seem like far too much of a hassle for any but the most desperate blackie to tangle with. "YAW! GIT! GIT ON OUT OF HERE!" he shouted.

He figured if that thing was anywhere near, it'd most likely be pulling up stakes and getting out of Dodge after that display. What he didn't count on was the screaming roar that answered him. It was unlike anything he had ever heard in his life. It made his yelling seem like little more than a peep in comparison. Whatever it was, it was big and it was *close.*

A goddamned grizzly. Sweat broke out on his brow despite the coolness of the weather. They weren't supposed to be down this far south. It must be all that global warming everyone kept hollering about on the TV.

There came the sound of wood being splintered as something moved in his direction. Joel quickly sobered up and considered his options. There was no use in running from a mad grizzly. You might as well try to outrun a car; a car with six-inch claws. No way was he getting his ass up a tree anytime soon either. He wasn't in that kind of shape anymore. Since his yelling and screaming had apparently pissed it off, that left only one option. Joel had never tried to play dead for a bear before, but there was a first time for everything.

He quickly lay on his stomach and put his hands behind his head to protect his neck. With any luck, it would just sniff him and be off. He was well aware of how ripe he probably smelled, thus he was fairly confident there weren't too many things that would consider him a good meal.

He was wrong.

He squinted through partially closed eyes in the direction of the commotion. What stepped from the bushes was no bear. Large feet – only two of them, Joel's confused mind registered – supported by massively muscled legs entered his field of vision. Before he could begin to comprehend what was happening, he was grabbed by the back of his coat and hoisted into the air. Whatever had a hold of him was insanely strong. Joel was little more than a rag doll to it.

He had just enough time to notice the glassy red eyes and foam-encrusted mouth before he was slammed face-first into a nearby tree. He hit with enough force to shatter his skull like an overripe pumpkin.

He died instantly, his alcohol-soaked brain forced from his head like toothpaste from a tube. All things considered, it was a merciful fate compared to what the creature did to his body next.

Elmer Gentry was sitting on his back porch enjoying a cigar when he heard the roar. His eyesight hadn't been so great for the past couple years, necessitating the use of what he thought of as *coke bottles* to be able to read his mail or watch the TV. However, his ears were just as sharp as ever. They had never let him down: not while he was lying in a trench in France during the big one, not when he had pulled a tour of duty in Korea, and not in the many intervening years since. Old Man Gentry, as the kids called him — they didn't realize he could hear them talking; idiots always assumed old meant deaf — looked up when the sound came, a frown furrowing his brow.

It had been a long time since he had heard anything like it, but even if his mind wasn't still as sharp as his ears, his eighty-eight years of life hadn't left him senile or stupid either. He had spent a portion of the seventies living in a commune on the border of the Cascade Mountains in Oregon. He had never given two shits about the hippie lifestyle, but had been newly divorced at the time and had decided to take a stab at the whole *free love* thing that had been all the rage. When he wasn't busy getting tail from the potheads, he would often be up in the mountains hunting. If those hippies had known he kept his Winchester stored in his tent, they'd have given him the boot. But they were often so stoned; he could have probably fired it off in the middle of the place without too many of them noticing.

It was during one such hunting excursion that

he'd heard a sound not unlike that which reached his ears now. Curiosity had gotten the better of him, and he had decided to check it out. What he had seen that day convinced him to never again go hunting without plenty of extra ammo. He hadn't personally been threatened, but he knew animals. If ever something like that decided to turn on him, he'd best have enough bullets to put down a small platoon or, if that failed, keep at least one in reserve for himself.

Those thoughts all flitted through his wrinkled head before the cry's echoes had even died down. Elmer's ears were sharp. The sound was similar to the one from all those years ago, but the pitch was different. He had heard enough animal cries to know when something was angry. This sounded that way ... angry *and* mean. It was a good ways off, but that didn't mean anything. Elmer had no intention of sitting there like a jackass with a stogie in its mouth while that thing came waltzing in his direction.

He grabbed his cane and hobbled into the house. When he got in, he barred the door. As he did so, his wife, Vera, came out of the kitchen. She observed him locking things up and shuttering the windows.

"Storm coming?" she asked.

"You could say that," he replied, going about his business. "Now be a good woman and fetch me my shotgun."

Kurt Bachowski was walking along a game trail toward his home, his rifle slung over his shoulder. The day's catch had been disappointing. Only two of his traps had managed to snare anything, and one of those had been an undersized fox with mange. It couldn't be helped. Some days were winners, others not so much. He and his brother, Stanley, still had more than enough work ahead of them.

They lived in a cabin about a quarter mile into the woods west of Bonanza Creek – alone in their own little world, just the way the brothers liked it. They were lifelong bachelors and preferred their solitude. Sometimes it was for the peace and quiet, but more often it was for the fact that prying eyes would have eventually noticed the Bachowski brothers were not always on the up and up as far as the law was concerned.

As far as *they* were concerned, though, the law could go bugger itself sideways. It wasn't like they were hurting anyone. So what if they had a small *herbal* garden close to their cabin? They weren't selling the stuff to school kids, so why should anyone care? A few tokes after a hard day's work wasn't going to kill anyone. And was it really a big deal if they occasionally poached a few animals above their license limit? Would anyone *really* complain about a few less coons tipping over their trashcans?

Speaking of coons, Kurt thought, Stanley should be just about finished skinning those big fat suckers from yesterday. They sold the pelts to a local furrier, then shipped the skulls out to souvenir shops along the highway. It wasn't big money, but it kept their fridge stocked with beer. As far as Kurt was concerned, it was a good, honest living. They kept to themselves, didn't bother anybody, and minded their own damn business. If only everyone lived by that credo, he often considered, there'd be a lot less trouble in the world.

He entered the clearing where their cabin stood. It appeared somewhat ramshackle on the outside, but was sturdy and warm inside. It was a solid dwelling, more than enough for the brothers. As the cabin came into view, Kurt stopped. He didn't see anything coming from the chimney of their smokehouse out back. Stanley should have been boiling those coon skulls by then.

Goddamned lazy sonofabitch, he thought, continuing toward his home. He wouldn't put it past his brother to have drunken their last six-pack and then gone off for a nap. Kurt loved his younger brother, but sometimes Stanley needed a boot in the ass to remind him that work wasn't going to take care of itself.

Kurt walked up to their cabin and then, seeing no sign of his brother, decided to go around back just to give him the benefit of the doubt before assuming he was loafing off again.

He was halfway to the smokehouse when he spotted the remains of fur and flesh on the ground. He went over to investigate. It was one of the raccoons they had caught, or at least he thought it was. It had been ripped to shreds, like someone had tossed the thing into a wood chipper. Forget skinning it – there wasn't enough left to wrap around a toothpick.

That in itself was odd. It hadn't been eaten, just

torn apart. Most wild animals wouldn't do that. A pet was another story, though. Kurt considered that maybe some fool's dog had gotten away. That hot-titted bitch who ran the general store owned a hound, he remembered. If that were the case, he'd put a load of shot in its ass the next time he saw it. It'd serve her right for not keeping a closer eye on the thing.

Though he had never married and never planned to – "*What's the useless piece of skin around a pussy? A woman.*" was his favorite joke – he was still a man. The thought of the store clerk brought a nice stirring to his crotch. After he found his brother and chewed him a new asshole, he might have to go sit back and rub one out in her name.

All thoughts of masturbation fled his mind, though, as he spied the mess lying in the grass about ten yards away. As he got closer, he saw blood and entrails strewn about. It was like something had stepped on a landmine. This was no raccoon. *Hell*, he noted, *you'd need to gut five raccoons to make this mess.*

That was when he saw the hand, the letters **S T A N** tattooed across the knuckles. It had been Stanley's joke. He had seen it in some stupid movie years back and had gotten it done. It had irked him to no end when Kurt refused to do the same.

"H-holy s-shit!" he managed to sputter right before his breakfast came bubbling up out of his mouth. He doubled over and emptied his stomach's contents. When the realization hit that he was vomiting onto parts of what used to be his brother, he began retching again. He backed away from Stan's remains and fell to his knees, still coughing up bile.

Soon, all he was left with were dry heaves, and in a few moments even those ceased. Finally, he was able to rise, still shaky, but at least his knees didn't buckle.

He slowly walked back over to his brother's remains. Kurt was usually not squeamish, nor was he a particularly sensitive man. His pa had beaten that out of him and Stan at an early age. No tears came to his eyes. He reacted the only way he knew how. He began to inspect the carnage, the woodsman in him coming to the forefront, looking for signs of what had done this. There would be time to get shitfaced to his brother's memory later, the only form of grieving Kurt Bachowski understood. For now, there was work to be done.

He examined the offal, then began looking for tracks of whatever had done this to Stan. Surely it had been some animal. As much as it looked like his brother had simply exploded, he knew that wasn't the case. They kept plenty of ammo in the house, some of it fairly heavy caliber, but nothing that would have done this to a man. Besides which, there were no scorch marks on the ground.

As for a person, it would have taken far more than one to do this. Even then, the ground would have shown signs of a struggle of that magnitude. That left a predator ... a big one.

The only question was: *what?* The damage didn't seem consistent with anything he had ever seen before. It was too much violence for a cougar. A wolf pack could have done it, but they didn't kill what they didn't eat, and while he couldn't say for certain that his brother hadn't been gnawed on, there was far too much flesh remaining for that to seem plausible.

That was when he saw the footprint.

How he had missed it before, he had no idea; probably the shock of finding his brother like this. Under normal circumstances, he would have found it with his eyes closed. Now that he did see it, though, he noticed others, too. They were huge. His first thought was a bear, but he didn't see the telltale claw marks. No, these looked human ... almost anyway. They were broader than a man's, and a lot deeper, too. Whatever made these must have weighed hundreds of pounds.

Studying the prints, he began to get an idea of what had happened. Whatever made these tracks had emerged from the woods behind the smokehouse. From the look of things, it had first gone after the coon. His brother had most likely hung it up, then gone back into the house for a skinning knife. As Kurt viewed the scene, Stan's fate began to take shape in his mind. His brother had come out to find something tearing into the dead raccoon. Either he had been too stunned by what he saw, or the dumb sonofabitch had decided to stand his ground. Stan could be stupidly stubborn when he wanted to.

Either way, the thing had come for him. Judging by the length of the stride, it had been fast, too. His brother never stood a chance. The thing had been on him within seconds.

He examined the area where he believed his brother had stopped upon first seeing the intruder. Sure enough, lying a few feet away in the tall grass was one of their knives. He picked it up. There was a thin smear of blood on the blade. His brother had only enough time for one slash before being disarmed, literally.

There were no more of Stan's prints between there and his final resting spot, only the creature's. Perhaps it had picked him up and carried him there, or maybe it had thrown him. Either way, it had been hell-bent on finishing the job. As much as it pained Kurt to do so, the tracker in him began to piece together what happened next. From the look of things, the intruder had fallen upon his brother and torn him to shreds. Judging by the splatter, this had been no feeding. Whatever had done this to Stan had grabbed handful after handful of his flesh and thrown it to and fro until there wasn't anything left of the man.

It was over quickly, but there was no doubt it had been an utmost brutal way to die. What the hell possessed either man or beast to do such a thing? Even in Kurt's sickest fantasies, he had never envisioned doing something like this to another man. He could imagine gut-sticking someone, then watching them die. Hell, he could even picture dismembering another person. But this? This was an act of such pure violence and hatred that even he could barely comprehend it.

Whatever this was, he'd be doing the world a favor by hunting it down and killing it. Hell, they might even give him a medal – not that he cared much. All he cared about was making sure his brother's killer met a violent end of its own. He planned to go inside, arm himself with as many guns and traps as he could carry, then set off in the direction it had gone. It had left a clear trail leading back into the woods.

He'd find it. It couldn't hide from him.

He turned back toward the cabin and froze in his tracks. He didn't need to find it. It had found him. The creature was standing at the same corner of the house he had just come from. It watched him, neither moving nor making a sound. Kurt wasn't an easily frightened man either, but he felt the hairs on his arm and neck stand straight up. Somehow, it had doubled back on his trail and done so without him ever suspecting it. How could something so large be so quiet?

This bitch ape killed my brother, he thought as the shock started to wear off – for surely this thing was female. It was over seven feet tall and covered in matted brown fur, but what he noticed most were the large breasts that hung from its chest nearly down to its waist. *Someone needs a little support,* his mind quipped before the dire seriousness of the situation set in. Red eyes peered at him from its ape-like face. As they locked gazes, its blood-stained lips peeled back to show teeth that looked very sharp.

Slowly, so as to not provoke it further, he unslung his rifle from his shoulder. It was all he could think to do. There was no way he could make it inside before this monkey intercepted him and repeated what it had done to Stan. Unfortunately, he grimly noted, the rifle he had with him that day was only a .22 varmint gun. He'd be lucky to do much more than annoy it.

R. GUALTIERI

There was no way it was going to be enough to stop this thing.

The beast watched him shoulder the rifle, then let out a howl. *My God! It knows what I'm doing!* The monstrosity charged forward. Before it got to him, he pulled the trigger.

He was right. It *wasn't* enough.

19

"There are the cars," Harrison said, pointing toward a break in the trees.

"It's about time," Mitchell replied, eager to get back to the town, if one could even call it that. He wanted to make sure the injured got off their feet, but, just as important, he also wanted to get to their van and start running tests on the samples. He had been dismissive to Derek earlier regarding his thoughts of illness. However, the squatch's behavior had been so far out of normal that there had to be *something* wrong with it. He intended to find out what that something was.

"Heh! With our luck, that squatch got to the rides first," Chuck joked, hobbling up alongside of them.

"Don't jinx us, man," Harrison said. "I'd like to think we've had our fill of bad luck today. Anymore and I'll start to wonder whether I pissed off someone important in a previous life."

"Maybe you angered the Great Spirit," Paula said from Phil's side.

Harrison and Rob both rolled their eyes at her. They assumed she was joking.

She wasn't.

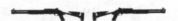

They found the vehicles sitting just off the logging trail, right where they'd left them. Both were thankfully untouched.

As they reached the cars, Danni said, "Don't forget we have two extra people to fit."

"And two injured bodies," added Greg, his face pale from exertion.

Danni put a hand on his good shoulder. He gave her a tired smile in return, then she continued, "I'm thinking Greg and Chuck get the back of my car. We'll tie as much as we can to the roof rack to free up some space."

"Good idea," Harrison said. "Allison, Phil, why don't you guys join me? If you all smoosh yourselves, I think we can fit three across in the back."

"Are you sure?" asked Danni. "I can probably hold one more."

"I'll go with her," Rob replied with almost no hesitation. "I have a few more questions for Mitch."

Mitchell, for his part, managed to not sigh. The kid had been talking nonstop since they had started walking. He was all for enthusiasm, but this was getting crazy. *Oh well*, he thought. *No matter what way you put it, the accommodations aren't exactly going to be ideal for the next hour or so.*

"Do you mind, hon?" Rob quickly asked Paula. She gave him a grin in return and shook her head. He turned back to the others so quickly, he didn't register that the smile never reached her eyes.

They finished loading up as quickly as possible in the fading light of the afternoon. Though it was unspoken amongst them, none of the campers were particularly eager to still be out in the woods come nightfall. They had seen enough adventure for one day.

Danni got behind the wheel of the Xterra while Mitchell took shotgun. Chuck and Greg took up the majority of the back while Rob managed to wedge himself into a corner.

Over in the Wrangler, Paula suggested Allison take the front with Harrison. She had agreed, and everyone took their respective seats. As they started to drive, neither of the two upfront noticed Paula's hand slide across the back seat to entwine with Phil's.

They were too late. Their sense of purpose, of clan, had been dulled by the fever. It had taken far longer to intercept the two-legged things than it might otherwise have. They were still hundreds of yards away when the growl of the two-legged things' beasts filled their ears. To the

Alpha's now overly sensitive hearing, it was like something sharp had been speared into his brain. He growled in frustration, then turned and swiped his claws at a female who had wandered too close. She fell back with a hiss, blood welling up from her freshly ruined eye socket.

Finally, the noise of the beasts diminished. They were leaving the clan's territory. A fading memory in the Alpha's mind reminded him they had once considered that a good thing — that not too long ago they had been glad when the two-legged things left their lands. However, the memory was cloudy and scattered. The rage was taking over, and it had different motives. It whispered to the Alpha that the two-legged things mocked him by escaping. It said that he should not allow such a thing, that he should pursue them. The existence of the two-legged things had been tolerated for long enough. He would tolerate it no longer.

He turned to his subordinates and growled to them in his guttural tongue. Soon, the rest of the clan grunted in return. They would follow him as they had done before, but this time he would lead them on a trail of blood and death.

By the time they were finished, there would be screaming ... so much screaming.

The Wrangler slowed as they came upon the same debris field from the previous day. Harrison eased the vehicle into low gear as he prepared to cross the sea of downed logs once more. "Guess now we know what caused this."

Phil remained quiet. Paula merely grunted in acknowledgement.

Harrison tried not to envision the potential fate that could have befallen them had Derek and his crew not arrived when they did. Maybe Rob had a point after all. Once they got back to school, he might even make an effort to try and watch that crappy show ... maybe.

"Hard to believe one creature did all of this," Allison answered. "We got off real lucky back there."

"Depends on what you mean by 'lucky,'" Paula responded in a small voice. It was the first words she had spoken in a while.

Allison gave Harrison a worried glance out of the corner of her eye. She was concerned Paula had been more deeply traumatized by the experience than she was letting on. Despite her anger at Phil, she wondered the same about him, too. Regardless, their continued silence was starting to creep her out. She needed a break from them. "Why don't I get out and spot you?" she said to Harrison.

"Good idea. It'd be just our luck to get a flat on the way out."

She opened the door. "Once you're across, I'll do the same for Danni. Just don't leave without me."

She quickly found a comparatively smooth path and started to wave them on. He nodded and gave the Jeep some gas.

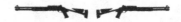

The ride across the logs was slow and bumpy. Harrison's full concentration was required to keep things slow and steady while following Allison's directions.

The jeep bounced with each tree it crossed. As they were passing over one, Phil decided to take a gamble. While the car rocked up and down, he slowly took his hand from Paula's and moved it over her crotch.

She glanced down at it, then back at him, but did nothing to remove it.

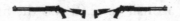

While they waited for the Wrangler to cross the debris field, Rob asked, "So do you think the squatch did all of this by itself?"

Mitchell grinned at his adoption of their nickname for the creatures. He was nerdy and a little annoying, but despite his earlier thoughts, Mitchell found himself warming to the boy. He didn't normally see enthusiasm like his in this field, so he decided it shouldn't be squashed. "I'd say so. Sasquatches are closer to humans than gorillas, but they still exhibit ape-like behaviors. They'll break branches and knock down small trees to mark their territory, during mating season and sometimes to show off to rivals."

"This guy must have had lots of rivals," Danni commented as she once more surveyed the destruction.

"I'll admit, this is a bit extreme." Upon looking

into the rearview mirror and seeing Chuck glare at him, he added, "Well, okay, a *lot* extreme."

"They don't normally act like this, do they?" Rob asked.

This kid definitely isn't stupid. "As I said, squatches are closer to people than apes. In a lot of ways, they act like people, too. For the most part, they want to just mind their own business. If you leave them alone, they'll leave you alone. But, just like people..."

"Some are assholes?" Greg offered.

"Not how I'd normally put it, but essentially correct. These creatures are smart and have distinct personalities. Unfortunately, that means sometimes you wind up with one with a mental disorder."

"And when that happens?" Danni asked.

"When that happens, we get called in."

Rob asked, "Just you guys, or the rest of the Department of Cryptid Containment?"

Chuck started laughing. He continued until his hands clutched his stomach, then he began coughing instead.

"Easy there!" Mitchell said in a warning tone.

"Only hurts when I laugh," he weakly replied. "Sorry, Mitch, that one always gets me, that stupid name DJ made up."

"What do you mean, '*made up*'?" Danni asked, an edge working into her voice. "Are you saying all that stuff about you guys being feds is bullshit?"

"No," Mitchell replied in an even voice. "That's all true. We're duly appointed deputies of the U.S. Forest Service. As for that other part, there aren't any other members of the Department of Cryptid Containment. We're the whole shebang."

"I'm not sure I'm following you."

"I am," Rob said excitedly. "This is turning out better than I ever hoped. You guys are like their *X-Files* or *Fringe Division*, right?"

Chuck sighed. "You watch too much TV, kid."

"Be nice," Mitchell said before turning back to Rob. "No, it's not quite like that..."

"Best watch what you're saying, man," Chuck interrupted. "Derek might kick your ass for spilling the beans."

"Whatever. It doesn't change the facts, and besides, who are they gonna tell? Even TMZ wouldn't run a story like this." He turned to address Rob. "Anyway, kid, we basically have an agreement with the government. Think of us as specialists of a sort."

"Specialists?" Danni asked, now fully engaged – so much so that she didn't realize that Harrison had already made it across. Allison was impatiently waving her on. "Oh crap! Sorry." She put the Xterra in gear and tried to divert some of her attention to the task at hand.

"Yeah, what kind of specialists?" Rob asked, picking up where she left off.

"It basically works like this ... *oof!* Careful, girl!" Chuck complained as the vehicle lurched.

"Sorry."

"The U.S. government doesn't like messes," he continued. "At least messes they don't make themselves."

"More or less," Mitchell said, jumping back in.

"Basically, when people go missing in inordinate numbers, especially in places where cryptid activity is suspected, they give us a call. We go in, assess the situation..."

"...and clean things up in our own *special* way." Chuck held up his hand and made the shape of a gun with it.

"Exactly. We make the problem go away. In return, the government gives us nice shiny badges and the authority to use them."

"And what about that stupid show?" Danni asked, again diverting her attention from driving.

"Thank you!" exclaimed Chuck from the backseat.

Mitchell ignored him. He knew Chuck had always hated the show. "It's the perfect cover. If we're around interviewing the locals, the real press isn't gonna want to touch it with a ten-foot pole. Showing up could give us legitimacy, something they couldn't care less about, but it would also take away from theirs which I guarantee they care a *lot* about. Hell, people just barely believe Fox News these days as it is."

"So, let me get this straight..." Rob said. "You guys get a call telling you that thunderbirds have been stealing kids from their backyards. You swoop in, kill the monster, and then stick around to interview a bunch of yokels to purposely throw people off?"

"Don't forget about all the blurry photographs," Chuck added.

"In a nutshell, yes," Mitchell said. "Although, in a lot of cases, the people we've interviewed are actual survivors. They're just now under gag order. For example: did you see episode twenty-two ... the one where we were tracking the Fouke Monster?"

"Of course," replied Rob to the surprise of nobody in the car.

"Well, remember that redneck hunter near the end? The one who said he'd lived in the swamp for decades and had never seen anything?"

"Yeah."

"We saved his ass," Chuck interjected smugly. "The squatches in that area are a bit more ornery than usual, something in the water maybe. Seems we have to go down there at least once a year and plug one that's gotten too uppity."

"So, why are you telling us all of this?" Danni asked, again taking her eyes off the path ahead. The SUV jolted as she rolled off a log. "Oh shit! Sorry."

"Well for starters, we're not exactly the men in black," replied Chuck, wincing as the vehicle hit another bump.

"Besides, think about it," Mitchell continued. "If someone told you that the hosts of some dinky reality show were actually part of a government cover-up to hide the fact that monsters are real, what would you think?"

Danni mused on that for a second. She'd never given much quarter to the conspiracy nuts before. The only ones who did were usually other conspiracy nuts. It really was quite clever. "Point taken," she said as she navigated over the last of the debris.

Unfortunately, they had all been too distracted by

the conversation to notice the scraping noise coming from beneath them a few moments prior. As Danni's vehicle once more drove onto solid ground, Allison climbed back into the Wrangler. Within minutes, they were once again headed toward Bonanza Creek, a thin stream of hydraulic fluid trailing the Xterra in their wake.

A short time later, the sounds of the forest ceased. For many minutes, nothing but the wind could be heard. A pin drop would have been like a shotgun blast in such oppressive quiet.

Finally, a twig snapped, followed by another. Soon, several large figures strode from the tree line and stood upon the old logging road. They observed the carnage that one of their own had done not too long ago.

They could smell lingering traces of the male. He had been the first to succumb to the rage. Before that, he had been both young and strong. If things had been different, perhaps one day he might have even made a successful challenge to become the new Alpha. Instead, he had been driven off, an outcast, to find new territories for himself. Whatever his fate had been, his scent was vanishing from the woods now. He might have wandered away, or he might be dead. The clan did not know, nor did they care. Any outsider they met, whether it be one of their own

kind or not, would be savaged on sight. The rage was now too strong to fight.

There was no sign of the two-legged things. Despite their attempts to catch them, they had once again missed their chance. The Alpha growled at their failure. He was on the verge of lashing out at them again when a different scent caught his attention.

He wetly sniffed the air for its source. Thick pus had already started to collect in his sinuses, but the sickness had not as of yet dulled his senses. He caught a whiff of something strange and followed it. At the edge of the debris, he found the source. A strange liquid was pooled here and a thin, almost invisible trail of it led further away.

Blood! One of the two-legged things' beasts was injured. If it had been hobbled, then they could run it to ground and tear at it until it died. The Alpha bent down and licked at the puddle. He immediately spat, then roared his frustration. This blood was like nothing he had ever tasted. It was entirely inedible. Stupid beasts of the two-legged things!

Enough of his mind remained for him to still be cunning, though. He looked at the trail of blood. He knew what to do. The injured beast of the two-legged things would lead the clan to its masters. There would be no escape for any of them now.

20

The old trail finally started to widen in front of the Jeep. Ahead, through the trees, the passengers could see the small town of Bonanza Creek. Harrison checked his rear-view mirror and saw the Xterra right behind them. He was momentarily tempted to bolt for it, to drive straight through town and onward toward 160, but he couldn't leave his sister – or his friends, for that matter – behind. Besides which, he just wasn't getting that kind of vibe from Derek and his group. Maybe it was foolish, but he felt that things were going to turn out okay for them.

He turned his head to say, "All right everyone…" As he did, there was a quick movement from the backseat, just on the fringe of his periphery. He turned all the way to find Paula and Phil sitting in their respective seats, seemingly minding their own business.

"You guys okay back there?" he asked. It was an

honest question. They had both been quiet for the trip back, and he was worried about them. Even so, mixed in with the worry was also a bit of curiosity regarding what he thought he had just glimpsed.

"We're fine!" Paula said, a little sharply. She seemed to realize this and toned her voice down. "I'm just glad to be out of those God-awful woods. I am never so much as even stepping into my own back-yard ever again."

"Don't worry, same here. It's gonna be a while before I even consider a picnic at the park," he joked back. "What about you, Allie?"

Phil raised a quick eyebrow, but Harrison didn't notice.

"I'm not sure. I mean, I practically grew up in a tent," she replied. "Although I'm definitely gonna rethink my stance on a few things, guns being first on the list."

"I know what you mean," Harrison said. "I might have to ask that Jenner guy for a few lessons with the cannon he had strapped to his side. Speaking of which, let's play this next part cool. I don't get the feeling that these guys are going to give us too much trouble. If we cooperate and don't give them any shit in return, I'm hoping we'll be in the free and clear."

He pulled to the side and waved the Xterra past. Mitchell was going to direct Danni where to go. Once they had parked, Harrison would pull in along-side them.

"What then?" Allison asked.

"What do you mean?"

"Camping is over. I get that, trust me. But we still have the rest of the week free," she pointed out.

"No idea," he replied truthfully. "I haven't thought that far ahead yet."

"Well, maybe we should discuss it," she replied with a smile.

In the backseat, Paula turned ever so slightly toward Phil and rolled her eyes.

"Where to?" Danni asked, pulling ahead of her brother's Jeep.

"Drive down the main street," replied Mitchell. "Park next to our vehicles. You can't miss them."

"Black with D.C. plates?"

"You got it," he said. Just then, the vehicle shuddered. "Whoa! What was that?"

"I don't know," she replied. "Maybe we busted something back on the trail. Good thing this is just a rental."

"I'm just glad we made it back to civilization first," Greg said from the back. "Knowing what we know, I'm not so sure I'd want to be broken down in the middle of nowhere."

Michell gestured at the town before them. "I hate to point it out to you, kid, but we're still in the middle of nowhere."

"You know what I meant."

"Sorry, just messing with you. There they are," he said, pointing toward the trio of ominous black vehicles. "Well, I'll be damned, they beat us here." He indicated Derek and Francis, who were loading a pair of ATV's onto trailers.

"How the hell did they do that?"

"We took a different path in," Chuck replied. "Narrower, but no graveyard of trees either."

Danni pulled in alongside the van. A few moments later, the Wrangler parked next to them.

"So, what now?" she asked Mitchell.

"Well, unless Derek says differently, three things. First, we figure out where the local doctor is so we can get Chuck and your friend checked out properly." He turned to his injured teammate and said, "No arguments," then back to Danni, "You and your friends should grab rooms at whatever passes for a motel in this place, and then get some rest. We'll hold onto your car keys for now. As for myself, I'm going to get my butt into the van and start analyzing these samples. The rest can sort itself out in the morning."

"Need any help?" Rob asked.

"Is there any chance of me getting any work done without you knocking every five minutes?"

"Not really," he answered, a grin spreading across his face.

Mitchell gave an exaggerated sigh. "Okay, then I guess I need some help. But I swear, if you touch *anything* without my say so, I'll use you as bait on our next mission."

Rob nodded eagerly and made a crossing his heart gesture.

Who am I kidding? This kid would probably enjoy that, Mitchell thought, stepping from the car.

Derek waved to Mitchell as he finished loading up the ATVs. He was pleased to see that the other vehicle was parking as well. That was a small relief. Sometimes his crew would rescue someone, only to have them go all paranoid and make a run for it. That was always a pain in the ass. As far as Derek was concerned, some people had watched The Bourne Identity one too many times. They assumed that anyone associated with the government must also be some sort of black-ops hitman.

The truth, as some were no doubt disappointed to learn, was far more mundane. There was lots of paperwork, signatures in triplicate, and then a few veiled warnings about loose lips sinking ships. That was it. The most exciting part was usually the interviews for The Crypto Hunter show that took place afterwards. Although, Derek thought, tonight's business might be a wee bit more interesting, considering the tests that Mitchell was supposed to be running through the CDC's computers. That was another nice perk of pulling a government paycheck. If they needed extra resources, at least computer-wise, it was available.

He had his fingers crossed that any results they got back would be negative. A disease amongst the local sasquatch population would be bad. They'd all need to be put down if that were the case. It would be a shame because their numbers placed them well within the endangered species range. But that wasn't the worst of it. If the local clan were infected, that meant potential danger for other humans. There had been enough of that already.

A negative would be good. Then they could fly out to film their next *episode*. He was looking forward to it. They were being loaned out to the Australian government for a mission. Fortunately, this time it was for conservation, not search and destroy. There had been several Thylacine sightings in Queensland over the past few months, enough so that a hefty reward had been posted for the capture of one, dead or alive. They'd be heading down to do the dual duty of disproving that the creatures still existed while also trapping and relocating any resident Tasmanian Tigers. It was so much nicer when they were able to save something rather than put a bullet through its skull.

For now, though, he pushed the thought away. It was pointless to think ahead to the next job while the current one was still wrapping up. If he did that, he would also be forced to consider the planned meeting in L.A. next month with the suits from the Adventure Channel. The show was their cover, but it was also a deep one. As far as their producers were concerned, they were just a bunch of deluded yahoos, albeit ones who brought in the ratings. They wanted to discuss adding a female cohost to increase the demographic appeal. Prior to this, they had been happy so long as Derek's crew got good footage, a few one-liners, and maybe the occasional inconclusive night shot. But now they were going to try adding some vapid swim-suit model to the mix.

Derek still hadn't figured out how to fight that

one. He couldn't exactly come out and say that sexing up the show wasn't worth the risk of someone ending up in a body bag on their first outing. But, once again, that was a problem for the future. For now, he needed to get these kids debriefed, his man patched up, and the all-clear from the germ guys. If he could accomplish that, all would be right with his world for a few days.

Mona and Josh Hildegard had no idea they were so close to Bonanza Creek. It had been two and a half days since they'd gotten lost on what was supposed to be a couple hours of light hiking. When they hadn't reappeared by nightfall, their adult daughter, Veronica, had called the police.

The next day, the search party had formed. That was where the police cruiser, the one Harrison and his friends passed the previous day, had been headed. However, the Hildegards weren't aware of that either.

By now, they were both fairly exhausted. Mona was also still pissed. It had been her husband's bright idea to take the *shortcut* that had gotten them hopelessly lost in the first place. That they were still alive was a matter of both good luck and a little bit of paranoia on her part. At her insistence, they had both dressed warmly for the outing. Also at her prodding, they had brought extra supplies. Josh had originally griped about their packs being too heavy, but by now even he had to admit the extra food and water had probably saved their asses.

Thanks to his compass, which they realized hours too late was broken, they had veered north instead of south and now found themselves far from where the search party focused its efforts. Though they had been rationing, their food situation was starting to get worrisome

Their luck hadn't been all bad, though. They'd found a shallow creek several hours earlier, from which they had refilled their water bottles. They were also now headed in a general direction that would take them right toward Old Man Gentry's front porch within the space of a few hours or, assuming they missed that, the old logging road a short while later. However, this was something they would never know.

Before they could reach such salvation, luck abandoned them altogether. Mona was too busy bitching Josh out for the thousandth time to notice how silent the forest had grown. By the time she realized it, it had been too late. Within seconds, the attack began. Their screams echoed for some distance before cutting off abruptly.

It would still be another two days before the search for them was called off. By then, between their attackers and the scavengers that came later, there wasn't much left to find.

The rage had settled down again. It was never truly gone, not now and not ever again, but for the moment, it was sated. The clan had been steadily following the trail of blood. The scent of two-legged things had been growing

stronger, much stronger. The beasts were bringing their masters back to their own clan. There were many of them ahead, no doubt huddled in their fragile dwellings. They would destroy the clan of two-legged things. Its existence was now an affront to theirs.

Just then, though, the wind had changed direction and they caught another scent: more two-legged things – this time to the west, although they had no name for direction. They were close, very close. It had been too tempting to ignore, thus the Alpha had turned in their direction.

Several times along the way, he had been forced to stop and bare his teeth at the clan in challenge. They were getting unruly. The rage was starting to supersede their sense of hierarchy. A few had wanted to tear after the two-legged things, heedless of stealth, and run them down like prey. But the Alpha was still the largest and strongest. The small bit of sanity that remained amongst the clan caused them to heed his commands ... for now.

The two-legged things had been chattering amongst themselves while the clan approached. They were stupid creatures, but they weren't entirely devoid of instinct. Eventually, one of them had sensed that something was wrong, that they were now being stalked. By then, they were surrounded.

The Alpha gave a short grunt, foam-laden spittle flying from his lips, and the clan descended upon the two-legged things. The rage took over. Even had the Alpha wanted to do things differently, which he did not, he would have been unable to exert any control at that moment.

Hands, claws, and teeth latched onto the two-legged

things from all directions. The presumed male had been the first to die when one of the clan had bitten into the top of its skull. The other, a female – or so their senses told them – died more slowly, although its end came only moments later. Its limbs were wrenched from its tiny body as the claws of the clan then began to tear into its rib cage. The two-legged thing lived just long enough to see its own insides ripped from its body, right before the massive fingers of the Alpha gouged through its eyes.

The next few minutes were like a drunken orgy of hate. Flesh was torn and eaten, viscera thrown in every direction. The coverings of the two-legged things were discarded to the side, where they were defecated upon. Amongst all of this, the clan also fought each other. Their bloodlust still running high, several of them clashed over the remains, trampling what little was left into the ground as they clawed and bit at one another.

It was several more minutes before they managed to get a tentative handhold on control again. The rage retreated a little, and the Alpha was once more able to assert dominance. He grunted and spat at the clan. Though their language was crude, he was still able to communicate a message of the carnage to come ... carnage which would make this kill seem like nothing in comparison.

The clan once more began to move, toward the trail, toward Bonanza Creek.

21

If the town had earlier reminded Danni of Little House on the Prairie, then Dr. Hanscomb cemented the deal. His practice had the distinct feel of a place that had been ripped out of its time and deposited into the twenty-first century, so much so that she had almost been surprised when he opened a cabinet and removed modern medical equipment rather than a jar of leeches.

As for the doctor himself, *old-timey* seemed to be the best way to describe him. He appeared to be about in his mid-fifties and was dressed warmly in jeans and flannel, as if he weren't quite sure whether his next emergency would involve a person or a horse. Despite his quaint appearance, Danni had seen the degree from Johns Hopkins hanging in his office. She began to form a picture of him as someone who wasn't quite ready to retire, yet had long grown tired of the steady inflow of patients that a hospital or big city practice would bring. That they had interrupted him in the middle of a game of Yahtzee with his wife seemed to confirm this.

After ascertaining the location of the town's doctor, Danni had accompanied Mitchell and the injured men. Regardless of the fact that neither appeared to be gravely wounded, she nevertheless still felt responsible, at least for Greg. It turned out to be a good decision, as Mitchell ended up having his hands full with Chuck – more or less having to drag the man there. Greg, at least, hadn't offered any objection to receiving medical treatment.

Once the two were safely inside of the examination room, Mitchell had given the doctor his field diagnosis, then left to resume his research. Before departing, though, he had asked Danni to do him a favor and make sure Chuck didn't leave before being treated. She agreed with no hesitation. As far as she was concerned, it was the least she could do for the people who had saved them all.

She had been in the waiting room for about half an hour when Dr. Hanscomb emerged, a grim look upon his face. He sat down next to her and, without any preamble, said, "I have bad news. Your friend didn't make it."

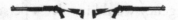

Conroy McStanish hadn't expected such a bonanza, excuse the pun, of business. He was the owner and oftentimes lone employee of the Bonanza Bed & Breakfast. During hunting season, he did a respectable trade, and often had at least one boarder at any given time during the rest of the year: usually hikers, road-trippers, or salesmen. It was rare, though, that he found himself with a full house – all six rooms rented out. He had been forced to send his wife on an emergency run to pick up supplies for dinner and breakfast. Still, it was worth it. The extra income would make a nice little addition to his and Susan's vacation fund. He had been promising her a Hawaii trip these last five years, and now it was looking more likely that he might finally be able to give it to her. Yes, things were finally going his way.

Even to Rob, who was still all starry-eyed at meeting Dr. Jenner and crew, the sleeping arrangements seemed a little off. Derek and his men had split two rooms, nothing odd there. Rob had assumed his group would pair off as they had done the night before. He had been wrong. Allison had grabbed a room to share with Danni. When he had started to book one for Paula and himself, though, she had demurred and instead asked for her own accommodations. Before he could raise a protest, she had cut him off with a curt, "I need some time to myself," and then gone ahead with the credit card transaction.

Phil had reluctantly agreed to room with Greg. He had tried to get his own as well, but upon hearing of the limited space available, had offered to share one with Greg and Greg only. That left Harrison and Rob. *Roomies again*, he thought, carrying his bags to the second floor. Odd or not, he quickly shrugged it off.

For the time being, it didn't seem like too big of a deal. He had been planning on just dropping his stuff, then going to assist Mitch anyway.

"You're an asshole!" Danni told Greg, who was trying and failing to suppress a smirk. Chuck wasn't even bothering. He was holding his freshly sutured midsection and laughing outright.

"What?" Greg replied. "It was just a joke. I figured you could use one. You've been a little mopey since we started the drive back."

"It wasn't funny," she said, poking a finger into his chest. "And if I've been mopey, it's because maybe I've been worried about you two idiots being hurt."

"If anyone should be sorry, it's me," Dr. Hanscomb interrupted. "I normally wouldn't go for a tasteless gag like that, but your friends assured me you'd be up for it."

She rounded on him. "Yeah, well I wasn't."

"But you should be," said Chuck, getting the laughter under control. "Seriously, little lady, you should be the happiest person on the planet. Think about it. You and your friends just danced with the devil, and all you got in return were a few bumps and bruises. Not everyone is that lucky."

She considered that and was about to reply when the doctor again interjected. "Danced with the devil? I thought you said you startled a bear and her cubs."

Chuck gave the others a quick warning glance. "Yeah, doc. I'm maybe exaggerating just a little bit."

Danni sighed and tried to change the subject. "So, they're okay?"

"For the most part. A hairline fracture and some nasty bruising on this fellow. I only had an air cast handy, but that should be fine for this type of break." He indicated Greg's arm, then turned to Chuck. "As for your other friend, I had to do a lot of stitching, not to mention pump a ton of antibiotics into him. I highly recommend he check himself in at the hospital down in Pagosa Springs to have some X-rays done. However, I don't think there's any danger as long as he doesn't try overdoing it."

"No worries on that one, doc," Chuck replied with a wink.

Oh well, he's not my problem, Danni thought.

"Great," Hanscomb said. "Now unless there's anything else, let's talk payment. I'd really love to get back to my game."

Mitchell was locked inside the back of the van. As always, he was a bit in awe of the place. *Amazing what you can buy when the feds are footing the bill.* He prepped the samples for testing. Between the equipment and the full communications array, including satellite uplink, he figured one could practically sequence the genome from here. He was just a field researcher, but he sometimes wondered what a true lab rat could accomplish in this rig.

He had just finished separating the samples onto slides when there was a knock at the back. He sighed.

Sure, he knew the kid was coming. Hell, he had even invited him. Still, he'd thought that perhaps Rob would be tired and might forget about it. *Oh well*, he mused, *maybe it's for the best*. He had been known to get a little too into his work at times, especially when he was sequestered away like he was now. Maybe a little company would be good. At the very least, having a guest might serve as a reminder that he needed to eat every now and then.

He stood up in the cramped quarters and opened the back door. Rob climbed in, an eager look on his face, as Mitchell locked up the van again behind him.

"You sure you're up for this? This stuff is gonna get a bit dense."

"You bet," Rob said. "Let's see what makes this sucker tick."

The curtain of the first floor window moved ever so slightly as the hand pulled away from it. Paula had been keeping an eye out ever since locking herself in her room. Sure enough, just as she knew he would, Rob had emerged from the front door and walked directly toward the van. He'd probably be in there for hours, maybe even all night. *A nerd to the very end.* She gave a small sigh, then walked away from the window and lay down on the bed.

She let her thoughts drift away. The thought of cuddling next to him in the little room turned her off more than ever. Even using the word "boyfriend" to describe him had begun to feel a little icky as of the last several hours. No, she had *better* things to occupy herself with for the time being.

The others would probably be grabbing some dinner right about now. She had no interest in joining them. Her appetite for food was nonexistent, and she definitely had no desire to reminisce about the events of the day. Even the barest recollection of that *monster* sent shudders of revulsion through her. She had other things to distract her, though. What she had in mind might make her shudder, too, but in a much more pleasant way.

As she let her thoughts drift toward clearings, loincloths, and savage cries in the wilderness, she slowly moved her hand down her body. She was well adept at the use of her own fingers. She had done so quite often while in the grip of one of her fantasies. Today had been the first time she had let someone else touch her *down there*. She remembered the long ride back to town and began to imagine it was his hand that was slowly unbuckling her pants.

Almost as if in response to her carnal thoughts, there came a soft knock on the door. She smiled, expecting that, too. If it was who she hoped, perhaps there would be no need for further fantasizing.

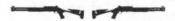

Harrison entered the pub just as darkness fully enveloped Bonanza Creek. It wasn't much, just a small bar and a few tables, but it would do. Frat boy or not, he usually wasn't a heavy drinker. Sure, he had attended his fair share of parties and had even woken up once or twice facedown in a toilet, but typically those moments were rare. Right now, though, he figured he had earned himself a couple beers. Although they had escaped mostly unscathed – physically, at least – there were probably deeper scars that would need mending.

Paula, in particular, was worrying him. He had gone into this weekend thinking he would soon be a single man again. Now he was wondering if Rob might wind up in the same boat. He wasn't too worried about himself. He was relatively certain he was going to ask Allison out. He was likewise pretty sure she'd say yes. Rob's dating prospects, on the other hand, had never been particularly strong. At least he was fairly well distracted at the moment. Even if Paula did dump him, it would probably be a good while before Rob finished yapping about the Crypto Hunter and noticed.

Speaking of the show, Harrison was none too shocked to see Derek and his cameraman seated at one of the tables. What did surprise him, though, was when they both waved him over. He had figured, with the excitement over, they'd be all business now and barely give him and his friends the time of day. His curiosity piqued, he walked over to them. "Hey, guys."

"Have a seat," Derek replied amicably enough. "I'm buying."

"Really?" Harrison sat down. "Thanks. I appreciate it."

"Forget that. You deserve it," Francis said. "You'd

be surprised how few people we meet that can keep it together once the shit hits the fan."

"Frank's right. You and your sister both showed a lot of character out there. If it weren't for the two of you, I think your friends might have scattered like rabbits."

"Agreed," Francis said, draining his glass. "Also, the way you stared down that squatch with just a can of pepper spray was pretty damn badass."

Harrison chuckled. "Probably a lot more crazy than badass. By the way, do you think it would've worked if you guys hadn't shown up?"

Derek didn't hesitate with his reply. "Not even for a second."

There was a moment of silence at the table, then all three men burst into laughter.

Mitchell linked the van's systems to the Denver CDC's computers via satellite. He set up an automated scan to match the samples against known animal and hominid contagions. The search queries were narrowed to only include results known to induce behavioral changes or neurological side effects. It didn't guarantee success, but it meant the time spent combing through the mainframe's vast database would be relatively short. If those results came up negative, he would expand the parameters. If that still didn't pan out, he explained, then next would be a full toxicological examination of the squatch's stomach contents.

"So, what do we do now?" Rob asked.

Despite his earlier reservations, Mitchell found himself smiling. Though the kid was enthusiastic to the point of almost being obnoxious, he had kept out of the way and asked mostly intelligent questions. "Now we wait a bit. Let the computer do the heavy lifting. If the first pass doesn't give us anything to work with, then we start again. Rinse and repeat."

"What if you don't find anything?"

"If the pathogen and tox screens all come back negative, then I wrap it up. At that point, I send the samples to the guys in the lab and let them do their thing."

"But what about..."

Mitchell lifted a hand. "Don't worry. If there're no matches with anything on file, then that probably means we're dealing with a unique case. That's a good thing. It means the problem most likely died with our hairy friend."

Rob seemed to consider this for a moment. He had read that the CDC had data on every disease known to man, including many that the general public wasn't aware of. If Mitchell was confident in those results, then he could be, too. He nodded, then decided to try his luck a bit. "So, while we're waiting..."

"Yes?"

"What does the rest of this stuff do?" His eyes swept over one of the many control panels in the small space. "I know a thing or two about computers. Maybe it's just me, but some of this equipment doesn't seem like it'd really be at home in a lab."

"You have sharp eyes. This here van is a Frankenstein's monster, if ever there was one. Before we got it, the bureau had this baby all decked out for undercover surveillance. We added all the medical stuff, but Derek had us keep some of the older equipment just in case it came in handy."

"Like what?"

"Well, for starters, did you notice how low the ceiling in here is?"

Rob raised his eyebrows. "Now that you mention it..."

"Exactly. It's a false roof. There's about a foot of space above us, literally packed with cameras and sensors."

"Cool! Like what?"

"Well, okay. Since we have time." Mitchell spun in his chair and began hitting buttons. Monitors came to life, and static began to hiss from hidden speakers. He indicated one of the monitors. "Check it out. Thermal night scope." He then grabbed a control stick and panned the video. "Full three-hundred and sixty degrees of freedom."

"Awesome!"

"That's not even the best part. There's a full acoustic array – pretty advanced stuff. We could hear a bear shit in the woods from a mile away if we wanted to. What's really wild, though, is that these systems can piggyback off each other. It's really not much use out in the forest, but if we were to point this thing at a building, we'd be able to hear the conversations going on and even see movement through the walls."

"Seriously?"

"Yep, and this isn't even top of the line anymore. Makes you wonder what toys the real spooks have at their disposal."

"Show me."

Mitchell appeared to consider this for a moment, then he smiled and said, "Well, these things aren't toys, but what the hell?" He started punching buttons and turning dials. "Derek mentioned something about going to that bar down the block. Let's see what he's up to."

The hiss of static coming through the speakers gradually gave way to garbled voices. He turned a few more knobs, and they became intelligible. They listened in for a few seconds before Mitchell said, "Sounds like Derek and Frank are chatting with your buddy."

"Heh! They're wasting their time. Harrison doesn't even like your show. Let's see what else is going on in this town."

"Sure thing. What'd you have in mind?"

"Everyone else is at the B&B," Rob said with a big grin. "I know. Let's check out Paula's room, see if she's talking smack about me."

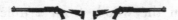

Paula let out a gasp as Wild Feather slid his full length into her. Pleasure, pain, and desire simultaneously flooded her senses. Mingled in with it all was a slight sense of disbelief. She couldn't believe she was letting this ... this ... *savage* use her like this. *So this is what it's*

like to be taken, to be tamed, like an animal. She arched her back and bit into his shoulder. He grunted in return and began to thrust even more furiously into her.

She gasped again and began to move her hips to match his. A smile crossed her lips as another thought struck her. How disappointed would her parents be if they knew what she was doing right now? Her father would probably disown her, especially if he knew she had spread her legs – eagerly, too – for a minority. Her mother would probably call her a filthy whore.

A giggle escaped from her lips at the thought. Wouldn't that be ironic, especially considering that's *exactly* what her mother often begged to be treated like? Their house was old, and the ductwork carried sound quite well. Late at night, when her parents assumed she and her brothers were asleep, her mother's breathless cries would carry up to Paula's room, often followed by the crack of her father's belt.

I can see the appeal, Mom, she thought, before turning her full attention back to Wild Feather, his naked body continuing to slide against hers. "Harder!" she moaned. "Fuck me harder, mighty warrior!"

Phil couldn't believe how well things had worked out. His roommate still hadn't gotten back by the time he left for Paula's room. He was probably playing things up for Danni. To his surprise, he found himself actually rooting for Greg. Hopefully, the fucking pothead knocked her up or gave her the clap. Maybe both.

Assholes! Either way, it was probably for the best that he was gone. Less questions that way, not that it was any of their fucking business what he was up to.

He decided to make his move while Paula's dweeb boyfriend was still nerding it up with his heroes. He had thought to take her on a moonlit walk so he could start putting the moves on her with more of his "Great Spirit" bullshit. She had shown herself to be receptive. Better yet, she seemed determined to believe in his Indian charade. It was pretty hilarious, considering his mother was Columbian while his father was a salesman of Dominican descent. He was about as Native American as Paula was. Still, it wouldn't hurt to play that up. He spent a little extra time in the mirror putting a feather back into his hair and donning his fake deerskin jacket.

What he hadn't expected, though, was the condition he had found her in. He had no more than said "Hi" before she had dragged him into the room and locked the door behind them. She pushed him onto the bed, and it was only then that he realized her pants were already halfway off. Had she really been waiting for him? It seemed so, and he was more than happy to oblige her. Within minutes, their clothes were strewn on the floor.

Considering the hunger with which she attacked him, he never had even a moment's consideration that she might still be a virgin. Had he suspected, he would have enjoyed it even more – although, he was greatly enjoying it as it were. It was as if he were figuratively fucking her boyfriend and that asshole, Harrison, by literally fucking her.

The only downside was her loud animalistic grunting amidst continual cries for him to take her like a savage. That part was weirding him out a little.

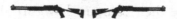

Inside the van, there was stunned silence for many moments. Finally, Mitchell reached over and muted the audio.

"I don't suppose there's any chance we accidentally tuned into Cinemax, is there?" Rob asked numbly.

"I'm so sorry, kid."

Rob was a cluster of confused emotions. There was definitely anger and hurt, a lot of that. There was also a sickening sense of resignation. Hadn't he suspected for a while now that he and Paula weren't right for each other? Surely, several of his friends had dropped hints of such. Even Harrison had suggested he play the field a bit. Perhaps ... although he realized that these thoughts might just be hindsight.

However, hindsight or not, mixed in with the jumble of other emotions was also an odd sense of relief. For a few minutes, he couldn't believe it, but yes, there was definitely a feeling of satisfaction in knowing. He would never have suspected Paula of such deceit on his own. He had bought her good little Catholic girl routine completely. There had never been any reason not to. She had always seemed genuine in her beliefs. Her family was devout, but not oppressively so, which might have dropped hints at a rebellious nature of sorts.

Most convincing of all was that the college rumor mill was entirely silent on the subject of Paula. No matter how innocent one acted or how hard one tried to keep a lid on things, gossip spread in a closed ecosystem like their campus. It wasn't always correct, but if someone was screwing around with someone else, there was usually a third party who knew about it and was happy to spread the word.

No, he wouldn't have suspected Paula, and thus, barring some tearful confession from her after the fact, she would have gotten away with it. She hadn't exactly sounded like she'd been forced into it, thus he didn't think such a confession would have been forthcoming. Even if it was, he found himself doubtful it would be all that sincere. He had to face facts: the bitch was cheating on him, and she was enjoying it.

He turned back toward Mitchell and grinned, but this time there was a predatory quality to it.

"So, tell me, does this thing have a 'Record' button?"

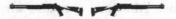

Kate Barrows wasn't much of a drinker. She enjoyed the occasional glass of wine with dinner and was known to drink a beer while she watched the Broncos with her dad, but that was it. However, after closing up shop that night, she decided maybe a shot of something stronger wouldn't be a bad idea. She was rattled from the earlier scare with her father, and she was most definitely still upset that Gus seemed to be missing. Adding to it all, she was also tired out from all the walking.

Earlier in the day, after talking with Grace Clemons and finding her curiosity piqued, she had decided to lock up the store and accompany her back to her home. Grace, for her part, hadn't objected to the company. After discovering the damage, her husband, Byron, had set out with their truck for the Home Depot all the way over in Durango. Considering the distance and that he tended to get a little distracted in that store, he wasn't expected back until sometime that night.

Grace had spent some time showing Kate what had happened. She had been right, it *was* weird. The coop had been torn wide open from top to bottom. Even stranger was the condition of some of the bodies. Grace had been too focused on the damage to pay the chickens much more attention other than to note they were all dead. Kate immediately saw that while a few were partially eaten, most were torn completely to shreds. Whatever had gotten into them had been in one hell of a mood. This wasn't a feeding – more like a mass poultry murder.

She found herself as stumped as Grace. She wasn't even sure it was an animal that had done this. Unpleasant thoughts had begun to form in her head. She began to wonder if her father hadn't been right about Joel Bean. Maybe he had downed one too many shots of cheap liquor and gone nuts.

She had assured Grace that she would send Mark Watson out her way immediately if she saw him. Grace had thanked her, then politely escorted her back to the edge of her property. Kate's mind was so preoccupied by then, wondering what was going on, that she didn't find it odd to be shooed off without even an offer to come inside for coffee.

Before leaving, though, she had stopped and turned to the other woman. There had been a nagging feeling in the back of her head. Something was wrong, and it was bothering her. "Grace, are you sure you don't wanna come back to the store with me, at least until Byron gets home?"

"That's sweet of you, Kate. But my place is here," had been the unsurprising reply.

"Well then, please be careful. Whatever did that could come back."

"Don't you worry about me, sweetie. I'm gonna go and lock myself inside with my good friends, Smith & Wesson."

As Kate started walking again, she had found herself oddly lamenting her own lack of a *friend* by her side.

Those memories were all still flitting through her mind when she walked into the town's lone pub. "Bar and Grill" was probably a bit of a stretch, she thought. Ben Reeves, the owner, had a good-sized barbecue pit out back, but this time of the year she'd probably be lucky to get a microwaved plate of hot wings.

It was still too early for the locals to fill the place, and even then, a good chunk of them might be down south helping the search party. Regardless, she wasn't surprised to see a few people sitting around. It was *who* she saw, though, that caught her off guard. She saw the college kid, the cute one from the day before. Hadn't he been heading out into the woods for a week of camping with his friends? Apparently not, as he was sitting there with two of those reporters who had rolled into town the other day.

They appeared to be having a fairly animated conversation, but it immediately quieted down as they noticed her. One of the men had a bit of an unkempt lumberjack look to him. The other, the one who had seen her, was another prospect to her liking. Well-built, with dark sandy hair, a chiseled jaw line, mid-thirties – maybe early forties. That same voice in her head that she constantly seemed to be shushing said, *Two cuties in as many days. This town is turning into a regular man-candy outlet.*

The college kid, "Harry-something" she vaguely remembered, turned his head toward her and smiled. Stepping up to the bar, she inwardly sighed. She could remember that he had a cute ass, but his name, nope, no dice on that one. *Definitely turning into an old cougar,* the voice whispered.

"Hey!" the college kid called to her. "Kate, wasn't it?"

"Hey, yourself," she replied back. She sensed the bartender at her elbow and addressed him, "Tequila shooter, if you will, Ben." *That ought to steady the nerves a bit.* Turning back toward the group, she said, "I thought you were off camping with your buddies."

For a moment, it seemed as if the other men at the table shot him a warning glance, but then again, she could have just been paranoid. Considering the day she'd had, that seemed the more likely scenario, so she dismissed the thought as he began to speak.

"Yeah ... well, that got cut short. We had a little bit of an accident," Harrison – that was his name – replied.

"Oh. Was anyone hurt?"

"Not too badly," he told her. "Bumps, bruises, and scratches mostly."

"What happened?" she asked. She retrieved the tumbler of Cuervo Gold from Ben, then took a step in the trio's direction.

"Bear," Chiseled Jaw said.

"Cougar," replied the lumberjack simultaneously.

There was a momentary silence, during which she distinctly saw Harrison roll his eyes, then Chiseled Jaw quickly added, "It was hard to tell. It happened fast, and it was a bit chaotic." He didn't sound all too convincing.

"And you are?" she asked.

"Oh, sorry," he said, getting to his feet and holding out a hand. "Derek, Derek Jenner."

She shook his hand then asked, "You guys are those reporters, right?"

Derek glanced at the lumberjack and replied, "Something like that."

Chuck should have been back at the bed and breakfast, specifically partaking of the *bed* part. Those were the doctor's orders, and he was sure it would have been Mitch's, too. Too bad neither of them was around to say it to his face.

He knew where Mitchell was holed up. He was also fairly sure Derek would be at the local watering hole, probably with Frank, celebrating another job well done. It was a tradition with them. The more difficult the job, the longer the celebration would go on. Considering the FUBAR this one had almost been, he didn't expect to see them around for a while. Nor did he consider joining them, as he'd probably just be shooed back to bed like some goddamn baby.

Well, he wasn't about to let a few little scratches stop him. He'd seen far worse in the service. Hell, he'd almost gotten his damn leg blown off in Iraq. As far as he was concerned, the best thing was to walk it off before his muscles started stiffening up. He decided a few circuits of the tiny town would do the job without the worry of pulling any stitches. If he had to go slinking back to the doc and the others found out, he wouldn't hear the end of it for a long time.

To be on the safe side, he had veered off the main road and taken a little side street, not much more than a dirt trail itself. Here, the houses were spaced out amongst the trees. There were no streetlights, and he had to navigate via his night vision, a task he didn't mind at all. He was nearing what he thought might be the city limits when he stopped. His body might be banged up, but his senses weren't. He wasn't sure what it was, but some instinct was telling him things weren't right.

The air was still and quiet, a little too quiet. He stopped and listened. Chuck didn't have a gun on him, but he never went anywhere without his combat knife. His hand slowly closed around the handle of the six-inch blade, and that was when the silence broke.

A loud *CRACK* came from the direction he'd come. It sounded as if a tree had been knocked down. It was followed moments later by another. *What the hell!?*

A scant second later, Chuck heard movement behind him. He turned, but his injuries had slowed him. He was a second too late as something large barreled into him.

Rob and Mitchell were busy arguing. The medic had reluctantly tuned the van's microphones back to Paula's room. He had been on the receiving end of a few cheating girlfriends in his day and could understand. However, he regretted doing so almost immediately and began trying to talk Rob down. "Think about what you're doing."

"What *I'm* doing? I don't think I should be worrying about what, or more precisely *who*, I'm doing," Rob countered.

"Seriously, what are you hoping to accomplish?" the older man shot back.

Rob was in the middle of opening his mouth to reply when a beeping noise diverted both of their attentions.

"Hold that thought," Mitchell said, turning to find one of the monitors rapidly filling up with data.

He pressed a button, and sheets of paper began flowing out of a laser printer bolted to the wall.

"What's going on?" asked Rob, momentarily distracted from thoughts of petty revenge against his soon to be ex-girlfriend.

"CDC. Looks like their computer found a match."

"What is it?"

"Hold on a minute," Mitchell replied, collecting the pages. "Give me a second to read through it. Unfortunately, this thing doesn't just spit out one-line answers."

He tried his best to be patient while Mitchell paged through the results. As he neared the end of the stack, though, Rob became aware that the other man was frowning. By the time he had finished, a thin sheen of perspiration had appeared on Mitchell's forehead.

"What's wrong?" Rob asked.

"I think we're in deep shit."

The lab was powered by its own generator, thus neither was aware that — at that exact moment — all the lights in Bonanza Creek had just gone out.

22

I t's debatable whether any of the occupants of Bonanza Creek that night, human or otherwise, would have appreciated that they were about to reenact one of the pivotal moments in human evolution – an occurrence that had, in essence, set the stage for the world as we know it.

It's doubtful the humans would have appreciated it. Though we as a people pride ourselves on our rich texts full of histories, we are a forgetful species. Our few millennia of written knowledge pale in comparison to the ten thousand years of oral history that have been forgotten. Even that is a minor blip compared to the race memories we all share, but have long since repressed in our minds – save perhaps for when we dream.

What has largely been forgotten by man is that thirty-thousand years ago, the battle for dominance amongst this planet's hominids hadn't yet been decided. Our ancestors, Cro-Magnon man, had waged a bloody centuries-long war of genocide against their closest competitors. Science assumes this much, but has gotten many of the details wrong.

For instance, despite our arrogance in assuming that our superior brains made our rise inevitable, for a long time the scales were tipped quite evenly amongst those vying for the top of the food chain. The second mistake is in assuming that this was strictly a war between us and the Neanderthals. It was not. There were more players on the board, the Megathropi chief amongst them. There had originally been more combatants in this battle for species dominance, and their remnants still existed, but they were no longer true threats. Homo erectus had all but been rendered extinct by then. As for the diminutive Homo flore-siensis, even then they had been scrambling for the relative safety that island living provided.

All throughout Europe, Asia, and eventually North America – by way of the Siberian land bridge – a three-way war had been waged. Primitive tools, clothing, dwellings, and even the basics of agriculture had been known to all three species. What did it matter if the spear of a human was slightly sharper, if the arm of a Neanderthal could throw his twice as far? As such, each race brought its own unique strengths to the battle. Had events played out just slightly different, our world would be a greatly changed place today.

The humans were smart and cunning, but they were physically weak. If caught alone with no weapons, there were few animals that could not take them. They were clever enough to realize this, though, and were thus heavily social creatures. Where there was one human, there were many. They also had the advantage of being a warlike race. Peace with them never lasted for long.

The Megathropi were large, strong, and swift. Not as physically imposing as they would eventually evolve to be, but more than enough to take any three humans in unarmed combat. When they waged war against their rivals, they hefted clubs the size of small tree stumps, However, they weren't wrathful by nature and only fought when provoked.

The Neanderthals were an intermediary species. Though they embodied many of the best physical characteristics of the other two races, what doomed them was that they also embodied the worst as well. They could not compete against the Megathropi in power, and they could not best the humans with cunning. They were also a solitary people, preferring small, nomadic families. When another species decided to do battle against them, there were often not enough in any one area to mount an effective defense.

In the end, it had been the humans' social nature and their eagerness for battle that had decided the fate of the planet. They decimated the Neanderthals in Europe and slowly drove back the Megathropi through aggressiveness and sheer force of numbers.

The Neanderthal tribes were eventually destroyed and their remnants absorbed into the human population. As for the Megathropi, they became a fractured people. They were driven into the deepest forests and the highest mountains. It was only in these places that the humans' greater numbers could be countered and they were able to make a stand. Eventually, mankind grew disinterested in these inhospitable territories and retreated back to the prime lands they had won. In time, they forgot.

The Megathropi were left in peace. Time passed, and they evolved. They became larger and stronger, better suited to the harsh climates they had been forced into. Their senses heightened, and they became warier. Despite their size, they adapted to a life of stealth. Sadly, all that they gained did not compare to what had been lost. Fire, tools, dwellings ... all was forgotten. In many ways, the remaining clans once more became the animals they had long ago risen above.

As for this history between the two species, it is also doubtful the clan would have shown much appreciation for it either. Their racial memory was strong, and the lessons of their defeat had been passed down through the generations. Who knows what they might have thought under different circumstances. Some of them might have felt disgust at this replaying of events long past. Others might have had vague feelings of vindication. However, none of this mattered to them in the slightest. By the time the lights had gone out at Bonanza Creek, each and every one of them was quite insane.

23

"**A**re you a fucking retard!?" Chuck screamed at the dirty man he'd just shoved off him. "I almost gutted you."

"Wouldn't..." the man gasped as he rose back to his feet, looking exhausted, "...be the first time I almost got gutted today."

Chuck had no idea what he was talking about. All he knew was that it still didn't feel right. If he had been a few hundred yards further back in the direction he had come, his suspicions would have been confirmed. He would have seen nothing but darkness where the town of Bonanza Creek should have been.

"Can you walk?" he asked, vaguely aware of the throbbing in his own gut. The collision hadn't done his wound any good. He could walk, but at the moment he wasn't sure he could do much more.

"Walking doesn't concern me so much as running." The man eyed the knife that Chuck was still holding. "Don't suppose you got anything bigger than that pig sticker on you."

"Not with me. Why?" Chuck asked, hoping the answer wasn't going to further ruin his already shitty day.

"You ain't gonna believe this," replied Kurt Bachowski, "but there's a big-ass ape out there, and it's gonna be up both our shitters if we don't get moving."

The blackout was just the excuse Phil had been looking for. He hadn't expected Paula to be such an — *animal,* and a freaky one at that. They had just finished up their second go at it, and he was breathing hard. He felt like he could pass out right then and there. Paula, on the other hand, was almost immediately ready for round three. She had started pawing at him and was once more weirding him out with her bizarre demands.

"Tame me, oh mighty chief. Make me your squaw," she had grunted, lowering her head beneath the covers and starting to work her way down.

Jesus, this bitch has some fucked up fantasies, he thought, trying to pry her off.

He grabbed her by the hair and yanked her back up, hoping she got the hint. However, she had just grinned at him and purred, "Oh, please don't scalp me, young brave. The other settlers are dead. I have no defense against you, should you wish to violate me."

She started grinding her body against him again. Amazingly, he was the one feeling violated. He was getting close to decking the freaky bitch – although a small voice in his head warned she might like that – when the lights had blinked out.

In the perfect darkness, she didn't see the look of relief that crossed over his face.

"What's going on?" she asked, dropping out of whatever crazed fantasy had been playing out in her mind.

"I don't know. I'd better go check." Before she could protest, he quickly rolled out from under her and began grabbing for his clothes in the dark.

"You don't have to go. This dump probably just blew a fuse. Why don't you come back here and we can pretend you just dragged me back to your teepee?"

Oh shit. He hopped back into his pants as quickly as he could. "I should get going anyway," he told her, a slight note of desperation in his voice. "Your boyfriend will probably be worried."

She sighed in the darkness. "I guess you're right. Although the twerp is probably busy jerking himself off to those assholes' every word."

Phil heard shuffling on the bed. It sounded like she was getting up, too. "I'll come with you. Maybe we can find a quiet corner and you can show me your *great spirit* again," she purred.

He involuntarily gulped. Even in the dark, he could imagine the insatiable look in her eyes. This was definitely not going as he had imagined. "You know, I'm not really an Indian," he confessed, fumbling into his sneakers and starting toward the door.

"Of course not," her voice came from right in front of him. "Your people have been scattered by the white man," she said in a throaty voice as she moved between him and the door. "You have no home, no identity of your own. All you have is vengeance for your own personal Trail of Tears, a chance to take it out on some poor, helpless maiden."

"Not quite what I meant," he replied in a small voice. *Christ, this chick won't take the hint.* He backed up and found himself leaning against one of the windows. Unsurprisingly, he heard her footsteps following.

Unfortunately, that wasn't all he heard.

He noticed a strange chuffing sound that didn't seem to be coming from her direction.

"Did I tire you out that much?" Paula asked, walking up to him.

"What do you mean?"

"You're panting like a dog."

"That's not me."

"Then what..." She didn't get a chance to finish the question, though, for at that moment, the window exploded.

Phil screamed out as shards of glass embedded themselves in his skin, but that wasn't the worst. No, that was *far* from the worst. He felt the nails of an impossibly strong hand dig into his back. There was a wet tearing sound, followed by a crunch as his spine shattered. It was the last thing he heard before a much darker blackness took him.

Inside the Bonanza Creek Bar and Grill, there wasn't any sense of worry, at least not initially. The three men had been talking with Kate when the lights went out. Before anyone could react, Ben Reeves had cursed, "Goddamnit! This place is wired worse than a ten-cent whore." Derek had been tempted to ask what he meant by that, when Ben turned on a flashlight from his spot behind the bar. "No need to panic, folks."

Moving with the speed of a man who knows a place like the back of his hand, he procured some candles from beneath the counter and lit them. At last, he seemed satisfied that he had given his customers enough light for the moment. He then said, "Hold tight and I'll go check on the genny," before walking around the bar and heading toward the rear of the room.

Harrison gave a worried look as the bartender disappeared into the back, but Derek smiled at him reassuringly in the dim light. "There *is* such a thing as coincidence," he said.

Kate looked between them for a second. "Coincidence about what?"

Harrison took another sip of his beer. "Sorry. I'm being jumpy. Just because I got a good scare is probably no reason to freak out the second anything weird happens."

"I'll say," she replied. "And trust me, there's been a lot of weird going on the last day or two."

"How so?" Derek asked, his interest piqued.

"Those hikers that got lost?" Harrison offered.

"No. It has nothing to do with them or the search party. I'm probably all worked up because my dog's gone missing."

Derek and Francis exchanged a quick glance. "When did this happen?"

"I don't know," she replied. "I haven't seen him since I left the house this morning. It's not like him. He's usually a lazy bugger. Then there was that blood on my porch."

"Blood?" She suddenly had Derek's full attention.

"Yeah, a whole puddle of it. My dad thought one of the locals got drunk, then maybe stepped on some broken glass. I don't know, though. It was a lot of blood for that. Whoever they were, I just hope they got themselves over to Doc Hanscomb's place."

Harrison's eyes went wide. Derek was about to tell him to calm down and not jump to conclusions, but the younger man spoke first. "What do you mean by 'stepped on glass?'"

"Well, there were bloody footprints. Big ones, too, and the damnedest thing was they were barefoot, just like it was the middle of summer."

Derek held up a hand to Harrison. "I'm sure it's just a…"

Just then, there was a loud thump from the back-room. All heads turned in that direction. Ben could be heard yelling, "Use the front door, you…" but his shout was interrupted by the sound of splintering wood. The entire building shuddered as if from an impact.

Then the screaming started.

"Let me guess, just another coincidence?" Harrison asked.

Derek looked between them all. "I've been known to be wrong on occasion."

"What's wrong?" asked Rob. "What does the report say?"

Even in the glow of the monitors, Mitchell's face appeared to have taken on an ashen sheen. "It says that I'm a goddamned fool."

"I'm not following you."

"The results," he said, holding up the printouts. "The biopsy samples came back with a match."

"For what?"

"Rabies," Mitchell replied. "The goddamn thing was rabid."

"Okay, okay. Don't panic," Rob said, trying to calm the other man down. This wasn't his area of expertise, but he was a quick thinker and wanted to make sure they weren't jumping the gun on anything. "Are you sure the sample was okay? Maybe they made a mistake. Maybe it got corrupted."

Mitchell rolled his eyes at the younger man. "Don't you think I thought of that? I sent over multiple samples, all prepared separately. *All* of them came back with similar results. If there was an outlier, the report would've listed it."

Rob listened with a growing sense of panic. "Harrison got that thing's blood all over him and Woodchuck got slashed up."

"I know. We're going to need to get them to a real hospital. Hell, we'll probably all need to be treated, just to be safe. And that's not even the worst of it."

"How is that not the worst?"

"Remember what Derek said? There's probably a whole clan of them in the area. What if that thing was a kind of Typhoid Mary?"

Now it was Rob's turn to look ill. He stood up and grabbed the printouts. "We need to tell him about this *now*."

He stepped toward the rear of the van. Suddenly, the entire vehicle lurched as if it had been broadsided. He fell to the floor, and Mitchell landed beside him.

"What the hell?" Mitchell barked. Just as he did, there came a second impact. If the first had rocked the heavy vehicle, this one was enough to finish the job.

The van tumbled onto its side. The sensitive communications array on top was smashed in the impact. Inside, equipment sparked, warning lights flashed, and then, after a few seconds of chaos, it all went dark.

Danni jolted awake in bed, disoriented in the unfamiliar surroundings. After escorting Greg back to his room, she had retired to her own. She had found Allison already out cold, still fully dressed, lying across one of the beds. Upon seeing her, Danni had realized how good a little bit of sleep sounded. Everything else could wait until morning.

She had covered her friend with a blanket before climbing into the other bed and doing the same. She initially wasn't sure if she'd be able to sleep, despite the weariness of her body. She needn't have worried, though. She was snoring within three minutes of hitting the pillow.

Though it was already starting to fade from memory, she knew she had been reliving the day's events in a dream. In it, she had been alone as the creature pursued her through the woods. It had been even larger than life, more like being run down by a dinosaur. With each monstrous stride, it gained on her. With each step it took, the ground beneath her feet shook a little more. Finally, she had looked back and realized it was right on top of her. The creature let out an earth-shattering scream, and that was when she had awoken. It had seemed so real.

"Danni?" a voice called from the darkness. She realized, after a second or two, it was Allison. She reached over and flicked the switch on the lamp next to her bed. Nothing happened.

"Danni, are you awake?"

"Yeah."

"You heard it too, huh?"

That got her attention. "Heard what?"

"I don't know. It sounded like someone screamed. I thought I was dreaming, but then I heard you sit up."

A dull feeling of unease shot up Danni's spine. "Turn on your light, okay? Mine's not working."

There was a shuffling noise as her friend got up,

followed by a dull click. The darkness remained, though.

"Power's out," Allison said, a bit of wariness creeping into her voice.

"I'm sure it's nothing to..."

Her words trailed off as something started hammering on their door.

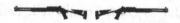

Both girls let out a cry of surprise.

The pounding ceased just as quickly as it began, and then a panicked voice on the other side of the door yelled, "Let me in!"

Danni swallowed the lump in her throat. She felt a bit foolish and was kind of glad that Allison couldn't see her. Judging by the deep breath that came from the other girl's direction, she was probably thinking the same thing.

"Is that Paula?"

"Sounds like it," Allison replied. "Can you get the door and see what she wants? I'll find my flashlight."

"On it." Danni walked toward the door, feeling in front of herself with her hands. The pounding and shouting started up again as she reached it. Fumbling with the lock, she yelled back, "Okay! We heard you the first time! For Christ's sake, Paula..." The door flung open, and she was pushed back by its force. A scant second later, someone, presumably Paula, grabbed her in a bear hug.

"Thank God! Thank God!" she panted over and over again.

Danni somehow managed to keep from falling over. She was confused, but she could tell the other girl was extremely upset. Instinctively, she put her arms around Paula, then felt her backside.

"Paula, are you...," she started to say when the bright LEDs of a flashlight lit up the room.

"Naked?" Allison finished.

Sure enough, she was – naked and completely hysterical, as far as Danni could tell. Paula continued to hug her with almost manic strength, then she started stuttering in an attempt to speak.

"Slow down," Danni said in a comforting tone. "It's okay. Take a breath and tell us what happened."

Paula continued shaking, but at last managed to blurt out, "Wild ... Feather!"

Allison stepped up to them. "What?" She looked Paula up and down. "What did that asshole do to you?"

Danni and her friend shared a glance. They were probably thinking the same thing. Had the whole ordeal caused Wild Feather to snap? She almost couldn't believe it. He was normally so together, so serene, so gentle.

No, that was all bullshit, she reminded herself. She had to remember that she obviously didn't know him at all. Now it looked like the little bastard had stepped way over the line. If so, he was going down hard. She'd see him behind bars and hopefully some convict's bitch before this was over.

"Get me a blanket," Danni instructed.

Allison grabbed one off the bed and wrapped it around Paula's still trembling shoulders. Danni then gently pulled away and looked her in the eye. "It's okay. He can't hurt you."

"He..." the other girl trembled.

"Tell us. What did he do?"

Finally, something seemed to snap in Paula. She grabbed Danni's arms in a manic grip and stared back at her, her pupils wide despite Allison's light. "DEAD!" she finally screamed. "HE'S DEAD!"

The two other girls once again exchanged confused glances. "What do you mean 'he's dead?'" Even as Danni asked the question, she realized how stupid it sounded. It was a bad line straight out of a Law & Order episode.

Paula didn't seem to notice, though. She was far beyond that. "IT KILLED HIM! IT KILLED HIM – AND NOW IT'S COMING FOR US!"

Greg slept like the dead. Despite his outward good cheer, his arm had been hurting like a motherfucker. The good doctor, knowing the nearest pharmacy was over an hour's drive away, had taken pity and handed him a small vial of codeine tablets before showing them out.

After Danni walked him back to his room – politely declining his offer to come in – he had immediately swallowed two of the pills. He had just been going through the motions with her anyway. He couldn't let a pretty girl walk away without at least trying any more than he could give up breathing. The truth was, he hadn't been particularly miffed by her refusal. In fact, he was pretty fine with it. The only company he really wanted tonight was the pain pills.

It turned out that what the doctor gave him had been the good stuff. Within a few minutes, he either didn't feel the pain anymore or didn't care, he wasn't sure which. He decided that his last joint would be the perfect chaser. By the time he had finished it, he had been high as a kite. Hell, someone could've sawed off his good arm with a dull butter knife and he would have been absolutely cool with it.

He had been lying on his bed, watching the room swirl around him, when the lights went out. "But I don't wanna go to bed yet, Dad," he had giggled to nobody in particular before completely passing out.

His room was directly above Paula's, yet he didn't hear the crash as the creature came through the window. Nor did he hear the wet tearing of meat followed by her piteous screams. He was completely oblivious when Conroy McStanish came walking down the hall to investigate. Conroy's grunts of irritation would have been far too low for Greg to have heard, even had he been awake, but he would have probably noticed the man's surprised yelp as Paula came tearing bare-assed out of the room and past him. He would almost certainly have heard the sound of her door being torn off its hinges just moments later.

He likewise missed Conroy McStanish's last moments on earth. Had he been awake, he most likely would not have heard the man's surprised gasp of, "Dear mother in heaven!" as a beast straight out of his worst nightmares strode down the hall toward him. The floors of the Bonanza Bed & Breakfast were not quite solid enough to mute the sound of Conroy's collar bone shattering as the creature slammed both its fists down onto the unlucky man. Even if they had been, Greg surely would have heard the high-pitched squeal that the bed and breakfast owner made as his head was ripped from his shoulders.

The only indication that Greg noticed anything at all was the rippling fart that he let loose as the now headless body of Conroy McStanish slammed into the wall hard enough to splatter like a crushed insect. It wasn't much of a eulogy to mark the end of a life, but it was more than most in Bonanza Creek received that night.

His tribute to the late Mr. McStanish done, Greg grunted in his sleep and turned over. He missed the sound of Paula begging to be let into Danni's room. He missed her weeping cries as they tried to comfort her. He even missed the heavy footsteps that came plodding up the stairs and past his room.

24

There was no longer any order within the clan. The very last act they performed as social creatures had been to bring darkness to the two-legged things. For creatures with night vision, even a small place such as Bonanza Creek stood out like a beacon. For the clan, whose eyes and ears had grown overly sensitive in the grip of the fever, it was a source of pain as well. The light bore into their dilated pupils as they approached, causing them to cry out.

That might have been the end of the attack. The lights of the small town may very well have been enough to turn them away and send them mewling back into the depths of the forest. If so, things would have ended differently. Some of the clan would have scattered. Others would have turned on each other. The survivors would have eventually succumbed to the sickness. Perhaps a few more wayward hikers would have perished at their crazed hands, but the worst would have been averted.

But the Alpha was old and had seen much. His

mind wasn't so far gone yet that he wasn't able to remember. He had traveled far in his lifetime, migrating as the weather changed and as more of their habitat was encroached upon. He had seen the clans of the two-legged things. Before the rage, there had been curiosity. He had observed them as they worked, as they played, and as they lived.

Though he did not understand how, he knew the false trees, the ones the two-legged things planted, carried fire within their vines. He had once seen a false tree felled by a storm. Its vines had snapped and flames had sprayed from their ends. The dwellings that housed the two-legged things had gone dark when that had happened, their source of fire cut off.

He remembered this, although rage had since replaced all of his former curiosity. Knowing what to do, he had barked and grunted to the clan to follow him. When they had hesitated, a few showing their teeth in defiance, he had torn off a tree limb and beaten them with it. That seemed to temporarily restore their sense of clan.

Once order had been reestablished, he had shown them what to do. The false trees were flimsy things. They lacked roots and could be toppled easily. The clan did not care much beyond that. All they cared was that they were finally able to let loose their rage. It was not nearly as satisfying as making something scream. When they saw the results, though – that the hurtful lights died when the false trees were felled – they attacked them in earnest.

Despite the Alpha's warning grunts, a young female had been stupid. When the vines fell, she had gotten too close. Her body had spasmed wildly at first, and then the *fire had touched her fur. She immediately burst aflame. She died, burning and convulsing, as the others watched. However, the lesson had been learned. None of the rest ventured near the vines.*

There had been no hooting of remorse at her passing. The clan was too far gone for that. If anything, her death had only excited them for the bloodshed to come. Their rage had been just barely kept in check until then. Watching her die, and the promise of more death to come, finally caused them to snap.

As the last of the light died, the clan spread out. There was neither rhyme nor reason to their pattern. Their individual goals were simple: find and kill as many of the two-legged things as they could. By then, the Alpha could not have stopped them, even had he wanted to. He didn't want to stop them, though. All he cared was that they stay out of his way. He was looking forward to the screaming, and it didn't particularly matter much the source.

25

Byron Clemons was happily whistling along to some Bob Dylan as he drove toward home. All the building supplies he and Grace would need to rebuild the chicken coop stronger than ever filled the bed of his Dodge Ram. In actuality, there were quite a few excess purchases as well. She would probably chew him out for it, but he just couldn't help himself. He had a high credit limit on his Home Depot card, and nobody had been around to tell him no. He wasn't too worried, though, having also picked up the new vanity set for the downstairs bathroom that she'd been bugging him about. If he tossed her a bone by installing it, all would be well.

As he drove along the former logging road, he passed a few other cars – most of them state troopers heading toward 160. Most likely, they were members of the search party calling it quits for the night. *Damn stupid hikers are always getting lost*, he mused. It had been years since he'd volunteered to help in one of those searches. Despite the fact that he and Grace were more than capable of adding their expertise, he had a bad taste in his mouth about the whole thing. Unless there were missing kids involved – and stupid ass teenagers didn't count as kids in Byron Clemons' book – then the damn fools could take care of themselves. Not only was it almost always their own damn fault, but most of the time they were ingrates about it after you went out of your way to drag their sorry asses back to civilization.

"I'm sure I'd have found my way eventually," one such idiot had proclaimed haughtily, as if he were Davey Crockett himself. The fat bastard had been missing for about eighteen hours. He'd been heading in exactly the wrong direction when they had found him, lost and scared – tears of joy streaming down his face at being rescued.

"Well if that's the case, mister," Byron had replied at the time, "howsabout I take you right back in there and you show me what for?" That shut the son of a bitch right up.

He was about a mile south of the outskirts of Bonanza Creek when he suddenly slammed on the brakes. Byron was usually a careful driver, but he had been caught up in his reverie. A stopped car loomed in his headlights, causing him to jam his foot on the brake pedal. Fortunately, his truck was kept in good repair. He managed to skid to a halt with plenty of room to spare.

He sat there for a few moments, breathing hard and cursing himself for not paying better attention. When he had himself under control, he took a good look through the windshield at the other vehicle. There was no mistaking it. It was wholly unremarkable for the most part, a grey Ford Taurus a couple years old. The bubble light stuck to the top, though, identified it immediately as Mark Watson's car.

Putting his truck in park, he remembered that Grace had been planning on tracking Mark down on account of their chickens. It was doubtful she had caught up to him, though. The part-time deputy had obviously been on his way back from a day of combing the woods.

He's probably off taking a piss in the bushes, Byron thought, getting out of his truck. He left the lights on. No point in wandering around blind. He decided to go and wait by Mark's car for his return. If he could chat with him about their chickens right now, it'd save Grace the effort of doing so tomorrow.

It wasn't until he had walked around the Taurus that he realized it wasn't just parked. The front of the car was badly dented and partially crumpled. Stepping closer, he could see there were streaks of blood on the hood and grill. *Unlucky bastard probably hit a buck. Big one by the looks of things.* It wasn't uncommon around these parts, especially after dark. Deer were everywhere, and they almost seemed to love jumping out in front of cars. "The stupid things must have a death wish," he had told Grace one night after stopping just in time as a small herd leapt from the surrounding forest.

He leaned against the side of the car and began looking toward the woods. If Mark hadn't walked too far, Byron figured he'd be able to pick out the beam from his cop Maglite pretty easily. It's not like there were a lot of other light sources out there. He had scanned perhaps a quarter of his field of vision, seeing no light other than his truck's, when he felt an emptiness where his elbow should have been touching glass. Turning, his first thought was to wonder why Mark had left the driver's side window rolled down.

He put his hand on the door, then quickly pulled it back as something sharp jabbed him. He lifted it and saw a shallow cut on his palm, a small sliver of jagged glass stuck in it. *Safety glass, my left ass cheek.* He pulled the shard out and tossed it aside. Leaning in, he took a closer look at the door. In the darkness, he had initially missed all the bits of broken glass littering the front seat. The window had been broken inward, pretty violently, too, by the look of things.

He was just starting to consider this, his mind going over more scenarios, when he was suddenly plunged into darkness. At first, he thought that maybe his truck battery had up and died. It would be just his luck. Then he realized the light was still there, it was just being blocked.

He turned back toward his Dodge and saw that someone was standing directly in front of it. He couldn't see who — all he could see was their silhouette, a dark outline against the light.

"Mark?" he called out, even as his brain made the connection that Mark Watson was a man of medium height and build. Whoever was standing in front of his truck was built like one of those wrestlers he and Grace sometimes liked to watch on TV.

His thoughts turned to that fool drunk, Joel

Bean, just as the figure took a lurching step toward him. Whoever he was, he was limping badly. Byron Clemons was not an overly kind man, but he wasn't a bastard either. He took a step forward to offer assistance. As the figure neared him, Byron held out a helping hand and touched what felt like slick fur. Before his mind could process this, a hand much larger than his own reached back toward him. It was fast and strong, far stronger than Byron would have been able to imagine had he been given time.

Sadly, he wasn't.

The hand grasped the front of his face, and its jagged nails dug into his scalp. He barely had time for a muffled scream before the fingers cracked through the bone of his skull and pulled. The front of Byron's head – face, eyes, bone, and muscle – was peeled like a ripe banana.

The creature leaned forward toward the raw bleeding cavern that had been Byron Clemons' face. Its mouth closed around the gaping wound. For the next few minutes, the only sound that penetrated the dark woods was a thick slurping as it gorged itself.

Grace Clemons wasn't psychic, nor did she even believe in such silliness. She had a cousin from Nebraska, Natalie, who claimed to have the sight. After a few drinks, she could always be counted on to pull out her tarot cards and give grand proclamations for love, money, or both. As far as Grace was concerned, though, she was full of shit up to her beady brown eyes.

If pressed for an answer to the strange feeling in her gut, Grace would have claimed woman's intuition – or perhaps the simple knowing that develops when couples had been together as long as she'd been with Byron. Regardless of how or why, though, she felt something was wrong.

She had been feeling it all day. First, there was the incident with the chickens. Later on, their hunting dog, Zeke, had nosed around near the coop. Without any warning, he had then scampered down into the basement, tail between his legs, and huddled in a corner, whimpering. Since then, he had refused to budge from down there. Finally, the lights had gone out, although that wasn't really an issue. Their generator had kicked in almost immediately, but something still didn't feel quite right.

There had been plenty of outages before. Tree branches were always coming down on a power line somewhere. But even with the low hum of the genny out back, something still felt wrong. She and Byron had always laughed at those silly TV shows about haunted houses, especially when people claimed to feel like they were being watched. Now she understood. It was like a prickling sensation at the back of her neck. It was an odd feeling, something she had never felt before – not even during the many hunting excursions she'd taken with her husband.

That must be it. She was spooked because Byron had been gone all day. If it had just been that, then maybe there wouldn't have been an issue. But all of the strangeness of the day, coupled with his being out, must be having a cumulative effect on her. "That's me. Getting old and jumpy," she mused out loud with a laugh that didn't sound all that convincing to her.

Oh, this is stupid, Grace thought, disgusted with herself. *Best to nip this in the bud before I wind up in the basement cowering with that fool dog.* She decided to do a quick perimeter sweep of her property. The generator kept the lights on in the house, but the external system was still off due to the earlier damage. However, the darkness itself didn't bother her. She knew the area around their house like the back of her hand.

She debated reaching for her thirty-aught-six, but then dismissed it as being overly paranoid. Still, she had no intention of being stupid about it either. She opted to strap on the holster holding her nine millimeter semi-automatic. It didn't have much stopping power – not that she was expecting to need it – but it was light, fast, and quick to reload.

She tossed on her jacket and grabbed the three-cell flashlight that hung near the back door, checking first to make sure the batteries were fresh. She turned it on, then stepped out into the cool night. It would be the last time she ever walked out of her house. Had she known, she might have stopped to take one last look around. It was a comfortable home, and she had been happy there. She had never been blessed with children, but that had been fine because she and Byron had been good company to each other. It had been enough for her.

Grace walked straight toward the tree line at the

back edge of her property. If there were any threats to be found, she reasoned that was where they would likely be. Had she gone the opposite way, or even made a circuit of her house first, she might have heard the footsteps approaching from the direction of town – along with the wet snuffling sounds as the apelike creature breathed through its increasingly congested nostrils.

She was a full fifty yards away when it came around the house and spotted her. She was facing away from it, her flashlight beam lancing out toward the trees. Once more, if there had been just a slight change in the events that followed, Grace Clemons might have lived to see another day. Unfortunately, luck was not with her that night. In fact, had her cousin been there with her tarot cards, she might have told Grace her luck had plain ole skedaddled out of town.

The creature let loose with an earsplitting roar as it began to race toward her. Grace, already on frayed nerves, jumped at the sound and lost her grip on the flashlight. It fell to the ground and rolled a few feet away. It was here that she made her final mistake of the night. Rather than pull her gun and unload it in the creature's direction, she bent down to retrieve the light. Maybe it was nerves or an instinctive need to see the source of her torment. Whatever it was, it was a mistake that cost Grace Clemons her life.

She did manage to retrieve the flashlight first, though, bringing it up just as the beast was upon her. She was given a momentary glimpse of fur, dripping mouth, and red eyes before being plunged into darkness again. A hand – easily three times the size of her own – tore the light away, along with the rest of Grace's arm.

Clutching at the ragged stump, she fell with a cry. She hit the cold ground, and the beast brought its foot down onto her torso. Her ribcage gave way as if it had been made of balsa wood. Bone fragments shredded whatever organs of hers weren't outright crushed on impact.

With her last thoughts, she considered that maybe there *had* been something to the feeling of dread that had been building all day. All at once, she realized what it meant: her husband was dead, and she was going to join him. *See you soon, hon...*

As the glimmer of life faded from her eyes, she never knew that her first intuition regarding the absurdity of psychic powers had been correct. She *wasn't* going to join her husband. In fact, he was coming to join her. It was still half an hour until Byron Clemons' final face-off with another of the creatures out on the lonely country road.

"Why can't I turn on the light, Elmer?" Vera Gentry asked her husband for what, to him, felt like the hundredth time. The only illumination in their small cabin came from the living room fireplace. He would have preferred it pitch dark so as to make it look like nothing was alive in the place. Sadly, their old oil furnace hadn't kicked over for some reason. He'd made the concession to get a fire going, not keen on freezing his ass off while he kept listen for whatever was screaming like a banshee out in the woods.

"No lights! I already told you, woman," he spat from his favorite chair. He had moved it to the center of the room where he now sat, – a loaded double-barreled shotgun resting on his lap. Next to Elmer, on the tray table where he normally kept the TV remote, sat a full box of ammo.

"And I'm telling you you're being a darn old fool," she shot back. "No lights. No TV. Heck, I can't even see enough to knit. All for what? You probably just heard a wildcat yowling out back."

"Weren't no cat made that noise," he said with grim finality. "Now pipe down, I'm listening. Can't hear nothing with you clucking like a hen."

She made a sound of disgust and got up from the couch where she had sat, complaining nonstop, since supper. Elmer breathed a quiet sigh. She was his third wife and by far his favorite. She could cook and she kept the house clean, but once she got on a nagging kick, the bitch just didn't shut up. He'd never been a violent man. He believed a sharp tongue lashing was always the better solution. Regardless, every so often, he found himself wondering if maybe a good smack upside the head might be in order. Now was one of those times. His sharp ears didn't mean squat while she was cawing like a bird.

She walked over to the closed shutters. "Well, at least let me open the window a crack. It's getting stuffy in here. If I have to be cooped up in the dark, I might as well be able to breathe."

He opened his mouth, meaning to tell her to sit

back down and, for the last time, shut the hell up, but in the split second between the end of her rant and his intake of breath, he heard it. It wasn't much, just the crunch of some dead leaves. Regardless, he definitely heard *something*. Elmer Gentry's ears were sharp. They had never failed him ... until now.

"VERA, GET AWAY FROM..."

The window exploded inward before he could finish.

The spray of wood and shattered glass caused his wife to back up a step, but it wasn't far enough. An arm, muscular and covered in brown hair, shot through the opening.

Elmer's eyes weren't that good, especially in the dim light. He couldn't see exactly what was standing outside the window except to tell that it was big. He didn't need to, though. He already knew what it was.

Before he could steady the shotgun against his shoulder, the hand grasped the front of Vera's housedress and hauled her toward the opening. She was dragged halfway out, her slippered feet kicking wildly in the air. Under other circumstances, it might have been comical, her legs flailing away while her dress rode up to show her bloomers. However, there was nothing funny about what happened next.

An animalistic snarl came from outside, followed by a wet ripping sound. Vera's feet stopped moving and fell limp after one last twitch. A second later, her lower half fell to the floor, the rest of her having been torn clean off. She hadn't even had time to scream.

Elmer raised the gun. There would be time to mourn later. For now, though, there was business to attend to. Unfortunately, even as he brought the gun to bear, he could tell there was nothing standing at the window. Another soft crunch outside alerted him that it was moving. Still seated, he quickly pointed the shotgun toward the front door.

Oh no you don't, you sneaky son of a bitch. The creature possessed impressive natural stealth for its size. It was moving quickly and quietly, but it hadn't counted on Elmer Gentry's uncanny hearing.

He watched calmly while his front door was literally torn from its hinges, as if it were made of nothing sturdier than tissue paper. The creature stepped through with a grunt. Runny red eyes locked first on Elmer, then on the barrel of his gun. They opened wide as if in surprise – the last bit of sanity in its hairy head asserting itself at the very end.

Elmer unloaded with both barrels. Had he been standing, the recoil would have knocked him flat on his old ass. Either way, he was going to have a nasty bruise on his shoulder. It more than did the job, though. The only thing left of the beast's head was a fine red mist. The rest of it crumpled unceremoniously to the floor.

"That was for you, Vera," he said to the empty room once the echoes from the blast died down.

He sat back in his chair with a sigh and closed his eyes.

That was when he heard it ... when he heard *them*.

With the door now wide open and Vera's incessant prattling silenced – permanently – he began to understand. Roars, cries, snarls – all of them reached Elmer's sharp ears. Soon enough, more of the creatures would come, many more. Had he been a younger man, he might have tried to make a stand, but he was old ... old and suddenly very tired.

As he listened to the sounds of Bonanza Creek dying, he lit his pipe for one last smoke. He took several deep, satisfying drags, then grabbed some shells from the table beside him. He calmly reloaded his shotgun, his wrinkled hands steady – moving as if he had all the time in the world.

He took one last puff from his pipe before setting it down. He kicked the loafer from his right foot, noting with some amusement that it landed on the body of the slain beast. *Kicked yer ass all the way to Hell,* he thought with a grin.

Elmer placed the barrel of the loaded gun under his chin, then positioned his big toe on the trigger. His had been a good life. He found he had no regrets. If anything, the anticipation of seeing Vera again so soon gave him one last smile.

Moments later, another thunderous blast shook the house, then all was quiet ... this time for good.

Some might have called it the coward's way out, while to others it would have been a good death. Regardless, Elmer Gentry checked out on his own terms. He was the only one in Bonanza Creek that night who could make such a claim.

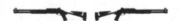

Many such events played out across the small town that night. People, both young and old, died. Some went quickly. Others weren't granted that mercy. A few died knowing what had come for them, but more went to the grave with no understanding of what had killed them. A handful of lucky souls even managed to fight back before being laid low. Regardless of how its occupants died, though, as the night wore on, Bonanza Creek became less of a town and more a graveyard.

26

Kurt Bachowski didn't like being yelled at. He didn't like being yelled at by women. He really didn't like being yelled at by foreigners. And he *especially* didn't like being yelled at by niggers. That he was being bawled out by one now was just icing on the cake, as far as he was concerned.

The disappointing hunt that morning had been just the start of a big dump that life decided to take on his head. His brother's death had been awful, but that seemed like almost a lifetime ago now. The bitch ape that killed Stan had charged him, and he'd emptied his rifle at it. Had he been given time, he might have been able to put one through its eye and end it right there. He hadn't been nearly so lucky, though. All of the low caliber bullets had struck home, but they'd barely slowed the thing down. But barely was better than not at all.

The creature had paused to put a hand over one of the small bullet wounds in its stomach, and Kurt had used the opportunity to throw the now empty rifle at it – hitting it in the face with a satisfying thud. He then turned tail and ran like hell.

It had been close. The damn thing was fast, and it apparently knew the woods as well as he did, maybe better. At one point, he'd practically felt it breathing down his neck. He had turned his head and looked straight into its hellish red eyes. He was sure he was a goner, but then the creature had made a mad lunge for him and stumbled over a tree root instead. It went down, and he hadn't waited around for it to get back up.

Since then, Kurt had been trying every trick he knew to make sure it didn't pick up his trail again, all while making his way toward town. Though he and his brother kept plenty of firepower in their cabin – *his* cabin now, he mentally corrected himself – he didn't want to risk doubling back. Animal or not, the thing was smart, and that made it all the more dangerous.

As if all that wasn't bad enough, he had come within inches of being gutted by the loud-mouthed spook in front of him. Now the son of a bitch was barking orders like this was the goddamned military.

"When did you see the squatch!?"

Kurt spat on the ground. "I don't know what the hell a *squatch* is. All I know is that there's a fucking gorilla loose out there, a goddamned big one."

"Not a gorilla ... sasquatch."

"What?"

"Sasquatch. You know, bigfoot? When did you see it?"

Under normal circumstances, Kurt would have laughed at that shit and continued walking. Under slightly less than normal circumstances, he might have decked the asshole for getting in his face. Unfortunately, the circumstances were so far from normal right now as to be in a whole other state. Kurt considered this for a moment.

"Left my Rolex in my other suit," he answered snidely, "but I guess it started chasing me a couple hours ago."

The man grabbed him by the shoulders. "Are you sure?"

Kurt shoved him away. He didn't like being touched either. "Yeah, I'm sure!"

The bastard pulled out his knife again. Kurt eyed him warily, but the man started scanning the area instead.

"Damn," he said to himself. "More than one."

"More than one?" Kurt asked. "You mean there are others?"

"It would seem so. I think we should get back to town. There are people who need to know this."

Kurt spat again. "Shit. That's the first sensible thing you've said."

If the screaming hadn't told the group that something was wrong, then the primal roar coming from the rear of the structure certainly did. Derek didn't hesitate for more than a moment. He stood and turned to his cameraman. "Stay with them, Frank." He then strode toward the backroom as the bartender had done.

Francis started to address the others. "Okay, let's all stay calm. He knows what he's..."

Derek returned just as quickly as he'd left. "Scratch that! Get them out of here."

"Why? What's going on?" Kate asked as Derek leaped over the bar. "Hey! This isn't your place."

Derek spoke while grabbing bottles from the back shelf. "Somehow, I don't think the owner is going to mind. Get them moving, Frank!"

The big cameraman stood and tried to usher the others toward the front door. Harrison didn't need to be told twice. However, Kate wasn't about to be dismissed so easily.

"Ben's back there. If he's hurt, we have to help him."

Without turning to face her, Derek replied, "He's beyond our help right now." He threw the bottles toward the rear of the room, shattering them against the door frame.

"What the hell are you doing!?"

"Having a fire sale," he answered, tossing one of the lit candles from the bar. Within seconds, the back of the room was engulfed in flames.

He hopped back over the bar and joined the group. Grabbing Kate by the arm, he began to drag her toward the front door.

She struggled against him. "We can't leave Ben."

Harrison turned to face her, unable to believe she could be so thick. "He's dead, lady. Get the hint." He didn't like being so blunt, but he was at the end of his rope. The creature's roar a few seconds earlier had gone a long way toward unnerving him.

"All right, enough," Derek barked. "Outside *now*! There's a lot of alcohol in this place, and we really *don't* want to be here when the fire reaches it."

"Do you think that'll stop it?" Francis asked, pushing the front door open.

"Not really." Derek stepped out into the night air, the rest following him. He took no more than three steps before stopping dead in his tracks.

"What is it?" asked Harrison, although as the sounds reached his ears, he understood.

The darkness around them was anything but quiet. Roars, screams, and hoots filled the air. They seemed to be coming from everywhere at once.

"Offhand," said Derek with a sigh, "I'd say this job just got a bit more complicated."

"Mitch ... Mitchell!" Rob called out. With all of the equipment that had been packed into it, the van had barely enough extra room for the two of them. In the dark, though, the toppled space seemed nearly cavernous.

He took a deep breath and calmed himself. He was lying on his back against something smooth. It felt like a monitor. Reaching out to either side, he began feeling around.

Again, the van shuddered. There was a hollow boom against the side, now the roof from Rob's perspective, and then any questions he might have had as to the reason were answered. A shrill scream pierced the night, disturbingly loud even in the enclosed space.

But we killed it, his mind childishly insisted. *Well, okay, 'we' might be a tad generous.* However, then logic took over, and he remembered what they'd been discussing before things went all topsy-turvy. *Rabies! Mitchell was right to be afraid.*

A low moan to his right caught his attention. He reached over as the van lurched again. Whatever was out there was angry and apparently not taking no for an answer.

A part of Rob wanted to curl up into a little ball, but then he remembered who he was in town with. Would the Crypto Hunter crawl into a corner and cry? Of course not, and neither would he.

He groped around until he found Mitchell's shoulder. He gave it a shake, and the moan came again. "Mitch! Are you okay?"

"Ugh! What the hell?" a slurred voice responded from the darkness.

"Are you all right?"

"Yeah. I think one of the damn printers fell on my head. Hurts like hell, but I'll live. You?"

"I'm as okay as I can probably be right now."

"What happened?"

"I'm thinking that you were right about the rabies," Rob answered.

The entire vehicle shook. In the small confined space, it felt like an earthquake. Metal began to groan, and the equipment that was now above them sparked. In the intermittent light, they saw that the side of the van was starting to cave in, as if a great weight were standing on it. Upon consideration, Rob realized that was exactly what was happening.

Neither Danni nor Allison needed any further answers from Paula, not that she had any left to give. The loud growl coming from the hallway told them everything they needed to know.

Before either of the other two girls could react, though, Paula let loose with a frightened squeal and bolted for the bathroom. She closed the door, and Danni heard a click from the inside.

She ran over and tried turning the knob – locked. "Paula? Paula, open the door," she said in a voice that she hoped was loud enough to be heard, but low enough so as not to alert the thing that was outside the room.

All she heard in reply was a whimper.

"Paula! Come on, open the door. You're not safe in there."

"Danni," Allison said, "I don't think there's time for that."

She turned back toward her friend. In the glow of the flashlight, she could see Allison backing away from the door. Then she heard it: heavy footsteps that stopped right outside. They were followed by a snuffling sound.

There was a moment of silence, then Allison said, "Come on!" She dashed to the opposite end of the room and threw open the window, the flashlight tumbling from her hands in the process.

"We can't leave Paula," Danni pleaded, even as she followed her friend.

"I don't think we have a choice." Allison looked out of the second-floor window in the direction of their cars. There was only a quarter-crescent moon that night, but it cast just enough light for her to know there was nothing out there to improve her mood. From her vantage point, it appeared as if all the vehicles had been beaten to hell, but the van was by far the worst. It was now on its side, and she could see another of those things leaping up and down upon it, trying to get in. Even from where she stood, the beast looked huge.

She turned and spoke quickly. "We jump and hit the ground running. Turn left, and just go. Trust me on this."

Danni shook her head. "But Paula..."

Whatever she had started to say, though, was answered by the door splintering into pieces – as if someone had driven a truck through it. A large shape growled at them from just inside the now open portal.

Neither girl said anything; they didn't need to. Allison was the first through the window. Danni followed less than a second later. Through some minor miracle, neither of them broke or sprained anything in the landing. By the time the creature reached the window, they were both running at an all-out sprint.

Paula didn't hear it come through the door. She had huddled in the bathtub and closed the curtain as if it were some magic talisman instead of just a cheap shower liner. She curled herself into as small of a ball as she could and began to make a low keening noise.

Outside, Danni and Allison made their escape. Furniture was overturned and glass broke, all combined with the creature's guttural snarls, but none of this registered in her mind. She was too far gone by then. Though she looked fine on the outside, the pursuit through the woods earlier in the day had damaged her mind. Her grasp on reality had been tenuous, at best, for the past several hours. Given time, she might have mended. Perhaps she might have even been able to eventually patch things up with Rob and move on. Sadly, her mind wasn't equipped to handle two such events in such a short time.

This last one had been even worse. She had been in high emotion when the attack came. She hadn't seen all of what had happened to Wild Feather, but she'd heard everything with excruciating clarity. She had heard his screams, followed by the awful sounds of his bones breaking and flesh tearing. Somehow, that had made it worse than actually seeing because it forced her mind to fill in the blanks, which it did with painful detail. Even had she been able to help him, she wouldn't have. Within the space of no more than a few seconds, the only part of her mind that was still functioning was the part that commanded her to flee. The excitement of the sex and the adrenaline of the attack had given her brain a little extra jolt of chemicals, just enough to allow her legs to run and her mouth to scream.

However, even that was now gone. She whimpered, neither knowing nor caring if the girls outside lived or died, not even really aware of it happening. She didn't even have enough sense left to hope that the creature would just pass by, leaving her undiscovered. Her eyes began to glaze over as she retreated deep within herself.

Wet snuffling could be heard in the bedroom outside. She didn't know – nor was she capable of understanding at that point – that the creature that had killed her lover was a male in the prime of its life. Under different circumstances, it might have passed by the locked door without even noticing her. However, Paula had just been recently deflowered. She smelled of blood and absolutely reeked of sex. Within moments, the sniffing noises took on an earnest, almost excited quality. She didn't notice this, either, for she was locked away in a safe fantasy.

She was six, and her parents had taken her and her brothers on a picnic one Sunday following church. What a fine day that had been, sunny with just enough breeze to keep the bugs at bay.

As the flimsy bathroom door was torn from its frame, she was in the middle of a game of badminton – her and mother on one side, her brothers on the other, while father cheered them all on. Her brothers had eventually won the game, but it had been close. Afterwards, they had all laughed and hugged.

As the creature advanced on her, its breathing turning to frenzied grunts, she was enjoying a sandwich and a glass of her mother's wonderful home brewed tea.

Paula died badly. However, fate paid her one small kindness in that: by the time she drew her last breath, she was too far gone to notice.

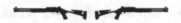

The Alpha's screams conveyed both triumph and frustration. He had killed one of the two-legged things' stupid beasts – had toppled it and was now attempting to get at the two-legged things that were still inside. That was proving to be infuriatingly difficult. He smashed it with his massive fists, leapt upon it, and even bit it – gouging the armored sides of the beast, but painfully chipping his teeth in the process. Though he had damaged it greatly, its shell proved to be formidable.

Driven into a rage by his inability to tear into the two-legged things inside, he redoubled his efforts. He climbed onto the beast's side and began to pound and jump, bringing all of his size and strength to bear. The beast's shell groaned in protest. Soon it would shatter, and he would drag the two-legged things from it, piece by piece if need be.

Before that could happen, though, movement caught his attention. Was one of the clan coming to challenge him? If so, they would be dealt with accordingly. He turned his head, foam flying from his jaws as he did so. No, it wasn't one of the clan, although he could smell one of them nearby. A pair of the two-legged things leaped down from one of their dwellings. They landed clumsily but appeared unhurt by the fall. They both turned and began to run.

The Alpha let out a satisfied grunt. If he could not have the two-legged things inside of the stupid beast, he would have the two now fleeing from him.

He jumped down and began to move in their direction. They were quick, but he would eventually run them to ground. There was no doubt in his mind of that.

Just as he began to put on speed, something else caught his attention, though. Sound, loud enough to cause the Alpha to cry out in pain, washed over him. Again and again it thundered, nearly driving him to his knees by its intensity. Finally, after what seemed to him an eternity of pain, it ended. Flickers of memory stirred in the Alpha's damaged mind. He knew that sound. It was the noise the fire sticks of the two-legged things made. The two-legged things used them to kill. They were fighting back ... they were challenging him.

He turned in the direction the challenge had issued from, the rage burning stronger than ever in him. He forgot the small running things. The challenger, perhaps the alpha of the two-legged things, needed to be dealt with. The Alpha would hunt it down. He would find it, and it would die screaming at his hands.

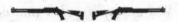

"What now?" Francis asked as the group stepped away from the bar.

"I'll tell you what we do now," Harrison said. "We

try to get back to the motel. Danni, Rob, and the rest are all back there."

"Screw this!" Kate spat. "I don't know what the hell is wrong with you people, but I'm gonna call the police."

"Enough!" Derek barked, momentarily silencing them all. He turned to her. "You aren't going anywhere, at least not until we know it's safe." Then to the rest, he said, "We'll find your friends, Harrison, but first we need to get to the trucks. Most of our gear is there. Once we're loaded up, then we can help the others."

"How are we gonna get there? It sounds like there's more than one of those things."

"What *things*!?" Kate cried, her frustration boiling over.

Derek ignored her. He opened his jacket, revealing a shoulder holster. The gun he pulled out was like nothing Harrison had ever seen. It was a large handgun with a ridiculously short muzzle. Derek smiled at him. "Ruger Alaskan, snub-nosed 454. Never leave home without it."

Francis gave a thumbs up, but Harrison wasn't quite convinced, "You have enough bullets?"

Almost as if on cue, the front door of the bar burst open. Smoke and flame escaped from the open maw, but that wasn't the worst of it.

"What the hell is that!?" Kate shrieked, instinctively stepping behind the others.

Even to Derek, who had seen his fair share of the weird, it was like something that had stepped straight from the gates of Hades. All four of them were momentarily stunned as eight and a half feet of angry man-ape pushed through the doorway. Its arms and torso were ablaze, but it either didn't notice or didn't care.

It growled at them and curled its lips back to reveal blood-soaked teeth. Foamy drool dripped from its mouth and began to sizzle as it made contact with the flames. Red eyes widened as it took them in. Derek usually wasn't one to assign human traits to animals, but he could have sworn the look was one of insane glee.

The creature screamed and charged them. For something so large, it was inhumanly fast. This close up, it was as if a freight train made of fire were advancing upon them.

Harrison and Kate both shouted, "Kill it!" as Derek raised the gun. There was no time to aim. He emptied the Ruger point blank into its torso, pulling the trigger over and over again – not even feeling the recoil as the heavy slugs flew from the barrel and hit home deep in the creature's flesh.

The high caliber bullets met the beast head-on and cancelled out its momentum. For a second, it seemed to stand still, flames rising from its body and blood dripping from half-a-dozen fist-sized holes in its chest.

Then, just as the sound of the last shot was beginning to fade, the creature toppled over and fell into the dirt, the fire continuing to claim its body.

There were two more clicks as Derek continued to squeeze the trigger of the now empty gun, then he took a deep breath and lowered it.

"Holy shit," Francis said.

"You can say that again," Harrison agreed.

Kate wasn't impressed nearly as much, as she was edging closer to outright terror. It was as if a nightmare had taken on life and stepped right out of her dreams. "Was that..." she managed to sputter.

Derek turned to her. "Well, it was almost certainly not a man in a gorilla suit."

"You mean it's real?"

"*Was* real," Francis said. "That one, anyway."

"Exactly. Unfortunately, it sounds like he brought his buddies to the party." Derek holstered the gun. "Let's get moving and make sure we have some noise makers waiting for them."

He began walking down the street, closely followed by the others, but hadn't gone more than ten paces when he stopped again. Before anyone could say a word, a howl of pure rage rose up from the darkness ahead of them.

"I think we're gonna need to find a detour."

Emerging from the shadows in front of them was another of the beasts, even larger than the last. It didn't look anywhere remotely close to calm. It stopped as soon as it saw them and bared its teeth as if in challenge.

"I don't suppose you have any bullets left, boss?" Francis asked.

"All out, sadly. I didn't quite expect this place to turn into the O.K. Corral tonight. You packing?"

"Nope. I don't carry when I'm drinking. Bad combo ... under most circumstances."

Derek sighed as he continued to face the creature. It seemed that they were locked in a Mexican standoff of sorts.

"*If* we can get to my store, I might have some ammo that'll fit your gun," Kate chimed in. The General Mart was about halfway between the bar and the B&B ... putting it just slightly beyond where the thing in front of them was standing.

"That's a mighty big 'if,'" Derek said, eyes still on the creature. The tension appeared to be rising in their battle of wills. He didn't have faith it would last more than a few seconds longer. When it finally broke, he wasn't sure what would...

"Just do me a favor, and save my sister," Harrison said, a tone of determination in his voice. Before anyone could question what he meant, he broke from the group and sprinted across the street. He started jumping up and down, waving his arms at the creature. "Hey! Yeah you, you ugly motherfucker!"

Both Derek and the beast turned toward him.

"Get back here, you stupid..." But his protest was cut short by the angry sasquatch. It let loose with a high-pitched scream and charged the young man.

Harrison stood his ground for a moment longer, then took off down an alleyway.

For a second, Derek thought the distraction might be all for naught. The creature paused in its pursuit, as if momentarily at odds as to what to do. It appeared to actually be considering its options, then it gave one last snarl in his direction, turned, and took off after Harrison.

"Oh my God!" gasped Kate. "That thing'll tear him apart."

Derek looked her in the eye. "Not if I have anything to say about it. Come on! That kid gave us a chance, and we're gonna make good use of it."

"What's the plan, boss?" asked Francis.

"The plan?" he replied, starting again in the direction of their vehicles. "The plan is to get all the guns we can carry, then kill each and every one of those goddamned things."

27

The pounding had stopped. *Thank God, too,* Mitchell noted, because the sides of the van were damn close to caving in. He and Rob were already wedged in pretty tight. Much more, and they'd be crushed like bugs between the two walls of computer equipment.

"I think I know how a sandwich feels," Rob said. It was gallows humor, but Mitchell uttered a laugh anyway. Considering the circumstances, it seemed that their choices were either to laugh or scream. He had a sinking sensation that if the screaming started, it wouldn't end until either their tormentor broke in or they were pounded into paste.

"What do you think it's doing?" Rob asked.

"That's the sixty-four thousand dollar question. I don't hear it anymore, though."

"Do you think it's maybe waiting to see what we'll do?"

"I don't know. Under normal circumstances, these

things are all about stealth. But there was nothing subtle about the way it attacked this van. If I were a betting man – and my bookie in Vegas says I am – I'd say this one was infected, too. If that's the case, then it's probably not even remotely sane enough to consider a trap."

"You're sure it's a different one, right? I mean, you guys are certain you killed it?"

"Trust me, it was dead. Since I'm not quite ready to start believing in zombie sasquatches, I'd say we have another one on our hands."

Amazingly, Rob started laughing.

"What's so funny?"

"You are! Lake monsters, dinosaurs, giant bats, et cetera. You guys have no problem believing any of that on the show, but now you're turning your nose up at a *zombie bigfoot*?" He started laughing again. After a few seconds, the medic joined him.

After the laughter, which had a bit of a hysterical quality to it, died down, Mitchell said, "Okay, maybe you have a point there."

"So how many do you think are out there?" Rob asked, serious once more.

"At least one more than I'd prefer. No idea, sadly. If the whole clan is infected, then we could be dealing with anywhere from three to a dozen."

"If it's all the same to you, I'm going to hope it's closer to three."

"Me too."

"So, what do we do?"

Mitchell had been waiting for that one. He wished he had a good answer for the kid. Unfortunately, he didn't. "You're not gonna like this, but right now I see two choices: get out and try to run for it, or stay here and get smashed like sardines."

"I was afraid you were gonna say that. Are there any guns in here?"

"There's a rack with a shotgun behind the driver's seat, but..." In the darkness, Rob heard movement from the other man's position. "No good. The door up front is crushed. You probably don't want to hear this, kid, but you're gonna have to try the back."

He was right: Rob didn't want to hear that. He could envision the creature standing out there, waiting for them. The second he pushed open the double doors, it would reach in and tear him apart.

That unpleasant imagery kept him frozen in place for several seconds. Then he remembered who else was out there. He softly whispered to himself, "Dr. Jenner wouldn't hesitate. The Crypto Hunter would go out there and kick some ass."

"Kid? You okay?"

"Sorry, just thinking out loud." He crawled to the back of the van and grasped for the handle in the dark.

"Okay. As soon as it's open, you bolt," Mitchell said. "Don't worry about me. Just run in whatever direction you don't see a squatch looking back at you from."

"Got it," Rob answered. "On three. One ... Two ..." He turned the handle and shoved. The door moved maybe half an inch, then no more. He pushed again, and this time there was no give. "Shit!" he cried into the darkness. "It's stuck."

"I was afraid of that," Mitchell replied. "They make these damn things bulletproof, but nobody takes into account an attack by a half-ton monster when they're drawing up the blueprints."

"So, what now?"

"Now? Now we sit tight, wait, and hope that Derek gets here before that thing comes back."

"Slow down!" whispered Allison from a few paces back. Though Danni had been the second on the ground, she had quickly passed her friend. Both girls were in good shape, but she had run track in high school and still jogged whenever she had the chance.

Though every instinct in her body was telling her to push on as fast as she could, she had no intention of leaving yet another friend behind. Danni slowed a little and let her friend catch up. She looked around, saw nothing behind them, then slowed further to a more even trot, – figuring there was no point in exhausting themselves now, in case they ran into another of those things later.

After leaping from the second story window of the B&B, the girls had turned down a series of side streets so as to try to throw off any pursuit. As they ran, they could hear the sounds of the creatures roaring and screaming into the night. Earlier, they had also heard what they thought might be gunfire, but it had been so brief that they weren't hopeful about it. Regardless, so far they'd been lucky and not seen another of the beasts. In the back of Danni's mind, though, she was wondering how long that luck would last.

Still running, she said, "We shouldn't have left Paula."

"That thing didn't give us a choice."

"Do you think there's any chance it didn't find her?"

"Maybe," Allison replied solemnly.

"Do you *really* believe that?"

There was no answer. Danni wasn't surprised. She didn't believe it either. She felt the sting of tears in her eyes, but wiped them away with the back of her hand. She couldn't afford the luxury of crying right now. Any lapse in their attention could get them both killed if another of those monsters was out there stalking them.

"What about the others?"

"Huh?" Danni asked.

"The others. Do you think anyone else made it out?"

Thoughts of her brother immediately weighed upon Danni, bringing fresh twinges of guilt to her gut. She hadn't given him a single thought since they had fled from the creature. *God, what a selfish bitch I am.* On the other hand, it wasn't like she was equipped to do much to help him. For now, all she could do was hope.

"My brother's a survivor," she said, praying she could believe that long enough to hold herself together.

Allison nodded and didn't mention it again. Unfortunately, neither had grabbed their cell phones in the chaos of running for their lives. For all they knew, help could be on its way right now, or they could be the last ones left alive for miles in every direction. They didn't know, and worrying about it wouldn't help their situation.

"So, what do we do?" Allison asked. "We can't keep running forever. At least, I can't."

Danni thought for a few moments, then replied, "You're right. We need to find some place to hole up until either morning or someone finds us." She left unspoken the possibility of something else finding them first.

Before either of them could ponder that latter scenario, a shape began to take form out of the darkness in front of them. It was a small house.

"There!" said Danni. "Let's take a look and see if anyone's home."

"Where the hell are you going?" Chuck asked, following Kurt as he zigged back and forth through the trees. He'd taken an instant dislike to the man. He reminded Chuck of the local rednecks from when he'd been stationed down in Louisiana. Those men had lived all their lives deep in the bayou. If you ever got lost in the swamp, there was no better person to be with, but that was the end of their usefulness. Overall, he had found them to be an inbred, ignorant, and intolerant people. The dumb bastard who was leading him through a dense copse of trees could have fit right in with them.

Chuck was no stranger to the woods. He was an accomplished tracker and knew how to survive. If his enemy had been human, he would have gladly faded into the brush and lain in wait to take them out.

But what was out there wasn't a man. This was its natural habitat. Here, it had every advantage. Unarmed, against a creature with near human intelligence and the superior senses of a wild animal, all the training in the world wouldn't be enough to even the odds. Chuck had seen his fair share of these monsters. His knife might as well be a toothpick for all the good it would do him. Yet here he was, letting this fool lead them deeper into the forest.

As he struggled to catch up, he felt wetness at his side. He didn't have to be told what it was. He'd pulled at least some of his stitches. *Great, just what I need.* "The town's back *this* way!" he protested, trying to push thoughts of his injuries out of his mind.

The other man stopped and turned to address him. "No, *the road* is back that way. You walk along it if you want. If that thing spots you, good luck beating it in a foot race. I'd say you'd last just long enough to piss it off real good."

"I have friends back in town..."

"Well, then you'll get to say 'hi' to your gang-banger buddies because that's where we're headed."

Chuck ignored the snide comment. "Then why are we..."

"Shortcut. The Barrows' place is just about a quarter-mile straight on. If we turn west about halfway, we'll come out right behind the bar."

"Doesn't feel short."

"Well, maybe it ain't. But if that thing's still tracking me, this'll slow it down enough for us to..."

"Get to my friends?"

"If you want. Me, I was gonna bust a window in the general store and see if I could liberate myself a rifle."

Chuck smiled back. "Think I can do better than that."

Kurt eyed him warily. "Your friends packing?"

"Oh yeah. And then some."

Just then, a bellow came from off in the distance, from the direction they'd been heading.

Kurt inclined his head to listen. "How in hell did it get in front of us?"

Before Chuck could offer an answer, six quick shots rang out in the night. Judging from the sound, it was a heavy caliber handgun. *Derek,* he thought with a smile.

Kurt likewise grinned. "Sounds like they started the party without us. Let's get moving before they're finished with things. I got me some payback to take on that bitch."

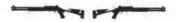

Thank God for lacrosse. Harrison thought, fleeing blindly through the back roads of the little town. Coach Connors, who ran the team at Alamosa University, was a mean old bastard. He often gave his players endless drills until they felt they were about to fall down dead. For the first time ever, though, Harrison was feeling some appreciation for it. If he had been in lesser shape, that thing might have caught him by now. As it was, he could still hear it occasionally letting loose with one of those God-awful screams that just about made you want to wet yourself.

He still couldn't believe what he was doing. There was a part of him that was sure he'd gone insane. Maybe he had. Taunting a creature that was, by all accounts, his physical superior many times over was definitely not something a fully sane person did. Maybe this was how Jeff Goldblum's character from Jurassic Park had felt when he decided to lead the T-Rex away from the kids. "Well, at least he survived," he mumbled to himself, hoping he'd be as lucky.

The creature was large, powerful, and fast, but Harrison was counting on it being more at home in the forest than in a town. Hopefully, it wouldn't have the stamina to keep up in an all-out race. If that failed, he could potentially duck inside of a store or house and attempt to lose it there. He reminded himself that he didn't need to win this. He just needed to keep going long enough for the others to get to their guns.

After that, they just need to find me ... although, considering how much noise this bastard is making, that shouldn't be a prob...

Harrison didn't get a chance to finish the thought. As he ducked around the side of another building in an attempt to lead it back toward Main Street, a large hairy arm swung out. It was only a glancing blow, but he was sent flying. He landed in the middle of the street, dazed.

A form materialized from the shadows. It had large, ponderous breasts and was still bleeding from half-a-dozen small wounds in its torso. It began to walk toward the downed boy, drool pouring from its lips.

"Holy shit, when did the demolition derby pull into town?" Francis asked as they reached their vehicles.

It wasn't entirely surprising. They had passed a few other cars that had suffered similar damage. Derek just wasn't sure if it had been random or if the creatures somehow knew that the cars could be used to escape. He hoped for the former. The latter was a little too frightening to contemplate.

Harrison's Wrangler and the Xterra had both been tipped over onto their sides. His team's SUVs, though heavier, had taken a beating, too. The hood on one of them was smashed and the front left axel broken. The other sat upon shredded tires. All of that, though, paled in comparison to what they saw of the van – if it could even be called that anymore. It was like someone had first sideswiped it, pushed it nearly half a block down the street, then dropped a wrecking ball on it.

"I hope Mitch wasn't in there. Frank, get to the truck and grab some ordinance. Kate, go with him. I'm gonna go check the van."

Neither of the others put up any argument against going to get some guns. Derek took a quick look around. He didn't see any movement, so he quietly walked over to the remains of the smashed vehicle.

He made a full circuit around the wreckage. It was a mess. There was virtually no chance of it ever being drivable again. *The auditors are gonna love this one.*

Walking around back, he gave one of the doors a yank. Unsurprisingly, it was stuck shut. He turned to rejoin the others when he thought he heard a noise. It sounded as if something had shifted inside of the van.

He couldn't believe anything could still be alive in there, but he had to be sure it wasn't just his imagination. He banged on the back of the damaged vehicle. In the silence, it sounded terribly loud. *Oh well, in for a penny...* "Hey, anyone in there!?"

He was startled to be met with a reply. A muffled voice called from within, "Derek, is that you?" It was Mitchell.

Derek grinned, glad that his friend was alive. "Hold tight! We'll get you out."

"We're not going anywhere," a second voice replied. It sounded like that kid, Rob. They were *both* wedged in there? *That must be a bit close for comfort,* he mused.

"I'll be right back," Derek said to them, then left to make his way toward where Francis and Kate were hopefully arming themselves.

He was too far away to hear the growl that came from the second story window of the bed and breakfast.

28

Was it possible there were no limits to the rage? It would seem so. At the sight before him, he felt it swell, doubling itself until he was certain he'd surely burst.

The two-legged things' alpha had fled from him. Its challenge had been nothing more than a ruse. The stupid thing knew it could not best him for dominance. In its panic, it had run, seeking a safe place to hide, but there was no place that was safe from the Alpha.

He could smell its fear as it ran from him, albeit not nearly as well as he should. He didn't realize that the disease was progressing rapidly now. It was beginning to clog up his nasal passages and eat away at the neurons connected to his optic nerve. Even had he known this, it wouldn't have changed anything. He was still fast and strong. The creature that fled before him had dared mark itself as his equal. However, first it had tried to fool him. It would pay for both affronts.

He had come across the small clan of two-legged

things as he sought out the source of the noise, the sound that told him the stupid things were attempting to fight back. The one in the lead had dared to lock eyes with him, a challenge to his dominance.

Before he moved to kill the insolent creature, though, a scent had caught his nostrils, smoke. Buried within it, however, was another smell. It took longer than usual to identify, bits and pieces of his brain having started to die. At last, he made the connection that the smoke carried on it the faint scent of one of the clan. It was enough information to let the Alpha know that his clan-brother was no more — albeit he didn't care. All emotions other than rage were but distant memories to him now.

He was still cunning, though. If one of the clan were dead, that might mean these two-legged things had killed it with their fire sticks. A brief conflict was fought in his mind over this. The rage insisted the fire sticks were nothing to him now. He was supreme in the forest, perhaps in the world. The two-legged things were weak, and so were their weapons. His faltering memories, though, said otherwise. If the fire sticks of the stupid things had felled one of the clan, couldn't they potentially hurt the Alpha, too? For perhaps the last time in his life, caution won out.

He had stopped and observed them, especially the challenger. If they were the holders of fire sticks, they would no doubt attempt to use them now. That didn't happen, though. They just stood there, looking stupidly back at him. He quickly grew tired of the game. He had been just about to charge what he thought to be their alpha when one of them had broken from the pack, chattering in its stupid language.

It stopped a short distance away to wave its arms and scream at the Alpha. For a moment, he was confused, but then he realized the ruse. What he'd assumed to be the alpha of the two-legged things was nothing of the sort. He'd thought the stupid thing had challenged him, but now saw that it had merely been frozen by fear. However, this other two-legged thing was bold. It threw an undeniable challenge toward the Alpha. The last vestiges of instinct took over. The other two-legged things were meaningless. He would kill them in due time, but first, their alpha must be laid low.

He had charged, and their alpha had fled in the face of his superiority – stupid thing. It would not escape. Thus the chase had begun, the scent of its fear wafting behind as it ran.

The Alpha had come round a corner, ready to pounce upon the two-legged thing and listen to its screams, when he saw his kill was about to be stolen. The two-legged alpha was on the ground. One of the clan stood above it, daring to usurp what was rightfully his. Even worse, it was an outcast – one of those who had fled into the night in the early days of the rage.

A flickering memory whispered to him that this outcast had once been his mate. However, to the Alpha, that had been a long time ago. He was no longer capable of feeling such foolish things as warmth or compassion toward even his own kind. Besides, she was even now advancing upon his rightful kill. That could not be tolerated.

He roared a challenge toward the outcast. She turned toward him hissing, no recognition in her eyes. The Alpha didn't know, nor would he have cared, that the female before him was even more fully in the grasp of the disease than he. She bared her teeth, foamy spittle raining down over her lips, and screamed her defiance at the Alpha — refusing to acknowledge him as anything other than an enemy.

Even in the midst of the rage, instinct can be a strong thing to overcome. The Alpha beat his chest and growled toward his former clan-mate. He swung a massive hand toward one of the two-legged things' dwellings, shattering wood in the process. The outcast, though, was long past such displays of dominance. The rage's hold over her was complete. As he persisted in his attempt to intimidate her into submission, she charged him.

Several hundred pounds of muscle flew into the Alpha. He fell to the ground with the outcast on top — clawing, biting, and tearing.

Neither of them noticed when the two-legged thing got back to its feet and limped away into the night.

29

Richard Barrows had been startled out of a pleasant dream involving him and his late wife, Emma. As soon as he awoke, the dream faded from his memory – a small kindness of fate. It spared him from any undo heartache the lingering memories might have caused. Had he remembered, though, it would have surely struck him as ironic once the circumstances surrounding his awakening became known. In the dream, he and his wife – a dyed-in-the-wool movie buff – had gone to a drive-in theater to see a double feature of King Kong and Mighty Joe Young.

He'd gone to bed early that evening. Despite having taken a nap, he had been tuckered out. After reassuring his daughter, he had sent her back to mind the store. He'd then spent the rest of the afternoon cleaning off the front porch. It had been quite the mess, and he put a good hurt into his back mopping it up. He had been so intent on the task that, as he scrubbed away, he failed to notice a few small tufts of grey-brown fur lying in the blood. Had Kate seen them, she would have surely recognized it as matching the coat of her dog, Gus. Despite Richard Barrows' earlier assertion that the dog would come home when it got hungry, Gus would not be coming home that night or ever again.

He didn't know this as he got up out of bed, though. In fact, he was pretty sure the ruckus that had awoken him was none other than that fool dog pawing at the front door. He let out a cry as he barked his shin against the night table, more a result of being half-awake than from the dark. He then uttered a curse after trying the light switch and realizing that the power was out.

He briefly considered heading toward the electrical panel at the back of the house – the stupid dog could wait – when he stepped outside of his bedroom and realized that he was wrong to blame Gus. What he had thought was scratching at the door was actually the knob being jiggled. Unless the mutt had grown opposable thumbs, it was unlikely to be the cause.

He walked to the front door to investigate, navigating his way through the dark house with an ease born from decades of familiarity. He was more curious than worried. He knew it wouldn't be Kate. Even had she forgotten her keys, she knew where the spare was hidden. So that meant someone else. Maybe that fool drunk, Joel Bean, had come back. If so,

Richard was going to give the big lummox a piece of his mind.

He reached to unlock the door, and the movement of the handle became a little more frantic. He unbolted it and turned the doorknob.

"Goddamn it, Bean! If that's you, I'll..."

He didn't get to finish. As soon as the door unlatched, it was shoved open from the outside. It hit the startled man and knocked him backwards, causing him to lose his footing and fall flat on his rump.

Before he could react, a shadowy figure crossed the threshold and came toward him.

"Where are you going?" Francis asked, keeping watch at the door of the General Mart. He alternated between training the night scope of the powerful rifle between their ruined van, where Derek waited, and the street in case any more hairy visitors decided to show up.

"One must have their priorities straight," Derek had said, grabbing an enormous revolver from the back of the SUV, then filling his pockets full of 50 caliber cartridges. After duly rearming themselves, they'd realized that they didn't have the proper tools with which to pry open the van's smashed doors.

"My place isn't exactly a hardware store, but I think I can scare up a mallet and crowbar," Kate had offered after they handed her a pump-action shotgun.

She had accepted it gladly. Though normally not endeared to guns, she would sooner have walked through the streets naked than turn down some fire-power at that moment.

Francis protested them splitting up, but Derek had insisted. He didn't want Kate going alone, but he also refused to abandon the van for even a few minutes. If one of the beasts came back to finish the job, neither Mitchell nor the kid would last long, and they all knew it.

"The stuff we need is in the storage room. Just keep an eye out, and I'll be back in a second," she said, grabbing a flashlight from a shelf then walking toward the rear of the store.

A minute or two later, she reappeared carrying the tools. "Take these," she called out to him before once more walking behind the counter.

"What are you doing now?" he whispered after her.

"Something I should have done the second this started," she replied, rooting through some drawers. "Ah, here it is." Kate stood and flipped something open in her hand. A keypad and small screen lit up on it.

"No offense, lady, but now might not be the best time to check Twitter. Come on, Derek needs this stuff."

"One sec," she said, pressing keys. "Once upon a time, people actually used these things to make phone calls, you know." There was a pause, then she slammed it angrily onto the countertop. "No goddamned signal!"

Francis shrugged. "What did you expect? These things were smart enough to knock out the power. Who knows what else they did?"

"Are you for real?"

"Hell yeah. Squatches make chimps look like they belong on the short bus."

She stalked over to him and pointed the flashlight in his face. "Just who the hell are you people anyway? How do you know about these things?"

He gently pushed the light aside. "Let me guess, you don't watch the Adventure Channel, do you?"

"*What?*"

"Never mind," he replied, pushing open the door and stepping back out into the night.

"Are you sure you know where you're going?"

"Like the back of my hand," Kurt replied smugly. "This trail will let us out right behind the bar. Used to come this way all the time when I got me my first fake ID." He stopped and sniffed the air. "Ol' Ben must have the barbecue pit cranked up."

"I don't think so," Chuck replied, pushing through the dense foliage. He'd noticed the flickering glow ahead of them as Kurt spoke.

He was proven right a few moments later when they stepped from the brush and the heat hit them. The structure standing before them, across a small open area, was rapidly being consumed by flames.

"What the fuck?" Kurt muttered, stopping in his tracks.

Chuck was able to take in the scene with a more detached eye. As far as he could tell, the bar was doomed. Thankfully, a good-sized back lot separated it from the tree line, although that might not mean much if the wind changed. Unfortunately, only narrow alleyways stood between it and the buildings on either side. Unless something was done to put it out, there was a decent chance the entire town – hell, maybe even the whole damned forest – would burn to the ground before the night was through.

He was considering possible worst case scenarios when he stopped in mid-thought, a sinking sensation hitting his already sore gut. "Listen."

"I don't hear anything," Kurt replied irritably. "I haven't heard a goddamned thing since those shots were fired."

"Exactly! There's no sirens, no hollering, nothing. Wouldn't someone have noticed this place burning down?"

"It's the only bar in town." Worry began to work its way into his voice. "Something like that catches fire and people typically come running."

"That's not all."

Kurt turned to look at him. "Well, are you gonna spill it, or do I have to play Twenty Questions?"

"The lights. I didn't notice before because I was busy following your ass through the woods."

"Seems pretty darn bright here."

"That's just the fire. Take a look around. There's nothing else. The rest of this place is dark."

"...and quiet as a tomb," Kurt added.

"Poor choice of words, I'm thinking."

"Oh, come on! You don't think one ape did all of this, do you?"

"No I don't. Not *one* ape."

"Power probably just spiked," Kurt said. "Shorted everything out and caused that fire, too."

"Do you really believe that?"

Silence followed. It was all the answer that Chuck needed. "Neither do I."

"Do you think your friends got it?"

"I hope so," he answered.

As if to refute him, another screaming bellow pierced the night, this one coming from further in the town.

"That sounds like a big negative to me," Kurt said, before turning back toward the trees.

"Where are you going now? My friends are *this* way."

"Son, your friends are dead," he replied evenly, beginning to walk away. "As far as I can tell, the whole goddamn town is. No way am I waltzing in there. Change of plans."

"Oh, and what would that be?"

"Grace and Byron Clemons," Kurt said over his shoulder. "I don't normally have much use for them, but they do a lot of hunting. I'd bet my Aunt Sarah's right tit that they have guns. Plenty of them, too. I say we cut back to the edge of town, then make our way there."

"And how the hell long will *that* take?"

"In the dark ... I'd say about an hour."

"Shit on that. You don't know my friends. They're probably holed up with enough ammo to blow a hole in the moon. Not to mention they know what they're up against."

"Man, you know what? You sound crazier than a shithouse rat. You can follow me if you want, but you're on your own if you decide to go and get yourself killed. No way am I walking out there and sounding the dinner bell for that thing."

With that, he continued walking away – barely making any noise as he went. Even Chuck had to admit the man was good, for a stupid redneck anyway. On the other hand, he reminded himself, he wasn't exactly chopped liver either. He felt another twinge from his stomach. *Well, some of me might be.*

He began to move left, parallel to the burning building and the street beyond it. He wasn't about to leave his team. However, he also had no intention of being caught with his back against the fire should that squatch – or squatches, he silently reminded himself – be lurking close by.

Within a few seconds he, too, disappeared back into the night.

Putting all of his weight against the crowbar, Derek finally felt some give. It had been hard work in the dark – he'd insisted on flashlights off so as to not attract undue attention. With a final squeal of metal – a very *loud* squeal, he thought – one of the back doors of the van was finally forced open. Hopefully, it would be enough. Things had fallen deathly silent in the small town of Bonanza Creek. The only other sounds were the growls and screams that pierced the night every so often. To him, it sounded as if every squatch in the area had gone crazy.

While Francis and Kate had gone off to get the tools, Mitchell had communicated his findings to Derek from inside. It was not good news. A rabid dog or raccoon was a bad enough scenario. The average sasquatch, though, was nearly eight feet tall and over seven hundred pounds. Some were considerably larger. Just one of them going nuts would make Cujo seem like a pleasant Sunday afternoon in comparison. A whole clan of them ... well, that was the stuff of nightmares.

Unfortunately, that nightmare was now a reality. Judging by the differing pitch and positions of the cries that sounded across the area, Derek estimated there had to be at least four more of them running around, maybe more. His team had walked into a worst-case scenario with their flies down. God knew how many people were dead because they had been unprepared.

His thoughts turned to Chuck. There had been no sign of him since the shit had hit the fan. For that matter, outside of Rob, he had no idea what had befallen the rest of the kids they had rescued earlier.

Enough of that, Derek commanded himself. He needed to stow the blame for now. It wasn't going to solve their problems. As soon as Mitchell and Rob were free, it would be time to go on the offensive. These creatures had been running around unchecked for long enough. It was time for him to take the name of his show to heart.

A hand reached out from the van interrupting his thoughts. Francis stood guard while Derek and Kate reached in to help Rob out.

"Can you make it?"

Rob's head and shoulders began to emerge from the wreck. "Yeah, I think so. Glad I skipped dinner."

Little by little, with their help, he shimmied from the small opening. At last, he made it out. Derek helped him to his feet. "Are you okay?"

"Yeah, I think so. Just glad to be out of that accordion."

"Great," Derek replied. "Now stand back so we can get Mitch out. Oh, and don't wander off, kid."

Mitchell wasn't a big man, but he was larger than Rob and had been trapped further in. He attempted to scoot toward the exit but found he was wedged pretty tight. Even with the others' help, there wasn't much progress to be had.

"Shit!" Derek exclaimed. "We're gonna have to pry the other door, Frank."

"I'm on it," the big man replied.

"Can you both keep a look out?" Derek asked the other two.

"I'll try," Kate replied nervously.

"Just don't shoot us by mistake."

"Like I said, I'll try."

"I guess that'll have to be good enough." He sighed and turned back to the task at hand.

Rob initially had no intention of wandering off, but then his eyes turned toward the nearby bed and breakfast. He'd been so caught up in the terror of his own ordeal that he had forgotten about his friends.

Squinting, he noticed the damage at the front of the building. *Is that Paula's room?* Yes, it *was* the same room she'd rented – the one where she'd cheated on him, the place he and Mitchell had spied on. He felt a momentary stab of anger at the entire thing. For now, though, he tried to push it away. He was pissed at her and pretty sure that it was over between them, but that didn't mean he wanted to see her hurt. Hell, he didn't want to see *any* of them hurt – Phil, the asshole who'd seduced his girlfriend, included.

Although, he mused, perhaps *seduced* was too strong of a word for it. Hadn't she sounded like she was enjoying it ... quite a bit, actually? Rob tried to push that thought away, too. There would be plenty of time for confrontation later on, he hoped.

While Derek and Francis hammered away at the stuck door, with Kate performing some semblance of guard duty, he found himself wandering closer to the entrance of the small B&B. He wasn't even really aware he was doing so. It was like his legs had a mind of their own.

The structure was dark. A small voice in the back of his mind noted that *everything* was dark. The building in front of him was the only thing he was focused on, though.

He found himself standing just a few feet in front

of the entrance, not quite daring to get any closer. "Paula," he whispered, barely loud enough to hear, certainly not loud enough to get the attention of anyone inside. Even so, a few seconds later he heard a sound, as if something had shifted in the building. "Paula? Is that you?" he whispered. Again, he heard movement as if in response. Feeling illogically hopeful, he took a step closer.

There came a screech of metal against metal from behind him. Rob turned and watched as the other door of the van was finally pried open. It was a fatal distraction. He didn't notice the hulking figure looming in the second story window right above his head.

"Gotcha!" exclaimed Derek, finally pulling Mitchell from the wreckage. While Francis helped the medic to his feet, he turned to the others. "Good job, Kate, Rob ... Rob?" His tone changed as he noticed that the kid wasn't standing with Kate. Her eyes widened at the realization he had slipped away without her notice.

Derek looked over her shoulder and saw him about thirty feet down the road. "Hey, kid!" he called – and that was when he saw *it*.

The creature was little more than a shadow of movement at first. Then it flung itself with reckless abandon through the open window, shattering the frame as its bulk pushed through. Rob had just enough time to look up before eight-hundred pounds of angry monster descended upon him.

Derek knew it was over instantly for the boy. He heard the sickening crunch of bone as the squatch landed squarely on top of Rob in a fury of clawing and slashing.

Kate started screaming, the shotgun in her hands forgotten. She was standing directly between Derek and the beast. They both watched as the bigfoot began to rend the misshapen lump of flesh that had been the eager college student.

Without any further hesitation, Derek shoved her to the side and raised his rifle. He pulled the trigger, but the shot went wide, impacting the masonry of the building.

The creature heard the shot and lifted its head toward the group, screaming its defiance at them. Derek used the opportunity to chamber another round. He aimed the rifle, centering the scope directly in the middle of its body just as it began to charge.

It was able to take three steps, enough to bring it frighteningly closer to the group, before Derek pulled the trigger. A gaping maw opened up in its chest. Blood and bone flew in all directions as the high-powered bullet tore straight through it. A second later, another hole, nearly as large, was blown open in its stomach. Derek turned his head to see that Francis had brought his own gun to bear on the sasquatch.

That was all it took for the creature. They had loaded up on heavy bore ammunition, powerful enough to put down an elephant. The beast landed in the street with a satisfying thud and stayed down.

The echo from the shots faded, but Kate's screams continued. Derek paid her no mind, though, as he walked over to where Rob lay. He bent down in the dim hope that there might still be a chance, but it was a futile gesture. There was still some movement from his body, but Derek could tell it was just the final sporadic twitching of his nerves as they shut down. "Sorry, kid. You didn't deserve this," he quietly said.

Hearing footsteps behind him, he stood and turned. It was Mitchell. He was limping slightly and holding a bandage to his head, but otherwise seemed okay. Behind him, Francis was tending to Kate, whose screams had quieted to a pathetic whimpering.

Derek held up a hand and gave a brief shake of his head. The other man stopped, realization dawning on his face.

"Goddammit!" Mitchell yelled. "This is my fault. I should have listened to you earlier, Derek."

"You had no way of knowing," Derek replied in a consoling tone. "And *none* of us could have known that the entire clan was so far gone."

"That doesn't mean much to that kid, his friends, or probably a whole lot of other people in this town. Who knows how many are dead because we didn't stop this sooner?"

"Then let's make it right and stop it now."

For a long moment, they looked at each other, then finally Mitchell nodded.

Together, they turned back toward the others.

"Want me to give her something to quiet her down?" asked Mitchell.

"Don't bother. Between the shots and the screaming, every squatch in this town is gonna know where we are. Saves us the trouble of finding them. And when they get here, we're going to want every available hand holding a gun."

30

"I'm going to be perfectly frank with you girls. I need to know, have you been taking drugs?"

Danni's eyes widened at the question as the older man continued tending to the fireplace. He had thrown a few logs on and was now busy positioning them in the flame with a poker.

Allison started to laugh, though.

"I say something funny, little lady?" Richard Barrows asked. He had been surprised as all hell when they had come rushing into his house like the devil was on their tails. All at once, they'd started squawking like a bunch of frightened hens.

At first, he'd been suspicious that he had caught them in the middle of a break-in. However, he had to admit that they didn't quite fit his image of hardened criminals. Then he had caught snippets of their story. It was hard to follow, the way they were carrying on, but it seemed they were pretty well spooked.

He had finally held up his hands and told them to

pipe down. Leading them to the living room, he'd commanded them to sit. He then attempted to light a few old oil lamps he kept around, but that seemed to agitate them more. So instead, he got a fire going. It provided enough light to see, but not enough to set them off.

At last, he had asked them to explain what was going on – slowly and one at a time – but it hadn't sounded any saner to him than when they were chattering away. Once they'd finished, Richard had considered maybe holding onto the fireplace poker just in case. They didn't look all that threatening. Hell, if he had been a few years younger, he might have admitted they looked quite the opposite. Still, he had read stories in the news about how people on PCP sometimes had crazy strength. If these two kids were high as a kite, he had no intention of being their victim.

"Sorry, sir," Allison replied, still giggling. "It's just that I almost wish we had been."

"What she means is," Danni interrupted, "what's going on out there would be a lot easier to explain if it was just some drug trip. But it's not. People are dead. My brother and friends are still out there. And those things..." She shuddered before she could finish the sentence. Now that she and Allison had a moment to collect their thoughts, the adrenalin was starting to fade, and the unpleasant reality was hitting home.

"Yeah. Bigfoot you said, didn't ya?" Richard replied. "Sure it wasn't some joker in a gorilla suit?"

"You don't believe us, do you?"

"Now, I'm not exactly saying that. All I'm saying is that I've lived here most of my adult life – spent my fair share of time walking through the woods. I've seen deer, bear, even seen a few mountain lions here and there. However, I've never seen anything like what you're talking about. I'd have remembered it."

"Listen, mister," Allison said, "you're preaching to the choir. My parents have been dragging me out camping since before I could walk. On any other day, I'd be sitting there with you, thinking the same thing. Hell, the first time I saw that bigfoot movie ... you know the famous one, I forget what it's called."

"The Patterson-Gimlin tape?" he offered. When she raised her eyebrows, he added, "Just because I never seen one doesn't mean I don't watch TV."

She nodded. "Yeah, that one. My first thought was that it was the fakest looking thing I'd ever seen."

"Guess you were wrong on that one," Danni commented.

"Tell me about it," Allison said to her. Then, turning back to the older man, "All I know is that I've had to throw everything I thought I knew out the window today. First out there in the woods..."

"Are we talking about the one that fellow from that TV show shot?" he asked with a dubious tone.

"When you put it that way..." Allison grinned sheepishly.

"Obviously, not the *same* one," Danni chimed in. "But maybe it had family. I don't know, and I don't care. The bottom line is that it's out there somewhere. Listen, even if you don't believe us, call the cops. If we're lying, they can arrest us. We'll go quietly, happily even."

Allison added, "Yeah. If you hand me your cell phone, I'll even dial 911 for you."

Richard shook his head. "Don't own one. Damn things give you cancer."

The two girls exchanged worried looks when he said that. That went a long way to allaying his fear of them being burglars. Thieves normally didn't look scared after hearing you had no way of contacting the police. He decided that even if they *were* on drugs, it was probably that harmless stuff the hippies used.

He put the poker down and stood up. "Now, don't be worrying. I didn't lie when I said I didn't own one of those mobile phones. I got enough aches and pains without needing to worry about a brain tumor. But I do have an old rotary in the kitchen. You're both a little young to remember them, but they run off the juice in the phone lines. Kate ... she's my daughter ... has been bugging me to replace it with something newer. Damn glad I've been holding out. Once the power goes out, them things are as useless as tits on a bull, excuse my language for saying so."

"That'd be great!" Danni said, brightening up. If it worked, they could call the authorities and get some help out here. For the first time in hours, she was beginning to feel a flicker of hope.

"Okay, then," he said. "You both sit tight, and I'll go see if I can round up the deputy."

"Kitchen you said, right?" Allison asked. "I don't suppose you have anything to drink? I mean, like water or something," she quickly added. "Danni and I have been running for a while. I'm parched."

"There's some lemonade in the fridge. Don't know how long the power's been out, but it should still be cold."

"That would be wonderful, thanks," She stood to follow him. "You want a glass?" she asked her friend.

Danni shook her head. "I'm good. Well, maybe not good, but no thanks."

The kitchen was a neat little room near the rear of the house. A long counter ran along two sides of it, forming an L shape on the right side of the room. Richard placed a few lit candles on top of it. They illuminated the space just enough to see what one was doing. To the left of the entrance was the refrigerator, where Allison found the pitcher of lemonade Richard had mentioned. She found a cup in the dish drain and filled it.

There was a small table on the far side of the room. It sat in front of a large picture window, currently covered by a thin curtain. Under better circumstances, Allison thought it might be nice to eat breakfast there while looking out at the yard beyond. Right now, though, with the exception of a little bit of moonlight, there was nothing to see outside but darkness.

Richard was seated on one side of the table, the receiver of the phone to his ear. She walked over with her drink and sat across from him. Even in the dim light, she could see the frown on his face. He reached over to the base and clicked on the cradle a few times. The frown deepened. At last, he put the headset back down.

"No good. Can't get a dial tone," he told her.

Allison almost choked on her drink. She started to speak, but he held up a hand.

"Don't go getting all panicky. Phone lines run on the same poles as the power. Probably a tree down somewhere. It's happened before."

"Yeah, but..."

"But *nothing*," he said, his voice stern. "We've had plenty of blackouts over the years. As far as I know, none of them were caused by monkey men."

"First time for everything."

"So you and your friend keep saying. I'll tell you what, though. My daughter should be home soon. Darn girl loves to work late. Once she gets here, we'll fix us up some supper. You and your friend are welcome to stay the night. We don't have much space, but the living room is warm enough. Come the morning, one of us will drive you over to the deputy."

"You have a car?"

He chuckled in response. "'Course I have a car. Bonanza Creek may be small, but we're not cavemen here."

"But I didn't see a..."

"Got a garage in the back. I keep my Buick in there. One of the good things about a small town, everything's in walking distance."

"Well then, let's go get it." She stood up and

leaned across the table toward him. "We can find your daughter and then get help."

"Settle down, missy. My eyes aren't so good at night. I'm just as liable to put us in a ditch as keep us on the road. And before you ask, nobody drives my baby but me and Kate."

"Fine, then when Kate..."

"Enough, girl," Richard said, rising to his feet and facing her. "Matter's settled. Morning will come soon enough. If you and your friend can't wait it out, then I may just have to ask you to leave. I don't want to. It's easy to get lost in the dark if you don't know the area, but I will if you push me."

Allison was about to protest, but she could tell he'd made up his mind. She could see it in his eyes as a shadow crossed over his face. In fact, his whole body seemed to darken.

It took a second for realization to set in. It wasn't just him. It seemed as if a wall of gloom had settled over their spot in the kitchen ... as if something was blocking out the meager starlight from outside.

Richard noticed it, too. His eyebrows raised in surprise right before the window shattered. Shards of broken glass flew everywhere, one cutting a nasty furrow across his right cheek. It was the least of his worries.

A set of frying pan-sized hands came through the broken portal. One seized the back of Richard's head in a vice-like grip. The other grabbed a fistful of Allison's hair. Before either of them could comprehend what was happening, much less struggle against it, the hands swung together with unearthly strength. Their faces rushed toward one another, as if overeager to meet in a kiss. Bone and cartilage were crushed in the impact.

As she died, one of Allison's arms flailed out and struck her lemonade. The glass fell to the floor, where it shattered and became indistinguishable from the remnants of the window.

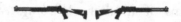

Danni desperately wanted to run. The sound of breaking glass and the dull thump afterwards were more than enough. Now there were other sounds, too – thick grunts followed by a wet slurping. She didn't want to fool herself that things might be all right. She had seen far too much that day. However, her rational mind childishly insisted that it was probably nothing. They just dropped a glass and maybe the man had a dog that was lapping it up.

Only, there had been no dog. One would have surely barked earlier when they had feebly attempted to pick the lock on the door. There was no denying that something was very wrong. Yet, she was unwilling to leave her friend behind. She had already done that too many times today. If there was any chance that Allison was still alive, she had to take it.

Danni grabbed the poker from the fireplace. She stood up with it held out before her. She was just one frightened girl making a stand against the unknown, thus she would've been quite surprised to know that the shadows cast by the fire told a different story. In them, she appeared a mighty warrior of days' past, wielding perhaps Excalibur itself.

She slowly made her way to the kitchen. Nearing the entrance, the slurping became louder and somehow more frenzied. A small thought flitted through her head: what if they had stumbled upon the home of some deranged serial killer? That would be just their luck, to run from one monster and end up in the arms of another. *All things considered, I'd probably be happy to deal with a psycho.* She stepped through the doorway, the poker held out before her.

The sight that greeted her was almost enough to make her drop the meager weapon and embrace the warm darkness that fainting offered. One of the creatures, perhaps the same that had chased them, was leaning halfway inside the broken window. That was far from the worst of it.

In the candlelight, she could see far more than she ever wanted to. Allison and Richard were both slumped at a table in front of the window, the same window in which the creature was leaning in. The same table that it had its face pressed to. It appeared to be lapping something up. She didn't need to get any closer to make an educated guess what that something was. In the flickering light, she could see the ruined remains of their heads. Whatever it had done, it had nearly decapitated them, and now it was eating the remains with a gusto that bordered on manic.

Danni couldn't help what happened next. She hadn't had much to eat that day, but whatever was left in her stomach came rushing out of her. She staggered back, retching. The creature heard the sound and looked up.

Their eyes met. It took one last greedy slurp from its awful meal, then bared its teeth. It was still hungry. A growl escaped from its lips, the remains of its last mouthful dripping out onto the table.

That was enough for Danni. She began to back out of the room, her eyes never leaving the creature's. It held her gaze, but didn't move. She took another step, but then her foot landed in the gorge she had just vomited up. It slid out from under her, and she went down, cutting her hand on a shard of glass as she landed.

The standoff broken, the creature sprang into action. It began to climb in the window. Danni watched in horrific fascination as the beast pulled its body inside, revealing its full bulk. *My God, it's huge!* Upright, it would be over eight feet tall.

As the creature clambered in, one of its feet became caught in the remains of the window frame. For one almost comical moment, its eyes widened in surprise. Then it came crashing down face first, shattering the table and sending the bodies of its two victims tumbling away. It landed on the floor only a few short feet from where Danni still sat.

She dimly realized that if it reached out with one of its hands, she would be caught and it would be all over. Something else about hands flashed through her mind, but in her terror she had no idea what her subconscious was trying to tell her.

The creature lifted its head and growled at her. It raised itself to its hands and knees, and that's when

Danni's mind clicked. It wasn't the creature's hands, it was *hers* ... more specifically, the one still holding the poker. Quickly, without truly realizing what she was doing, she jabbed her arm forward with a snarl of her own. Her aim was true, and the point of the fireplace poker punctured the creature's right eye.

There was a strangled screech of pain from the beast. It attempted to pull back, but one of its legs slipped in the very gore it had been lapping up only seconds ago. Before it could escape, Danni leaned forward and put her entire weight behind the makeshift spear, driving it in deeper.

"Eat this, asshole!" she screamed, grabbing the handle with both hands and giving it a sickening twist.

The creature began to convulse. It reared up, pulling the weapon from her grasp in the process. She scuttled back as far as she could while the monster struggled to make it back to its feet. It finally stood, and then, just as suddenly, stopped. Without further warning, it pitched forward and fell face first onto the floor. The poker was driven through the back of its skull by the impact. Its body spasmed once, then all was still again.

Danni waited, unmoving, for a few minutes. At last, she realized that the creature wasn't playing possum. It was dead. Inching closer, she was surprised by the calm coldness she felt inside. She supposed she should be hysterical. Despite the fact that one of her best friends was lying brutally savaged less than ten feet away, she couldn't bring herself to cry. Instead, she actually began to giggle. It wasn't a mirthful laugh, though. It was a hard chuckle with little humor behind it. She had stared down the devil, and the devil had blinked.

No, that wasn't right. This creature wasn't the devil. It wasn't even a monster. It was just an animal. It was big, strong, and fast, but it could be killed just the same. That realization brought resolve to Danni. She had run enough for one day – enough for one life, perhaps. She was done with that. She still had a brother out there who needed her.

Danni got to her feet and walked over to the dead creature. She grabbed the end of the poker sticking through the back of its head and gave a yank. The only movement was an involuntary twitch from the dead sasquatch. The makeshift weapon was stuck fast in its thick skull.

No matter. She spent the next fifteen minutes searching the now quiet house. She felt a little guilty about doing so, but realized the owner was beyond caring at this point. Unfortunately, her search didn't turn up any firearms as she'd hoped. Richard Barrows appeared to have been more fisherman than hunter. However, she did find a hand axe and a sturdy looking filet knife. It wasn't much, but she tucked them into her belt nevertheless.

She turned, meaning to go, but then hesitated – finding she couldn't just leave Allison lying there in the kitchen. The thought that the beast had been eating her friend threatened to make her retch again. There was always the possibility that something else might make its way into the house to finish the job. The smell of blood and death might lure another of the creatures. She wouldn't allow that.

Danni took a candle from the kitchen and placed it beneath a curtain in the living room. Within seconds, it ignited and began to spread. She felt a momentary twinge of regret in doing so. She was wantonly destroying someone else's property. Didn't Richard say he had a daughter ... Kate? A vague memory reminded her that had been the name of the woman running the general store. Were they the same person? Sadly, she had no idea. Whoever Kate was, though, assuming she was even still alive in this damned town, Danni felt that perhaps she was doing her a small favor. Burning the place to the ground was kinder than leaving her to find her father's remains. The sight in the kitchen would probably be enough to unhinge anyone. No, it was better this way – a fitting funeral pyre to her friend and the man who had welcomed them both into his home. It was the best she could do.

As the fire began to spread in the small home, Danni walked out the front door, not bothering to close it behind her. Her eyes were dry, a look of determination in them, as she strode into the darkness.

I'm coming, Harrison.

31

The fire at the Barrows' residence wasn't the first in Bonanza Creek that night, nor would it be the last. At the edge of Main Street, the blaze at the late Ben Reeves' bar looked like it might be starting to burn itself out. However, then the flames found several barrels of home-brewed liquor that he sold to a few of his regulars. This was hi-test hooch, more than capable of pulling double duty as both beverage and engine degreaser. The barrels exploded with a dull boom, the contents fueling the fire and causing it to flare up higher. Embers were thrown high up into the air, some landing on neighboring buildings, where they began to smolder.

Across town, something similar was about to occur. It would be more remote than what happened at the bar. Although, had the lone witness to its occurrence been able to speak, he would have certainly agreed that it was far more spectacular.

Kurt Bachowski, last of the Bachowski clan who

had settled in Bonanza Creek over a hundred years ago, or so his father used to claim – despite having moved there just a year before Kurt's birth, after a few run-ins with California's finest – didn't know that, though. He continued toward his destination with absolutely no thought as to whether it would be nothing more than a smoking crater just a few minutes later.

He saw the lights in the Clemons' place from fairly far away. The trail he'd been following wasn't particularly dense, and in the darkness of the night, their house had shone like a beacon. He'd never gotten along particularly well with either Grace or Byron, nor they with him. They considered the Bachowskis to be little more than poachers. In turn, Kurt saw them as a bunch of sissified survivalists. As far as he was concerned, take away their fancy equipment and they'd be useless.

All things considered, though, he was glad to see their place. As long as they had a gun for him to use, and he suspected they had plenty, he could deal with them looking down their nose at him. He had heard via the Barrows bitch about the gun shows that they frequented. Supposedly, they were always coming back home with new *toys*. It didn't matter much to Kurt. So long as they didn't hand him some Chinese piece of shit that'd jam just as soon as shoot, he'd be happy. Then he could make his way back to his own place and get to his own stash of firearms. Maybe his weren't as fancy, but they were well cared for and dependable.

He took a look around before abandoning his

concealment. He didn't see or hear anything out of the ordinary, so he made his way to their front door – giving a quick knock on it. "Grace, Byron," he said in as loud a voice as he dared. He then knocked again. For a moment, he thought he heard movement inside, but it might have been his imagination. The blinds were drawn, so there was no way to be sure.

He decided to try the back door instead. Walking around the house, he noticed that their truck was missing from the driveway. That figured. They were out, probably off somewhere sleeping in one of their fancy tents complete with air conditioning. *Shit on that.* He wasn't above a little breaking and entering if it meant saving his own ass.

He got to the back door, unaware that Grace Clemons' mangled body lay in the grass only a few yards away. He'd been considering breaking a window or just kicking the damn door in, but it wasn't necessary. The back door was ajar, lying closed against the jamb.

He was busy thinking *damn fools are practically begging to be robbed* as he pushed it open. Thus, he was caught completely by surprise when something charged out of the house at him. He fell back with a cry, raising his arms in a defensive gesture – prepared to give it hell for what it had done to Stan. It might kill him, but he'd do his damnedest to gouge its eyes out first.

However, the Clemons' dog, Zeke, had no interest in any conflict with Kurt. It bounded past him and ran off baying into the night.

He cursed and threw a rock in the direction of the

fleeing dog, missing it by a country mile. Damn thing had nearly given him a heart attack. "I hope you get eaten by a bear!" he yelled after it. Oh well. Yet another thing that served the Clemonses right, as far as he was concerned.

He collected himself then stepped inside, immediately regretting the decision. The place was trashed. It was like a bomb had gone off. Furniture was overturned, shelves had been torn from the walls, and their table had been smashed. Either Grace and Byron had gotten into the mother of all fights, or he wasn't the first intruder in their home that evening. No wonder the damn dog had bolted like a bat out of hell.

He briefly considered that he should probably follow the mutt, but being so close to salvation was ultimately too tempting. He'd spoken to them enough times to know they probably had a stocked gun cabinet in their basement. A decent cache of firepower was probably less than twenty feet away. He considered his options and decided to chance it.

Kurt stopped in the doorway and listened. Hearing nothing, he took a tentative step further in. It was still dead silent, so he continued. He stepped over a small pile of debris, never knowing that beneath it lay the very same rifle that Grace Clemons had decided against bringing on her ill-fated perimeter sweep.

He came to a hallway. Before him lay the Clemons' living room. It was likewise in shambles, but no movement came from within. To his right, at the end of the hall, was a doorway. Kurt didn't need to get any closer to tell that whatever else had been in here wasn't too fond of politely knocking. The door had been ripped right off its hinges. He looked to the left and saw three more doors, all intact. He turned in that direction. *Might as well go with the odds.*

Kurt had barely taken a step when he heard a thump coming from the far end of the hall. He froze. What followed was the sound of wood being splintered. He looked back toward the open doorway and saw a shadow move. Something was still in there.

He was too far in to make a retreat now. It was all or nothing. He tried the first door he came to. It opened smoothly and quietly. Kurt peered inside and silently cursed. It was just a closet.

He crept further down the hall as a ripping noise came from the room behind him. *I hope those are just curtains,* he thought, coming to the second door. It was ajar, which was a small miracle as far as he was concerned. *If not, then third time's gotta be the charm.* Thankfully, though, that wasn't necessary. He pulled it open and saw stairs leading downward. He blew out a quick sigh of relief and clicked the light. The switch flipped to the on position with a loud clack. Immediately, the sounds in the other room stopped, as if whatever was in there was listening.

Deciding not to wait around to see if it was curious, he bolted down the stairs. The bottom two creaked as he stepped on them. If the thing upstairs had suspected something before, it definitely knew he was here now. As if in confirmation, a bellowing roar came from above. He had a moment to consider that if hatred could be vocalized, this was what it would sound like.

Kurt looked around. He was in a game room of sorts. A few stuffed trophies hung on the walls. There was a comfortable looking loveseat on one end, facing toward a big screen TV. There was even a foosball table off to one side. Where were the goddamned guns, though?

He could hear it coming, and like a fool, he had left the damn cellar door open. Quickly scanning the room, he saw there was still hope. There was another door, this one leading toward the back of the house.

He ran to it and tried the handle, finding the goddamned thing locked. The beast roared again, now at the top of the stairs.

"The hell with this," he said and savagely kicked the door. It held. He did it again, and that time the lock broke with a loud *crack*. The door swung open. He chanced a look behind him and saw hairy legs descending the stairs.

Thinking quickly, he turned and shoved the TV to the floor. The screen shattered, spreading glass and electronics. Hopefully, it would be enough to slow the creature down.

Kurt bolted into the other room and stopped dead in his tracks at what he saw. He had earlier joked about the Clemonses being a pair of hack survivalists, but he didn't know the half of it. Two entire walls were covered in ordinance of various calibers. He wasn't particularly up on the finer points of gun control, but was pretty certain some of the stuff there was illegal.

Scratch that, he was *very* certain. On the far wall was what appeared to be a rocket launcher. He had seen one in a Rambo movie once. Beneath it was a box covered in lettering he couldn't read.

"Shit on toast," he muttered to himself in disbelief.

Had the creature not bellowed again, this time with a slight note of pain as it stepped on the broken glass, Kurt might have stood there gawking until such time as it came up behind him and tore his head off. The noise – *Dear God, it sounds like it's right behind me* – spurred him into action.

Fortunately for him, the Clemonses were well-organized. Beneath where the guns hung were neatly labeled cabinets. He quickly opened a drawer and saw boxes of ammo corresponding with the pieces hanging above it. Unfortunately, the one he opened first was all small caliber.

Dashing across the room, he grabbed an assault rifle from the wall. He tore open the drawer beneath it and, sure enough, there was a whole stack of fully loaded magazines. Hearing movement behind him, he quickly grabbed one and slammed it home before turning to face the beast.

The creature was right there. It crouched slightly, too tall for the room they were in. At first, he thought it was the same one from before. Large breasts hung down almost to its waist, but there were no wounds in its torso. He'd peppered the creature that had killed Stan with a full load of .22's. This beast was untouched. *Holy hell, there really is more than one.*

He tried to swing the weapon toward it, but the

creature stepped in before he could do so. *Should've taken a goddamned pistol!* The beast grabbed the barrel of the gun with one hand and Kurt's right shoulder with the other. It was massively strong.

He screamed, feeling bone snap. As it dug its claws into the flesh of his arm, his finger pulled reflexively on the trigger, causing the gun to go off. The bullet slammed into an ammo box, the same one with Russian wording that Kurt couldn't read, and impacted with one of the RPG shells inside.

A hundred yards away, Zeke – his limited doggie brain already forgetting the danger behind him – had stopped to pee on the side of a tree. Suddenly, there came a bright flash of light through the trees followed by a tremendously loud noise, enough to make him whimper in pain. A few moments later, an uncomfortably warm breeze washed over the frightened dog. He watched as the place he knew as home was blown apart by the explosion. He whined again, turned, then ran off into the forest.

A few days and many miles later, he was found by a good-natured hiker. When nobody answered a newspaper ad for the lost dog, the man's family adopted him. He lived a good, long life with lots of love. His was a happy ending. The only remembrance of what happened in Bonanza Creek came late at night while Zeke sometimes dreamt. He would whine in his sleep, and his legs would move as his dream self ran from large hairy things in the woods.

32

The smell of smoke kept getting stronger, even as he continued moving away from the bar, but Chuck didn't stop to ruminate. That the fire was spreading wasn't exactly a surprise. As far as he was concerned, though, he had bigger fish to fry right then.

He kicked in the back door of what he thought was finally the bed and breakfast. He'd weaved in and out of the woods, crossing small side streets that weren't much more than overly wide deer trails. Normally, he'd have a good sense of his bearings. Unfortunately, he had gotten turned around pretty good while following that idiot redneck. It also wasn't helping that all the movement had continued to pull stitches in his shredded stomach, the blood flow gradually worsening. He could feel it trickling into his pants and down his legs. It might not be life-threatening yet, but he was definitely starting to get a little lightheaded.

He bit down on his lip. The pain cleared his head for the moment, and he was able to think. Yeah, this was definitely the B&B. Though he hadn't seen it from the rear, it was too big of a building to be anything else. This was the way. He was pretty sure his friends were somewhere on the other side of it. Not too long ago, he had heard a squatch bellowing into the night, its screams followed by a series of gunshots. Judging from the report, it might have been one of Derek's big elephant rifles.

In the end, though, caution won out over his desire to run up through one of the alleys and pop out onto the main stretch. For starters, he couldn't be certain they had killed it or that it was even the only one. Secondly, it would be just his luck to step out and get plugged by friendly fire. He didn't think that scenario likely. However, this situation was different than any other they had been in. Even the most seasoned veteran could get jumpy and start shooting at shadows.

No, this way is best, he thought, entering a dark room, a pantry from what he could tell. His plan was to cut through the building and recon the street from the windows. If he saw his friends, he'd get their attention and join them. If not, he'd make a go for the SUVs and get himself some proper firepower.

The pantry led into a kitchen. From there, the gloom of a hallway beckoned. Chuck stepped out and flattened himself against the wall. He listened for a moment. There was no sound, so he began to move again.

A moment later, he heard a hollow thud. It had

seemed to come from above him. A few seconds passed, and there came another noise. It could have been a grunt, although he wasn't sure.

Some of those kids from earlier had gotten rooms on the second floor. It might be one of them, or it might be something else.

He was split on what to do. A small part of him desperately wanted to find his teammates and get something more substantial than a knife in his hands. However, he also had his duty to do. If there were survivors, he should find them. If one of the creatures was in here with him, he should at least make sure so they could come back and flush it out later.

Continuing on, his foot landed in something wet, causing it to slip out from under him. He fell to the floor, agony coursing through his stomach as the last of his stitches popped. He gritted his teeth against the pain to keep from crying out. It was bad enough he'd potentially given his position away. He wouldn't exacerbate the situation by screaming.

He put his hand on the floor to steady himself and felt more of that wetness. It had a sticky, tacky feel to it. Chuck didn't need to see to know it was probably blood, a lot judging by how much was oozing through his fingers. He reached blindly in the darkness, there being no windows in the hall to light the way. Eventually, he found the body that he knew would be there. It didn't take more than a few quick touches to tell him all he needed. Whoever it had been, they had been pounded into pulp.

Chuck rose to his feet, momentarily ignoring the fire in his gut. He quietly unsheathed his knife with his right hand while his left went to his injured stomach. What he felt there didn't do anything to improve his mood. He was soaked in blood, although how much was his and how much was from the floor he didn't know.

He continued along and eventually came to the lobby. Just enough light filtered in to let him see the outline of the staircase leading to the second floor. *If that fire keeps spreading, light won't be an issue for much longer*. He gave one last longing look toward the windows, then started up the stairs.

"I'm not so sure we should let her keep the gun," Mitchell whispered to Derek as they made their way down the center of the dark street. It wasn't a wide road, especially by city standards, but if anything decided to come running out of the shadows, they'd hopefully have enough time to react against it.

Derek glanced back over his shoulder. Francis was walking with Kate. He held his rifle in his left hand. Derek was pretty certain he was keeping his other free in case he needed to stop her from accidentally shooting anyone. The kid's death had almost completely unraveled her. Her eyes kept darting from one side of the street to the other, one shaky finger resting on the trigger.

"Do you wanna try taking it away from her again?" Derek asked, remembering the panicked look in her eyes when he had first suggested she relinquish the weapon following Rob's death. Had he tried physically removing it from her grasp, he was pretty sure one of them would have gotten shot. "Besides..." He sighed. "She has a right to defend herself. I don't care how jumpy I am. No way would I want to be out here unarmed, knowing what we're dealing with."

"Speaking of which, you know we're all gonna need treatment when this is over, just to be safe."

"Don't remind me," Derek said. He'd been bitten by a raccoon as a child and remembered very well the painful rabies shot.

Mitchell opened his mouth to say more, but his words were lost as a thunderous sound shook the night. It reverberated through the town for a few seconds before silence once more descended. It had been close, surely inside of the town limits. Because of the way it echoed across the quiet streets, there was no way to tell which direction it had come from, though.

"Thunder?"

"Sounded more like dynamite," Derek commented. "Kate, any ideas?" When she didn't answer, he turned back toward her. "Kate!" Her eyes finally focused on his. She gave a small shake of her head, then went back to scanning the shadows.

He was about to ask, for probably the tenth time, if she was okay, when his eyes happened to glance over her shoulder and down the street.

"Uh oh," he said. "I think the fire's spreading."

Sure enough, the glow from the direction of the bar seemed to be getting brighter.

"What fire?" asked Mitchell.

"I might have burned down the bar to kill one of those squatches."

"Slick. Things too boring for you otherwise?"

Derek shrugged in response. "Seemed like a good idea at the time."

The upstairs hallway was quiet. In the darkness, Chuck couldn't locate the source of the noises he'd heard. Then he saw a dim glow from one of the rooms at the far end of the hall, its door open. He walked stealthily toward it, or as much as he could with his stomach paining him with every step.

He passed a few more rooms, all of them shut, making a mental note to give the upstairs a clean sweep on his way out. He came to the open door – no, open was the wrong word for it. It was missing from the frame entirely, jagged splinters poked out from where it had been torn asunder.

There was light coming from the floor over by the windows. It was just enough for Chuck to see that the room had been absolutely trashed. There were no sounds and he didn't sense any movement, but his nose told a different story. There was a musky scent in the air. One of the creatures had definitely been here, although someone could've probably guessed that just by looking at the place. Entering the room, he noticed that there was a stronger, more pungent smell on top of the rest. *It almost smells like...* He took a step and his boot squished down into something semi-solid. *Shit.*

He rolled his eyes in the dark room. *It figures. A bear shits in the woods, but a squatch will shit wherever the hell it pleases.* He lifted his foot out of the excrement with a faint sucking noise. Before he could continue his sweep of the room, a roaring boom sounded from outside. For a moment, the glass in one window shook. The other next to it, Chuck noted, had been shattered, along with a good chunk of the wall it was attached to.

"What the hell?" he whispered. If he didn't know better, he'd have sworn that was an explosion. Putting caution to the wind, he stepped to the window and looked out. The noise didn't come again, and he couldn't see the source from his vantage point. Had he leaned out further and looked to his left, he might have seen his teammates making their way down the street. As it was, he instead pulled back to examine the light source.

It was a small flashlight. It appeared to have been stepped on; however, one of the LEDs was still working. It wasn't much, but it was providing at least some light. He picked it up and used it to further survey the damage.

The condition of the room was every bit as bad as he'd suspected. Fortunately, all he saw was the debris of smashed bedroom furniture. *No bodies. That's a good sign.*

He began making his way back to the door, careful not to step in the sasquatch-sized *landmine* again. Playing the beam of light across the room, he saw that the bathroom likewise appeared to have been broken into.

He glanced at the pile of excrement on the floor and couldn't help but grin. "Guess he couldn't make it in time. When you gotta go, you gotta..." The joke died in his throat as he shined the light into the bathroom. *Why the hell is it painted red?* he briefly thought, before realizing it wasn't.

Chuck had seen a lot in his day, but what had been done to the body lying half in the tub was utterly inhuman. "My God," he whispered, the flashlight slipping from his suddenly numb fingers. He staggered back and tried to fight off the urge to vomit, afraid that he might literally puke his guts up.

So transfixed was he by the carnage before him that he didn't hear the click as one of the doors down the hall opened.

Chuck Wayans wasn't a religious man, but he crossed himself anyway. He just hoped whoever he was ... *she* was, he corrected himself – long brown hair and one ruined breast could be made out amidst the grizzly scene. He just hoped she had died quickly and that most of this had been done after the fact.

What the hell was wrong with these things? He had never seen one do anything even remotely like this. *This is more the work of a psychopath than a wild animal,* he thought, backing out of the bathroom.

Whatever's going on here, these things need to be put down and fast. The thought caught in his head as he heard a sound, a slight creaking of the floorboards behind him. He cursed himself for letting his guard down. At the same time, though, he drew his combat knife from its sheath. He'd been caught flatfooted like a rank amateur. He didn't give himself good odds, but hopefully he could take the ugly son of a bitch with him to Hell.

He felt a puff of breath on the back of his neck, then a hand fell upon his shoulder. Without hesitation, he spun with a battle cry and brought the razor-sharp blade up in an arc. Where it met flesh, it sank in like butter. Chuck gave the knife a vicious twist before launching his full weight at his attacker.

The creature went down under the assault with little more than a grunt. Chuck pressed his advantage, straddling its torso and continued to stab it, screaming obscenities all the while – until the blade finally became stuck in bone. He braced his other hand on the body to pull it out. That's when he realized he wasn't touching fur. It felt like ... fabric.

It took his mind a moment to register this fact. Finally, he scrambled back from it in a breathless gasp. He turned, feeling around with his hands. Where was the goddamned flashlight? Then he saw its glow coming from the bathroom, where he'd dropped it. He scuttled over to it on hands and knees and picked it up from the bloody floor.

Turning back, he played the feeble beam out toward the doorway. Two bare feet were visible in the illumination. Jeans covered the legs they were attached to.

"Oh God, no!" Chuck scrambled back to the fallen person.

It was too late. His first stab had been instantly

fatal, having driven the point of his blade straight up into the soft spot underneath Greg's chin. The poor kid had been dead before he'd even hit the floor.

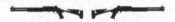

"Holy shit!" exclaimed Derek, peering down the small side street. There was something large lying in the middle of the road. "Shine that light up here!"

Francis flipped on a flashlight and played it out before them as he and his teammates stepped forward to investigate. The beam revealed fine brown hair covering a massive body. "Looks like somebody managed to fight back."

"More like *something*," corrected Derek, kneeling over the corpse. "More like a *lot* of somethings. This squatch has been shot up to hell ... wait a second. I don't think the bullets killed it. Too small of a caliber. Hell, it probably barely felt them."

The men were hunched over the body, busy examining it. They didn't notice Kate slowly stepping backwards – a look of horror spreading across her face following the realization that this was another of the things that were killing her town. *How many more are out there?*

Images of her own death at the hands of these creatures began to play in her mind. Her eyes went wide as she remembered the bloody footprints she'd found earlier in the day. It had to have been one of those things, and that blood ... Gus had been missing since that morning. There had been no sign of him.

Tears welled up in her eyes as she thought of her kindly old dog. He had gone up against a foe that he'd stood absolutely no chance against. He'd died defending her home and her sleeping father within.

Her father! She realized that, in the nightmare of the past few hours, she had completely forgotten about him. He was home alone in the dark. What if the thing that had taken Gus had come back?

She felt her legs quicken their pace, backing away from Derek's team. She didn't want to go – there was safety in their numbers – but she needed to get back to her father. He was the only one left in the world for her.

"Definitely female," Derek said. "Big one, too."

"So, what did this?"

"Something bigger."

"Yep," agreed Mitchell. "Look at her head. Neck's been snapped like a twig. I'd say a male probably took her out. Look at that indentation in her chest."

"Stomped on her after the fact," Derek said. "From the size of it, I'd guess we're dealing with at least a nine-footer."

"Well, it looks like he took care of some of our work for us. Maybe we should pin a medal on him."

Derek gave Francis a grim smile. "Don't worry, I have plenty of *metal* for that big boy right here," he said, patting his rifle. "The one we saw earlier was around that size, maybe a little bigger. Dollars to doughnuts says he's the alpha."

"Where do you think it is?"

"No idea. Last I saw, it'd taken off after that kid."

Francis whistled. "I sure hope he's a fast runner."

"Me too," Derek added. "He saved our bacon. I'd like to return the favor."

As if in response, a screaming roar split the night.

"That wasn't far," Mitchell said.

"No, it wasn't. If we're in luck, Harrison's still leading it on a merry chase. Let's get moving." Derek turned around, "Kate, come on..." The words died in his throat. She was gone.

"Where the hell did she go?"

"She was right here."

"KATE!" Derek shouted, his voice echoing in the empty streets. "Son of a bitch!"

"Should we go after her?"

Derek was silent for a moment. "No. We need to kill that thing before it gets away."

"What if one of them finds her?" Mitchell asked.

"She's armed. That Remington will teach some manners to anything dumb enough to stand in front of it. No. She's a big girl. She can take care of herself," Derek said, then silently added, *I hope.*

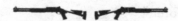

Chuck sat up, stifling a scream, the creature's roar still echoing from outside. He blinked and looked around, sure that it was about to gut him, but there was nothing except the darkness. Gradually, the fog in his brain cleared a little. He'd found a blanket in one of the closets and used it to cover Greg's body. It wasn't much, but he felt he needed to do *something*. The kid hadn't deserved it. *Why the hell did he sneak up behind me like that, especially with all this crap going on?*

He had no way of knowing that it was only the explosion at the Clemons' place that had finally stirred Greg. He'd slept through all the rest in a drug-induced haze. Even then, he'd still been pretty wrecked, and though his death had certainly come as a surprise, there hadn't been much pain. Chuck might have taken a little bit of comfort in knowing that.

He had covered the poor kid, then said a few words of apology over his body. Afterwards, he had slumped, exhausted, against a wall to catch his breath. His stomach had hurt quite badly and was bleeding even more profusely. He'd nodded his head for just a second and had immediately plunged into a half dream/half hallucination in which the entire clan of creatures had him surrounded. The scream from outside, though, had been real, real enough for Chuck to slap himself across the face in a bid to clear his head a little. There was still a job to do.

Pocketing the flashlight, he grabbed his knife in one hand and attempted to hold his gut closed with the other. He staggered to his feet, then shuddered in pain before slowly making his way back down the stairs.

Eventually, he found the front door, and spent several seconds fumbling with the locks – his fingers feeling slow and heavy. He opened the door and stepped out, surveying the scene as best he could. His eyes didn't seem to want to focus correctly. He could see well enough, though, to notice the two lumps on the ground in front of the B&B. He hobbled down the stairs as quickly as he dared and went over to them.

Two bodies, a human and a squatch. He didn't know what happened to the person, but the large bullet holes in the creature's corpse told him all he needed to know.

He was considering his next move, when he heard a sound ... footsteps. Looking up, he spied a figure across the street. It was moving quickly. Even in the moonlight, though, he could tell it was far too small and slim to be a squatch. The person was holding something; it looked like a gun.

Rising from the sasquatch corpse, he began painfully shuffling toward the direction of the newcomer. *Hot damn! Finally, a lucky break.*

He had no idea how wrong he was.

The creature's screams had finally broken the last of Kate's nerve, otherwise she might have heeded reason and stayed with those reporters. No, that wasn't right. They didn't act like any reporters she'd ever heard of, especially with all those guns. They were more like hunters, but that was insane. Who would hunt creatures like these? If there was a Hell, then those things must surely be from its deepest depths.

Still, some small part of her had rebelled against the mad need to find her father. Deep down, she knew it was in her best interest to remain with the men. However, the beast's cries had silenced all opposition in her mind. There was at least one more of them out there. Its wild bellowing had purged any rational thought while awakening a primal fear inside her. She'd turned away from them at once. Let them go forward and be slaughtered by that thing. She'd find her father, and together they'd somehow survive this nightmare.

Setting a quick pace, she tried to keep from outright running. The gun was heavy, and it was dark. It wouldn't do any good if she fell and broke something. She'd kept to the middle of the road, as the group had done earlier, until the dark form of the bed and breakfast loomed before her. Knowing what was waiting outside it, Kate was certain she wouldn't be able to handle seeing the beast's body again. She was barely holding on by a thread.

Unfortunately, that thread was about to snap.

Moving to the far side of the street, she quickened her steps to pass the dreadful scene. She was almost past when she heard something coming from its direction.

"Heeeeyyyy!" a slurred voice seemed to call out.

She stopped and shut her eyes. *No! It's just in my head.*

"Heeeyyyy ... yoooouuuu," the voice gasped again.

Almost against her will, her eyes opened. She turned toward the small hostel and immediately wished she hadn't, for what she saw wasn't possible.

The thing had risen from where the body of the monster lay and lurched in her direction. It took slow shambling steps, as if it weren't used to its legs. One hand was pressed tightly against its body, and in the other ... *Oh my God, it has a knife!*

"Stay back," she sputtered weakly.

It continued to shamble closer. Drawing near, she could see it better. There was enough moonlight to make out that it was covered, head to toe, in some dark ichor. She imagined some unspeakable offspring clawing its way out of the belly of the dead monster, a hideous abortion that refused to die. It was coming for her now, seeking vengeance for its slain mother.

"Heeeelllllppp meeeeee," it croaked, stepping to within ten feet of her,

That did it. The frayed tatters of her sanity snapped in that instant. She turned the barrel of the shotgun toward it, now close enough to see the whites of its eyes widen in surprise. It seemed an almost human gesture to her, perhaps *too* human. Her finger squeezed the trigger. Fire and thunder erupted from the gun, driving her back a few steps and almost knocking the wind from her.

Fate was far less kind to her *attacker*. The creature's chest and jaw disappeared in a spray of gore. It was blown backwards by the blast, landing on the ground twitching.

She didn't bother sticking around to see if it got back up. Ignoring all caution, Kate ran off into the night, smoke still trailing from the shotgun.

33

It was a small wonder that Kate Barrows didn't run into anyone, or anything, else as she fled. It was probably for the best. The sound of her shot caught the attention of the many ears in the area. Had another human come across her in the dark, they might have met the same fate as Chuck. Had she run across one of the clan, perhaps things would have ended in a different, if no less bloody, way. Whether through darkness, accident, or design, she didn't see another living thing as she ran blindly home in search of her father.

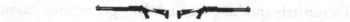

Derek and the two remaining members of his team were still down the side street where they'd found the female's corpse. The sound of the shotgun blast stopped them dead in their tracks. Unfortunately, the buildings around them played havoc with the acoustics. It took them several moments to realize that the shot had issued from the direction they'd come from. After that, it didn't take much considera-tion to conclude it had come from Kate.

Danni had been resting against a tree about halfway back from the Barrows' place when she heard the shot. She'd been pushing herself hard and was finally reaching her limit. When the blast sounded, though, she felt something she hadn't in several hours ... *hope*. Someone was out there, and they were fighting back. It might even be her brother. It was enough to get her moving again.

"It's about time," Harrison muttered. After fleeing the scene of the two battling monsters, he'd holed up in a tiny crawlspace beneath the first house he found. It was a tight fit, far too narrow for one of those things to manage. They'd have to tear the whole damn building apart to get to him, albeit he wasn't entirely doubtful of their ability to do so. Fortunately, nothing had tried to get at him. Soon after, tired and scared, he'd dozed off in the confined space. He didn't realize he had slept through a previous volley of gunfire, as well as the commotion made from the Clemons' house blowing up.

Now that he was roused, though, he decided to

chance it. If Derek and the others were armed, then that's who he wanted to be with.

He crawled out, looked around, then started back in the direction of Main Street.

The Alpha had been ready to scream his fury into the night again when he heard the noise. He refused to believe that the two-legged thing had escaped after the outcast had dared challenge him. He'd dispatched her with raw, brute savagery, being far larger and stronger than the outcast bitch. She was a fool to attack him and had been dealt with accordingly. Before dying, though, she had inflicted several minor, if annoying, wounds on him.

The two-legged thing had run off during the battle. When it was over, the Alpha pursued, but his pace was lessened by his injuries. Then, much to his surprise, he'd lost the stupid thing's scent. Little by little, the disease was taking its toll on the mighty creature. Thick, pus-like mucus had started to clog up his nasal passages. More of it was building up in his eyes, blurring his vision.

He'd howled in rage when he realized he couldn't locate the two-legged thing. Afterwards, he had taken out his frustration on the nearest of their dwellings. One entire wall of the Bonanza Creek Post Office had already been demolished, although he did not know it was called that. The building was groaning from the strain of his repeated attacks and wouldn't last much longer. Before he could topple it, though, a new sound filled the air. It was loud, like the bellow of some great beast.

Had his brain been in a less advanced state of decay, he would have remembered the two-legged things' fire sticks and the lessons of his ancestors, but he was beyond that now. He heard the sound through his semi-clogged ears and came to the only conclusion the rage would allow ... it was the cry of another challenger. It, too, would be killed. It, too, would scream.

34

The hunters became the hunted. They just didn't know it yet. It wasn't that they weren't being cautious, far from it. They'd simply been spotted first.

When the attack came, it came quickly and without warning. The Alpha's senses, though dulled by the disease, were still superior to any of the men whom it spied as it came looking for the source of the challenge.

Though it had long abandoned any notions of purposeful stealth, it still moved with a natural grace that belied its size. Had it bellowed its fury at the men, they would have turned and cut it down easily, though it didn't know this. For whatever reason — whether the very last vestiges of instinct remaining in its dying neurons or a total focus on the killing to come – it remained silent.

The two-legged things were moving away from him. Perhaps they were fleeing. It didn't matter. What did, was that their backs were to him. Soon, the only thing that would matter would be their dying screams and the hot wash of their blood as the Alpha drank it in great slurps. Foamy drool dripped from his lips in anticipation.

He closed to within ten yards, then could control himself no longer. He put on a burst of speed as the rage boiled over, screaming a cry of victory.

Derek thought perhaps a truck had hit them, some crazed survivor of this doomed town making a run for it. As he flew through the air, though, he realized there were two problems with that theory: he didn't recall hearing an engine, and the thing that hit them had been a little too hairy to be a truck. Then gravity reasserted itself, and he hit the ground, knocking the rifle from his hands. He skidded to a halt, scraping himself in a dozen places and momentarily scattering all coherent thought to the wind.

The creature had appeared behind them, seemingly from out of nowhere. So intent had they been on rushing to Kate's aid that they'd acted like a bunch of rank amateurs, forgetting that the threat could come from anywhere.

First, there had been its unearthly bellow, so loud and near it had practically rattled their teeth. Less than a second later, it was upon them, its sheer size alone allowing it to barrel them over all at once.

It caught Derek in the back with one of its meaty fists, sending him tumbling down the street. The others had both been hit by a wide, sweeping blow from its other arm. Mitchell was flung into the side of a wrecked pickup they'd been passing, slamming into the driver's side door before landing in an unmoving heap. The blow shattered Francis's right arm and sent him flying. He landed badly, pain immediately flaring through his left leg as it, too, snapped.

Though stunned, Derek was able to roll back to his feet out of instinct alone. He shook his head to clear it and saw the squatch. It was huge, over nine feet tall, and bristling with muscle. Where the other creatures had been covered in dirty brown fur, this one was distinct in its salt and pepper coloring. There was little doubt in Derek's mind this was the alpha. It was the largest and strongest of the clan. No doubt the craftiest, too, as it had taken out his entire squad with one hit.

It was in the act of advancing upon Francis, who was struggling weakly where he lay upon the sidewalk. He looked injured, perhaps badly. Shaken as he was, Derek wasn't about to let the creature have his friend. He gave an inarticulate shout as he rose, catching the beast's attention. It turned toward him, its eyes malevolent points of red in the moonlight. It bared its teeth at him and took a step forward.

It was only then that he realized he'd dropped his rifle. He could see it lying in the road about halfway between him and the squatch. There was no way he'd be able to retrieve it before the creature was upon him. Instead, he began fumbling for the heavy sidearm he wore. Unfortunately, he was still semi-dazed, and his fingers didn't seem to want to fully cooperate.

Sadly, before he could free the revolver, the creature launched itself at him. Though limping slightly, it still closed the gap with frightening speed. As the great beast lunged toward him, Derek did the only sensible thing he could think of: he turned and ran.

Despite being in a world of agony, Francis saw the squatch turn toward Derek. He dimly realized that the creature had been coming for him before it'd been distracted. Despite the pain, he wouldn't let the opportunity go to waste. His rifle strap was still around his right arm. Reaching for it with his functional hand, he gave it a tug. Pain flared in his broken appendage as he realized he was partially lying on the gun. He gritted his teeth while he shifted it out from under his body, the effort costing him greatly. Sweat stood out on his brow and tears obscured his vision as he leveled the rifle, one-handed, at the creature's back.

Just then, it launched itself into a loping run toward Derek. Francis steadied himself as best he could and pulled the trigger. The noise from the gunshot was nothing compared to the pain that exploded through his body from the recoil. Broken bones shifted against each other from the resulting shockwave. It was too much for him. He passed out before he got a chance to see whether the shot had hit the mark.

It hadn't. The bullet went wide, missing both cryptid and crypto hunter alike. However, it did serve to catch both of their attention.

The creature had closed on Derek with incredible speed. It had been only a few steps away from reaching him when the shot was fired. It stopped and raised its hands to its head with a piteous mewl of pain. Derek turned, saw this, and at first thought the shot had hit home. Unfortunately, though, the creature didn't go down. It just held its hands to its ears for a moment while it shook its head, sending drool and snot flying.

Derek used the distraction to free his handgun. As he unholstered it, the squatch took another lumbering step toward him. Simultaneously, he brought the gun up and shuffled a few steps backward.

Just as he squeezed the trigger, his leg struck something. Losing his balance, he fell – the shot going over the creature's head.

Derek landed on his ass with an "Oof!" Despite the impending threat, he glanced at what he'd tripped over ... his eyes opening wide once realization hit. Though the body was covered in blood and its upper half in ruins, he could see just enough to know it was his tracker. "Chuck! Jesus Christ!" he exhaled, despite it being a particularly poor time for even the simplest expression of grief. He looked up, again raising the weapon, and saw at once his distraction would be a costly one.

As he futilely tried to line up a kill shot, one of the creature's enormous hands closed over his. Its fist squeezed shut, and Derek screamed in pain. It had never even been a contest. The bones in his right hand might as well have been made of paper, as far as the beast's strength was concerned. It was crushed into pulp.

Even so, whether through force of will or pressure from the squatch's grip, his index finger somehow managed to squeeze the trigger.

The heavy caliber bullet flew from the barrel and slammed into the creature's shoulder. A spray of blood washed over Derek as the alpha screamed. It let go of him and the gun tumbled out of his now useless fingers.

The pain was incredible. Darkness played at the edge of his vision, causing him to bite down onto his tongue to keep from passing out. As much as he might have welcomed it, he knew it would be a *really* bad idea to let unconsciousness take him.

The bullet would have blown a man's arm most of the way off, but Derek was doubtful he'd done much more than piss off the already enraged beast. He needed to put some distance between them, and quickly, too.

He scanned the street, looking for something he could use to his advantage. He saw the ruined remains of the van a couple dozen yards away. That was no good. Even if he could wedge himself in the back, the squatch would most likely just finish the job of crushing it. Then his eyes glanced toward the bed and breakfast. It was right across the street, its front door wide open.

Beggars can't be choosers. Cradling his broken hand against his body, he used his good arm to scramble back to his feet. There was a moment when his eyes again locked with the creature's, and then he was off, running as quickly as his legs could carry him.

Behind him, the squatch's cries changed pitch. Gone was the pain and in its place pure hatred. Bounding up the stairs to the dark B&B, Derek silently hoped someone had left a spare howitzer lying about. He was beginning to doubt that anything less would stop the beast.

Harrison emerged from an alleyway, close to where he'd earlier gotten clobbered. He turned toward the main road and immediately saw the two men lying on the ground. Taking a quick look around and not spying any of the creatures, he ran over to them.

The first was Mitchell. Harrison rolled him over and saw that the side of his face was covered in blood. He groaned weakly when moved, but didn't awaken. He was alive, though. That was the important thing. Harrison then went to check on the other man. If anything, Francis looked to be in even worse shape than Mitchell. Fortunately, he, too, was still breathing.

He was debating how best to help them when he

heard the sound of a gunshot. Harrison instinctively ducked, although he was vaguely aware that the chance of someone mistaking him for one of those monsters was pretty slim. He crouched low, just in case he was wrong, and debated calling out to the shooter when a second gunshot rang out. A howl of pain rose up in response, and Harrison zeroed in on the sound. Straining his eyes in the darkness, he saw it. One of the creatures was standing further down the street, its size and shape unmistakable. From the look of things, it might've even been the same one that had chased him earlier.

It appeared to be clutching its arm as it let out another bellow. It didn't take a genius to figure out why. *Good! I hope that hurt, fucker!* Harrison thought, listening to its screams. Unfortunately, it didn't fall. A second later, a smaller figure darted out from the beast's shadow and ran for the place they'd been staying at. He couldn't see much detail from this distance, but it looked to be about Derek's size. The person ran up the stairs, disappearing inside the doorway as the creature roared again and took off in pursuit.

Harrison debated his course of action for a moment, then stepped to where Francis lay – not to help him but to reach for what he was still holding. He pulled the rifle from the unconscious man's limp grasp before turning back toward the bed and breakfast. Hefting the gun, he began walking down the street.

Time to return the favor.

35

D erek really hoped he hadn't just run into his
own tomb. He knew full well that at least
one of the creatures had been in there
tonight. If another was waiting for him, he'd be absolutely screwed. If not, though, then he might have a
chance. Out in the open, he knew he couldn't outrun
the squatch. Despite their immense size, they were
capable of hitting speeds only the best of Olympians
could match. Fortunately for him, most buildings
hadn't been designed with nine-foot giants in mind.
The low ceilings and narrow hallways of the B&B
would hopefully hamper its progress, or so Derek was
betting his life on.

He skidded on something slick, almost lost his
footing, but then managed to ride it out. *Glad I skate-
boarded as a kid,* he mused, his feet hitting dry floor
again, allowing him to continue onward. Entering a
large room, the lobby it seemed, he saw a choice of

either going up the stairs or continuing on toward the rear of the building.

He heard a noise behind him, the squatch no doubt. It was coming after him – quickly, too, from the sound of it. A moment later, there came a bellow, followed by a crash. "Watch your step!" he called over his shoulder with the manic laugh of a man close to coming unhinged.

Derek didn't like his chances going forward. If the back of the B&B was fenced in, that could be trouble. With his smashed hand, he wasn't in any shape to be climbing. There was also the fact that, out in the open, the creature had all the advantages. A thought hit him: *If it worked for that other squatch, maybe it'll work for me.* A second later, he was vaulting up the stairs.

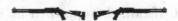

Two more shots rang out in the night. Danni didn't really know guns, but nevertheless it sounded different than the earlier one. The second gunshot was followed immediately by the scream of one of those monsters. There was no mistaking it. She was certain she'd be hearing that sound in her nightmares for the rest of her life.

Pushing herself onward, she realized she could see light ahead. Shortly thereafter, she noticed there was a flickering quality to it as the smell of smoke drifted toward her. Fire. She didn't know whether it was caused by the creatures or set by another survivor. Either way, there seemed to be a fight going on. Unfortunately, she had no idea who was winning.

Looking down at the axe in her hand, she realized how small it seemed – surely insignificant against one of those giant apes. *No!* She shook her head and cleared that thought out. It might be small, but that didn't mean it wouldn't be enough to tip the odds. She had to keep positive thoughts like that in mind. Holding her head up high, she continued toward the battleground.

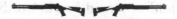

A mere scream wouldn't have done the pain justice. Fate, it seemed, had a cruel sense of irony insofar as Derek was concerned. As he had raced along the second floor, still chuckling at the spill the squatch had taken downstairs, he'd tripped over something in the hallway and tumbled ass over teakettle. Landing on his bad hand, the feeling had been so intense that, for a few moments, all he could do was lie there and gasp for breath. Tears were still streaming down his face when he heard it clambering up the stairs after him. Whatever it was he'd fallen over, it had erased his lead. The creature was mere moments from ending this in its favor.

He gritted his teeth to deal with the pain. It was incredible, but at least he was no longer in danger of passing out. *Not without half a bottle of Percocet.* Pulling his hand out from under himself, he used his intact appendages to crawl over whatever had tripped him up – focused on his own survival. Regardless, as he made his way slowly forward, he became aware that he was crawling over a body. If anything, that steeled his resolve to make it out of this alive. He had no intention of being another name on the mass grave this town had become.

He finally pulled himself over the corpse and found the floor again. It was slick and sticky, which didn't come as a particular surprise. At least it was solid, allowing him to get back to his feet. A creaking of the floor boards behind him, though, told him that he was out of time. The beast had caught up to him.

He felt a puff of rancid breath on the back of his neck and instinctively ducked. Just then, something large swung over his head, crashing into the wall. Studs cracked like toothpicks as a rain of drywall dust settled upon him, prickling his nose. *Great, I get to die sneezing,* he thought, launching himself forward out of its reach.

The creature snarled, still coming for him as he pushed himself into the bedroom. He saw the opening ahead of him, the frame grossly distorted from where the other beast had earlier forced itself through. Throwing caution to the wind, he jumped out of the same window that had seen almost as much traffic that night as the front door.

Several beings, both human and otherwise, had already used that egress successfully in their endeavors. Unfortunately, whatever luck was bestowed upon the previous wayfarers had been used up by the time Derek leaped from it. He hit the ground badly and felt a painful pop as his right ankle buckled beneath him. Toppling over, he once again landed on his broken hand, crying out as a rainbow of agonizing stars exploded in front of his eyes.

This is starting to become a habit. He rolled onto his back and glanced upward. The alpha was leaning out the window, watching him. Though he knew it was little more than an animal, a crazed one at that, he could have sworn he saw a look of triumph in its eyes. Had it been able to speak, Derek wouldn't have been surprised to hear it issue a pithy comment regarding *any last words.*

The situation had "hopeless" written all over it, but still he refused to accept his fate lying down. Using his good hand, he rolled to his knees and tested out his hurt ankle. He put some weight on it, and pain lanced up his leg. Fortunately, it was far less excruciating than what he'd felt from his hand. It wasn't broken, just badly sprained.

My luck is improving. If I get out of this, I'll have to play the lottery.

His ankle was already swelling inside of his boot; however, hobbling was better than crawling by any stretch of the imagination. He pushed himself to his feet just as he heard the dull thud behind him he'd been expecting. The creature had jumped out the window and landed only a few feet away.

Whatever gods protect against sprained ankles smiled more kindly on the squatch, Derek noted. Blood poured freely from the wound in its shoulder, but it still appeared to have a lot of fight left in it. *Probably*

enough to kill me, then go strangle half a dozen bulldozers.

It bared its teeth at him, then raised its head to howl. It was long and loud, splitting the quiet of the night like thunder. It sounded of rage, of hatred, of *victory*. At last, it lowered its gaze to meet Derek's. Its eyes were red and runny, but the look in them spoke volumes. *This must be what it's like to stare down a serial killer.*

It took a slow step forward. Derek contemplated his next action with the speed of thought. Running was out of the question. He would have to stand and fight. Unfortunately, he doubted the creature would feel even his best haymaker. That left just one thing, he mused, drawing back his injured leg. What he was about to do would hurt like a motherfucker – hopefully for the creature, too. As a man, Derek knew that in all the world there was one universal way to slow down a bipedal male: a good solid kick to the balls. He was preparing to do just that when a voice spoke out from behind the beast.

"Hey, you hairy asshole, forget about me?"

The challenge was won. The Alpha could see it in the two-legged thing's eyes. It had put up a good fight, had even wounded him, but there had been only one possible conclusion in the end. The Alpha was supreme, the Alpha of all other alphas. He would kill the two-legged thing slowly. Mercy was beyond his comprehension by that point. But first, he would make the stupid thing scream.

It would scream long and loud, so that all others knew the futility of challenging him.

He was about to unleash his fury upon it when there came another sound behind him. It was the chatter of another two-legged thing. He did not understand their words, but he could understand the tone. It was yet another challenge.

The Alpha turned his back on his current foe. The first two-legged thing was injured, weak. It could neither fight nor run. There would be plenty of time to deal with it.

He grunted in surprise as he saw what awaited him. He blinked some pus away, clearing his vision, and saw that it was true. The original alpha of the two-legged things – the one who had taunted him, challenged him, and then somehow managed to evade him – was back. It was standing in the entrance of the dwelling he had just leaped from. It chattered some more with that same insolent tone, then raised the fire stick it was holding.

"See you in Hell, *Chewbacca*," Harrison said, pulling the trigger.

The response was a dry click from the rifle.

The creature cocked its head to the side, as if confused.

For a moment, time seemed to stand still.

Derek looked past the beast and saw that Harrison, his eyes wide with fear, was holding Francis's bolt action rifle. In an instant, he realized what had happened. His cameraman had fired at the creature earlier, but for whatever reason hadn't been able to fire again or chamber his next shot. Harrison had at some point picked it up and never bothered to check. The kid wasn't a hunter. Hadn't he said something earlier about not knowing anything about guns?

Sadly, whatever momentary reprieve they'd been given was up. Time resumed its normal course.

He screamed, "The bolt! Pull it back!"

Harrison was frozen in place for another second. Finally, though, the words seemed to hit home. He began frantically working the lever on the gun, but Derek could see that he was going to be too late.

Launching himself at the sasquatch's back, he tried to buy the younger man another few seconds, but the creature was crafty. It heard his clumsy attack. Without breaking stride, it swung a backhand at him. It was only a glancing blow, but it sent Derek sprawling into the street.

As Harrison frantically tried to ready another shot, the creature advanced. The alpha wrapped its arms around him as if welcoming him home after a long time away. Bones crunched as the creature began to squeeze. Harrison made a gurgling noise, but it was all he could manage before his lungs collapsed.

From his vantage point, Derek saw the squatch's head descending, mouth open, toward the poor kid's neck. The sound that followed was almost too much for his mind to comprehend. He turned his eyes away in horror, but didn't close them. Something else had caught his attention.

Halfway across the street, he saw the glint of metal. It was the revolver that he'd dropped earlier.

He knew there should still be four shots left in it. Mustering the last of his reserves, he began to crawl.

He wasn't going to make it. It wasn't even going to be close. Derek heard a sound behind him, as if something wet and heavy had been tossed to the ground. He knew what it meant. There was a growl, then the creature took a heavy step forward. In another few seconds, it would be upon him.

Before that could happen, though, an unearthly scream pierced the night. For a second, he thought another of the creatures was still in the area. Then he realized he could understand it.

"HARRISON!!"

There was a primal quality to it. It was both a wail of horror and battle cry. For one surreal moment, Derek envisioned Valkyries descending from Valhalla to collect the souls of the fallen. Alas, no winged horses appeared from the heavens. Instead, a lithe form dashed past him, headed toward the creature.

"Danni?"

He was almost too stunned to process it. Sure enough, though, it was her. Not only that, but she was actually going after the squatch armed only with what appeared to be a hand axe.

Derek was almost certain that he'd gone mad. Surely, his mind had cracked in these last few seconds of life and was now filling in the blanks with some bizarre Xena: Warrior Princess fantasy to save him from the awful truth.

If that were the case, though, then it was one *hell* of a hallucination.

Danni dodged left at the last second, just outside of the creature's reach. She brought the blade of the axe up in an arc and it connected with the squatch's outstretched hand, severing two fingers in the process. The creature screamed in pain. She definitely had its full attention.

She turned, nimble as a cat, and raced back toward it.

I haven't gone crazy. She has, Derek thought, butt-scooting backwards toward his discarded weapon, unable to take his eyes off the battle.

The creature swung again, intending to remove Danni's head with one swipe, but she ducked underneath it and went into a baseball slide. She wasn't going for home plate, though. As her momentum carried her forward, she again swung the axe. This time, it lodged firmly in the creature's kneecap. The blade struck bone with a meaty thud and held fast. The beast stumbled, causing her to lose her grip on the weapon.

That was when Derek's hand touched something heavy and metallic.

"Over here!" he screamed at her.

Danni glanced over her shoulder at the sasquatch alpha. It stumbled again, but didn't fall. Seeing it was still very much a threat, she got back to her feet and ran toward Derek.

The creature wrenched the axe from its knee with a pained grunt. It took a step to test the leg, found that it held, then lurched after her.

They were out of time. As fast as she was, the creature's long stride more than made up the difference. It was right behind her as she reached Derek.

"Danni, left, NOW!" he barked, still on the ground, bringing the gun up with his good hand.

Staring down the barrel of the massive weapon, Danni's eyes widened, then she threw herself into a hard dive. Once she was out of the way, there was nothing before him except the massive form of the alpha squatch. This close up, it was enormous. Of far greater importance, though, was the fact that, in less than a second, it was going to squash him like a bug.

Derek couldn't shoot for shit with his left hand, but he didn't need to. The beast filled almost his entire field of vision. He fired.

The gunshot took its toll on both of them. Derek hadn't had time to steady the shot, thus the recoil sent a shock through his body and jolted his arm upward. The creature, though, fared even worse. Its stomach exploded in a shower of blood and intestines. Gutshot, it skidded to a halt and doubled over.

That action brought its face almost even with the barrel of the gun.

"Smile for the camera," Derek said as he pulled the trigger again.

EPILOGUE

Overnight, the small town of Bonanza Creek had been nearly wiped from the maps on which it just barely existed. By the time the sun came up, several buildings on the eastern side of Main Street had been burnt down to their foundations, a result of the fire at the bar. Several smaller blazes burned elsewhere in the town. Some were the result of the chaos that the rampaging beasts had caused. Others were purposely set to destroy evidence of what had occurred that night. The smoke that rose from these particular pyres carried the distinct scent of burning hair.

If the preceding weeks had been slightly dryer, a true disaster might have occurred. Had that happened, a much deeper investigation would've been inevitable and the truth might have been impossible to conceal. As it were, the fire didn't spread beyond the town limits, and thus interest outside of Bonanza

Creek was limited mostly to the friends and family of fallen and survivor alike.

And survivors there were. Some had, amazingly enough, slept through the whole ordeal. One couple had decided to take advantage of the power outage to retire to their bedroom for a night of carnal activity. They lived close to the Gentrys. Had Elmer not neatly removed the head of one of the creatures with a double blast from his shotgun, they might have been paid a visit soon after. Instead, the gunfire and subsequent screams of the beasts had been drowned out by both the R&B music playing from their battery powered radio and the loud creaking of their old queen-sized mattress.

Others had stayed in their homes behind locked doors. Huddled against the strange howls that filled the night, they did their best to convince themselves that nothing was wrong. Dr. Hanscomb and his wife, Myra, were one such couple. They lived in a small, cozy apartment above his practice. Though they were close to the heart of the conflict, they were left unharmed. A few of the creatures came within touching distance of their home. However, each time they passed it by. Though unknown to either the good doctor or his wife, the odor of the various antiseptics and medicines he kept in his office had served as the perfect mask to cover their scent.

Dr. Hanscomb was kept busy in the days to come. There were bodies to be identified, as well as injured to tend to. Amongst the latter was that odd group of reporters who had come into town the day before. He knew better than to question them, especially when the one in charge flashed a government I.D. They gave him some cock and bull story about grizzly bears, but he didn't dispute that either. He hadn't seen what occurred, and as far as he was concerned, he was too old to go stirring up trouble for himself.

Later that morning, before the surviving locals had much chance to talk amongst themselves, outside help began to arrive. It wasn't the aid that people would have expected, though. Representatives of either the nearby Pagosa Springs Sheriff or Fire departments were nowhere to be seen. Instead strangers, many of them in unmarked vehicles, arrived in the town. Some offered medical assistance to the survivors – treating them, taking blood samples, and, in all cases, administering painful shots of rabies vaccine. Some assisted in the cleanup efforts. Others scoured the surrounding woods, carrying weaponry that even the staunchest gun lover would've considered overkill for the known fauna. When pressed as to what really happened, the locals were given vague and often contradictory information: it was bears, wolves, or a rogue biker gang on the run from the law. By the end of the day, there'd been so many different theories spread that if someone had mentioned *Bigfoot*, they'd have gotten a laugh and been asked if he brought his friend, the *Loch Ness Monster*, along.

In the end, only one survivor of Bonanza Creek was absolutely sure of what had occurred. Kate Barrows was found outside of the burnt remains of her house. She was carrying on about monsters and appeared to be completely out of her mind to the point where she eventually had to be sedated. In the coming days, when her condition didn't appear to improve, she was taken to Denver, where she was put under psychiatric evaluation pending a hearing for commitment.

Derek was supervising the ATF agents while they packed his gear in the SUV. One of their vehicles had been salvageable. The other two had been towed away before any curious onlookers could get a chance to snoop around them. He sighed wearily, feeling his hand throb painfully at his side. The entire mission had turned out to be a gigantic clusterfuck. He wasn't being personally blamed. The few people who knew what he really did understood there was a certain element of uncertainty when dealing with creatures unclassified by science.

It didn't matter, though. He blamed himself more than enough. Mitch and Frank had been airlifted to Alamosa for medical care. They were going to be fine. However, Chuck wasn't. His death was almost certainly Derek's fault. He should've listened to Mitch and disarmed the Barrows woman when he had the chance.

That wasn't even scratching the surface of all the

casualties he felt weighing him down. Lots of people died who hadn't deserved it: his teammate, those kids they'd pulled out of the woods, and more folks from this poor town than he cared to think of. He glanced at the heavy cast around his hand. All things considered, he'd gotten off far more lightly than he deserved.

That it appeared to be over was small comfort. The agents had combed the woods for miles around the town and discovered only one of the creatures still alive. It had been a straggler from the clan, found a few miles to the south, wounded apparently by a car. Between that and the disease, it had been near death when the agents had come across it. They had immediately put it out of its misery, then burnt the body. Since then, nothing further had been found.

"Penny for your thoughts," said a somber voice from behind him, pulling him back into the present.

He turned to find Danni standing before him. He was more than surprised, as he'd given instructions that she be allowed to leave unhindered. She had been through more than enough, as far as he was concerned. That brought another pang of guilt. Her brother's cause of death had been listed as a bear mauling. Their parents would never know the truth. Even if they did, they probably wouldn't believe it, but the girl knew. In some ways, that made things even worse.

"Listen, Danni, I'm sorry..."

She stopped him with a wave of her hand. "You've said it a hundred times already, and I believe you." Though her eyes were puffy, her voice didn't waver.

"Yeah, well maybe *I* don't believe it." He sighed. "After this, I'm thinking of disbanding the team."

"What?"

"What we do ... it's borderline insane. And this time, a lot of people paid for it. If we hadn't been around..."

"We'd have died in the woods, *all* of us," she said, her voice taking on an edge. "There wouldn't be any survivors at all here. Who knows how far those things would've gotten before someone stopped them?"

"Danni, I..."

"Just stop it with the pity party! I have enough of that for myself right now. Yes, a lot of people died, but not as many as could have. And that's not even counting everyone you've ever saved before now ... unless you were lying about that part."

He let her words sink in for a few moments, then he slowly nodded. It was going to be a long time before he was at peace with himself, but she had a point. He almost laughed as a phrase flashed through his mind ... *the show must go on.*

"I just have one request." He thought she was going to ask for permission to let her parents know what had really happened to her brother. Instead, he was surprised, and a little horrified, when she said, "I want in."

"What!?"

"You heard me. This could happen again..."

"Danni, if this is about revenge..."

"It's not," she said emphatically. "I know enough not to hate all dogs if one bites me. I realize those things were sick. As much as I want to blame them, it wasn't their fault."

"Then what?"

"It's about Harrison." Her eyes began to glisten. "I couldn't save him. He was so brave out there in the woods..." She paused to wipe a few tears away. "Well, now it's my turn. I know what's out there now. I couldn't help him, but maybe I can help others. If I can do it enough, then maybe..."

"You can make it up to him?"

"Something like that. The funny thing is, if our positions were reversed, I know he'd be asking you the same thing."

Derek smiled at her. "From what I saw of him, I wouldn't doubt that for a second." He was amazed to find himself actually contemplating her request. It was insane, yet he couldn't help but remember how she had handled herself against the alpha.

He found himself remembering the Adventure Channel's demand for a cohost. There was little doubt she'd pass their muster in the looks department, and he'd sure as hell rather have someone who could handle herself watching his back than some airhead cosmetics model.

Still... "I don't know, Danni," he said. "You have no idea..."

"Yes, I do," she replied with a tone of finality. "I was studying to be a forest ranger anyway. I'm not afraid of the outdoors, and this seems a hell of a lot better way to apply myself than harassing people about their campfires."

"Well..."

"Besides, right now it seems like you could use the extra help."

He winced a little at the thought of Chuck, but again, she had a point. Just because he was a man short didn't mean that situations weren't going to pop up again.

"At the very least, you're in no condition to drive." She looked him in the eye expectantly.

He sighed. "You're right about that, and I do need to check on Mitch and Frank. Fine, I'll tell you what. We can discuss it on the ride over to Alamosa. No promises, though."

She smiled and held out her hand for the keys.

He handed them over, and she opened the driver's side. As she was getting in, he leaned over and asked, "You're not camera shy, are you?"

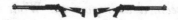

Several miles to the south, a Honda Pilot was parked on the side of route 160. Bernadette Hodgekins was sitting in the passenger seat, waiting for her husband, Darryl, to get back. He'd hastily pulled over and run off into the trees to take care of *business*. She was playing Angry Birds on her phone and thinking idly, *that man has the bladder of a mouse,* when she looked up and saw movement further down the road, near the edge of the woods.

At first, she thought it was her husband, then she realized her mistake. Whoever it was, they were far too small. The figure staggered out to the edge of the road, and she was able to make it out better.

"What are you looking at?" her husband asked from right outside the window, causing her to jump.

"Don't do that, jerk!"

"Sorry." He followed her gaze. "Is that a boy?"

"I think so," she replied, opening the door. "What's he doing out here?"

"Don't know."

"Poor thing might be lost."

"Well, let's go see if we can help," he said as they started walking.

He stared at the two figures through red-rimmed eyes, from within a world of pain. His body ached all over, and there was a fire burning in his brain. Suddenly, though, that seemed unimportant. What mattered was the rage. It took hold of him as they approached. They seemed unafraid, impudently walking toward him. They were stupid things and would soon learn their mistake.

He bared his teeth in what could have been mistaken for a smile but was, in fact, a snarl. Once – ages ago, it seemed – he had been camping with his parents when they had stepped into a nightmare. A brief flicker in his decaying mind whispered that his name had once been Carl Mercer, but the memory vanished just as quickly as it appeared. All that remained was the rage. It told him to deal with the two stupid things standing before him. It commanded him to make them hurt, to make them bleed ... to make them scream.

THE END

The Crypto-Hunter will return in
Devil Hunters

DEVIL HUNTERS
A Tale of the Crypto-Hunter

The golden eagle soared effortlessly above the frozen landscape, its wings barely moving, held aloft by the updraft that preceded the storm front. A clap of thunder sounded in the distance, but the mighty bird paid it no mind. It was far too preoccupied searching for prey.

Something on the snow-covered ground caught its sharp eyes and it banked its impressive six-foot wingspan to investigate. It moved with the easy grace of a super predator, certain in the mastery of its domain. Soon, it spotted the fresh kill. It was likely that wolves or maybe a bear had brought down the great antlered beast below, but none of that mattered to the eagle. It had few qualms about facing down either opponent over meat. It knew it had little to fear from even the largest of land predators.

In the fading sunlight, as the storm's approach quickened, it began to circle, slowly descending toward the appetizing prize.

All at once, movement registered in its vision from down below – a flash of yellow hair, followed by something stepping from the brush near the kill. Like many predators, the eagle did not outright fear a lone human. However, its instincts commanded it to be wary. It continued circling, waiting to see if the intruder would move off. That was when something else caught its eye.

The eagle had no fear of any creature that walked the land, but what came from the sky was a different matter entirely. Though it realized the newcomer was still far above it, the shadow it cast on the ground dwarfed its own.

Banking its wings, the eagle made a sharp turn. The prize on the ground wasn't worth it. The creature that had entered its airspace was an enemy against which it could not win. With one last shriek, the eagle headed west, hoping to try its luck elsewhere.

"What are you doing?" the voice from the Bluetooth headset demanded.

"My job," Daniella Kent – Danni to her friends – replied, stepping out of the hunting blind and approaching the dead moose.

"That's why we set the bait."

"This thing's already taken two kids from that village and it's started going after the adults, too. It's a man-eater and you know it, Derek. The bait isn't going to attract anything more than the usual scavengers." Danni rolled her eyes. It had been nearly a year since she'd joined the team and he *still* acted like she was a kid.

"We just need to be patient..." Derek began when another voice over the radio drowned him out.

"I see it!"

Danni was tempted to reply, "Told ya so!" but knew it would be childish. Besides, if the creature really was approaching, it would be unwise to engage in unnecessary banter.

"Can you get a shot, Frank?" Derek asked.

"No good," came the answer. "Still too far away, and the goddamned wind is picking up."

"They don't call them Thunderbirds for nothing," Danni said under her breath. She pushed an errant strand of blonde hair from her face, then lifted her rifle and scanned the sky through the scope.

"Danni..." Derek's voice warned.

"Where is it?" She lowered the rifle just as the oncoming clouds blotted out the sun. The dazzling brightness was immediately replaced by a shape much darker than the clouds above it.

The creature had been using the glare of the sun to mask its approach. With its cover gone, Danni could see the monstrous bird in all its glory. It was huge, with an eighteen-foot wingspan and a curved beak that looked like it could shatter bone. Worse, it was coming at her fast ... too fast.

Shit!

There wasn't time to line up a shot. Her training taking over, Danni threw herself into a hard dive, losing her grip on the gun in the process. Fortunately, big as the creature was, it was incapable of making a quick turn to compensate for her movement.

She had just enough time to think, *Where the hell are the others?* when the reports from multiple rifle shots reached her ears.

Danni hit the ground and rolled onto her back, hoping for the best. A splay of feathers fell from one of the creature's massive wings, but the monstrous bird remained airborne. *Damn it!*

It had been Derek's idea to split the team up at multiple bait sites so as to cover more ground, but still remain close enough to provide cover for each other. Not a bad plan, really. Unfortunately, the storm was moving in faster than expected and the erratic wind gusts were playing havoc with their ability to hit a moving target. *Even one as big as a Cessna*, Danni mused, getting back to her feet in time to see the creature bank for another pass at her.

Not afraid of people. That's gonna cost you, you ugly son of a bitch. Despite the danger, a small smile played out across her lips. She must have been hanging out with Francis too much. His attitude was obviously starting to rub off on her. It probably wasn't the healthiest mindset for living a long life, but it was better than running scared.

Speaking of running... "Danni, lead it toward me so I can get a head-on shot."

She didn't need to be told twice. Despite its size,

the bird was more maneuverable than she would have given it credit for. It was already positioned and building up speed for another run. Danni spotted her discarded rifle, determined there wasn't time to retrieve it, then turned and dashed toward Derek's position.

Thunder crashed overhead and suddenly the storm was upon them. The wind picked up and pinpricks of frozen rain began to pelt her.

"Just a little more," Derek said from over the headset.

A shriek from behind told her she didn't have a little more.

Screw this! She reached into her jacket and drew the semi-automatic pistol from the holster inside. Throwing herself into a dive, she spun, landed hard on her back, and took aim. There was almost no chance of missing at this range. The bird took up nearly her entire field of vision.

She squeezed the trigger over and over, unleashing a small volley of hellfire upon the beast. But then Danni realized she had a new problem. Regardless of whether she killed it, the small caliber bullets weren't going to stop the monster bird's momentum. Alive or dead, it was going to slam into her. Between its massive beak and outstretched talons, she was about to be impaled... The golden eagle soared effortlessly above the frozen landscape, its wings barely moving, held aloft by the updraft that preceded the storm front. A clap of thunder sounded in the distance, but the mighty bird paid it no mind. It was far too preoc-cupied searching for prey.

Something on the snow-covered ground caught its sharp eyes and it banked its impressive six-foot wingspan to investigate. It moved with the easy grace of a super predator, certain in the mastery of its domain. Soon, it spotted the fresh kill. It was likely that wolves or maybe a bear had brought down the great antlered beast below, but none of that mattered to the eagle. It had few qualms about facing down either opponent over meat. It knew it had little to fear from even the largest of land predators.

In the fading sunlight, as the storm's approach quickened, it began to circle, slowly descending toward the appetizing prize.

All at once, movement registered in its vision from down below – a flash of yellow hair, followed by something stepping from the brush near the kill. Like many predators, the eagle did not outright fear a lone human. However, its instincts commanded it to be wary. It continued circling, waiting to see if the intruder would move off. That was when something else caught its eye.

The eagle had no fear of any creature that walked the land, but what came from the sky was a different matter entirely. Though it realized the newcomer was still far above it, the shadow it cast on the ground dwarfed its own.

Banking its wings, the eagle made a sharp turn. The prize on the ground wasn't worth it. The creature that had entered its airspace was an enemy against which it could not win. With one last shriek, the eagle headed west, hoping to try its luck elsewhere.

"What are you doing?" the voice from the Bluetooth headset demanded.

"My job," Daniella Kent – Danni to her friends – replied, stepping out of the hunting blind and approaching the dead moose.

"That's why we set the bait."

"This thing's already taken two kids from that village and it's started going after the adults, too. It's a man-eater and you know it, Derek. The bait isn't going to attract anything more than the usual scavengers." Danni rolled her eyes. It had been nearly a year since she'd joined the team and he *still* acted like she was a kid.

"We just need to be patient..." Derek began when another voice over the radio drowned him out.

"I see it!"

Danni was tempted to reply, "Told ya so!" but knew it would be childish. Besides, if the creature really was approaching, it would be unwise to engage in unnecessary banter.

"Can you get a shot, Frank?" Derek asked.

"No good," came the answer. "Still too far away, and the goddamned wind is picking up."

"They don't call them Thunderbirds for nothing," Danni said under her breath. She pushed an errant strand of blonde hair from her face, then lifted her rifle and scanned the sky through the scope.

"Danni..." Derek's voice warned.

"Where is it?" She lowered the rifle just as the oncoming clouds blotted out the sun. The dazzling brightness was immediately replaced by a shape much darker than the clouds above it.

The creature had been using the glare of the sun to mask its approach. With its cover gone, Danni could see the monstrous bird in all its glory. It was huge, with an eighteen-foot wingspan and a curved beak that looked like it could shatter bone. Worse, it was coming at her fast ... too fast.

Shit!

There wasn't time to line up a shot. Her training taking over, Danni threw herself into a hard dive, losing her grip on the gun in the process. Fortunately, big as the creature was, it was incapable of making a quick turn to compensate for her movement.

She had just enough time to think, *Where the hell are the others?* when the reports from multiple rifle shots reached her ears.

Danni hit the ground and rolled onto her back, hoping for the best. A splay of feathers fell from one of the creature's massive wings, but the monstrous bird remained airborne. *Damn it!*

It had been Derek's idea to split the team up at multiple bait sites so as to cover more ground, but still remain close enough to provide cover for each other. Not a bad plan, really. Unfortunately, the storm was moving in faster than expected and the erratic wind gusts were playing havoc with their ability to hit a moving target. *Even one as big as a Cessna*, Danni mused, getting back to her feet in time to see the creature bank for another pass at her.

Not afraid of people. That's gonna cost you, you ugly son of a bitch. Despite the danger, a small smile played out across her lips. She must have been hanging out with Francis too much. His attitude was obviously starting to rub off on her. It probably wasn't the healthiest mindset for living a long life, but it was better than running scared.

Speaking of running... "Danni, lead it toward me so I can get a head-on shot."

She didn't need to be told twice. Despite its size, the bird was more maneuverable than she would have given it credit for. It was already positioned and building up speed for another run. Danni spotted her discarded rifle, determined there wasn't time to retrieve it, then turned and dashed toward Derek's position.

Thunder crashed overhead and suddenly the storm was upon them. The wind picked up and pinpricks of frozen rain began to pelt her.

"Just a little more," Derek said from over the headset.

A shriek from behind told her she didn't have a little more.

Screw this! She reached into her jacket and drew the semi-automatic pistol from the holster inside. Throwing herself into a dive, she spun, landed hard on her back, and took aim. There was almost no chance of missing at this range. The bird took up nearly her entire field of vision.

She squeezed the trigger over and over, unleashing a small volley of hellfire upon the beast. But then Danni realized she had a new problem. Regardless of whether she killed it, the small caliber bullets weren't going to stop the monster bird's momentum. Alive or dead, it was going to slam into her. Between its massive beak and outstretched talons, she was about to be impaled...

DEVIL HUNTERS
Available Now!

AUTHOR'S NOTE

I've always been fascinated by the field of Crypto-zoology. Personally, I would hope there isn't too much argument against the existence of animals that have yet to be discovered by science. Hell, even as I write this, there was a new species of crab discovered just a few days ago. That some of these undiscovered creatures might actually be true monsters – straight out of our wildest imaginations – is one that makes me as giddy as a child. However, I'm split on my thoughts with regards to the outcome of searching for these legendary beasts.

On the one hand, there's a part of me that *needs* to know. That part insists that one day the Bigfeet and Loch Ness Monsters of the world must either be revealed or proven false beyond a shadow of a doubt. The truth is out there, and I *must* know it.

But, there's also a flip side. Another part of me loves the mystery, the *what if* aspect of it all. Discovering such creatures would go a long way toward dispelling that feeling of wonder.

Despite how incredible it would be for science to prove that Sasquatch exists, how long would it be before they became mundane? Think about it: a scant hundred years ago, there were nightmarish rumors of man-beasts in Africa. Today, though, people barely give the gorilla cage at the zoo a second glance. How quickly would Bigfoot go from being the legendary wild man of the woods to *those annoying apes that keep eating out of my trash can*?

That's what I mean. There's the need to know versus the need for something to remain fantastic. Quite the conundrum, isn't it?

Fortunately, it's not one we have to worry about right now. For within the realm of fantasy, which I assure you this book strictly is, there need be no such quandary. The unknown can be discovered, yet still be as awe-inspiring as ever.

In writing this book, I decided to merge my interest in Cryptozoology with a few of the staples I crave in my entertainment: monsters and the people who fight them. After all, vampires and demons are lots of fun all by themselves, but, for me at least, it is so much cooler knowing that *Blade* and *Buffy* are busy kicking their asses.

Hence this book. *Bigfoot Hunters* is a horror adventure that merges all of the above. There's the thrill of discovery, the mayhem of monsters running amok, and a few brave souls who aren't going to surrender without a fight.

I had a lot of fun getting to know the characters

in this story. I had even more with their furry antagonists. I hope you did too.

In closing, I will just say: if, having finished this book, you find yourself walking in the woods and hear a branch snap behind you, relax. It's probably just a deer ... *probably*.

Rick G.

ABOUT THE AUTHOR

Rick Gualtieri lives alone in central New Jersey with only his wife, three kids, and countless pets to both keep him company and constantly plot against him. When he's not busy monkey-clicking words, he can typically be found jealously guarding his collection of vintage Transformers from all who would seek to defile them.

Defilers Beware!

Also by Rick Gualtieri:
TALES OF THE CRYPTO-HUNTER
Bigfoot Hunters
Devil Hunters
Kraken Hunters

THE HYBRID OF HIGH MOON
Get Bent!
Bent Outta Shape
Bent On Destruction

THE TOME OF BILL UNIVERSE
THE TOME OF BILL
Bill the Vampire
Scary Dead Things

The Mourning Woods
Holier Than Thou
Sunset Strip
Goddamned Freaky Monsters
Half A Prayer
The Wicked Dead
Shining Fury
The Last Coven

BILL OF THE DEAD
Strange Days
Everyday Horrors